PEAKS OF COLOR

A RIGGS ROMANCE
BOOK 1

VICTORIA WILDER

Edited by NiceGirlNaughtyEdits

Cover by Echo Grayce, Wildheart Graphics

To those who are courageously curious, smart enough to take a chance, and bold enough to pivot.

A NOTE TO READERS

This book contains adult material, including references to drug abuse, child abandonment, child neglect, as well as violence. You should also be aware that this romance story is open-door, which means there are multiple descriptive sex scenes. The adults in this story also frequently use profanity.

PROLOGUE

THE COLOR ORANGE HAS BEEN MY FAVORITE FOR AS LONG AS I can remember. My clothes, though limited, always had something orange woven throughout. It's also the only color that you can taste. When you're left alone with too many thoughts as a kid and then you discover this tidbit, that a color can have a specific flavor...poof! It's life-changing. Orange has always brought me a little bit of happiness, in a reality that rarely ever provided that emotion.

I jerk awake, slightly dazed, but quickly remember where I am. The hardwood floor has earned its name. The left side of my body completely numb from lying on it for what feels like forever. My little sister is still asleep in my arms, shaped like a tiny ball sprouting curly hair. Thank goodness I didn't wake her. I pray she stays that way because the footsteps keep coming and I know eventually they'll find what they're looking for. They always do. It's been almost an entire day. The sleep fog has lifted. I've only peed in my pants twice. I hope that the smell doesn't give us away.

My baby sister is four, but she wears a diaper so anything that she's done is kept there. She's also learned that while we hide, we must be brave, and even more importantly, we must be quiet. I've had to teach her that being quiet is the only way that we get to be happy and safe.

I'm still so tired, but I can't fall asleep again. If they look under here, I'll need to be ready. I always pray they never come back, but as Mama has told me repeatedly, *"It doesn't pay to pray. Nobody is listening."*

We usually can get to the closet in time, but it's my fault that we didn't. I was busy trying to get an old camera I found in the dumpster down the street to work. It's still broken, but maybe I can figure out how to fix it. I've never had anything like it, so I had to hide it. If she found it, she'd sell it or throw it away. I was distracted, and that's the reason why we're under the bed right now.

I won't make that mistake again. The closet is where I can breathe. There's also a place for me to pee, some extra diapers for my sister, and granola bars. What I wouldn't give for a granola bar right now. I didn't get to eat yesterday. Mama said she needed her medicine instead of food for her "little mistakes."

The door slams shut, and I can tell by the scuffed patent leather shoes that scurry to the bed that it's Mama.

"Motha' fuckerz," she slurs.

I know she's not right again. Too much medicine. The only good thing when she's slurring is that she should be asleep soon, and then I can move around the apartment before the men return. I can get something for my sister to drink and eat.

I'll be able to change my pants.

Then, the door swings back open so violently that it makes a slamming sound against the wall. I'm so very good at being quiet, but I move back slightly so that the light from the hallway can't touch us. If we stay in the shadows under the bed, I'm almost positive they won't see us.

"You make me sick. Look at yourself. You smell like piss too," the deep-voiced man snarls at Mama.

I tune out everything else that follows. My mama always says to me that I have selective hearing, but it's true; I can turn my ears off when I know the deep-voiced man is going to hurt her. This time, however, my ears turn back on moments later when I hear a loud piercing screech and the sound of gargling.

"You cost me tonight. As usual. But never again, you fucking cunt."

The man stomps out of the room, and I know he's left because I hear the front door slam shut, and then car doors close outside shortly after. I know whatever just happened is bad.

The only thing I see in the darkness of the room from where I lie is a flashing orange light. It flashes every three seconds.

Orange. One, two, three.

Orange. One, two, three.

Orange. One, two, three.

I stay on the hardwood floor, underneath the bed, safe in the dark, watching the orange light. It keeps time for me. Helps me to gather my brave face.

Mama doesn't move above me. The apartment is quiet enough that I hear only the city sounds outside. A warm liquid drips from the mattress above and onto my arm. But I lie there for a little longer, knowing that when I move, I'll wake my sister, and then I'll have to see what the deep-voiced man has done to my mother.

I know she's not going to wake up this time.

Orange. One, two, three.

Orange is my favorite color.

1

Jack

"Tilt your ass out and grip the pole. More. Keep going. Put a little more into it. I know you have it in you, man. That's it."

Click-pop, Click-pop.

I press down harder because I'm finally getting what I've been trying to coax out of him for the past two hours. The force of my finger enlists the clicks to run in fast succession as the shutter on my camera collects what I require. Perfection.

"Marcus, *finally*, man."

"Hey, boss, cut me some slack here. This isn't my usual rodeo." I just start laughing quietly and shaking my head, because he's right. As the top NFL draft pick this season, he's barely wet behind the ears when it comes to anything that isn't on the football field or in the training room.

"If you keep playing the way you have been, then you'll

be *very* used to rodeos like this in no time. But yeah"—I look down at my camera, which needs a new battery and some lens adjustments—"let's take a few minutes."

"Marcus, darling, that was incredible. You're even more of a vision here than on the field," the very ostentatious rep from one of the big five sports brands yells, as he plows farther onto my set. I can never keep track of what rep belongs to which brand when we're doing these sessions. Most of these athletes are my friends at this point. Kissing ass is no longer part of the job description for me. My work speaks for itself, and they pay a pretty price for my time, in some instances more than what they're paying the athletes for a sponsorship.

"Bridgette, get the fans set up and the rest of the scene prepped for our next group. I'll be back in 30."

"It's Katie, sir. My name."

I stop and turn back to look at her. "And?"

"And I've been working with you for the past two weeks. You should know my name by now. My name is Katie." She shifts closer. "We had drinks last week."

I don't shift my gaze, still giving her a blank stare that asks why I should care.

"We had sex, like, two nights ago. Why are you looking at me like you're not remembering any of it? Or me?" She's clearly getting frustrated. I remember, and it wasn't great. Lots of asking me, *"Do you like that?"* and most of the time, I didn't. I almost fell asleep when she was giving me head. Very mediocre. And incredibly predictable. I can't remember the last person that I've slept with that enticed me for a second round, never mind kept me interested enough to bother remembering their name.

"Maybe you should think about *why* I don't remember

your name." I walk away and yell over my shoulder, "Set needs to be ready in 27 minutes now. Everybody better be ready when I get back."

I can hear her huff and call me an asshole. "I quit, you dickhead," she yells back at me.

Waving over my head, I pull out my phone, yelling back, "Get your ass off my set by the time I'm back, then."

I send a text to my agent.

JACK

Get me a new assistant for today's shoot. They need to be on set in 20mins ready to work. I have 3 more athletes coming in that need to be coddled, so I will NOT be holding any additional hands.

LUCIFER

On it.

Professional advice...stop fucking them.

JACK

I don't need your advice. You have 17mins now.

LUCIFER

Done. This shoot wraps tomorrow, then you're out to Colorado the day after that. Try to keep it in your pants.

JACK

Where am I staying?

LUCIFER

They're handling accommodations.

7

JACK

Really? Why? I better not end up at some shitty B&B.

LUCIFER

Their marketing guy was annoying, so I filled the contract with dumb asks.

Oh! And no assistant for the Colorado job. It's just you and the clients. You're there for a while, so please, DO NOT FUCK THE CLIENT.

JACK

You say that as if I can't help myself.

LUCIFER

If the title fits.

JACK

Stop slut-shaming me.

LUCIFER

Keep the rest of this shoot professional, please? I'd like to end the year with no more lawsuits or social media smears.

#TheJackDeaconOrgy just stopped trending. Thanks.

JACK

There needed to be more than three people for it to be considered an orgy. That was false advertising.

LUCIFER

Your assistant is on his way to set. He'll be ready when you are.

JACK

Thanks, Luce.

You can go back to eating small children or sacrificing goats now.

LUCIFER

Just doing my part.

The only person who keeps my business life, and personal life for that matter, in check, is my fire-wielding agent, Luce. You'd never know that she stands at just about five feet tall since her bark and her bite scare the shit out of most people. That includes me, but she's fiercely loyal and has dug me out of plenty of shit over the years. And while I throw her a fair share of things that most agents don't have to deal with, she does it all. I pay her an insane amount of money, but she deserves every penny. We've both built up each other's careers, and along the way, we've built respect for one another as well.

After grabbing an espresso from the Illy Caffè around the corner, I feel refreshed and ready to tackle the rest of the day's session.

"What brand is up next? I need the heaters on. This place is fucking freezing. I don't want to over-enhance anyone's junk in post so let's go people!" I yell out. Shuffling feet and chattering voices surround me. Their maestro is ready!

"Mr. Deacon, thank you, sir. I appreciate what you did earlier."

I turn toward my equipment as my lighting director fixes a piece of blue filament over the foreground lights. I give him a nod and don't move any closer to address what I know he's referring to.

"Girls like Katie are one social media post away from self-destruction and an empty apology tour. Who calls people fags anymore? Like, seriously?"

I just smile and turn back to the chaos of the set.

"Let's get to work, people. I need makeup and hair cleared out. Here we go!"

2

Everly

"ARE YOU ALIVE IN THERE?" I DON'T MOVE. I DON'T WANT TO answer.

"Everly, love, you want some coffee?" He knocks again. I dunk my head back under the shower stream. I want to avoid any kind of interaction for just a few more minutes. Is that too much to ask?

He double-taps the door *again*. "Everly, did you hear me? I'm making some coffee. Do you want some? I can do an Americano..."

I should have left last night and never fallen asleep. Stupid move.

"Ah, yeah, no. I mean, yes, I heard you and no to the coffee. I have a brunch meeting. I'm probably running late." I'm such a dick. I should just have coffee with him.

"Okay, no problem." He pauses, so I assume he's walked away.

Another tap on the door happens a moment later, and I suppress a huff. "Everly?"

"Yes?" I sing-song, louder this time.

"Stop overthinking in there, yeah?"

"Okay. I'm...I'm just trying to hurry up, Jin. I'll be out in a few."

I rush through washing my hair and body, all with the same kind of soap. Men have it too easy. One and done. I smell like citrus pine from top to toes now. Margaritas must have altered my state of smell last night because this morning it's like a floor cleaner and Christmas tree water had a baby and I'm coated in it.

After the hot shower, I glob toothpaste on my finger and run it around my mouth, trying to rid that tequila-tasting reflux from my tongue, and remove that nice morning fur from my teeth. When I step out of the ensuite bathroom, I grab my black pencil skirt and pull it up and over my still-damp hips. Jin left out a gray Riggs Outdoor sweatshirt for me instead of the rumpled blouse I wore over here last night, so I throw that on next. I'm pretty sure I busted some buttons on the blouse while trying to get off, now that I think of it.

Last night was an entirely different tone than what I'm putting off right now. When you're ecstatic about the turn your life is taking, naturally, you celebrate. So, that's what we did.

Yesterday my life felt put together. Organized. The polar opposite of today. Yesterday, I woke up alone. And that's not a complaint. I was prepared for the day ahead. I was nervous as hell, but I felt confident in the level of work my brothers and I had done in preparation for our board of directors meeting that evening. Today, I woke up to one of the board members of my father's company face down on the pillow next to me.

Jin and I are colleagues. Friendly. Flirty. It's happened a few times before, but it's never been a hot and heavy affair, more like an agreement or transaction. *How depressing does that sound?* There was thought behind it, and when there's thought, you lose the heat. Instead, I settled for a warm bed. Not even a spark. And I want fire.

Shit, what time is it right now?

Riggs Outdoor Sports & Apparel is a family business. My father leads the company, but it's my brothers and me that have made it the most successful outdoor sports business in Colorado. I'm not exaggerating when I say we have become the most sought-after brand in the industry. My father opened the company as a small storefront long before he had any of us. That's more than thirty years ago now. It all happened shortly after falling in love with my mother, and in addition, our home in Strutt's Peak. It started as a simple rental and sporting goods store on Main Street, catering to the winter sports goers. As our family grew up and the tourists kept pouring in year-round, there was so much more to offer, and money to be made. Throw that in with one of the smartest businessmen you'll ever meet, and it's a jackpot.

I've been working for the business since I was twelve, helping out in the store where I could, but when I came back from New York City where I finished my undergrad, I decided I could turn it into something even more spectacular. That was more than a decade ago now.

My father navigates all of it as President and CEO, but I

drive it forward as his VP. My hands are in all aspects, from budget numbers to client bookings. It's how I like it. Organized and in control. My three brothers have carved out their roles and are great at what they do, but in the end, it's all for the same goals: continue to grow the business, do it together, and support the small town that we all call home.

I hear my phone chime from somewhere in the pile of blankets on the bed. Buried under the mess of sheets and a very fluffy duvet, I see that it was already 11 a.m., and my best girl, Giselle, texted me.

GISELLE

> Tell me you overslept from a night of dirty sex. That is the only reason I'll forgive you for making me wait in this coffee shop alone right now.

G is one of those people with whom everyone falls in love. She's outgoing and unapologetically curious, and it took barely any time to realize that she's my person. She's my Christina Yang. I never understood what a ride or die meant until her. And damn, do we have a good time. When you see us together, you'd never assume it. We're opposites in every obvious way, but the same in all the ways that count. We balance each other out, and at a time in our lives when we needed an unapologetically real and rowdy friendship, we met each other. That was just about twelve years ago now, after I moved back home, and she strolled into our small town.

In my very biased opinion, my best friend is the full package. She's funny as hell, kind without even trying to be, whip-smart, and is always there for me when I need her. But she is not someone who falls in line or subscribes to conventional thinking. She's never in a relationship and prefers it that way. We joke all the time about how she's the master of the meaningless hookup. She almost has it down to a science and makes no apologies for wanting what she does. Usually, the men she meets are all for it at the start, but then many of them tend to catch feelings and she's already begun her exit strategy. I think it's brilliant, a woman who knows what she wants, and more importantly, what she doesn't. I wish I was built like that. I'm just not.

Every time Jin and I do this, I hate myself a little more for it. If I'm being honest, it's solely because of the need to be with someone in the moment. The sex is okay-ish. It scratches an itch. It's very vanilla. Vanilla is a great flavor. But, when you know there are other flavors you want to try, then vanilla just gets the job done. Now that I think of it, every time I came last night, it was because I was pushing my own button. We simply don't have chemistry.

We make sense on paper. We're both good-looking, great businesspeople, smart in the boardroom, decently wealthy, and single. God, even saying that sounds pathetic. It's more like a resume than a compatibility list.

After so many years of refusing to make time to date and letting work come first, I'm here. In my *almost* mid-thirties with a fabulous career and bank account, but a less than mediocre sex life. And a barely there dating life. What's even more depressing is there is not a single person in my past that was *the one that got away*. I haven't met anyone that I'd even try to make room for. It's a barren landscape of men. Strutt's Peak has a roster of mediocrity, but then when I lived in Manhattan it was a lot of bros, trust fund douches, and artsy disappointments. I thirst for the idea of falling into a maddening lust and that soul-level kind of love with someone who could match my ambition but still relish in the closeness of family.

I've resigned myself to thinking that maybe that kind of partner isn't the one I'm destined to be with. Someone like Jin, who isn't cringe-worthy, is a totally decent guy. Then that's what gets me here, and I'm reminded the next morning that there's nothing exceptional when we're together. That's where I'm at in my life right now. On the cusp of becoming a cliché and settling for average versus being utterly alone.

There's probably an ample number of women who would love to be where I am right now. You don't settle for a guy like Jin. He's a catch. He intimidates people from a business perspective, but it's his kind eyes and the dimple on his chin that made me want to cross the line. Looking is where I should have stopped. Now, I'm trying to talk myself into a relationship with someone I know I should want. But I don't.

"Get your shit together," I whisper to myself, then take a breath and open the bedroom door. I walk down the long hallway and into the brightly lit main space of Jin's loft. His wealth is obvious, and the decor understated, but he flaunts it where it counts. A view of the mountains splashes across the floor-to-ceiling windows as I make my way into the living room. The view is almost as nice as the one from my place. *Almost.*

The smell of espresso loosens the knot in my stomach, as I'm greeted with a wide smile and a shirtless Jin Cormick standing in the kitchen.

"Whatever you're thinking of saying as an excuse to get out of here as fast as possible, just don't." He smiles and raises his hand up before I can respond. "I'm happy I got to wake up with you this morning. But I can take a hint, Everly. We both know last night was about filling some open space for each other, right?"

I blow out the breath I hadn't realized I was holding. "I'm hoping you really do feel that way. I-I don't want to admit that I used you as a celebratory sex toy last night, but-"

He laughs and says, "Everly." Shaking his head and looking down, he pauses and then continues. "You should already know any man would happily volunteer as tribute to be a sex toy for you." He leans back on the counter, effortless confidence always oozing from him. "You're fantastic, but we mixed pleasure with business again, and we both know we shouldn't have."

I'm so relieved that I actually feel my body relax at his words. The way he peeks up at me and smirks...I wish I wanted more from him. For me. I want the kinds of things that Jin is all about, but I just don't feel that *zing*. I want that fire, the electricity that I worry so few people ever get. I still want it. I'm stubborn like that.

Instead, I agree with him. "Does that make me a cold-hearted asshole?"

He smiles back at me. "No, darlin', that makes you, us, human. And we're choosing to be smart." Popping a raspberry into his mouth and letting out another laugh, he adds, "Go ahead. I know you're dying to get out of here."

I walk over, kiss him on the cheek, and wrap my arms around his shoulders. "You're a good man, Jin. Friends?" I ask.

He nods and smiles back.

"Oh, and thank you for the vote yesterday. I know it was unanimous, but I'm happy you're on board with what we have planned for the company."

"It's really smart moves, Ev. You and the guys are something to watch out for." He smiles and swats my ass as I walk away toward the door. "Go on, get outta here."

"See ya, handsome." I take a deep breath as I leave. That went better than I expected.

3

Everly

I'M JUST ABOUT TO WALK INTO BREWS & BOOKS, WHEN MY phone simultaneously chimes with text alerts and an incoming phone call. I see Law's name on my caller ID. I'll call my baby brother back later. Instead, I open my text messages and see a full paragraph from my brother Michael.

MICHAEL

You missed the gym this AM. Are you hungover, or are you just avoiding a weekend workout?

When I left you guys last night, I thought you said you were heading out early so you could be up for the gym.

So now I'm worried because you didn't show.

Oh, gross, did you go home with someone? Are you "walk of shame-ing" back home right now? Nvm, don't wanna know. Unless you've been kidnapped.

Ev, I'm at the house and you're not here. Law said you didn't come home. If I don't hear from you in the next few minutes, I'm going to assume you've been kidnapped and I'm calling the sheriff.

In most situations, it's Law that would be freaking out that I didn't text him that I wouldn't be home last night, but Law and I left the bar around the same time so he knew where I was going, or rather who I was leaving with. I forgot in my tequila-haze that I promised Michael I would be at the gym this morning. Routines and plans with Michael are important. He lives with OCD and high anxiety, so along with therapy and meds, consistency and routines are some of the tools he uses. And now I've unintentionally messed with his day.

EVERLY

I'm alive. Not kidnapped. I'm sorry, I completely forgot to text you that I wasn't going to make it.

MICHAEL

Dick.

EVERLY

I know. On my way to meet with G for some brunch at that new coffee shop. Can I shave off some grovel time with a chocolate croissant or a Kouign-Amann, if they have them?

I wait a few minutes, and when I don't see a response, I decide to call Law back quickly before I get to the corner up ahead.

Picking up on the first ring, Law answers, "Everly! We fucking did it, didn't we?" Law laughs in my ear. "Ev, we handled that board like fucking bosses."

As the youngest, most people would assume that he would turn out to be the lazy lackey, but not Law. No, the youngest Riggs is pure optimism and excitement, wrapped in charm. It doesn't hurt that he's a brilliant mind, of which I'm still in awe.

No matter the season or mood, he can always make me smile. Even now, I'm giving him my proud, goofy grin as I think about the win we just had in that boardroom. "We did it. But listen, I'm about to walk into a coffee shop to meet up with G right now. Why'd you call me?"

He exaggeratedly scoffs. "Well, fine. I'm going to assume your booty call didn't remove that nicely wedged stick up your ass. I'm calling for two reasons: One, Michael has been pacing for the last hour and it took every drop of my willpower not to tell him that you went home with," he pauses and loudly whispers, "Jin, last night, and that's why you skipped your plans this morning."

I hear Michael chime in from the background. "Tell her she can get me two chocolate croissants and as many Kouign-Amanns that they have left. And I expect her to be in the gym with me tomorrow." Then he yells into the phone, over Law's shoulder, I assume, "She's doing the climbing wall! No excuses!"

"Yeah, okay. Tell him *fine*. What was the second thing?" I huff, waiting to get off this call so I can get some caffeine in my blood and see my friend.

"What? Oh, yeah, so that photographer that we booked for our rebranding is arriving today. And, um," he pauses, clearing his throat. "He had a section in his contract that I didn't realize until he called to confirm his arrival with me, and, uh, well...there's no room at any rentals that aren't total shit at the moment because of the film festival, and then there're the early snow seasoners too." I know where this is going, so I cut him off.

"What are you telling me here, Law? Cut to it."

"I think we should give him the pool house for his stay. It's convenient and we might be able to get even more done by having him close by to shoot ideas around with, or approve things he might have and-"

"That's my studio, Law. How am I supposed to finish up what I need for the spring line-up if I can't have access to all my stuff?"

I moved in with two of my three brothers a handful of years ago. Instead of each of us just shelling out money on cleaners, landscapers, and food services individually, we thought it made more sense to do it together. We spend so much time working and none of us were in relationships, at least not serious enough to move in with them, so it made sense. Buy a big enough place together. Part of that deal was the pool house was mine. I could escape there and nurture my creative side without having to deal with what comes with living with two men.

"It's not ideal. I get it, but I'm really stuck here, Ev. I don't want to be in breach of contract before we even begin. Not to mention, his agent is frightening, and I don't want to call her. He's not the guy to mess up with. He just finished an NFL Rookie spread, and you know that elite athletes body issue? That's him. Plus, he's connected. Just having him here is going to open some new conversations for us. It would suck if we couldn't provide him with a place. It was part of the contract, and I don't know how much of a dick he'd be if we said, 'Oh yeah, figure out where you're staying.'" Law just keeps rambling, but all I hear is, *"I messed up and now you have to suffer."*

"Law, I don't have enough energy this morning to deal with this, but I'm not happy. I'm fucking pissed off. You didn't read the whole contract through, did you? It would be one thing if it was just a few days, but you want a stranger to take over my personal space for the next month?"

"Yeah, pretty much. C'mon, Ev." I can hear the pleading in his voice. I hate this.

"Figure out something once the film festival is out of town. You should be able to move him elsewhere. Just know that I'm not going to get any work done on the spring line otherwise."

He blows out a breath, loudly. "Ev, I'll figure it out. Just for the record, you could find a space somewhere else to do your work while he's there."

"No! This is you fucking up and spinning it around on me because I'm mad about your dumbass solution. I'll go along with it for the short term, but fix it."

"Alright, okay! Can you get me a few of th-" I hang up before agreeing to take home any more baked goodies than necessary.

4

Everly

An electronic bell chimes as I enter through the opened double doors. Cinnamon and coffee assault my nose, and it smells so good I want to lick the air. A warm breeze nudges me forward and kicks the door closed behind me. Autumn in Colorado is host to some of the most beautiful weather in the world. The air is crisp, with no hint of snow just yet, only the promise of cool mornings and warm sunshine throughout the day. It's one of the many things that makes me love where I live so much.

Brews & Books is the newest shop downtown and the only coffee shop in the area that serves more than black coffee. It's gotten some major tourist chatter for its unique vibe. An entire location dedicated to coffee, beer, and romance books. My marketing team also swears by their pastries and their version of a black eye coffee, called a Hungry Eye, which is the typical two shots of espresso in a regular coffee, but they add something sweet with cinnamon to their version. I look around the space as I step into a line that's about a handful of people deep. Soft jazzy piano and saxophone music is playing in the background and some laughter fills the space from the banks of seats along the front window.

I spot G in an oversized fluffy swivel chair and wave to grab her attention. She points at her drink and a giant pastry on the short table in front of her. Thank goodness she didn't opt for avocado toast or something healthy. My hang-over needs some grease and sugar. Anything that looks or presumes to be healthy has no place in my life right now. There's something so comforting when your bestie can support your choices subconsciously and that giant pastry is doing just that.

The short line lets me take in the surroundings. What a small slice of heaven; it's like a warm, cozy hug, and I want to snuggle up to it. All of the seating is mismatched, but it works here. Oversized and comfortable, as if the goal is for everyone to eat, read, and nap. The front walls that aren't windows have a modern feel with beautiful black and white photography of men and women, some with just men, and two in the front with one woman and three men holding each other in various ways. It's incredibly sexy.

There are short and tall bookcases decorating the unused space, each distinguished by romance tropes. I lean around the corner and see the back of the room lined with more lounging chairs and walls chock full of books. The hissing of the milk steamer brings my attention back to the menu boards above the counter as I step forward.

Sweet-seeming ocean-blue eyes greet me, along with an awkward stammer. "Ah, hey! Hi there. Um, what can I get started for you?"

"Hi. I think I'll try your Hungry Eye coffee. And, I need something to eat for now, but then I'm also going to take home some Kouign-Amann pastries. It looks like you have only about four left, so I'll just take those."

"Sure. How about the bacon and brie croissant for your right-now food?" he suggests with a full-watt smile that shows off well taken care of teeth and a very cute, dimpled chin. This kid is still in high school and is already trying to flirt his way into a sale.

"I think that sounds great"—I look at his name tag— "Benny. Are you at Strutt's Central, or are you already out of school?"

"Central. I'm set to graduate this winter. We just moved here, so I decided I'll start my final classes at the end of next month and then graduate in the spring with everyone else."

He moves around the coffee bar quickly, pulling the pastries out of the cases and boxing them up for me to-go, then warms up my savory croissant and finishes up my drink.

"Well, I love the vibe already. Oh! I know your landlord too, so I'm not surprised." I'm not sure why I offer that information, but everyone knows everyone's business in this town, and I've been here long enough now to follow suit, I suppose. "Nice to meet you, Benny. And welcome to Strutt's Peak. I'm sure I'll see you here again."

He just nods and smiles back. I probably scared the kid with so many compliments. There's nothing like a teenager to remind you how uncool you can be when you're beyond a decade older than they are.

I make my way over to G, who's twirling a piece of her long platinum blonde hair and smiling. "Seriously, how hot is that kid?" she whisper-shouts.

I place my drink and box of pastries down and wave my hand at her. "He's in high school. That's a decent age gap, you damn cougar."

She shrugs. "I didn't say I was going to take his virginity," she says while looking at him over my shoulder.

"Okay, no way is that kid a virgin, but I wasn't going to lure him into my tattoo shop and fuck him. I was just appreciating an insanely adorable face."

"He's working that charm, for sure. How cute is this place?" I sip on my drink, my eyes closing in appreciation. "Oh my gosh, yup. This is the most delicious take on a black eye coffee I think I've ever had."

"I bet his dad is ridiculously hot," G spouts from behind her oversized mug. "What? I said it, but you thought it. It's the same thing. Okay, enough about the eye candy, and tell me what happened this morning."

I start from when we secured the approval of the entire board of directors for our expansion plans for the family business, and then to the celebratory dinner. From there, I keep the details brief about the too much tequila with Law, then the texts, and the eventual booty call with Jin sometime later.

She's quiet for a few seconds too long before I hear a huff. "You've been telling me that this 'relationship'—she uses air quotes to prove a point—"you have with Jin is just friends sleeping together to fill a void. Is that true, or do you have feelings for the guy? I mean, he's nice to look at...not my flute of champagne, but-"

I cut her off. "No! Not the kind of feelings you mean. I'm not in love with Jin. I've never been in love with him. He's never been in love with me either. We're honest with each other and we hook up when it's necessary. The rest of the time, we're friends, colleagues."

"Whether you want to admit it or not, you are both using each other as a parachute, and I don't understand why. You have told me, *repeatedly*, that you, and I quote, 'Sometimes get bored in bed.'"

"True. But sometimes a girl just needs some, even if it's mediocre. And I'm not the type of person to go home with people I don't know. That leaves a lot of blank space, ya know?"

She takes a bite of her pastry while shaking her head back-and-forth at me, "Agree to disagree on that one, Ev. Buy a better vibrator and read some reverse harem or kink romance. Don't keep calling someone to be dicked if you already know it's not gonna do it for you."

I laugh and take a deep breath. I know she's right.

"Forget about Jin. Move your life forward. Have a few great orgasms with a sexy stranger. Nobody is watching. Do you, boo. But stop wasting your time with repeat placeholders. Jin is a good guy, but that good guy can't satisfy you. And that's just as important, if not more, than good guy status." She laughs at her own joke. "Let me talk this out for a second...the guys you've gone after for as long as I've known you are always friends first."

"That's true."

She ticks off the rest of her fingers. "They get bored, you get bored, sometimes you want more, sometimes not. Oh shit, I remember the guy from your gym who just moved without telling you. It was the greatest ghosting of all time! And you didn't even get upset about it." I know what she's getting at here, but I let her continue. She's on a roll. "Ev, my darling sister from another silver fox mister, it's time to say *it's really not you, it's me.* And mean it."

"Take a page from my book for a little while. Test out different men and see what you might like. I love you and I love that we're different, but why not try looking at men as temporary for a little while. I know you want the relationship, the husband, but why not pause that high-standard job description for a little while?"

"I'm listening." Maybe she has a point here. If I don't try something else, I'm going to keep ending up in the same place. Settling. And I'm so scared I will end up settling for someone that's just barely enough. What she's suggesting isn't that crazy. Harden up my heart, soften the hard limits for the type of men I find suitable, and just go for it.

"I can see you having a real coming to goddess moment here, but I'm just making a suggestion. I'm not saying you need to adopt my mentality completely. I know full well that my approach is not a guide for how to find the love of your life, but it is a shake-up for how to find some of the best sex of your life."

"I hear everything you're saying, but I don't know how to do all of that."

"Stop thinking about the future. Stop trying to check all the boxes that you want in a life partner and instead just feel it." She takes a bite of her pastry, then points her finger at my lap and says, "Ev, you gotta let that kitty purr."

She shimmies forward in her seat, readying to stand. "I have to open the shop for a few hours. I have some scheduled touch-ups to do this afternoon and a couple of customers coming in tonight. Sunday dinner tomorrow?"

I pout. "Want to come over for a glass of something after your appointments tonight?"

"I'm planning to have a few orgasms tonight. It's been a bit, ya know?" She pops the last of her croissant into her mouth and brushes the flakey crumbs off her fingers. "That guy with the mosaic stained glass design I've been working on for months across his chest and down his back is looking to dip it farther into that nice V-cut and I feel like if he's not interested in some bumpin' and thumpin' afterward, then I'm going to hit up my vibration station for a little relief."

Sometimes I can't respond fast enough to what comes out of her mouth, so I just laugh and shake my head. "Okay, fair enough. And yes, Sunday dinner is on."

We get up together to head out, and as G's pulling on her jacket, she whips her head back to me and points her finger in my direction.

"You didn't say what we're having, which means it's barbeque, which also means dickhead is cooking."

"Smoking, actually. He's doing a smoked duck and maybe a brisket thing."

"Of course he is. Fucking show-off. Who's he bringing?"

"I have no idea. I don't think anybody, but you know Henry, he's so tight-lipped about who he's seeing after he broke up with 'the one who we shall not name' that I have no clue."

"I can't stand the brooding oaf, obviously. But I still hate that redheaded wildebeest with such passion. I'm glad I don't have to endure any more discussions about juice cleanses and why art should be hung and not worn. She was such a pretentious, condescending bitch. I don't know what he saw in her."

As we walk out of the shop, I can't keep from laughing. "I'll probably never know. I mean, she was beautiful. I'll give her that, but it was only skin deep. She was awful, wasn't she?"

G and Henry really can't stand to be in the same space for too long. They were instant hate from the moment I brought G around.

We stop at the front of G's tattoo shop, which is conveniently right next to Brews & Books. "Love you. I'll see you tomorrow, then?"

She wraps her arms around me, never shying away from affection. "You will. And think about what I said. Sometimes you just need to flirt and fuck your way out of a funk. You never know, maybe you'll find that what you're looking for is something or *someone* you never would have tried."

I wave at her over my shoulder and start the trek back to my house.

A short gondola ride, a heap of overthinking, and then ten more blocks, and I'm strolling into our driveway. Wearing my Jimmy Choos, an oversized Riggs Outdoor sweatshirt, and my black pencil skirt, with my hair piled high in a messy bun, I'm embodying the *leftovers from last night* look. My tired and hungover brain is ready for a shower and a nap. I can strategize about my lackluster love life later.

5

Everly

As soon as I open the front door, I'm assaulted by the smell of oranges, which means Law is making Old Fashioneds. Most people would assume juice or maybe a fruit salad, but I know my baby brother; it's the weekend, and oranges mean Old Fashioneds.

I trip over a pile of black duffels and garment bags in the front foyer. Then I hear laughing from the kitchen and Law shouting from somewhere in the house. The negative to living with roommates is that you have to deal with their habits, and Law has a knack for not thinking ahead. Like, *I shouldn't leave stuff in front of the door in case someone else walks in...*

"LAW! Why is your shit all over the floor? C'mon! I almost just fell on my face. And whose motorcycle is that? Who drives a Harley up here?"

I'm tired and cranky. The walk home, while beautiful, was also just a bit too far, and at the peak point of the day, with the sun high, getting me nice and sweaty, my thighs chafed, and a blister started on my right foot.

I'm still yelling while I walk into the kitchen. "Law, my boobs are sweating, I have no idea where my underwear went, and I'm-"

I stop dead in my tracks. My brain can't register all of the parts that make up the stranger that's leaning casually on our marble counter.

Are we being robbed? Are we being robbed by the world's hottest robber? Is he here to kidnap me? *Take me, please. I'll go willingly.*

Looking at this dish of a man is like ticking off a list of the most delicious features on a menu made up of all the fixins that are about to result in a hands-free orgasm.

Sexy smile. Oh, there's a dimple, nope, two. *I'll tick that box.*

Light eyes. Are they sparkling? *Yup, check.*

Dark brown, nope, black hair, cut tight. *Check. Is it wet?*

Tight black t-shirt showing off nicely sized biceps. Yup, and sculpted shoulders. *We'll just go ahead and select that too.*

Don't look down. *Damnit.* He's wearing dark, faded jeans. *Those fit nicely.*

My eyes rove over to his hands resting on the counter and a leather cuff wraps around his wrist. *Why is that sexy?*

No wedding ring. *Check.*

No tan line or indentation from a pocketed wedding ring either. *Double-check.*

And he's just waiting in my kitchen to be visually assaulted. My face feels hot, and I realize I haven't said anything since I plowed into the room less than thirty seconds ago. He's staring back at me now, with no reaction, just an intimidating, stoic gaze. The corner of his very pretty mouth twitches slightly. If I had blinked right then, I would have missed it. This tall drink of sex water is very aware that he has me flustered.

Sex water? No idea what that is, but I'm thirsty and want a big ol' sip.

I imagine this happens to him often, but for me, this is new. Not many people catch me off guard. Even fewer kick-start a ticker-tape parade of dirty thoughts that begins and ends with a very suckable lower lip, like the one on that man's mouth.

The robber slash live-action thirst trap licks it, as if I needed another reason to change my not-even-there underwear, and says, "The Harley and bags are mine." His smooth, deep voice drops an octave lower as he continues. "Would it make you feel more comfortable knowing that I'm not wearing any either?"

Of course, without thinking, like a reflex, I look down at his crotch. Did his dick just flex and wave at me? Look away. Look. Away. D*amn it.* I looked again.

"Everly! Finally!" Law shouts as he jogs down the stairs and across the room.

That knocks me right out of the eye-fucking haze.

Law stops mid-stride and stares at me. "Did you *walk* home?" And before I can even answer, he continues. "I'm making afternoon drinks." He turns back and ignores, or just completely misses, the fact that I was rattled by the stranger standing mere feet from me. "I was just going to give Jack a tour, but we thought it would be better with a drink. Want one?"

I shift my gaze back to our supposed houseguest, who has managed to completely throw me off any type of game. He crosses his arms over his chest like he's amused and I'm his entertainment. I spot his dimple again as the left corner of his mouth kicks up. This man is so beautiful, it's impossible to not acknowledge it, even if I'm annoyed by it. Even if I hadn't already dragged my attention over every inch of this man's body, it would have been impossible to not notice that with his arms crossed, his shoulders and biceps strain under his shirt, and I'm all of a sudden very appreciative of his upper body workouts. What does it feel like to be overpowered by those arms? Grabbed by his hands? Held tight against him?

I keep trying to shake myself out of these thoughts, but the universe decided to have a good laugh in my honor today. Is this an *ask and you shall receive,* or *complainers are fools* moment? My heart rate won't slow down, racing so fast it feels like I just finished a warm-up sprint at the gym. I'm fairly certain my cheeks are still shades of pink, and *if* there were panties involved, they'd be long ruined by now.

6

Jack

"Everly." I nod and smile at her again. She still looks flustered by our exchange, and I can't say that rattling the steel reserve that she portrays, at least in business, based on her reputation, definitely turns me on. But I'm fucked up like that. I wonder how often someone catches her off guard? My guess is practically never.

Righting herself, she takes on an entirely new stance, as if she's ready to strike. Her body language changes, standing taller, her expression blank. She doesn't say anything else. Instead, she grabs an apple from the oversized refrigerator and takes a bite, leaning back against the counter next to it. With still reddened cheeks, she lifts her eyes and gives me a tight-lipped smile. She's going to try and knock me down now, and I'm watching as she readies to go full alpha on me. *Bring it, beautiful.*

"Jack. The photographer." She says it accusingly. Almost

disrespectfully. Unaware of the level of success I've achieved, I'll let her have her moment. Gain her footing.

"Among other things, but yes. The photographer," I say right back.

"I know my brother has high expectations for what you're able to do with our brand." Lifting her left shoulder, she takes another bite. "I'm not so easily convinced." She leans forward to speak more softly, just to me. "I'm also not interested in flirting, Mr. Deacon. Keep it professional, and we'll be good. 'Kay?" Her voice kicks up more cheerfully, and she smiles widely.

I nod. "It's your show, Miss Riggs."

The truth is, I know as much as there is to know about the Riggs family. Luce is a cross between an agent, personal assistant, and detective. She does thorough research on all the businesses before I sign any contracts. Riggs Outdoor Sports and Adventures has a board of directors that encourages the company's growth and approves big moves. Asher Riggs, however, holds fifty-one percent share. That means he can veto when the board tries to take his legacy in the wrong direction. He hasn't let it happen yet. I say *yet* because, at some point, most if not all companies fall off their proverbial cliff.

It started as a little storefront, renting and selling winter sports gear, but over the past decade, it has more than grown, it's flourished. Now, with all four of the kids taking hold of different seasonal sports and departments, the company has expanded into multiple categories, far beyond where it first started. Part of the company's appeal is that it offers extreme sporting adventures all year long. And there is also an indoor facility at Riggs headquarters for prep and training.

On top of that, the company sells a unique clothing apparel line, with new styles for each season, all with the Riggs name attached. The apparel is a hot commodity, and it's completely original from an unknown source. Riggs stopped selling competitor clothing and accessories altogether, and now they only sell their own brand. And the brand sells wildly. It's made a splash with a ton of professional, elite-level athletes, giving the big brands a nervous tick. A disruption I haven't witnessed before, and it has the industry buzzing with anxious excitement. I know most of the athletes who swear by the Riggs brand. I've seen the goods up close. Hell, I have a pair of their sweats and they're nice, better than nice, if I'm being honest.

The fact of the matter is, Riggs Outdoor is on the cusp of being the hot ticket, and it's the name on everyone's lists as a business to mimic. When Law reached out to Luce, I was already half sold on the job just by hearing their name. Needless to say, its projection for growth is on track, but it needs a visual and branding upgrade to keep that momentum. That's why I'm here. Elevating what a company is already good at is an area in which I'm well-versed. Most of the time, it's why I'm hired. Law knows it, but without ruffling too many feathers internally, he asked for that evaluation and plan discreetly. As far as the rest of the Riggs team knows, I'm simply a photographer and designer, here to amplify their appeal.

The internet only provided surface-level details about each of the Riggs siblings. The details mostly listed well-curated public relations, including some charity items the company participates in annually and collaborations with sponsored athletes. And because it's a family business, with a handful of thirty-somethings who are all very good looking, the social media chatter was heavy. Even heavier with pictures of the Riggs men. Ranging from their countless dates to working out, and even more on slopes, rivers, and hikes, doing what they do best. Playing in and selling the fun of the outdoors. It's done well, but I can help them do it better.

The brunette standing across from me, squared off as if she's about to either climb me or kick me, had the least personal information to find. She didn't have many pictures available, and the ones that were posted didn't do her much justice. Most of the pictures were headshots for the business and an old resume profile, a random few of her climbing or skiing with her brothers, and then a couple with her father at industry events. I have a feeling even if there were more to find, I still wouldn't have been prepared to face off with this kamikaze of a woman. She's pure confidence and fire. But I'm just arrogant enough to know that I set her off-balance, and now I can't help but think about pushing the kinds of buttons that might just make her keep her attention in my direction.

She's impressive, to begin with, but also knowing that she's been at the helm of this business for the past handful of years is intimidating. Everly is the one in the driver's seat, moving it all forward. They don't cut corners. Anyone who has done business with Riggs Outdoor raves about their ethics and the return, and because of that, she's widely respected. There aren't many people who can remain well respected within their company, have a high retention rate, and still procure the kind of growth she has. She's a force.

I can't stop looking at her. I keep noticing small things that emphasize her beauty, like the fullness of her mouth, with a perfectly shaped bow making it look like a plump heart, and the dip of her waist that tells me her hips and ass are bite-worthy. If you add the physical to all that I know about her professionally, I'm left with a hard-on and a blooming crush. *Not my style.*

And it's only been about five minutes. I've already imagined what it would feel like to rub my hands along her body. Explore what kinds of things she likes. How her voice would change when she's turned on. Does she get breathy, or more talkative? Is she shy, or would she tell me what she wants?

She knows that I can't stop looking at her and she's trying incredibly hard to *not* look at me now. *Cute.*

She clears her throat, knocking me out of my head. "Where's Michael?"

Law doesn't turn or even respond to her right away. Instead, he concentrates on making our drinks. "He's around here somewhere. Here!" Law places two scotch glasses in front of us. "Tell me if this isn't the best Old Fashioned you've ever had."

She mumbles, "Almost," before taking a sip.

"Everly!" another voice yells from somewhere else in the house. Maybe from upstairs? I haven't figured out how many people actually live here. Apparently, a few of them. Maybe all of the Riggs siblings?

"We are set for the gym after dinner. I've got our climbing gear in my car." A succession of thumping sounds comes barreling down the main stairs from the other side of the house. A tall, lean guy with a top-knot charges into the kitchen without acknowledging that I'm in the room, then continues. "You blew me off, so I decided you're also going to go back to the gym with me again today to make up for making me worry."

"Dude, don't be rude." Law stares at him. He doesn't look

at Law, only at Everly, but Law keeps talking. "Jack is the brand guy, the photographer. He had the proposal for the new look that we all really liked. He's staying in the pool house. Remember, we talked about this."

Michael continues to ignore Law. I don't know why, but it makes me laugh. Instead of responding to his brother, he stares at Everly and says, "Ev, I can't answer Law until you confirm that you're not blowing me off again. Gym. Climbing. You had your *sex* time. Now, back to business. Why aren't you answering me?"

Her eyes widen at him. And then she glances at me with flushed cheeks. "Michael, you know better."

He just looks at her, tilting his chin up.

She lets out a harsh breath. "Fine! I'll go. *You're* buying dinner. And what are you, a teenager? Who says sex time?"

I'm trying so hard not to laugh. The awkwardness of this entire discussion makes the elusive Riggs family much more human. Not at all what you'd expect in a business meeting, but exactly what you find between siblings. I can tell this isn't how Everly does business. She's very clearly pissed off and trying to mask her discomfort.

Michael doesn't smile, but the change in his tone is obvious, now more pleasant than annoyed, as he turns to me and says, "Jack. Nice to meet you." He holds out a hand to shake. "Michael. Most of what you're shooting next week is in my arena..." Ticking off on his fingers, he goes on. "Hiking, climbing, base jumping, fishing, and ATVs. I don't like spending my personal time with people I don't know, so I'd like to keep things professional. I'm sure Law can keep your social time busy when we're not at the office. No offense, I just like to do my own thing. I feel like it's better to lay that out instead of you wondering if I just don't like you."

"All good. I'm happy to keep it professional." I flick my eyes over to the gorgeous brunette who has my pulse ticking up. "I appreciate you opening your home to me, but I'm here to work. I won't be in anyone's way."

Everly clears her throat, and I think I even hear her scoff. Likely at my comment about being professional. The noise draws my attention back in her direction. Damn, she's beautiful. Her hair is a wild mess on the top of her head, but it allows me to take in her big hazel eyes, swirling with browns and greens, and that plush mouth. She has a small beauty mark above her lip that screams sexy. The tight black skirt, which seems like it's leftover from the night before, frames the lower half of her hourglass shape. Her calves are toned and...*Shit*. She catches me raking my eyes down her body.

With her gaze now locked on mine, she says, "I use the pool house apartment as my home office too, so can you let me know if you're not going to be there for long stretches?"

"Not a problem." I smile. She drags her eyes from my lips down my body and back up again, almost as a response to my obvious gawking. She smirks and leaves the kitchen. Touché.

Law claps me on the shoulder. "Let's give you the tour, and then I can help you get settled. Oh, and we should definitely grab drinks after dinner tonight. It's the best time to go out. The film festival is in town, which means fresh faces." He wiggles his eyebrows.

"I'm in."

7

....

Everly

THERE ARE A SELECT FEW THINGS THAT CAN HELP ME ZONE out and relax, make me stop thinking about work emails, end-of-quarter numbers, and overzealous vendors. I never understood the importance of finding the things that make me turn off the internal scrutiny I'm so very good at unleashing on myself.

I can sit down for hours and read a book straight through; forgo sleep and even snacks if a romance book has the right balance of steam and anticipation for that happily ever after. And a great upside-down latte, or my new favorite, a Hungry Eye. Iced is always preferred. I can escape with caffeine and dirty words. It's so simple and it can act as such a source of therapy for me. I'm already itching to go back to Brews & Books, explore some of the new indie authors, and maybe add more to my already overflowing bookshelves.

Beyond books, this town and the mountains are what

ground me. The sunrises and fresh air are something I always took for granted when I was younger, like most kids tend to do, I suppose. It wasn't until I lived in New York City and I couldn't see many, if any, stars, that I realized how much I missed the bigness of a starry sky. Loud, busy cities have their own kind of beauty, but for me, it wasn't enough. I missed my mountains and my views too much to only see them on holidays and long weekends.

That choice also meant I left behind opportunities. I always loved to draw. Sweaters, dresses, even swimwear sometimes, and accessories. I turned the drawings into actual garments for my Barbie dolls and eventually was making dresses for prom. I adored the movie *Pretty in Pink*. I never had a Ducky, but I definitely had a crush on *that* pink dress that Molly Ringwald had spun together. I had tried and somewhat succeeded in making my own for prom but with more of a 90s flair. I was damn proud of that dress at the time.

Awards shows like the Oscars, or the Met Gala are my special brand of porn. When it came time to decide if I was going to take it seriously and go to school to see if my talent could evolve and be nurtured, I jumped. I was homesick for the first semester, so far away from everything I knew, but Manhattan and design school were all I had my sights on at that point in my life, so I was going to do it no matter how much I wanted to run back home. It took the entirety of my four years to realize that while I did have talent, the world was a big place, and talent was subjective. Someone was always better, and the industry that held my attention spit on my excitement enough times that I knew I had to improvise what success for me looked like.

Lizzo croons away through the speakers, stamping down

truths like being her own soulmate, and I can't help but smile while I work away on my latest drafts of loungewear for our spring line. Designing, sketching, and creating something on paper that I can sew to life is truly what makes my heart beat faster. And just because I didn't follow the path that gets you into a world-renowned design house as a top designer, it didn't mean I was going to stop doing it.

The styles I'm working on lately are what Law has coined "sexy loungewear." It's meant for both men and women to wear right after they come in from outdoor sports. My take is that after an adrenaline-induced session outdoors, it's a shame to throw on an ugly shirt or sweats, but instead to opt for the same comfort just in a cut and color variety that induces a sexier vibe.

Two years ago, Law was so excited to show off my men's sweats that he and some of his fraternity brothers, after one of their bachelor parties, decided to model them in a few photos on Instagram. One of Law's buddies is an agent for some pretty hot professional football players, and he shared the photos. Needless to say, it snowballed, and the hype for my men's loungewear started. Our brand of apparel now represents a third of our profits. The online portion of our business exploded and has made Riggs a brand name and not just an outdoor sports company in Colorado.

Law and I decided we'd try to create more hype by pushing the designs to the athletes his best friend had known, and we've been growing ever since. The best part is the world has no idea who's behind it and that's exactly how I want it to stay. I want to be known for my business skills and take the Riggs name to an entirely new level. I never wanted to be scrutinized for something creative that has a little piece of my heart in it, so everybody wins. I've worked hard to be where I am at the company, and to be honest, the apparel is too much fun, too easy to be anything more than a lucrative hobby. The mystery of who designs it all plays in our favor. I get to design, and we make a full profit without having to outsource.

I dig a pencil out of the wet knot of hair I threw up after my gym session with Michael and then make a few changes to the women's off-the-shoulder sweatshirt in front of me. Thinking about whether I want it to be full cotton or a poly-blend, I look around the space and notice the mess. Jack's things are thrown around; shirts draped over the couch, a few pairs of shoes in the living room area, camera equipment taking up the full length of the coffee table, and chargers with cords on the side tables. *Invasion of my space!*

How am I just noticing it all now? The pool house is a 2,000 sq. ft. room with high ceilings and large windows that overlook the pool, hence why we call it the pool house. My design area is separate from the bedroom, living room, and kitchenette. It runs the length of the north-facing wall and overlooks our back property and the most prominent mountain ridge in all of Strutt's Peak. The view is breathtaking. It's *my* haven and I'm a little anxious to have a stranger taking it over. Regardless of how hot that stranger might be.

"I'm gone for less than an hour and you're already working your way into my space, Miss Riggs?" I snap my head up to get an eyeful of a very sweaty Jack Deacon chugging a bottle of water. Keeping his eyes on me, head tilted back as he swallows large gulps, his Adam's apple bobs up and down. It's like I'm in a damn trance. He walks over to where my phone is perched on my drafting table to turn down the music that's pumping through the entire pool house.

"*My* space, you mean?"

He gives me a slow, devious smile that runs chills down my arms.

"I thought you were out for the night already, otherwise I wouldn't be here." I was just getting into my zone and now I'm interrupted by this distractingly sexy man who's going to ask me questions that I have zero interest in answering. "I'll get out of your way. Let me just grab a few things."

"Went for a run. I'm heading out with Law in about twenty minutes." He leans back against the counter of the kitchenette, curiously looking at what I'm doing. I throw my portfolio case over my large drafting table to keep him from seeing what I've been working on. "Don't bother leaving. I'm showering and then I'll be out for the night."

Too quickly, I respond, "You can shower at our place. That outdoor shower is only fun to use in the summertime."

He moves to the other side of the room, reaching back and pulling his sweaty t-shirt over his head. I'm assaulted with tight, lean muscles and broad shoulders. His waist tapers inward and my mouth goes dry. There's not a bit of fat on this man, but he's so large that he's still incredibly intimidating. It takes every ounce of my sanity to not let out a nervous giggle in response to how attractive that move just was. And wildly inappropriate.

"The hot water right now is questionable."

He turns around from his suitcase, which is splayed on the bed across the room. "It's going to take a little more effort on your part, Miss Riggs, to get me naked and in your shower. I am worth the effort, but I don't think we should be mixing business and pleasure." He rakes his eyes over me, and I feel it from the backs of my knees all the way to my shoulders.

I have no words. I'm not sure if I'm embarrassed, pissed off, or just short-circuiting from being so turned on by the forwardness of this guy.

"That's not..." I get up, shaking my head, and start pushing my designs and swatch samples back into their oversized leather drawing bag. "Believe me, Jack, if I wanted anything to do with you, naked or otherwise, you'd know. But in case it's not clear. I like men, not boys. And certainly not boys who work for me." I make my way to the door, and without another glance back at the walking thirst trap, I shut the door behind me. There goes my calm.

I pull my phone from my yoga pants pocket and text G.

EVERLY

> I need you to abandon your plans tonight. I
> need to drink and flirt. Please?

I know she had plans, but I never say please about either thing. My phone vibrates back almost immediately.

GISELLE

> Giddyup! Your thirsty bitch is just wrapping
> up. Meet you in an hour.

8

<hr>

Jack

"WE'LL TAKE ANOTHER ROUND, HONEY." LAW WINKS AT THE cocktail waitress that's been serving us for the past couple of hours. She's been flirting with him since we walked in, and by the way he's paid her extra attention, I'm guessing they know each other rather well.

He checks his phone for the time. "We can make this our last round and move on if you want. There's a ridge-side bar with an incredible view. Pretty decent local bands play on weekends. Original stuff too, not just overplayed covers."

Looking up, he waves at the two women who just walked by us for the third time. We've been at this cigar bar talking about his marketing vision for the Riggs brand for about an hour, and now that business is out of the way, I can tell he wants the night to move on.

"Should I ask them to join us?"

I give him a nonchalant tilt of my head. I'm not interested, but if he is, then I'll go with the flow. Instead of asking them over, he carries on talking about The Strutt's Peak Film Festival that hits their town every year. Also, it's part of the reason that I've gathered as to why I'm staying at their place and not near the office or in a condo, with which ski towns tend to be riddled.

"The two women who just waved, the brunette is a director, and the redhead is her PA. Best friends turned lovers. Great girls. Definitely not interested in me joining them for any after-hours party. I got that message loud and clear when the redhead threw a coffee in my face last year."

I look at him in a little disbelief at the douchebag assumption and can't hold back a laugh.

"I'm lucky it was iced." The memory has him wincing, and I only refrain from laughing until he continues with a shrug. "It's fine. I apologized, and by the end of the night, I was helping them with their social media issues and talking about the best wine to pair with potato chips."

"They're not all they're cracked up to be." He raises his eyebrows. "Two women at once. It's hot as hell, but if you do it right and make sure they're satisfied first, it ends up being really fucking exhausting."

"No offense, but I'm not taking your word for it. I'd rather test it out and see if I share in that theory. Life goals, ya know?"

"Fair enough." I cough out a laugh. It's not the typical colleague chatter, but I'm learning that Law isn't like most of the people I've worked with. None of the Riggs family that I've met so far are what I was expecting.

The last threesome I participated in ended up being a social media scandal that followed me around for far too long. I knew they were wealthy, but I had no clue they were technically royalty and any kind of sexualizing of royalty is very frowned upon. Let's just say it wasn't worth the headache it created in the long run. My phone vibrates in my pocket. *Speaking of headaches.*

LUCIFER

> Your sister texted me asking where you are, so I'm assuming you haven't been by to see them yet. She's only texting me, because she knows I'll respond immediately. Please tell me you are, in fact, in Colorado, like you're supposed to be.

JACK

> Yes, I'm here. I'll call her first thing tomorrow. I'm just getting settled.

LUCIFER

> Today! Make it a priority, Jack. Or she's going to text me again. I'm not your therapist or your secretary. Please handle your family shit.

She's right. Not that there's been much time since I've arrived in Strutt's Peak to see my sister or nephew, but I did get distracted. They've been through enough shit lately, and the fact that they're in the same town as this job means I get much-needed time with the most important people in my life. I should have made time to see them already, let alone tell her I was here already. Women and work never get in the way with what little family I have.

JACK

> Can you do some digging for me?

LUCIFER

> No.

JACK

I need some details on Everly Riggs. What I
can't find on Google.

LUCIFER

No. Do the fucking job and keep your dick
in your pants, man-child.

Law hits my knee with the toe of his shoe to draw my attention back. "I'm a big fan of your work. Obviously. What should I know about you that isn't properly curated online?"

I prefer to keep conversations like this one light and simple. The heavily edited online details are the only things I want people to find. The world doesn't need to know too much, *dig too deep.*

I always take a minute to decide what version of my life I'm willing to share with someone. Do they deserve the bird's-eye view, the glossy version, or the truth?

"I grew up on the east coast, a small town in Connecticut not far from New York." *Bird's-eye view, it is.* "I went to RISD." He raises his eyebrow. It's not ivy, so pretty-boy here might not know it. "Rhode Island School of Design. I studied photography. I decided to stay in the Northeast and head into Manhattan. For the business I'm in, it makes the most sense. Got my MBA from Columbia and decided to stay in the city. It was either New York or L.A. I love the change in seasons. And the east coast does winters better than California ever can."

"You haven't seen a Colorado winter, then."

"I haven't, you're right. And what about you?"

"I'm from here, but you already knew that." He looks at me and knows that I'm already aware of where he's from, but I know he'll entertain the question. "Everyone assumes

my old man pushed us all to be a part of the family business. He has a strong personality. You'll know what I mean
when you meet him, but it wasn't like that. My dad never
pushed his dream on any of us. We were all just smart
enough to know a great thing to stand behind."

The waitress's voice cuts in. "Law, you want me to close
out your tab?"

He takes a sip from his Manhattan and smiles at her
again. "You bet, honey. Tell Frank I said nice job on the cocktails tonight. He *almost* got the Manhattan perfect. Text me if
you get off early, yeah?" He winks at her.

The brunette squeezes his forearm. "Maybe." She looks
my way after attempting to play coy, but we all know she'll
be texting him later. "Jack, good to meet you. Come back
and see me again?"

I just smile and salute her with my drink.

Law's phone must buzz, as he pulls it from his jacket and
texts someone back while smiling. "Alright, what was I
saying? Oh yeah, so about two years after grinding away in
agency life, I took a swift look at my options and decided I
was wasting my time. It made more sense to dedicate my
time to growing the family business. I'm the youngest and
everyone else had already carved out places where they
would be instrumental in its growth. It was my sister who
talked me into coming back home and running marketing."

Just the mention of her and I'm picturing her in the
kitchen all over again. Flushed and vulnerable, looking at
me as if she wanted to lick every inch of me. I sure as shit
wanted to steal a taste of her, especially after thinking about
her lack of panties. *Damn.*

Law continues. "She told me if I could run award-
winning campaigns to sell people water, a product that can

be free from your tap, then I could kick ass for the family business, where we had a carved-out market, location, and superior shit." He laughs and pauses, maybe remembering the discussion. "She said it, not me, and that was it." He claps his hands together. "That was about five years ago now, and we're finally in a place where our visions for growth have been approved by the board and my dad. It was the right move."

I can appreciate their dynamics and the relationships they have with each other. To have someone inside your family that you grew up with recognize a talent and cheer them on, but also support how they lead their life. It's inspiring, and I have a pang of jealousy for not being a part of it. "So Everly is the ringleader, then? Or is your father still at the helm?"

Before answering me, Law leans back in his seat and thinks for a beat. "Everly's more like the hero. My dad isn't ready to let go completely, and Ev gets that, but it also doesn't stop her from getting her way. My sister is the best person you'll ever meet. She's tough as hell and can run the shit out of this company."

I'm half hard just thinking about the woman, but beyond that, I'm realizing she's in an entirely different league than the type of women I'm used to being around. There's danger in that, I can feel it, but it just makes me think about her full lips and the way her tongue swiped along them when she dragged her eyes down my body in the pool house.

"She's a badass." Law pulls my attention back to our conversation. "Over the last handful of years, she's managed to grow our team efficiently and has doubled sales every quarter. Except for last year. Last year, we tripled our numbers when Henry finally got his way and we incorporated two choppers into our heli-skiing program. Not to mention, she's creative as hell...if you saw some of the stuff she wasn't getting credit for..." He blows out a breath. "Eh, anyway, that's enough shop talk. What do ya say, want to hit up the next spot with me?"

I look at my watch. It's just about ten-thirty, and I'm starting to fade fast. Law can tell I'm going to say no and decides to seal the deal by telling me, "That was her, by the way, who just texted me. Ev and her best friend, G, are at the bar right now. Want to push some of her buttons and check out the view?"

He saw us together today. He knows what he's doing by dangling his sister as bait to keep the night going. While a good night's sleep is the smarter option, I'd rather check out the view. That realization pisses me off more than anything, but not enough to change my mind.

"Let's go."

9

Everly

"It hits just the right spot. I'm telling you, Ev. It's like when you grind down all the way, it's a clit-hitter." G sips her vodka and lemons on the rocks. She keeps going on about her last appointment of the day.

"Now they just need to make vibrating piercings. Oh! Or can you imagine if you could do matching piercings, like those Best Friend heart necklaces when we were kids, but these are like the adult versions, and every time they meet, they'd start vibrating?" G is on a roll once again, and I'm laughing my ass off.

"I feel like there's a business idea here...What? Stop laughing at me. I'm being serious."

"I'm not laughing at you, I promise. Is this guy good enough for round two?" I look around the bar, surveying who we might know here, and to be sure we haven't attracted too much attention between my laughing and G's loud, sexual business ideas.

"Ev, round two was when I discovered the clit-hitter. Then we had round three in the break room. Then you texted and I decided you were my perfect escape. The guy was starting to talk about getting breakfast together in the morning. I thought it was very clear when I was finishing his tattoo that we were going to see each other's O-faces and then the only aftercare necessary was for his new ink."

"You know, one of these days, you're going to find one that matches *your* wants and you're going to be the one planning breakfast."

"Doubtful." She laughs, but then instantly scowls after looking over my shoulder. "Fucking, great," she says in a deadpan tone.

I look toward what's turned her mood into an instant downer. Around the outdoor firepit is my brother, Law, making exaggerated arm gestures, narrating some kind of story that has about half a dozen women laughing. Next to him is my brother, Henry, looking as pissed off as ever. Always stoic, rarely showing any kind of emotion other than disdain, but for some reason, women still flock to him. That very beautiful redhead included, who is whispering some-thing in his ear. *Gross.* I love my brothers, but I could do without seeing women throw themselves all over them. Having a thing with a Riggs boy is like a rite of passage in this town. *Double ick.*

"Henry looks like he's sized up his butt plug this evening, based on that scowl he's sporting. Ew, is that girl nibbling on his ear? It's not even after midnight, for fuck's sake."

G waves the cocktail waitress over to us for another round, then she drags her annoyed attention back to my brothers and Jack. "Are you fucking kidding me, Ev? Tell me *that's* the photographer that has your panties in a frontal wedgie." She grabs my arm and squeezes as if to draw more details out of me.

On the other side of the firepit is Jack talking to another annoyingly pretty woman, but instead of looking at her and returning her flirtatious body language, he's staring right back at me. "Yes. That would be him."

"Cheezus, Everly Riggs, you had better get that man to spank your ass and tell you to be his good girl, or I'm calling dibs. What, is he just staring at you?"

"He's staring." Jack looks away for a minute to answer something the Chatty Cathy to his left just said, then resumes his attention back to me.

"I'm staring now. Please tell me he has, like, a whiny voice or is dumb as rocks or something to offset that face. Oh, wow, and that body."

He winks, then smiles; he knows we're talking about and objectifying him. His dimples flash and it's as if he's unleashed some sort of hidden sexual weapon of mass destruction. I'm speechless and need more vodka in my mouth, immediately.

"I either just came or I've peed myself," G deadpans.

I practically choke on my sip.

G continues. "*That's* the asshole in your pool house for the next month? Hell, Ev, it's like God herself decided to call the *Holy Hot as Fuck Division*, and said, 'Everly Riggs needs to be good and thoroughly fucked. Send in the big guns.'"

I drag my attention away from him and gape at my friend. Sometimes the things that come out of her mouth are pure comedic gold.

"What? You do *not* want to get on Her bad side. When

the universe sends you a gift, you take it. And, girl, you need to TAKE. IT! This is exactly the kind of person we were just talking about. Gorgeous, fire-inducing, and temporary."

"G, I worry about you sometimes."

"Don't. I have plenty of money, my business is incredibly fulfilling, and I am a liberated woman who enjoys men, sometimes women, in all shapes and sizes. You, my fabulous friend, have been telling me for the past year that your fuck buddy is, and I quote, 'Okay-*ish* in bed.' I mean, what is that? It wasn't even okay, you added the *ish*! I'm the one concerned about *you*. And now you have a living, breathing men's cologne and underwear advertisement just existing mere feet away from where you sleep at night and you're asking me what's wrong with me!? Girl, this is your opportunity to abandon your checked boxes and focus on your *lady box*. I'm sure she's annoyed you haven't presented her to him yet."

I can't argue with her there. For the next few minutes, I think about what she says as I steal glances at the newest visitor to grace our small town's presence. There are a few groups of women who walk up to the guys, flirt, and grab selfies. My brothers have a bit of a following on social media, but Jack is just ridiculously good looking, and it's not wrong to assume that he's some kind of celebrity. How can a person even be jealous? I mean, someone who looks like him needs to be experienced by many. And my guess is that he's experienced. It's not that we're in different leagues. We play different sports. I wonder if I can do this, play in his arena, with no strings and just great sex. Am I even built for it?

Getting up from the table, she grabs her drink and nods

for me to follow her. It looks like we're going to say hello after all. The brisk air outside hits with a bite when we open the doors to the firepit patio. Even though she came from a full afternoon of work and a post-appointment hook-up, Giselle still manages to look flawlessly confident.

My girl rocks a tight black leather skirt and vintage cropped Nina Simone concert t-shirt, with black combat boots. Her colorful wildflower tattoos cascade from her shoulders down to her hands. If she emerged from the ocean right now, I'd be certain she was a siren waiting to devour the next man to glance her way.

There's always a sense of fun woven into what she wears. It's a stark contrast to my black-on-black attire, but don't get me wrong, I feel the most confident in the basics of black and white. The only trace of color I'm sporting tonight is the crushed velvet red lipstick I stained my lips with earlier. My favorite black cocktail dress hits just below the knee, but hugs my boobs, hips, and waist just perfectly. It's sexy and understated. I put more attention into the material and the cut instead of color. The one similarity between us physically is that we both rock long hair. I have dark waves, with some lighter caramel highlights that run past my shoulders, while G has white-blonde, almost silver, tresses that drape down her back in loose curls.

"There she is! Get over here, Everly, and help me talk Henry into making those duck fat potatoes with his smoked meat this weekend." Law likes to use me as the negotiator between him and Henry. I have a really good relationship with each of them, but with each other, it's very competitive. At least that's the case with Henry and Law. I kiss Law on the cheek, then I lean down to Henry and do the same.

"Be nice today. She's in a good mood, so don't ruin my night," I whisper to him, referring to Giselle.

Henry looks over my shoulder to G. "Ev, she's the one who can't turn her mouth off. It's not me."

I look to the left of where Henry is sitting, and Jack is busy listening to two women tell him a story about the magic that is golden hour in the desert. I give him a smile and a short wave, not wanting to interrupt his discussion. Instead of a friendly smile as a greeting, he stares right at me. No smile, no returned wave or sense of acknowledgment. I just see the muscles in his jaw flex as if he's biting down hard on something. So much for flirting with the new guy tonight.

"Jizz." Henry nods in Giselle's direction.

Damn it, Henry.

"I've told you repeatedly not to call me that, Hanky." She looks at the redhead that's practically sitting on his lap. "He's hot, but don't let it fool you into some of the depraved things that get his rocks off. I've heard he likes to piss on girls, and don't be surprised if he asks about pegging. Just warning you if you're on the prude side." She smiles like the Cheshire Cat and the redhead looks back and forth between the two of them. Poor girl, getting caught in that crossfire. She whispers in Henry's ear and leaves to join a group of her friends.

"Fuck off, Jizz. That's really...that's real fucking mature. Such a brat." Henry stands up, walking toward the bar, knocking her shoulder as he passes by.

"You started it, you fucking dick-stick. She probably has chlamydia anyway," she shouts, as he's just out of earshot. "You're welcome!"

I just look at her. She knows what I'm going to say, and before I get the chance, Jack chimes in, "Are you alright? Giselle, is it?"

"Well, I am now. Hi. Please, call me G." She takes his extended hand and pulls him in to kiss the side of his cheek. "Everly hasn't said too much about the hot photographer who is here to revitalize her brand and invade her," she pauses, "*space.*"

Jack just looks at me and raises his eyebrows. "Well, if she's talking about me at all, then that must mean something. Everly, you thinking about me?" He wiggles his eyebrows and smiles as if he's caught me with my pants down. And he kind of did. I'm speechless. I stare back at Jack, willing some kind of smart response to come to me, but when I open my mouth, nothing comes out. I don't like being taken aback or teased like that. Especially when he's spot on.

Law breaks up the embarrassment by interrupting. "Stick around and have a drink with us, Ev. I was just telling Jack about the new heli-skiing adventures we're implementing. He had some good ideas about how to cater to different groups." Figurative brakes screech to a halt. Law, bless his little heart, but there's no way in hell I'm going to take business advice from someone I've known for less than twenty-four hours.

G knows exactly what I'm thinking too, because she sees my face and gives me a smile. She's enjoying this. When I'm caught off guard, I wear my feelings front and center. Right now, I'm annoyed that this guy would have any feedback about our brand, my brand. He should have stayed sitting pretty.

"Law-baby, we're going to pass. I have a gorgeous actor

friend I want Everly to meet before we leave. And I've spent enough time in such close proximity to Hanky, I'm nervous he might induce a resting bitch face upon me."

Without even thinking, I look at Jack, but he doesn't look phased. I can't distinguish what he's thinking. It's a blank, indifferent slate. I quickly look away, just as his eyes meet mine.

Walking quickly in front of me, G turns back to make sure I followed her. "You're welcome, by the way. I know what I'm doing. He'll be over in a minute, guaranteed."

We lean against the end of the outdoor bar. It's cold enough to see your breath now, but the overhead heaters from the bar roof keep us relatively warm. I wave over to the bartender. "Two shots of Grey Goose. One lemon slice. One orange slice."

"Don't ask why your brother and I are like oil and water. I don't want to spend any more brain cells thinking about his arrogant ass. And why wouldn't you want to climb that delicious man and capture him for a night of naughty things?" She wiggles her eyebrows at me. "Let him photograph you like one of his French girls, Ev. I feel like his dirty talk is on point. I know these things. I have a sixth sense about it." I just shake my head at her. "He's your fire, right there. A temporary fulfillment. Take advantage, you owe it to your neglected..." She looks down at my lap.

"G! He's hot. I'll give him that, but I guarantee he's a one-trick pony. One night is pretty good, but then that's it. There's no substance there."

"What's your point?" she asks, narrowing her eyes.

"He's the guy that talks about his art, spends too much time at the gym, bros out about sports, and then ends up with a twenty-something who's nothing more than mediocre, but tight and hot. I'm not about to flirt my way into bed with him. Vapid guys like that don't mix with women like me. Even if it is for just sex."

And it's right then that I feel it. I notice the shift of her body language, and the sudden uneasiness in the air. I turn my head slightly to my left, my eyes closing, knowing what I'm going to find as soon as I open them. *Jack.*

He looks forward, not meeting my gaze. "Ms. Riggs. I'm flattered to hear that you're attracted to me. It's not anything I haven't heard before."

"That's not what..."

He holds up his hand to stop me from speaking and that move alone makes me suck in a breath. The confidence, arrogance, his closeness. He leans into me and says, "Not to worry. I'm not interested anyway. You're just business."

He grabs my vodka shot and kicks it back, then slams the empty glass on the bar top, and before he walks away, he leans back into my space, so close that I feel his lips graze just behind my ear. With a rumble in his voice, he says, "Oh, and you are right. The *only* trick I have is to make my partner beg. Beg for my cock again and again, even after they've come so hard they can barely stand, beg to be touched in ways no other man has the balls enough to try. They beg to be allowed to touch me and taste me after I give them everything they need."

For the second time tonight, the man leaves me with no response, and while I'm embarrassed that he heard the presumptuous things I said about him, there's a bigger part of me that's turned on by his words. Nobody has ever spoken to me like that in public before. Or anywhere else, for that matter. I stare at his back as he walks away.

"I feel like this is what your face looks like after you've

been fucked, Ev. That man just verbally fucked you up. Girl, please don't avoid his sweet ass anymore. For the both of us. I need to hear that he lives up to the hype," G whisper-shouts at me. I can't respond, because while she's right, on so many levels, this is my red flag warning. I know it.

10

Everly

THE NEXT WEEK MOVES ALONG AS IF THE ASSHOLE-LEVEL assumptions I made and verbalized at the bar on Saturday night never happened. And I try hard to pretend like Jack's rebuttal didn't affect me the way that it has. I find moments to breathe when I'm with my family or working in my studio, but those are fleeting, as usual. I cling to my routines. I'm up early working out with Michael, then the workday starts at 8 a.m. and ends somewhere near 7 p.m. The guys and I make dinner or grab a bite out on the way home. It's our normal, well, except for one glaringly obvious six-foot-three difference. Mr. Blue Eyes and slap-yourself-senseless sexy dimples. Jack Deacon is everywhere. And he's dug his way into my thoughts.

The first couple of days he was in town, I only ran into him at the office, as he was paraded around by Law, taking pictures of our new building and turning our extra conference room into his studio. Our interaction was surface level, even a bit cold, but my body didn't get that message, because any time I was within a few feet of him, my face flushed with heat. It routed a course down my back and over my arms, behind my knees, and right to my core. I never thought I would be one of those women that would have a physical reaction like that to a man. You read about it, but I just assumed it was an exaggerated thing to say. It's not. I've been wearing panty liners because I can't keep changing underwear after I see his stupidly handsome face.

I'll see him at the gym when I'm working out with Michael, at the office again before my first meeting of the day, then at the house when I get home. He's either talking with Law about the latest way to ferment a beer or why LeBron is one of the greats. With Henry, they talk about NFL and MLB trades or the latest UFC fight. Needless to say, my space has been sufficiently invaded. My studio, my office, my home, and when I close my eyes at night, I find myself thinking about him.

By Wednesday, he was joining us for dinner, and by Friday, he found his way into my brother's inside jokes, which, to be honest, is impressive and annoying all at once. I've managed to find time inside my studio without running into him. There's something about finding him in my space that pisses me off more than anything. The way he so easily starts a conversation and flirts, even though he's made it quite clear he's not interested. I would have thought that overhearing the judgmental words I shared with G at the bar that night would have made him mad or had him ignoring me altogether, but I'm finding that he goes out of his way to drop comments. He's friend-zoned me and I'm entirely pissed off about it.

When was the last time a man seeped into every part of

my life? *Never*. I've never allowed it. I've always been focused on my career, my family, and just living my life at my own pace. Everything that I have, I've worked and planned for, which is why I thought finding someone exceptional in a partner would use that same formula. Then I have this big change in plans by the coaxing of my best friend to stop being so rigid and just fall into bed with men. See what I like. See if a spark would outplay the need for certain things I always look for in men. And as soon as Jack shows up, I'm flailing. I'm attracted to him. What woman wouldn't be? But before I can even wrap my head around that feeling, he takes it off the table. And now I'm feeling all the feelings that I try to avoid. But mostly, the biggest one is wanting something I can't have. Or maybe, *shouldn't* have anyway.

I watched him speak with a few of the marketing managers about their point of view on our brand. He did the listening and minimal talking, which for many, is a feat in and of itself, to listen instead of talk. That was yesterday, and by the end of the workday, I saw him leaving with those same team members, likely grabbing dinner and drinks. When he's not trying to be intimidating, I notice that he's actually very thoughtful. It's not a trait you typically see in a man that looks like him or has the kind of reputation that he does, being aggressive, artistic, and a complete gentleman. *With a dirty mouth.* And not easy to categorize. I squeeze my eyes shut to focus back on the tasks ahead of me and away from the sexiest man currently residing in Strutt's Peak.

And in an effort to punish me, like the universe knew I was thinking about the mechanics of his dimples and the way his hands flex the cords of his forearms, the door to my studio slides open. I jump up like I've been caught doing something I shouldn't be, and in the same movement, I knock over my entire water bottle onto my drafting table.

"Shit! Fuck."

Water drenches my samples for the new lounge sets that just came back from the manufacturer.

"I got it, here, here." Jack is immediately at my side, leaning over, throwing down a towel to sop up the water. The side of his body is leaning against mine, working to clean up the mess I just made, and I'm instantly stupid at the fact that he's touching me, making my arms break out in goosebumps.

"Thank you. I can't believe I did that." I laugh at myself, both for the clumsiness of it and at our sudden closeness. I'm distracted before I realize what we're hovering over.

"I'm sorry I scared you." He looks down at the pile of drawings and materials. "What are all of these?" He picks up a handful of papers that are still dry. I try to yank them out of his hand, but he's too quick and pulls back before I can swipe them.

"Nope, nope. Don't touch. These are, well, these are just some things I had to review. Please give them back to me."

He smiles, realizing he has the upper hand right now, but he surprises me and holds the papers out to pass them back to me. My relief is short-lived because in exchange for the sketches, he snags my iPad that sits on the charging stand. "You've officially piqued my interest. What are you working on?"

When I don't answer, he looks up. "Miss Riggs, I thought you were the head honcho at the office, not a designer." His smile grows even bigger, and I can't help but smile back at him. The way this man smiles, it's impossible not to mirror it.

"Please," I say dismissively. "I am the head honcho, you're not wrong. But, please just put it down, and forget it. It's a hobby, something personal, just for me." I sit back on my stool as he walks over to the kitchenette and grabs a bottle of water out of the refrigerator. He's ignoring me and I don't like it. I resent the fact that I even care. "This isn't any of your business, and I'd appreciate it if you stay away from everything over here on this side of the room."

I watch him swipe the screen as he looks through the accessories that Michael has been demanding and the menswear for next year's winter season. I shift my weight, anxiously waiting for him to put the iPad down and comment on what he's looking over. I don't know why all of a sudden his opinion matters.

Less than a minute later, after he's worked his way through more than a dozen swipes both left and right, he says, "I didn't see anything, but I'll be honest, if I'd known I'd get such a rise out of you on this stuff, I would have peeked a while ago." He winks at me, and I fight back smiling at him again. Instead, I take a grounding breath.

Charming isn't the right word for him, even though there are traces of that. It's more dangerous. A man that can manipulate my thoughts and my body's response just from a facial expression or provocative words. "I got you, Everly. It's not my business. Plus, I've signed an NDA, which has my lips zipped on all aspects of your business." He hands me the iPad and walks past me and toward the back of the room, an area that until now was completely off limits to him.

The oversized windows that run the full length of the back of the pool house show off an incredible view, a live portrait of the northern ridge. At this time of day, just after daybreak, the colors are still lingering before the sky decides to be blue or overcast. "The view back here is the most unexpected and beautiful thing I've seen since coming here."

I step closer to where he's looking and fold my arms. "It's one of the reasons I wanted this place. There are so many beautiful views in this town, but there was something special about claiming this as mine. You should ask Michael to take you to his favorite spot in Strutt's. It *almost* outdoes this view."

"What if I ask you to show me your favorite spot in Strutt's?" He gives me a side glance and holds it for a bit too long. Long enough so that I feel myself swaying closer to him, as if my body needs to touch his again.

His directness makes me think he's teasing me instead of asking for real. I'm not ready for a slap of rejection from him, especially after he was so clear about his lack of interest during our last interaction. "You wouldn't ask me that, remember? You're not interested." I finish with a smirk, claiming myself the winner of this round.

He looks down at his hands and hums a small laugh. I feel like I've missed something. Then, he walks away, and I watch as he grabs some clothes off the bed and his small toiletry bag.

My mind is reeling, searching for a response, because I realize I want to hear what he has to say about what he saw earlier. I'm realizing that I like being around him. But before I can come up with anything that doesn't sound pathetic, he pauses at the door.

"Everly?" he says. Turning his attention toward me, he looks over his shoulder. My eyes meet his, and his tongue kicks out to lick his bottom lip. "The view I mentioned? I wasn't talking about the ridge."

Before anything he just said registers, he opens the door and leaves. It takes me a minute to really digest what he was telling me. Did he just suggest that I was the most beautiful thing he's seen? *What the fuck happened to him not being interested?!*

11

Everly

THE PROBLEM WITH DECIDING TO CHASE YOUR PASSION IN unconventional ways isn't that you have to work really hard, because that's a given. It's coming to understand that the hardest work you put in isn't happening during working hours. Nope. It's the late nights, early mornings, moments you can collect in between, and, of course, the personal life sacrifices. Specifically, not having much of one.

After I came home from college, I decided that I wasn't just going to work for my dad's company. Henry had already had a career and then was forced to make a change working for the family business. I came into it with eyes wide open and eager. I knew that if I was going to be here, in Strutt's Peak, then I was going to be a force to be reckoned with at Riggs Outdoor. I wanted to be respected. To earn that respect, and a place at the table, it meant that I'd have to work in different aspects of the business to learn about the people and how it runs, from secretary, to sales, to operations.

Being a woman at a dominantly male-run business had, and still has, its hurdles. While I could outmaneuver most of these guys in all of the sports we supported, I had to make sure I was on an even playing field. That meant putting everyone in the colleague zone; no social relationships, or dating coworkers, which already ruled out half the town. I couldn't be anything other than all-business if I was going to be in charge someday. That has always been my plan. Working for my father was never the goal; it was to work alongside him. If I was going to be here, then I was going to make a name for myself and not just be "Asher's kid" or "The Riggs girl."

I dug in and made those late nights and early mornings count professionally. It just never left space for much more, especially to bar hop or other things that led people to meet-cutes and long-term relationships. A small town meant you knew everyone, and anyone you didn't was a tourist and only here for a fling. I crave connection. A sexy smile or well-intentioned drink, or even ill-intentioned, for that matter, wasn't enough to just go home with a guy. That's why flings or one-night stands just never seemed like the right thing for me.

Show me a single, successful woman who hasn't thought at some point, *"Did I just fall victim to the most patriarchal stereotype and force myself to choose work over love?"* I never thought I'd find myself here. I had always made space for the idea that both could exist. Could a few nights with men like Jack really have an impact on my expectations?

I drop my head to my forearms draped over my drafting table. I'm overthinking again, and when I overthink, my creative muscle decides that atrophy is the way to go. *Not helpful.*

"What material could the new lounge pants work best in?" I ask myself out loud. Immediately, my mind thinks of lightweight sweatpants and then veers off to thinking about Jack's perfectly biteable thighs and tight ass in his sweatpants after he came back from his run.

I feel indescribable energy from him. He's arrogant, brimming with confidence that is borderline a turnoff. *Borderline.* He's invaded my space, my thoughts. He's everywhere and leaves me with mixed signals that have me a little whiplashed and a lot confused.

His stupid-handsome face is now a part of my universe for another few weeks, whether I like it or not. If I indulge in anything more than a professional relationship with him, it has messy disaster written all over it. And yet, I say all of this while also being completely aroused by his words, turned on by his voice, and fucking lit up like a damn tree just from remembering what his body looks like, fully clothed, mind you.

A part of me wishes Jack Deacon had some kind of gross flaw to offset the perfection. But even as I think it, I know it's not true. He even smells incredible. Leather mixed with amber and cinnamon. And now I'm fantasizing about what he would taste like if I could lick my way down his abs, brush my lips across his hips. What's left of my sanity trails down to those V-lines directing all traffic to what is likely a very satisfyingly sized cock. I laugh at myself. I'm hopeless and wickedly distracted.

I refocus my attention on the ridge. The sun is just setting behind the mountains and the sky is burning orange with a billowing purple haze. It's as if grape and orange soda just spilled across the clouds.

The entire pool house is darker now, just the lamp leaning over my drafting table keeping the space lit, and *Skin* by Rihanna streams on the speakers throughout the room. The ambiance and my swirling thoughts have me feeling far more turned on than I should be for a Saturday night all alone.

I can't help but smile, thinking about the way Jack's tongue peeked out and wet his bottom lip as he left the pool house earlier. Just that singular thought about his mouth is making me warmer. I can feel my face flush with heat and my body is suddenly very aware of what a Jack-featured fantasy can do.

Is he messy when he dives into a woman? Is it his tongue that does most of the exploring when he goes down on a girl, or does he taste, smell, nudge, suck, and lap at a woman's pussy?

My right hand trails across the V-necked collar of my white t-shirt, my fingers brushing against my skin, and I palm my breast. My nipples harden as I play and roll it between my fingers. I get lost, and before I even realize it, I'm breathing out a moan.

Rummaging through the side tables next to the bed, I finally find my pocket-sized vibrator. Still charged, *phew*. If anyone found it, they'd have to click the button to understand what it was. It looks like a rainbow rocket lollipop, a gift from my best friend on my last birthday. When I told G not to buy me anything, she put up a fight, so I told her just to get me something sweet. Chocolate or Twizzlers are gifts I'd always welcome. I never knew there were so many sweets-themed sex toys, lubricants, and spa essentials. Her bag of birthday goodies was massive, and the lollipop-shaped vibrator was by far the tamest thing there.

I quickly scan the door and windows that lead to the main house. No lights on, which means Jack and Law are still out. Who knows where Michael is, but he rarely makes an appearance out here. So, I turn up the music. I want to get lost in this feeling for a little while. I've earned it.

12

Jack

I'M FINALLY GETTING USED TO THE ALTITUDE OF THIS TOWN. It's taken an entire week here to walk up this hill to the Riggs' house without being winded. I walk farther and faster than this in New York just to get from my apartment to my studio, but the air is different here. *I* feel different here. I miss my space and the energy that the city fuses into me, but I have to admit, Strutt's Peak is incredible. The brightness and big-ness of it.

Law is back at the cigar bar, hitting on a brunette that was more than happy to drink for free for the rest of the night. He's a good guy. What I wouldn't have given for a friend like him growing up. Any of the Riggs siblings would have been a breath of fresh air. They've all had things going on in their lives, I'm sure, but they also have a feel-good vibe that's easy to be around.

I double tap my knuckles on the front door before I punch in the code to open it, just to be courteous. I need to grab something to eat before I head back to the pool house. As I walk through the entryway, I look up to see if there are any lights on upstairs. Maybe Everly is up there by now and not in the pool house any longer.

I said more than I should have when I was leaving. The reality is, she's fucking beautiful, and I can't seem to keep myself from wanting to look at her every chance I get. Never mind the fact that pissing her off and seeing how far I can push her have become my favorite things to do since I set foot in this town. Riling her up, a woman who is so structured and stone-faced, is a little victory for me. Her entire face and neck flush. She can't keep her emotions in check when I'm around, no matter how hard I've seen her try. Everything she said at the bar about me was wrong, and she knew it, even before I interjected. She was trying to talk herself out of being attracted to me. Self-preservation, at its finest, and I know a thing or two about that.

Luce was right to remind me to be smart on this job. Keep my dick in my pants. It might be for different reasons, since Luce wants to avoid cleaning up a public fallout or the repercussions a family like The Riggs might cause, and I want to maintain the lifestyle I'm most comfortable with. That means steering away from someone who is far more than surface-level beauty. I'm not in the market for someone like that, regardless of how much I think about her or how much my cock wants to burrow into her for the winter.

I watched her rock the boss role this week as she laced into a new distributor. He told her that the newest of their signature snowboards has to ship to big box stores first based on their lead time or something like that. She was *not* happy and tore the guy a new asshole, threatened his business, called him out on his lack of local business support, and by the end of the conversation, she had her shipment and was making plans for drinks with him when he's in town after the holidays. To say she's a force is an understatement. It was impressive and sexy as hell.

And while my cock is semi-hard just thinking about how she can masterfully own the attention and adoration of a room full of people who work for her company, I know that a person like her isn't one you just have fun with. She's the kind of woman that changes a man's life. Unlucky for me that I like my life just as it is. Focused, simple, and void of people that'll end up disappointing me, or I, them.

I'm not looking for upheaval, even if it's got a beautiful mouth and an ass I'd love to sink my teeth into. It wouldn't be an easy getaway either. I'll be here again, often enough, since this is where Kathryn and Benny will be. Not to mention, I'd like to do more with the Riggs brand; I have other ventures that make sense to align with them, so giving the company's Vice President a good fuck on just about every surface I can touch is definitely an occupational hazard.

I walk into the kitchen and head for the refrigerator, but a clatter of a spoon against a bowl startles me. I thought the place was empty. "I don't understand why you're going to bring in random people to model the activities we offer."

"Michael. Hey, man, didn't see you there." I haven't gotten to know the middle Riggs brother very well. He's not the most welcoming and made it clear that we're supposed to keep our interactions professional. "We're about to set the schedule for your shoots this week, but if you want to make changes, it's your company, so let's talk about what you're not happy with."

He shifts in his seat and keeps his focus on eating the

cereal in his bowl. After an uncomfortably long pause, he laughs to himself. I look over his way again, and he says, "Law doesn't listen to me. Ev is the only one I can get through to and she's so..." he pauses to take another spoonful, then says, "distracted lately that I can't get a word in about work with her."

I grab the cold cuts out of the fridge and the sesame rolls out of the bread box to make a sandwich. "Well, I'm listening. What don't you like about the models we chose? I thought you picked out who you liked with Law this past week."

"I did."

I look at him to elaborate more. I don't want to spend time on a shoot if the one person who knows this part of the business the best isn't happy before we even start. Michael places his spoon down on the counter and adjusts it so that it's perpendicular to his bowl.

"I want my team to be in the images for the summer adventures. It should not be some guy who just looks good in cargo shorts and Oakleys." He looks up and finally makes eye contact. Michael is a good-looking guy. The entire Riggs clan is attractive, and not many people would be quick to kick any of them out of bed. His hair is the same sandy blonde as Law's, longer, but always pulled back. I gather that he's not the kind of guy that is okay with looking disheveled or unkempt. "Listen, I don't want to be in any of it, but I'm the one running that part of the business, and it should be my guys who are front and center. They've earned their spot in our business and I'd like them recognized for it."

He looks up at me as if I'm going to tell him no. "That works for me. There's no need to pay models if we've got the actual crew of people running it. Are your guys available and open to being photographed?"

"Yeah? I mean, yeah, yes. Some of them do the winter adventures too, but I can work with Henry to make sure those guys aren't scheduled. Do you think this is the right call? I know it's my family's company, but you're the creative guy. Will you be able to get what you need by making this kind of change?"

"As long as you clear it with whomever you need to, then yeah. I don't see why not. If anything, it'll show more authenticity, and people would be thrilled to see your team online, then in person once they book. It seems like a no-brainer." I'm genuinely excited to hear this from Michael. Out of everybody, I didn't expect much of an opinion on things from him. I feel like I should have suggested this from the start, utilizing the staff to tell their story and show off what sets this brand and company of people apart.

Michael stands up and walks over to me, extending his hand. "Thanks." He turns and walks toward the stairs after shaking my hand. He turns and rubs the back of his neck nervously. "And don't worry. Everyone is fit and can do this on my crew. But they're not models, so..."

"I think it's a better look for your brand if you show off some real people instead of polished versions. More authentic and, honestly, it'll allow people to connect better. I'd rather go climbing a mountainside with someone who looks like they know what they're doing instead of just a good-looking face."

He nods and doesn't say anything else, heading up the stairs while I'm left finishing my turkey club.

13

Jack

I WALK THROUGH THE LIVING ROOM AND NOTICE THERE'S STILL a light on in the pool house. I didn't leave that on, which means Everly is in there. The clock over my shoulder reads nine-thirty, and I'm trying to give myself a reason to bother her again. It's too early to head to bed, so I can't use that as an excuse. Maybe I can mention the need for some new equipment to be rented for this week's outdoor shoots.

Or I can stop trying to find excuses and just be in the same space as her. It's what I want anyway. To see her, be around her. She has that kind of energy about her. This feeling does more than not sit right with me. It scares me. I'm not interested in being with a person who could have that kind of power over me. Maybe I just need to stop flirting with her and riling her up, because the last thing I should do with this woman is sleep with her. Even though those pouty lips are seared into my mind and the curve of her ass, goddamn, the way it dips so beautifully is like a fleshy snake-charmer for my cock.

I shake my head. That's exactly what I don't need to be doing. Fantasizing about the delectable boss and fucking the sense out of her. I'll work on avoiding her. Maybe I just need to get laid. I should find a lonely snow bunny to fuck and fill the void. Steer clear of the locals. Everyone seems to be in everybody else's business here.

I've made up my mind on this. Everly Riggs is not going to get under my skin, and I will not be dipping any part of me into any part of her. Ugh, my dick kickstarts with the idea of dipping anywhere near her. Fucking traitor.

I flip the light switch off before I open the slider to the backyard and pull out my phone. As I make my way across the travertine patio surrounding the now covered in-ground pool, I send Kathryn a text about our plans tomorrow.

When I get closer, I can hear music playing rather loudly. I hit send, store my phone in my pocket, and tap my knuckles on the door. There's no response, so I check the handle to find that it's unlocked, which seems strange to me since all of my equipment is in here. I doubt Everly would have just left the place without locking up. At that thought, I don't hesitate to push the door open and walk right in, but it takes my eyes a minute to adjust to the darkness of the space. The one light that's on above Everly's drafting table illuminates that small room, but there's no Everly in sight.

Just as I'm thinking about her, The Weeknd is crooning to a girl that she's earned it on the surrounding speakers, and then there's a break in the music, and I hear it. A low, muffled moan. I jerk my head toward it. Toward *her*. Because when my eyes finally adjust to the room, that's when I see her.

Everly lying on the couch, with one hand in her shirt, palming her breast and pulling the material down enough that I can see her fingers tugging at her dark pink nipple. Her other hand hovers over her very naked lower half. No pants, no underwear. Knees bent and butterflied open, granting my eyes total access to see her bare, glistening pussy on full display. Her whole body rolls slowly, as if she's a living ocean wave.

My cock stood at full attention as soon as I heard the moan, and now I'm stuck in this spot, my body locked onto the siren's every movement in front of me. Everything I just promised myself about staying away from this woman is now irrelevant, null and void. I couldn't leave even if I wanted to; my brain turned off my common sense the second I heard her. I can't help but adjust my dick through my jeans for just an ounce of relief. Her silky hair is splayed carelessly above her, half draped over the arm of the couch. She moves her hand out of her shirt, trailing it down to her clit, and I can see her making small circles. In the other hand, she's gripping something, moving it in and out of her pussy.

This is the hottest moment I've ever unknowingly walked into. It's even more incredible that I'm watching the woman who I've been trying to *not* think about get herself off in the middle of my room. *So fucking sexy.* I lick my lips. I've watched plenty of women pleasure themselves. Hell, most of the time, I'm inside them, urging it on...but *this*? This is better than any fantasy I could have demanded of her.

"Fuuckkkk," she whimpers, and it's obvious she's moments away from coming. There's no way I'm leaving. A decent man would have left by now, but I'm not decent, so why start now. I accept that about myself. It would be so easy to drop to my knees in front of her and thrust my tongue into her warmth, lap up the pleasure she's been drawing out of herself, and find out if she tastes as delicious as she looks.

The wet sound coming from where she's playing is making this live, filthy moment feel exceptionally deviant. I'm not even thinking anymore; all of the blood has left my head and is now throbbing in my pants. She gasps for a breath, and I watch as her orgasm starts to take over her body. I bite my lip at the sight of her trembling, which reminds me to breathe, and then she opens her eyes.

And she stares right at me.

Breathily, she says my name. "Jack..." With her gaze on mine, her body starts to twitch. She moans again, louder, her body so wound up and releasing so strongly, she can't hold it back. Her hips rock toward me, her other hand thrusting harder into her cunt as her back bows off the couch and her mouth opens, silently screaming the crest of her release. I rub my aching cock through my jeans as she wrings out every last bit of pleasure she earned for herself, and it's incredible.

I'm so fucking turned on that it doesn't fully register for me that I've not only invaded an intimate moment, but that I stayed, and watched...and got caught.

I was seconds from demanding more from her, making her come again under my hands. All of my self-control was left at the door. That realization keeps my feet firmly planted, since if I move, I'm not sure what I might do. She saw me as her orgasm rang through her beautiful body, and she didn't stop it. Instead, she called my name. *I'm so fucked.*

She keeps one hand between her legs and throws the

other arm over her eyes. "I have no idea how to navigate this right now, Jack. I need you to leave and pretend you never saw it. Or, oh my God, or heard it."

Yea, no way is that going to be possible.

I pause for a minute. "I can't do that."

She abruptly moves her arm, looks at me, and sits up, pulling her knees to her chest in an attempt to cover her naked lower half.

"I'm not sure I want to forget how fucking sexy that just was. Jesus, Everly." I run my hand through my hair and shift. "I won't make you any more uncomfortable than you already are, so I'm going to walk out that door and go for a walk."

She looks down, and it's very clear she's embarrassed. The last thing I want is this confident, strong woman to ever be embarrassed with me, because what that just was, was practically poetic.

"Don't think for one fucking minute that I'm going to be able to forget what you look like when you come. And I plan to see it again. You hear me, beautiful?"

She looks up at me, her eyebrows raised, surprised by what I've said. How can this woman for one second think I'm not using all of the good guy left in me to not rush that couch right now and fuck her senseless.

Instead, I plaster a smile on, give her one last look, and walk to the door. I'm going to need a long walk to cool off. I don't wait for a response, but I hear her whisper, "Oh, I hear you," as I shut the door behind me.

14

Jack

"There is no way you're holding your side up high enough. You have to hold it higher if I'm going to clear the step." With sweat dripping down my back, I shift the over-sized chair higher.

"You're the muscle here, Jack. I'm carrying the most I can." Kathryn blows out a frustrated breath. "I thought you worked out, or is that just for show? That much arm bulk should be able to hoist a chair up some stairs." She's laughing, and it makes me laugh too.

"Benny! Your mom isn't helping here. Can you grab her side?" I shout up the stairs. Kathryn stalks up the stairs, and as I assumed, she wasn't carrying any part of this chair. "KATHRYN, get your ass back here right now!"

Five thumping footfalls echo in the staircase. "I got you, Uncle Jack." The kid grabs the upper side of the chair, and we move it quickly up the tight space and into the apartment at the top. "You know Mom isn't going to carry anything else up here now that you're here, right?"

"Yeah, bud, I just figured that out." Laughing, we make our way into the open loft to the floor-to-ceiling windows that overlook small-town Main Street downstairs. "You want this here?"

"Move it just to where that light hangs over. That's going to be my reading spot. I'm not sure where I want to put the TV, but I won't want to block the windows, so yeah, that's good right there." Kathryn stands in the middle of the living room, biting her thumbnail. "There's not that much stuff now that it's all in here."

Looking around the open loft, it pulls in a ton of natural light and has a great vibe with top-of-the-line appliances and a huge island that separates the kitchen from the dining space and living room.

"Ma, I'm going to finish unpacking my stuff. Uncle Jack, you stayin' for a bit?" Benny leans on his elbows, and I can't believe how grown up he looks. It's only been about a month since I saw him last, and he looks less like a boy and more like a man.

"Yup. I'll be out here annoying your mom. Let me know if you need any help assembling that shelf." I look back at my sister. "Is he going to unpack that whole room by himself?"

She shrugs her right shoulder. "I'll help hang up some of his clothes later. I know he wants to get as much done as he can so he can get to that ropes course before they close."

She grabs a box from the pile in the dining room and hoists it to the counter. I grab another and start opening some of the wrapped glasses. "Put all those in the upper cabinet next to the fridge."

We spend the next hour unpacking and talking about Benny. We purposely avoid the conversation, I know she's trying her hardest not to have with me. "So, are we going to talk about it, or are we going to keep avoiding it?"

She stops opening the box in front of her for a second and thinks about the question. "Would it be okay if we just do this for a bit longer and then we can talk about the disaster area that is my life? Preferably with some food and alcohol to numb the reality?" She laughs. I don't.

I continue to assemble the console stand that'll sit underneath her mounted television on the wall adjacent to the windows. My sister is complicated. Her life, like mine, was never easy and, more so lately, it's been hectic.

"The fact that this loft, which is pretty fucking amazing, by the way, was available to rent right above the shop down-stairs, makes your life so much easier."

She shifts and looks like she wants to tell me something, but I don't press it. I know how she is when she feels cornered or pressured into talking. "The shop is pretty incredible. I don't think I've ever been prouder of myself for actually doing something that I've always *wanted* to do. I'm probably crazy for opening something like that in a town I barely know, moving my kid here, and during the shitstorm that is my divorce right now..."

I stop what I'm doing for a moment because I really want her to hear me. "Don't do that, Kat. Don't minimize any of this. All of these things, moving, opening a business on your own, and leaving that piece of shit, are all good things. You're not crazy. You're living."

She looks at me with tears in her eyes. "Jack," she chokes out before she stops herself from saying more or sobbing.

I'm not sure which. "I feel like I'm coasting into this new life, and I don't deserve it, ya know?"

"Listen to me, Kat. Really hear me here. You're not coasting, you're working for it. You're strong and smart. You're raising a great kid, and on your own now, I might add. And you deserve good things. You and I have been dealt some shitty hands, but we deserve some good ones every once in a while. Okay?"

"I just don't know if I can do it. I feel like I'm just barely keeping my head above water."

I make my way to her and wrap her in a hug. Rubbing her back as her face buries in my chest, I decide not to say anything else. I get it. Sometimes people just need to feel their feelings and not be cheered up or given solutions. So we stand for a while, just holding each other, much like we did when we were kids. My job has always been to protect her. There wasn't anybody else to do it, and I take the job seriously.

I see Benny walk down the hallway from his room, and he smiles at me. He knows his mom is having a tough time right now. Kathryn hears him approach and pulls back, looking at me. She gives me her brave smile, but I know she's doing that for me, not for her. The hardest part of growing up isn't the responsibilities. I mean, yes, those suck a bit, but the hardest part of growing up for me has been watching my baby sister struggle.

We grew up in the system. Our mother was a drug addict, sold everything for her next fix—our furniture, food, our toys, and even herself. She was consumed by her addiction, and I'd like to think she was once a good person, but that's really just years of therapy helping me process the fucked up childhood I experienced. We were lucky though, because she died. Some would say it was horrible, but for me, it was the only outcome that allowed Kathryn and me to have a better life. If my mother had stayed alive any longer, Kathryn would have had to endure the nightmares I had to experience. The day my mother died was the scariest and best day of my life.

We were in a few foster homes for a while before we were placed with a really good family; one that made sure we were clean, had clothes on our backs, and were safe. One that did things like eat dinner together and watch movies on Friday nights after pizza. We had two lives. The before and the after. And while "the before" creeps into my dreams often, "the after" happened for much longer, and it did a good job of erasing as much of the darkness from our memories as possible.

Kathryn was only four years old during "the before." Foster care was tough on her. She didn't understand the times that we had to be separated, and she had been placed with a family that should have never been in the system. But that was brief, thank goodness. After we ended up with the Cormicks, life was boring for a while. Then Kathryn got pregnant with Benny when she was just a nineteen-year-old freshman in college. She needed to change perspective and look at life differently at that point, but she wanted that kid from the moment she found out she was pregnant. She had choices, but the only one she entertained was *how* she was going to do it, not *if*. She had my support, no matter what she chose. Benny's father was never in the picture, someone from the neighborhood. A part of me wonders if Kathryn ever told the guy she was even pregnant, but it didn't matter, not to me at least. As Benny has gotten older though, I'm sure he wonders who his biological father might be.

She struggled as a single mom for a while. I helped her financially so she could finish school, and our foster mom helped raise him. Kat met her ex-husband when Benny was eight. I thought he was a good man, but people change. He turned out to be a scumbag, had another woman on the side, and drank, heavily apparently. Kathryn dug him out of trouble repeatedly, and then once she found out about the other woman, that was the final straw and she left. She served him with papers and decided to move to Strutt's Peak. I have no idea why she chose it, but it ended up being perfect, especially considering I'm here for the next month on a job. I can help them settle in before I head back to New York.

"I'm going to head out, Ma." Benny pushes out from his chair and brings his plate to the sink. Grabbing his jacket, he comes back over, kisses her on the cheek, then hugs me.

"Love ya, kid. Are we still on for that hike after school on Monday?"

"Definitely. You bring the snacks. I got all the gear."

"You bet." I smile as he leaves.

I look over at my sister, and she pours the rest of the bottle of red into her glass. "He's such a great kid, Kat. You did good. A living, breathing reminder that ya did damn good."

She smiles at me, a little sadness still filling her eyes. "I know. He's the best parts of me and his father."

I look around the apartment. "I think we made some headway. This looks lived in now. I really can't believe everything is unpacked out here. That pile of boxes was pretty intimidating when I came in."

She looks at me. "Tell me about this job you're in town

for. I didn't think you'd take a job in a place like this. Most of your clients are in big cities."

"True, but it's for the Riggs family. Ever hear of them?"

"Oh, yeah. Everyone knows the Riggs family here, and it doesn't take much time to run into one of them. I've been here for a few weeks now, and I've heard all the gossip about those boys and their bossy sister. Benny said he met her when he was working in the shop the other day too." She looks at me, waiting. I know what she's waiting for.

Kathryn shifts in her chair, staring at me, smiling in her red wine haze. "Benny said she's smokin' hot."

I take a sip of my wine and look at my sister, hoping she can't read all over my face that I'm in complete agreement with my nephew's assessment. I can't help thinking about the last time I saw her, flushed after just coming. The way she moaned my name. The way her body moved when she was touching herself. The way I promised her I'd see her do that again. "Oh, yeah? Well, they're an interesting bunch. I'm staying in their pool house, so I've gotten to know the youngest brother pretty well. Law. He's a good guy."

"And?"

"And what?" I laugh and shrug my shoulders. "Okay, yes, she's probably the most beautiful woman I've ever met, but I'm not about to be stupid and pursue something with her." *I'm a fucking liar.*

"Why not?" She laughs.

"What do you mean, why not? She's the boss on this project, for one. And she's not the kind of woman you go after unless you plan on sticking around for a while. And I'm not. Plus, Luce would kill me if I fuck up this connection with the Riggs family. Too many casualties and other ventures that it could affect."

"Okay, well, all I heard there was, 'She's beautiful, blah blah blah. I'm scared of catching feelings, blah blah blah.' Hey!" Picking up the napkin I just launched at her head, she says something I didn't know I needed to hear. "And since when are you not interested in finding a woman to stick around for? Maybe you stop being this big shot person you've created and just be the guy you want to be for a change? You're not so damaged that you can't have something great with someone, big brother."

Leave it to my sister to throw a cold bucket of wisdom on me.

I have nothing more to say, so I kiss her on the forehead, and then head out to pick up a few things to bring to dinner tonight.

15

Everly

ASHER RIGGS IS A FORCE. THE KIND OF FORCE THAT EVERYONE should be so lucky to have in their lives. My father is smart, loving, loud, and always over the top. In all aspects, from his professional life to his hobbies. There's nothing subtle about Daddy. Most newcomers to Strutt's Peak assume he's the mayor, knowing everyone, and spending his time being actively involved in the community, but he's not. I think when we were in high school, maybe when I was a junior, enough people wrote his name on the ballot for mayor and he won. He declined it, though. He was too invested in building his business. Well, that, and raising four teenagers on his own. It was also the year that he donated enough money to re-turf the football field because Michael and Law decided to hold a horse race with some of Dad's prized thoroughbreds.

You would think he would have torn them a new asshole for that, but instead, he told them he was disappointed, and *that* from Ash Riggs is far more damaging than any berating or punishment. That's who he is, though. Respected. Influential. A badass.

He showed up in Strutt's Peak with a blown tire and met my mother at the diner across the street from the mechanic's shop. They fell madly in love. And he never left. Even when she did.

"Pumpkin! Get your ass in here. I need help with the fireplace. This damn flue won't stay open..." My dad's lower half is the only part I see as I open the door, walking into the oversized living room with a massive fireplace in the center. It's a spectacular house, and we were lucky enough to grow up in it. Most of the ranch my dad built and upgraded over the years, but this fireplace has been here from the beginning. He says it's what made him pull the trigger on buying. Well, and the acreage and views, of course.

"Pull the lever on that side, and I'll use the iron poker to hold this piece open. I need to have someone come out here and fix this."

"Fine, but I'm wearing a white sweater. I better not come out of this with soot all over me."

"There. All set." He ducks down and out of the chimney. "No soot. You look like a damn model in that, pumpkin. You have a date later?"

I kiss him on the cheek. "No date. Just wanted to wear a new sweater, that's all."

He looks at me with slightly narrowed eyes, wiping his hands on a cloth hanging from his belt, then walks into the kitchen. "So it wouldn't have anything to do with this Jack guy coming for dinner too?"

"What?! No. I didn't even know he was coming. And even if I did, no. You should know by now in your old age

97

that women dress for themselves these days, not men." I'm so clearly caught here. I didn't know Jack was coming for sure, but I know Law, and I knew he couldn't resist inviting him over to join us.

"Old age." He huffs. "I'm fifty-four, pumpkin. That's not old. Hey, where's my other girl? She didn't come with you?"

"G? She'll be here. She was planning on bringing dessert, I think."

"Good. I haven't seen her in a bit. I miss that firecracker."

I grab a glass and pour some water. "You have any lemon slices, Dad?"

"The lemon is for vodka or gin, not water, pumpkin. So, if you want lemon, you need to have a cocktail with your *old* man."

I smile wide and shake my head. There's no use in putting up a fight that I won't win. Plus, I could use a drink. "Fine. I've been wanting to try your last batch of Limoncello."

"Excellent choice." My dad's full bar is state-of-the-art. Aside from some local brews on tap, it has an ice machine that specializes in pellets, cubes, spheres. Not to mention, most of the cocktails he peddles at guests have some sort of infusion that he's perfected, like herbs or cedar smoke. He takes his cocktails very seriously.

"This is also a good time to tell you again how proud I am of you." He holds his drink up in the air as a toast. "You and your brothers made me so damn proud in that board meeting, and I'm genuinely excited to see what this business is going to look like over the next few years with you at the helm. I couldn't be prouder. Cheers, my darling girl." With watery eyes, my dad clinks my glass and we toast.

Before I can appreciate the moment, the side door off

the kitchen slams open. "You're not going to just make changes without talking with me first, man. This isn't how it works, Michael," Law says loudly as he walks in.

"This is the new plan," Michael replies plainly. I can't see them yet, but I can hear them. One of them drops a bunch of bags on the counter.

"Dude, why? Why not just talk to me first, and then we figure it out together? You can't just call people and tell them they're not needed. We might still have to pay some of them based on their contracts."

My dad looks at me in question. I shrug. I have an idea of what they're talking about, but I have no desire to talk about work right now. "Michael, bring in the firewood by the garage, please."

I look over my shoulder toward the dining table where Law is putting out bottles of wine for dinner. He looks up at me and shakes his head. "I'm not. I'm not talking about it now, I know. We can discuss later, but *someone* decided they were going to hijack my plans and not even tell me!" Law blows out a breath. "He just doesn't talk to me, ya know. I mean, we live in the same damn house, and he won't talk to me. I gotta find shit out from other people. Ugh...fuck it, never mind." He makes his way over to Dad, giving him a big hug and slap on the back. "I need one of those. What are you guys drinking?"

"Limoncello."

He makes a stink face. "Gross. I'll just do bourbon."

Dad gets up. "Here, let me pour. Want me to smoke it?"

My attention is pulled toward the kitchen again as Michael strolls in. I raise my eyebrows at him, silently asking him what he's done now to get Law so worked up.

"You okay?" I ask.

Law cuts in. "Why are you asking if he's okay? He's the one fucking *me* over right now."

I keep my eyes on Michael, waiting for him to meet mine. I know he's running circles in his mind about how to diffuse this. After a few seconds, he looks up at me, and I just smile at him, telling him I got this.

"We can talk about it at Monday's marketing meeting, but Michael had my approval. It's on me that I didn't bring it up yet. I've been...distracted trying to get the spring loungewear back from the new manufacturer, and I forgot to clear it with you. I told Michael just to move forward."

I don't meet Michael's attention, even though I can feel him staring at me, wondering why I'm going to bat for him.

"Ev, ya know..." In true Law fashion, he huffs and pauses for added drama. "Fine. It's not like I don't like the direction, I just don't like being the last person to know about a change that, technically, I need to approve before it happens."

Law drops into the chair next to mine, giving me a look as he scans my outfit. "Why do you look dressed up?"

"I'm not! I already told Dad it's just a new sweater, and I'm wearing jeans!"

I hear shuffling and clanking in the kitchen, and I know Henry is finally moving dinner along. I'd rather go see if he needs help and avoid any more discussion about work or the motivation behind my clothing choices today. Law is easy to talk into things, but he's not a dummy. He knows full well why I'm not wearing my typical Sunday dinner uniform of black yoga pants and a sweatshirt.

"If you're not in here to help, then get out," Henry grunts from behind the stove.

"I'll put the salad together. Pass me the cutting board

from the wall over there." I pull out the lettuce, cucumbers, and celery from the refrigerator and rinse them.

"You still entertaining those Olympic guys tonight, or do we have your charming attention all to ourselves?" I look up at Henry while peeling the cucumber. He pokes the popovers from the oven and starts cutting pads of honey butter to place over the top of each one. It smells so good here, like bread, cinnamon, and bacon had a salty and sweet carby baby.

Henry is complicated. A grumpy asshole most of the time, but he looks out for me. He's my protector, and truly the most selfless out of all of us. It takes a while to get to that part of him, but once you're there, it's like you've reached the inner circle. His short answers and grunts keep a lot of people at work in line. He can be scary if he needs to be, and it's nice to not be the only one that can be intimidating when needed.

I'm drooling over the little muffin-like bread he just pulled out of the oven, as the smell mixes deliciously with the smoked meat that's resting on the counter. Cooking is Henry's love language. I look forward to the Sunday dinners when he's the one in the kitchen, which tends to be a lot of them since the rest of us are a bit more basic with our meal planning.

"Those Olympic guys are the ones who are going to triple our Q4 profits, so yeah, if they call me and want me to go out with them, then I'm gonna do it, Ev."

"I know, I know."

Henry oversees all aspects of our Winter Sports business. Everything from the gear we sell, the brands we carry, to the excursions we cater to, like snowboarding, heli-skiing, powder cats, and fat biking. You name it, Henry does it. He's brought out some of the world's best in competitive sports to promote our adventures and to show him a thing or two. He says it's the best way to stay on top of everyone else. He and Michael work together a lot on building excursions or adventures since they're the ones planning the core sport, and they've done some crossover things too, like ice climbing, that have gotten a ton of attention.

I look up at him, gauging his mood tonight. He looks like he's in a decent mood compared to others. "Did you get Milo back from the wildebeest yet?"

He glances over at me, and I can see the sadness splash over his face. It quickly disappears, and he bites back at me, "Ev, I'm not in the mood to talk about her."

"I'll take that as a no. If you want, I can hire someone to just break into her house while she's working, and they could just take my furry nephew back. I bet she wouldn't even notice."

"He's being taken care of. She may be the worst person on the planet, but she treats that dog better than she ever treated me, so I'm not too worried."

Before I can say anything else, he grabs the cutting board that holds the slab of meat and heads toward the dining table. "Food's ready!"

I carry the basket of heavenly-smelling popovers and see that G has finally arrived. She's talking with her hands at my dad as he pours her a drink. Michael sits down across from where I usually sit and waits as everyone else makes their way over. "You good?"

Without looking up from pouring water into his cup, he smiles. "Yes, Everly."

"Everly!" Giselle sing-songs over to me with a big glass of

red wine in one hand and the other stretched out for a hug. "Why are you dressed up? Got a hot date after this?"

Before I can say anything, Law chimes in, trying to mimic how I speak. "She said she just wanted to wear a *new sweater*."

We both look up at the sounds of a motorcycle coming up the driveway. Law smiles at me and says, "But I think she's full of it, and she'd *hoped* that Jack was going to come tonight."

"What are you talking about? Seriously, Law, you're going to start a thing when there isn't a thing. I can look nice for dinner. Henry isn't wearing sweats. Wait, Henry, why aren't you wearing sweats?" I change the subject brilliantly and crane my neck back to my burly brother. Now everyone is focused on Henry and his worn jeans and charcoal gray dress shirt.

Before anyone can press Henry further, Law yells toward the front door, "Come on in!"

Jack waltzes into my father's house with a bottle in a velvet bag in one hand and some kind of boxed dessert in the other. I'm instantly heated. My cheeks are flushed. *He* looks like dessert, in all honesty. His black leather moto jacket over a white Henley shirt and jeans. I'm practically biting my fist as I take him in.

"Jack, I know you know most of this crew by now, but you haven't been introduced to my father, Asher Riggs."

My dad stands from his seat as Jack makes his way across the room to the head of the table. "Pleasure is all mine, sir."

"Jack, great to meet you, son. I hear you're the creative that's shaking up our brand a bit. I like your photography work." Dad leans into the handshake, then adds, "You're going to have to tell me what it's like to do that Body Issue every year. I'm sure you have some good stories."

Jack takes the seat next to my father, which is also next to me. "Absolutely. It's a lot of personality fluffing and strategically placed limbs." He smiles that megawatt smile, and those dimples make their appearance. Geez, those things really should be announced before they come out. "Maybe we can share a drink after dinner, sir. Law tells me you're the one who taught him to make his perfect Old Fashioned. I could go for another one of those."

Jack looks at me. I can see him out of my peripheral vision, and he's staring. Smiling at me, because he knows I'm trying my hardest to avoid meeting his eyes. I'm being so immature, but I don't know how to look at him after the other night. "Everly, good to see you. You look beautiful." I smile, still without looking him in the eye. He leans over, closer to me. "Mind passing me that bottle of red in front of you."

"Sh-mure. Sure. Yes. Red," I say, awkwardly loud. I grab it and pour the pinot blend into his glass. The heck was that, *schmure*? I have one sexual fantasy about the man...okay, *and* encounter, if I can even call it that, and I'm a blundering idiot. I am not this person. When I finally steal a glance at him, I find that he's still staring at me. I can't help but crack a smile, coupled with a nervous laugh that helps me breathe. Looking up, I see everyone watching our interaction. Law and my dad are smiling, Michael is scowling, and Henry is staring at me with narrowed eyes like I'm an idiot. *Nice.*

G breaks the silence and looks to Henry. "Is there a reason you're extra bear-like today, or have you just not met your quota of growling at people for the week?"

Ignoring her comment, Henry continues to dish out a serving of crispy Brussel sprouts with bacon onto his plate. "There's no quota. I'm not trying to be anything other than myself. Maybe it's just you that brings out the bear, *Jizz*. Here, eat your risotto."

There goes the calm and quiet dinner I was hoping for. If these two are already picking at each other, then it's just a matter of moments before it gets out of hand.

"Why is it that you insist on calling me *that*, Hankey?" G grits her teeth as she growls back at him.

"You can't go more than fifteen minutes before you're pushing my buttons. Why is that, Jizz? Are you only happy when everyone is only paying attention to you? You that hard-up for attention?" Henry turns and leans in toward her, spitting out an evil smile while he bats his lashes.

"Stay out of my personal space before I show you exactly how quickly I can go from being tolerant to my foot jamming its way into your tiny little excuse for a-"

"That's enough, you two," Dad chimes in.

Surprisingly, they quit for now. I look at my best friend with wide eyes, wordlessly asking what the heck that was. She just shrugs her shoulders and focuses back on the mushroom truffle risotto on her plate. As much as they can't stand to be in the same room with one another, Henry still made her a vegetarian plate of her very own, like always, and I'd bet a hundred bucks that there's a grilled cheese in the kitchen for her too, just in case. Not to mention that she goes out of her way to notice all the places he is or isn't.

The diversion only lasts a minute or two and my mind is brought back to the man candy next to me. I know I should be embarrassed that just a few nights ago he saw me masturbate, stood a few feet away as I orgasmed like it was a show for his personal viewing. I should feel embarrassed, but I'm not. Every time I think about it, the thought of him watching, studying me intently, just arouses me more. I'm not one to be shy about sex, but I'm also not the most well-versed. I never thought I'd be one to be an exhibitionist, or want to show my body off to someone I barely know.

He just stood there, watching me, and for how long, I don't even know. Heck, part of my fantasy was imagining him watching me and then fucking me, so when I opened my eyes and saw him standing there, it sent me over the edge and an orgasm ripped its way through me. There was no stopping it to freak out.

"What do you think, Ev?" Law asks.

I wasn't paying any attention.

"About what?" I look down at the table at my youngest brother. Before he answers, I feel a warm leg rest against the side of mine underneath the table and a current of excitement ripples through me. I have no interest in shifting away.

I'm turned on by the fact that Jack and I have this dirty little secret between us, and it's setting my skin on fire. I peek over at him. He looks back at me and nudges my leg slightly. Such a small movement that changes me from feeling a bit turned on to warm and cozy all over. Like I want to snuggle and nuzzle into him. I'm one more affection away from draping myself over him and purring. How did I become this person?

"What do you say we head to the Breakfast Nook in the morning before we head to the office?" Law suggests. "Jack's going to ride with us. That potential ice storm coming through won't be kind to his Harley. Oh, Jack, I think those two girls from the other night are working, and I wanna see if I can convince them to test out the hot tub." He wiggles his eyebrows at Jack. And just like that, I'm snapped back into the reality of the man next to me. World-renowned photographer, all-American playboy, whatever the stereotyped title GQ gives him. Jack is definitely one thing, and that's a temporary fixture. This means all of these feelings that are stirring need to remain surface level. He's not the kind of guy you keep.

And I know myself enough to know I'll want to keep him.

16

Jack

ABOUT AN HOUR LATER, THE DINNER IS WRAPPED UP, AND THE table cleared. They seem to have the clean-up part down to a structured routine with clearing, washing, and drying while Giselle informed me all about one of the techniques of tattooing she specializes in called watercoloring. When we step outside for a drink, it doesn't surprise me that the outdoor setup of this place is almost as expansive and impressive as what was indoors.

If someone asked me to name the most incredible place I've ever been, I always thought I would say somewhere iconic like a rooftop in Prague, a villa in Tuscany or the beaches in the Cayman Islands, but right now I can't imagine anywhere that I've already been that would top Asher Riggs' Ranch in Strutt's Peak. It's fucking spectacular, and I haven't even seen it during the day. I can only imagine the light this place gets in the morning, and then during sunset. Everything on the main floor of the house must bathe in perfect honey-colored warmth.

"So, Jack, what's it like to work with some of the best athletes in the world? Are they all just big egos?" Asher asks from his Adirondack chair next to me. We've made our way out to the oversized firepit that sits in the middle of the stone patio overlooking his sprawling property, the outline of mountains in the background. The only person still inside is Everly. It was obvious that she was rattled by seeing me since our last encounter, but I also can't ignore how she leaned into me as I brushed her leg under the table at dinner. I wanted to move closer, but didn't. I needed to touch her in some way.

"It's a mixed bag of personalities. There are some more attention-seeking than others. If you can believe it, the men's Olympic swim team is neck and neck with some NFL long-timers. Overall, most of the athletes are incredibly humble, down-to-earth. Minimal assholes. For the body image shoots, these athletes aren't shy. Most of them have honed their sport, and in doing so, their bodies have become their instruments. They're all proud of their strength and contours, and that honestly is what makes those issues so good. The confidence behind them. The positions can be..."

I smile and look down into my drink. "The way we ask them to move is uncomfortable, but the result is worth it. And not just from the popularity of them." I pause for a moment, trying to articulate this without sounding preten- tious. "These athletes have such a short window of being able to compete on a national or world stage. It takes their whole lives and then only these select few get to the level they're at and it's fleeting. So being in this issue, specifically, is just another way to increase their spotlight."

"You've become friends with a lot of these guys too, right?" Michael chimes into the discussion.

I nod. "Yeah, some of the best friends I've got I've met through work and are professional athletes. Some retired now, but most are still playing or competing. Henry, you probably met my buddy Shae McKenna a time or two. I know he comes up to Colorado to train pretty often."

Law coughs on his wine. "Are you shitting me right now? Henry, I'm going to kick you in the sack in a minute." He turns to me. "Please tell me we can flex this friendly arm and get his agent on the phone? I'd love to get him in some of the winter marketing for next year."

"Sure. Happy to introduce you guys."

"Henry Montana Riggs, you better speak now about what other world-class athletes you just so happen to know and have kept from me! I feel betrayed. I mean, c'mon, man!"

Giselle starts laughing so hard she practically chokes. "Henry Montana?! This...this can only be the best day ever. Please, please, tell me that's your middle name, Hankey? There is so much to unpack here."

Henry turns his head toward her slowly and leans into her ear, saying something that instantly quiets her laughter and turns her cheeks a shade of pink. I don't know what exactly is going on there, but whatever it is, it's pure entertainment.

I hear the sliding door open behind me and I sit a little taller, knowing she's joining us. An empty chair is across the firepit and part of me wishes she would sidle up next to me instead. Before I see her, I feel her. Her warm breath in the cool night air hits my ear. She smells like oranges and cinnamon, and I swallow a groan. Everly leans down toward me as Law and Michael talk about the famous people he may have come across. "You see that too, right?" She's looking over at a now embarrassed Giselle and a pissed-off Henry.

I smile and turn my head to look at her, only inches away from her beautiful mouth. "It's hard to miss," I say. God, this woman is so beautiful. I keep her stare a minute longer. She has a dimple on her left cheek that I'm just noticing. It makes her even more stunning; sweet mixed with sexy. I bring my gaze back up to hers, and alluring hazel eyes have me stuck. I take a second to enjoy the golden flecks that outline her pupils, morphing with brown and a little bit of green. She looks down at my mouth. *See something you like?* I can't help but smile a bit right before I take a sip of the cabernet she poured for me. She realizes what she just did and snaps her attention back, stands up from leaning over, and walks over to the open chair.

"There are plenty of people, rich people, I might add, that want an entire experience. Something that's an experience beyond a sport." Law is speaking passionately next to Everly and Henry. I can tell she isn't buying what he's selling, just based on her body language alone. She's not looking at him, staring into the firepit, and dropping sideways glances, which makes me think they've talked about this before and it never went any better.

"You're talking about creative excursions, which are nice. Hell, I'll go on one, but it's not what *we* specialize in. It's not our business model, and, quite frankly, with all the changes we already have a green light to tackle, adding something else seems like an unnecessary risk."

She can command a conversation, I'll give her that, but I

can tell that Law isn't satisfied with what she's shooting down. Everly looks across the pit toward her father, perhaps searching for someone to agree with her.

"Maybe it could be a passion project that he could lead. If you look at it as exploratory, then why not test it out to see where it goes?" Asher chimes in.

"That's not the point, Daddy. I just don't see the return on investment we'd have to make. Law, if you want to do it, then give me the numbers and not the fluff."

"Ev, give me a fucking break here. You know this is a great idea and I don't get why you're dragging your heels on it. I mean, if you want to get bitchy, then fine, I'll meet you there. How's *your* passion project? Who was your cheerleader on that? Hmm?"

"It's not the same thing and you know it. There was such limited risk and on top of that, *I* didn't want to do it. You were the one who pushed it along."

"See! I know a good thing when I see it. You're being too conservative. You know it, and I just don't get why." Law seems defeated and looks at me. Damn it, keep me out of this. I get what he's saying, but I'm not about to get involved here. "Jack, how would you feel about coming to Strutt's for your buddy's bachelor party, where the only thing you need to do is have a chat with my team and we plan the whole thing?" He leans forward, excited. "I'm talking about day adventures like heli-skiing and then mountainside cigars and scotch. Then at night, you don't want a typical raunchy party with tits in your face, so we plan a personal tasting menu at Strutt's Lodge, a pro-level poker game, and some eye candy. If it's wanted, of course."

"Sounds exclusive and expensive, but I'd be all about a

guy's weekend like that." Law looks like I just delivered him his favorite treat after a year of no sweets. And in the same moment, I realize I just stepped into a bear trap and it's going to hurt like a bitch.

I look across the fire to Everly, and she barely spares me a glance when she says, "Of course, you'd think that sounds great. Hell, I want to go on that trip, but again, that's not the point." She huffs. I study her for a minute. "Now imagine your expensive specialized guys' weekend has one or two guys that are prick drunks who decide they want to be snorting lines of coke and looking to hire hookers instead of just eye candy. We'd be opening ourselves to things I don't think we're equipped to handle."

"Ev, you say shit like this all the time. Why does-?" Law gets cut-off from the question.

"Jack, you can't tell me that the guys you hang with aren't looking for more fun by the end of the night. Whether that comes in the form of drugs or girls." She laughs sarcastically. "I'm sure *you* know exactly what I'm talking about. You are the target audience!"

Are you kidding me? That's how she sees me. I shouldn't be surprised. She doesn't know me, just my reputation, but it still burns. I shouldn't feel like I've been slapped in the face by that comment, but I do. I work hard not to give her any emotional response; I'm too pissed off. So instead, with my jaw clenched, I just look at her and take a minute to decide how to respond. Before I can make her choke back the words she spit like venom, she stands and leans down to her father. "Daddy, thank you, but I'm not interested in hearing any more about this tonight. I'm going to head home."

Not so fast, princess. "Listen, this isn't my company, so I don't know the first thing about the return or the investment involved, and I don't have the research in front of me to back it up, but I agree with Law. It sounds like a promising offshoot to what you guys are already offering. And just for the record, I don't do drugs. I don't monitor what all of my friends do, but the people I choose to spend my time with aren't the stereotype you just spit out. As far as women are concerned..." I shrug my shoulders. I don't need to offset her opinion of me in that department.

"Pumpkin, there's no reason to leave. We haven't even tried the dessert yet." Asher leans into her hug.

"I'll see most of you at home." She looks at me for a beat, and I want to back her into a corner and kiss the assumptions right out of her feisty mouth. Everly leans down to Giselle. "I'll talk to you later, love. It's been a long weekend, and I have some things I need to do before I head home. Text me when you get in, so I know you're home safe, yeah?" Giselle nods and steals a glance at me. She's watching as I watch her friend leave.

As soon as the sliding door closes, Law and Michael start arguing about the lingering conversation. Giselle walks over to my chair and sits on the arm. She leans in closer and says, "My rules dictate that I always side with her, even when she's being an asshole. So, I'm siding with her, but I'll say this"—she pauses for a minute, perhaps selecting her words carefully—"not many people challenge her or call her out. Even these guys." She takes a sip of her wine. "So be careful. Once she makes her mind up about someone, it sticks." After her next sip, she sing-songs, "You may have just made yourself an enemy, Jack Deacon."

I'm pissed off that she left, but I'm more pissed off at my choices that have led me to this moment. Regretting the reputation I've built, because for the first time, I actually care about what someone thinks of me.

17

Everly

"THERE ARE AT LEAST THREE DIFFERENT BRANDS THAT WANT to be the exclusive brand for next year's winter season, so why would we add yet another one to the list if it's just a version of the same thing?" I sit back in the conference room chair and stare at each one of the marketing team members for some kind of response. *Crickets.*

I'm still in a huff from last night's family dinner. I don't like when outsiders, specifically ones that are too good looking to keep my mind from wandering into *very* unprofessional territory, get involved in family business discussions. Even if he had a point and I was the one being kind of an asshole in making assumptions about him. I saw his face when I said it, and I immediately regretted it. I was ticked off that he even entered the discussion, but I shouldn't have been so nasty.

As if on cue, almost knowing that I'm already distracted by thoughts of him, Jack strolls into the conference room with one hand holding his camera by the lens, with the strap hanging casually by his side, and the other hand with a still steaming cup of coffee. From Brew & Books no less, I can tell by the cute logo on the cup. *I could go for another Hungry Eye coffee right about now.*

"Jack, thanks for making it to this meeting," Law says as he gets up from his chair and shakes his hand. "Perfect timing. Everly was just asking my team about the additional brand that wants exclusivity for next winter. I thought it made sense to have you here for it."

I look at Law, somewhat confused as to why Jack would need to be here for any other reason other than to take images of the team working and interacting for the website revamp.

"Law, I'm here only for creative reasons. I want to get a feel for your team interaction and maybe take a few shots throughout, but that's it."

Jack leans against the far back wall, which is directly in my line of sight. He sips his drink and just watches me. His attention is inescapable, and I'm brought back to him watching me touch myself. Once again. I can feel my cheeks warm, and I'm instantly turned on by just a flash of those thoughts. I need to get a handle on this.

"Fair enough. Jack brought the fourth company to my attention and some of the questions you have were in their proposal. We can recap it later."

I ignore Law and the rest of his team and ask, "Jack brought the fourth company?"

Jack chimes in, "I'm on the board. It's a small brand in comparison to the rest, but they're worth looking at. There might be more there beyond a winter exclusive. If you're thinking of acquiring some smaller companies in the future, they're primed for partnership now. Could be more later. Just a thought. I don't mean to walk into a scenario that I'm not supposed to, but I'm not the kind of man to stand by and just watch."

Did he just...

This fucking guy smiles into his cup of coffee.

"It's funny because I feel like that's exactly what I'm seeing. You, walking into a situation late in the game and just standing there with some big words and no action. It is very disappointing. This makes the third time now that you've walked into something late and did nothing but interrupt."

He chokes a bit on his sip.

I give him a snarky smile and ask that the team provide their recommendations by the end of the week. We carry on for another twenty minutes before leaving the conference room. I don't stick around. As much as I want to challenge that stupidly sexy man, I know it's a bad idea. Too complicated, too much of a reputation, and too many red flags. I also probably owe him an apology, which I'd like to give when I'm not annoyed at him. On the flip side, I'm going to have to change my underwear, because, after verbally sparring with secret innuendos, followed by a flash of those dimples he keeps whipping out, I was almost at the point of having to rub my thighs together just to calm myself down. Why does bickering with him feel like foreplay?

When I finally make my way back to my office, I'm greeted with a large cup from Brew & Books sitting on my desk. "Beautiful" is written on the side where someone's name would normally be. I can't help but smile. I take a sip. It's a Hungry Eye. *So good.*

Over the next week, every day after my first meeting of

the morning, I come back to my desk and find a cup of my favorite coffee from my new favorite coffee shop waiting for me. And every day, just the word *beautiful* is scribbled on the side, nothing else. I don't know why it would be from him, but my guess is that if it is, Jack is trying to change my perception of him. And it's starting to work.

18

Jack

"She has this gorgeous mouth, and I'll be honest, Uncle Jack, I don't think I've ever seen anything I want more in my entire life than to kiss this girl."

"Then do it. What's holding you back from asking her out and just going for it? Shit!" I grab at the rock above me. "You're such a shit. You told me this was going to be an easy, chill hike."

"First, I never said chill. And are you complaining? For real?"

I laugh and wipe the sweat from my forehead. "I don't complain, kid. I could run circles around you. I was just expecting something a little less intense. I didn't eat anything before I left this morning."

I pull my weight up the wall and meet Benny at the top of the trail. "Wow. This place keeps impressing me. You and your mom picked a helluva town to settle down in." I look over at my nephew and still see the little kid I taught to ride a bike, but staring back at me is a man.

"I hope she can be happy here." I grab his shoulder but don't say anything. I want him to be able to talk to me, so I make space for him to do that. "She wasn't happy with Dad for a long time, but I just don't—" He blows out a heavy breath, shaking his head. "I don't know that a new place is going to make her happy. I mean, she's taken on this shop and the stress that comes with it. I feel like she jumped into this."

"Your mom came here for a fresh start. Your dad wasn't the man she thought he was, and she needed to stop running into him everywhere she went. It wasn't healthy."

"I know that, but I don't think Dad was the only problem." He pulls a knee up toward his chest, draping his arm over it, and looks out over the horizon. It's well into the morning, but since it's fall, the air around us it's still chilled enough for us to see our breaths.

"How about we hike back down, and I'll make you some lunch at the coffee shop? We can hang in the back, and you can tell me your game plan for this girl with the beautiful mouth."

"Uncle Jack?" Benny looks at me, searching for some comfort. "You think Mom will be okay? I'm worried about her."

My nephew witnessed more than he needed to in that relationship. Instead of walking away a long time ago, Kathryn stayed. It was loyal, and it was a bad call, in my opinion, but it wasn't my life. She made choices I never agreed with, but always supported. That was who we were to each other. The other's anchor, but never the navigator.

"I can tell you one thing that I know to be true, and it's

that your mom is capable of so much. I know she's dealing with a lot, but that's how life hits her. She's always dealing with something big. Ever since we were kids, she had something running against her and now, well, now, it's her turn to do things that are going to make her happy." I nudge him with my shoulder to make sure he's really hearing me. "She came here for the both of you. You've been wanting to be in a place like this for years. Out of the city, with access to things like this. The fact that her dream shop just happened to fall into her lap was the push she needed to finally get out from under the weight of her life back east."

Benny just nods. He hears me. I stare into his brown eyes that are riddled with wisdom, far beyond his years. His features have slimmed, leaving him with more angles than cheeks, making him look far from the boy he used to be. For a seventeen-year-old kid, he's mature and much smarter than the lot of us. "I'm happy you're here, Uncle Jack. She needed to see you, spend time with you. Heck, I need to be around you too. Stuff with Mom and Dad has been exhausting. Then Dad just checked out. He hasn't wanted to hear much from us since the move either. Part of me understands and then part of me is pissed."

"Don't do that. You don't have to be okay with the way your mom or dad reacts to things if you're not. It's not okay that your dad isn't still there to listen to you, regardless of what's going on with your mom. That's on him. Don't be so quick to take the blame or forgive it so quickly."

"How long will you be in town? Any chance you're going to be here through the holidays?" Benny asks with a twinge of hopefulness in his voice.

"My contract runs for another few weeks, but after that, I hadn't thought about it. Maybe I will. I don't have any more jobs until the New Year that I can't get done remotely from here. I won't fit in your apartment though, so I'm going to need to find a place."

"What about just staying at the Riggs' house a bit longer? Can you just maybe rent the space?"

We start descending the last climb we just made, and I take a minute to think if that might be a real possibility. "It's, well, there are some complications there, so I'm not sure. I'll figure it out, don't worry. I can always just rent something else. I think I'd like to stay a bit longer. Make sure you and your mom feel settled, and I would have come back for Christmas anyway, so that'll just save me on the travel."

And just like that, I'll be in Strutt's Peak for longer than I'd planned. More time with my nephew, I'll help out my sister, and while they are the reason for my staying a bit longer, I'm immediately thinking about a smart and opinionated brunette who I'll have more chances to be around.

19

Everly

FOR THE MIDDLE OF THE WEEK, IT FEELS AN AWFUL LOT LIKE A Friday. I look up from my desk and notice the quiet of the office, slipping my heels back on. It's a good time to walk out the stiffness from sitting for hours and make a coffee. I look down toward the pit, an open space where the marketing team sits, and it's empty. They hightailed it out of here around three o'clock, something about the film festival promos, which I'm sure will prove to be a smart use of their attention.

Michael is with my father on some sort of horse tranquility ride they've been planning for weeks. Henry's office is empty, and only a few folks from the finance team are still trucking away.

My phone buzzes in my back pocket.

G

Is it pineapple for better-tasting jizz, or cranberry juice? I always get the jizz and the UTI mixed up.

I need a quick answer here, Ev.

EVERLY

Pineapple for Penis.

G

Got it. Thanks, love u.

EVERLY

Google also works for quick answers. Just sayin'.

G

Yes, but then Google doesn't ask me later what that was all about. So until Siri or Alexa or Google can make me feel good about my life choices the way you can, I will ask you the ridiculous things first.

She might be an acquired taste for some, but Giselle is the kind of friend I always hoped I'd find. How does a person make you love them even more after they ask about penises and urinary tract infections?

"Man or meme?" I look up and find Jack leaning against the door frame that leads to the creative studio. Instantly, I smile at him and feel my face flush.

"You're smiling at your phone in the middle of the hallway," he says with a smile mirroring mine.

I hold up my phone. "Giselle."

"Ah, yes. The passionate tattoo artist. She's funny. And a schmoozer. I left our conversation wanting another tattoo."

I shift, dropping my phone into my back pocket. "She is pretty wonderful. If you get on her good side and treat her people right, you'll have her in your corner for life. But, don't piss her off. It's never a good thing for whatever poor sucker is on the other end of her wrath."

"I guess your brother didn't get that memo."

"Missed it big time. Henry is the eternal pessimist, and it grinds at G. He's had to make some big life changes over the past decade and it's made him cranky. Everyone except G gives him a pass to be an asshole." I lift a shoulder. "I always thought maybe they'd get over the bickering and move on, but now we all just run defense when it's needed and hope for the least amount of fallout."

I brush past him and that current of electricity that exists between the two of us revs up, and I feel it roll right through me. "What are you still doing here? I thought you would be with Law and his team down at the film fest. Opening activities means most of the town is there celebrating and on the hunt for celebrity sightings."

He turns and smiles, but instead of answering right away, Jack walks into the room as if he owns it, and to be fair, this has been his workspace for the majority of his time here so far. I'm actually not sure why I'm in here right now, but I'm not quite ready to move away. Jumping up onto a box, he reaches up to a light surrounded by a black umbrella. As he does, I catch sight of his skin that peeks out as his shirt rides up in the front. I lick my lips and realize that I've never looked at a man's lower abs with such need.

I know I'm objectifying him, but at this moment, I couldn't care less, because I'm fairly positive the lines that cut in from his hips and dip into his pants are just pointing to what I'm practically panting for right now. *Snap out of it, Everly!*

He catches me checking him out, and instead of looking away, I choose not to care. Then he jumps down from the box and says, "I have more to get done here before I can call it a night. And celebrities aren't all that impressive."

I move my attention to the rest of the room and take a breath, hoping it'll get my head out of the crotch-region of Jack's body. Looking at him any longer isn't a smart idea. "What are you guys working through right now? Law keeps me updated, but I've been a bit nuts this week and haven't talked to him yet."

"We did a lot of flat lays on the clothing line, but I'm not loving them. I want to show these off on bodies, and I'm trying to figure out how I can do that best. These aren't a part of the sports side of things where the equipment is the focus, but I wanted to keep the flow of people versus just products. Making it feel more like a glimpse into Riggs and not just a catalog."

I move toward the flat lays of my loungewear samples. Some of my favorites are being displayed. Jack did an incredible job arranging the styles. "These look good. I love this one the most. It's my favorite."

Jack tilts his head, and I catch him looking me up and down, studying me. I move my attention back down to the table and run my fingers along the garments, feeling the materials I've spent so much time on.

Click-pop. Click-pop. The light he was just fiddling with goes off twice, and I look up quickly. "Did you just take my picture?"

He smiles. That's his answer. This fucking guy.

"Those three pieces. The one you're holding, the shorts and those undergarments."

I look down at what he's tilted his head toward. "They're lounge-bras. That's, that's what we're calling them."

"Okay. That lounge-bra, the shorts, and that sweatshirt." I point to them. "Yes, those. Put them on."

I look up at him, silently questioning. I'm instantly nervous.

He's already looking down at his camera, distracted by flipping through the pictures he just assaulted from me. Then he peers up, realizing I'm not responding, and says, "Put them on. Let's see if they look better on a body instead of just laying flat."

I shake my head no before any words come out. "I'm not putting anything on. I'm not. I don't want my picture taken, Jack."

He walks closer to me, leaning over, invading my personal space, then plucks the garments off the table and drops them in my arms. "I wasn't asking, Everly. Go put them on."

Who does this guy think he is? I don't move. "I'm not going to do that, Jack."

He turns from fiddling with his camera. "I want to see these on a body. There's no one else here right now, and you're not working at the moment." He quirks his brow, looks me up and down, surveying my body. "They'll fit. You just have to put them on and follow my directions."

I don't realize what I'm saying until it's already out. "Fine."

What the fuck am I thinking?

"Let me go grab something, and I'll be right back." Aside from not wanting to be featured in any of our marketing materials, I don't want to be wearing my designs, at least not in a promotional way, but there's a part of me that wants to have Jack's attention right now. What better way than to be in front of his lens.

I round the corner into my office bathroom, and somewhere between walking back to my office and pulling out my makeup bag, I decide I'm going to show this man exactly the type of woman I am. Nervous and vulnerable are not on the menu today. Nope, today Jack Deacon will see the boss he's working for.

I swipe mineral powder across every shiny part of my face. Cream blush for some color, since the tan I worked hard for this past summer is long gone, and then I clean up the smudged eyeliner from the day. After I brush through my waves, which are still looking decent, and add a swipe of color on my lips, I've got that boost of confidence I was hoping I'd find. And since I'm a smart woman, I grab the bottle of Johnny Walker Blue from my bar cart with two scotch glasses and stalk back to the creative studio. It'll be needed for this.

"I'm just moving a few lights and then we can talk about how we'll move you around this space." Jack jumps down from some scaffolding near the windows and eyes the bottle in my hand. "One of those for me?"

Without answering, I just pour us both two fingers and hand him his. I clink his glass and he starts to sip while I take the entire thing down with one gulp. It burns the whole way.

He looks at me quizzically, obviously not expecting that move. "I'm not sure if I should yell at you for shooting down Johnny Blue Label so fast or be impressed."

Again, I don't reply, and without even looking at him, I

take my heels off and start unbuttoning my pants. If Jack is going to push me out of my comfort zone, then I'm going to make him squirm a bit too. I pull my black suit pants off completely and drape them over the chair to my left. My blouse reaches low enough to be covering the very tops of my thighs. I pull on the thermal-like boy shorts up and over my thong, turning around so I can discard my shirt without giving him a full-frontal view. While the man has already seen some of my lady bits, I'm not ready to show him my tits in the middle of my creative studio. I slip off my white blouse and unclasp my white bra, flinging it over to the chair as well, my bare back exposed to him. Then I pull on the pink lace lounge bra, which is equally comfortable and sexy. Enough padding to boost my girls, but no wires to poke and leave marks, and just enough strap to evenly distribute weight while doubling as a part of the style. I've never felt prouder of something I've designed than I do at this moment wearing it. In front of him. I feel more excited than nervous now, small butterflies making their way into my stomach. I never shy away from this feeling; it's a reminder that I'm doing something daring.

Before I turn around, I grab the pale blush-colored sweatshirt, which matches the shorts, and I slip it over my head. The off-the-shoulder design of the sweatshirt also shows off the lacey straps of the bra, which is exactly how I wanted it to be paired. I catch Jack's eye and smile. That same electric current runs up my arms and down my legs, leaving goosebumps in its wake.

"I knew you were trouble, Miss Riggs, but until a minute ago, I didn't realize just how much." I start to walk toward his camera bench setup. "You need to put those on too." He points to the charcoal-colored thigh-high socks that are resting on the table to his right.

I grab them, jump up on the table, and start pulling on the first one. "Yes, sir!"

Jack groans loudly. I bite my lower lip to keep from smiling. *This is going to be fun.*

20

Jack

It's only been about ten minutes since I've started shooting and in that ten minutes, I don't think I've experienced a more uncomfortable hard-on in all my life. This woman is some sort of personalized drug and it's taking every ounce of willpower not to grab two handfuls of her ass and bury myself deep inside of her. I've photographed plenty of beautiful women. Models, athletes, lonely, powerful, and even celebrities but, right now, I feel like being focused on this woman is making me feel like I'm exactly where I'm meant to be. I can't explain it. While Everly and I have been teetering between flirting and spitting fire at one another over the past couple of weeks, I haven't felt this kind of attraction to anyone. Ever.

There have been a few times when I've had a post-shoot fool around and then a few one-night stands with a model or two, but I've always been able to keep the work moving along before I indulge in anything. Everly is testing my reserve simply by the way she moves her body and takes my direction. I can barely remember looking at a woman the way I'm looking at her. I'm fucking enchanted.

"Pull your arm over your head and maybe just play with your hair a bit. I want this to look relaxed. You need to relax, Miss Riggs. It's just me in here."

Rolling her eyes at me, she takes a deep breath and lets it out, draping one leg off the side of the couch and twirling a few strands of her hair around her fingers. And right there, my body is awake and thrumming in appreciation.

"That's it." And without thinking, I groan slightly while quietly praising. "So fucking beautiful."

Her head jerks up at the words. I can tell she's weighing how or if to respond. The corner of her mouth kicks up, which makes me think she didn't mind the slip. "If you want me truly relaxed, then you're going to need to give me a heavy pour from that bottle and throw on some music, Jack."

I make my way over to the bottle of Johnny and pour some into the mug on the coffee table. The mood is feeling an awful lot like what I walked into the other night at the pool house. Music with a relaxed Everly Riggs on a couch has my dick wide awake and doing one-armed pushups in my pants.

Making a quick adjustment, so that my eagerness isn't so obvious, I walk back to her, hand off the mug of booze, then pull a few pieces of hair away from her face. "May I?" I ask permission to touch her legs to move them the way I'd like. "Here you go, ladies' choice." I give her my phone, which is connected to the speakers in the room, and she scrolls through. She smiles, and a moment later Florence + The Machine is filtering through, crooning about the stars and the moon. It wasn't what I was expecting her to choose, and it makes me want to hear more.

"Have you ever seen her perform?"

"Florence + The Machine? No, I haven't."

"The music is just as good live as it is listening here. Maybe even better, which isn't always a guarantee. She has this presence on stage that's infectious. No, that's not the right word. She looks ethereal, but her voice has this power that makes you believe the words and practically absorb the instruments. When I saw her, she wore this flowing dress...I can't remember what color it was, but that dress, the way it moved with her red hair and, oh yeah, and she was barefoot. She danced around the stage, capturing the attention of every single person in the amphitheater. It was an incredible show, but I just left there feeling like she was one of the special ones. You know, to really see someone in their element, doing exactly what they were born to do and loving, like really loving it. It was beautiful. That concert was right after I took a seat on the board of directors for our family business. All of it was such a rush."

Click-pop. Click-pop. Click-pop.

Her head snaps up, catching me smiling at her story. "Keep talking. People relax more when they talk about things they enjoy or things they're proud of." Everly looks at me like I've just caught a glimpse of something she tries to keep out of sight. *Show me more of it, beautiful.* "Okay. Okay, I'm not going to push. Tell me the one thing that will always put you in a great mood. No matter what. It can be anything."

Click-pop. Click-pop.

I take a few more pictures of her thinking about what she's willing to share with me. The flashbulb goes off, casting a perfectly warm light on the scene. She's on the oversized couch, surrounded by blankets and pillows. The loungewear, after all, is meant to be marketed to outdoor athletes and their post-activity relaxation. The entire setup could be right out of anybody's cozy living room. Especially anybody vacationing in Strutt's Peak.

She smiles and sits up a bit. "Pedicures with my dad."

Again, not expecting that. "How often do you do those?"

"We've been going together at least once a month since I was about thirteen. Dad tried to make up for the fact that my mom wasn't in the picture, and then he realized how magical a good pedicure could be. Have you ever been?"

I look at the screen to my left, scrolling through the last few shots to review. "I haven't."

"You're missing out, Jack. It's so relaxing, the massage is heaven, and you walk out with pretty-looking feet."

Everly sits forward and grabs the mug, and holding it with two hands, she continues. "Outside of that, my brothers drive me nuts, but they make me happy. Oh! When I'm on fresh powder after a snowstorm. Skiing with Law and Henry down an unused trail is *almost* perfection. A good workout with Michael always puts me right. You'd never guess it about him, but he's super motivating to train with." She pauses and then says, "Those are all the things I can think of, well, at least all the things I can share." She looks off to the side, as if she's really seeing these things that make her smile, that make her happiest.

Turning her attention back to me, she asks, "What about you? What's the one thing that will put you in a great mood? Gives you complete pleasure?"

I raise my eyebrows.

She smiles. "You know what I mean."

I return her smile. That was a loaded question. "Like I said before, you're trouble, Ms. Riggs."

Conversations that shift to me are ones that I do my best to avoid. I connect with people through their stories and not my own. I have too many demons that hide and lurk in dark corners that I don't want peeking out. Nothing good ever comes out of unleashing them. How much do I share here? Bird's-eye view, glossy version, or the truth?

"Waffles." I'm not sure why, but the thought rolls out of me before I'm able to edit it.

"Waffles?" She laughs a bit and then stops when she notices I'm not making a joke of it, but truly answering her question. "Okay, I'll bite. Why waffles?"

"What's not to love about waffles?" I try to move on and play this off as just a love for great breakfast food. "Syrup, whipped cream, strawberries, throw some bacon on there too and it's instant happiness. I can always be in a great mood after I eat waffles."

"Mhm. I see you, Jack Deacon. Trying to make light of something that I could guess is a bit heavier than that. I answered your question, now answer mine." She pauses, treading lightly and watching my body language. "Why waffles?"

I lower my camera and my eyes connect with the swirl of browns and greens staring at me from a few feet away. "The first time I went to a waffle house, I was nine years old. I just had the worst night of my entire life, and not like I lost a toy kind of bad." I take a breath and try to remember. "A fireman took my sister and me to a waffle house and it was the first warm meal I had eaten that month and the best meal I had ever had in my whole life. It was a giant Belgian waffle."

She smiles at me. "Let me guess. Syrup, whipped cream, strawberries, and bacon."

I nod. "It was life changing." Telling her this doesn't change the mood. I feel good sharing this small piece of me. After those waffles, my new life began. Life before waffles was unpredictable. I was scared all the time. For my sister, for my mother. I was scared of the things that happened, as all those men would come to see my mother. I was frightened every moment of every day. After waffles, nothing seemed too horrible any longer.

I never share anything like this with people, and especially never with women. The last thing I want is for anyone to know too much about my life. The glossy version of it is far more palatable, even if it makes me look like an arrogant playboy. I don't open up like this. And I know that's exactly why I'm never in a relationship longer than a vacation. I've also never met anyone I truly wanted to tell.

This woman, with her confidence and the way she can own a room with an idea, is mesmerizing. I've seen the way people respect her in this office. But it's also the way she makes people feel comfortable. She makes it easy to be around her.

"Jack!?"

"Yea? Sorry." I zoned out. I pull myself back to the moment and realize I'm not ready to be done with this just yet.

"I said, are we all set here? I need to wrap a few things up before I head out for the night, and it's already...wow, yeah, it's already after six." She stands up and walks toward the far side of the room where her clothes are draped over a chair.

"I'll send these your way and you can decide if you want

us to include any in the new materials. If you don't, then we should bring in someone to model these pieces. I'll speak with Law about it, but these clothes should be worn, not just laid out, they're too good. It's better to show how they fall. That's the point, right? Comfortable and sexy." That's her in this moment, exactly. Comfortable and sexy as hell.

"Yes, that's exactly the point. I love everything about this line. I'm so excited for it to launch." She pulls the sweatshirt off her head and says, "I'm glad you pushed me to do this. It's so far out of my comfort zone, being on this side of things." She turns slightly toward me, smiling. "You're good at your job, Jack. It was fun, and believe it or not, I did relax."

Standing there paying compliments in nothing more than a glorified bra and boy shorts, I realize that Everly has no clue how incredibly beautiful she really is, and that alone turns me on even more. Her body is built to be looked at, touched, worshiped. She has toned legs that have seen plenty of hours playing outdoors, and a gorgeous peach-shaped ass that makes me want to bite it, mark it up a bit. Her breasts are magnificent and I'm craving to see what they look like out of the bra. I have to take a steadying breath just looking at the swell of her tits peeking over the top as she breathes. They make my mouth water, thinking about how I'd like to tease and explore, how they'd move under my hands and tongue.

She's watching me canvas her body from a few feet away, and she shifts uncomfortably, probably realizing the way I'm looking at her is dangerous. And right now, it is, because nothing else exists for me other than what's buzzing between the two of us. I take three steps toward her. She backs up, but I keep walking, closing the space between us.

"Wh-what are you doing?" She smiles tentatively, then says, "Oh, is this your thing? You make a move on your models after you take their photos? Jack, you're forgetting..." Her voice lowers in a teasing, low tone as she whispers, "I'm not one of your models. I'm your boss." She's trying to play off what she can see in my eyes, what I'm intent on doing to her. I've made her nervous, but a joke isn't going to save her right now.

I push my fingers against the seam of her shorts, guiding her backwards toward the wall. Her breathing picks up in time with my own. She knows exactly what's going to happen next, so I'm not going to answer her. If she doesn't want to kiss me, then she can tell me, because I'm not interested in reading between any lines or stopping this feeling between us. I'm crossing this line with her, and I've never wanted to taste someone's lips the way I want to devour hers right this second.

Her back meets the wall, and in one fluid motion, I push my fingers through her hair and frame her face with my hands. I rub my thumbs along her jawline. Her skin is warm, soft, and I want to touch her everywhere to feel all the things she might be feeling right now. Be able to absorb it. She looks at my lips and then back to my eyes, silently challenging me to keep going.

"Don't insult me, Miss Riggs. I'm far from a good guy, but don't think for one minute you're in the same league as any of the women I've fucked before." She flashes a confident smile. She took that as a compliment like I'd intended, whereas most women would have taken it as a negative. And *that* is the kind of woman she is, self-assured, powerful, and it's intoxicating. "I've been turned on since I walked in on you touching yourself the other night. It took every bit of my willpower not to crawl on my knees to you, slap your hands away, and taste that sexy pussy of yours." She moves her hands to my chest and her breathing picks up even more, as if she's just been running. "Tell me right now if you don't want this, because once I start, I'm not going to want to stop."

She stares up at me, lips parted. I can tell she's turned on and equally unsure if the next move is mine or hers. She leans forward, slowly, and as eager as I feel to capture her mouth, I want her to make this choice. Close the gap between us. She's in charge for now.

Finally, her mouth brushes against mine. She sweeps her lips softly, so lightly, as if she's making sure this line is worth crossing. The gentleness of it unleashes me. I flatten her body against the wall, my body pressing against hers, and I grip her hair tighter, tilting her head so I can deepen the kiss. She licks across my lower lip, and I can't help but groan. I grant her access, and our tongues collide in a frantic dance, making everything in my body come alive with need. I *need* this woman.

She smells like oranges and tastes like vanilla frosting with a hint of the smokiness left behind from the scotch she was sipping. Fucking delicious. My hands trail down the curves of her body, and finding the exaggerated rounds of her ass, I grab underneath, lifting her up. Wrapping her legs around my waist, she can feel exactly how turned on I am. I grind my hips into her, my cock rubbing against the seam of her shorts. I've hit her exactly where she wants, because she moans softly into my mouth. Even the smallest movement against her feels incredible, and I want more of it.

Suddenly, I hear a huge crash of something hitting the

ground behind us, and it jolts both of our attention toward the door.

"I leave you two alone for a few hours and you're practically fucking each other in the office. Geez, Ev!" Law says casually as he picks up the light kit equipment he just barreled over.

I hold on to her, even though she's trying to wiggle down out of my arms. Instead, I carry her over to the table where she left her sweatshirt, hold her up with one arm, and grab it for her. Ignoring Law, I make sure she's covering herself up and not embarrassed by being interrupted by her brother, of all people. But when I look her in the eye to make sure she's alright, she rolls her eyes at me, flicking her gaze to her brother. She gives me a quick, light kiss on the lips and then looks over her shoulder to address him.

"The fact that you're still standing there, cock-blocking me right now, Law, makes you an asshole, not a protective brother." A mostly dressed Everly stalks toward her brother and stops mid-stride, halfway between us. She holds her pointer finger up to him, indicating for him to wait, and whips back around to face me. Then, she walks back and leans into me with a huge smile on her face, whispering in my ear. "I'm sorry about the other night." I lean back to look her in the eyes. "I should have never said what I said, and if I hurt you in any way, I'm sorry." That hits me right in the gut. I wasn't expecting an apology from her, but I give her a nod. I wasn't holding any hard feelings, because while her assumptions weren't accurate and ticked me off at the time, the lifestyle I portray makes it easy to jump to conclusions. She brushes her lips softly against mine again and before she pulls away completely, she whispers, "We're nowhere near finished here, Jack." Then she pats my chest and turns back toward her brother, who is still hovering in the doorway. I can still feel her ass in my grip, her mouth exploring mine, and I quietly groan. She's right; we're nowhere near done.

Law stays where he is, looking back at me. He's trying to figure out how to navigate this. The guy likes me, but he's trying to be a good brother here. "She's a badass, but don't hurt her. I like you, Jack. Don't make it so I have to change my mind about that."

I give him a quick nod. Fucking cock-block.

"Want to grab beers and burgers?" His tone changes completely from just a moment ago.

I just laugh at the instant shift in conversation. "Nah, I'm going to hang here for a bit longer and then just grab something on my way back home."

"Alright, man. Text me if you want me to grab takeout for you. I'll be there for at least a couple of hours. I'm meeting up with this redhead who does visual effects for one of the movie finalists for the film fest. She had a friend, but well, a double date with her seems like a weird thing to do with you now."

I just give him a smile and nod. We've become friends, but I'm not about to tell him that I've been stuck on his sister since she walked into the kitchen on my first day in town.

My phone vibrates in my pocket.

BENNY

Need to talk, got a minute?

21

Everly

I CAN STILL FEEL HIS LIPS ON MINE. THE BURN OF HIS SCRUFF on my cheeks and chin. I can't believe I went there. Crossed that line, no, not even crossed. I friggin' twerked my ass so far past that line. And at the office...and then got caught. *What am I doing?*

"I'm thinking this year my pop-up shop should be like a date night theme. I can send out invites for tattoos and tacos or something with your partner. What do you think?" G asks as she digs her phone out from her bag.

The Strutt's Peak Film Festival is one of, if not *the* biggest, pre-season tourist draws in Colorado. It happens in advance of the big snowfalls and brings a certain vibe to town that I look forward to every year. The town takes it seriously with an accompanying vendor fair, all the local restaurants arrange specialty menus, and the small businesses in our downtown village thrive off of the foot traffic.

My phone buzzes in my back pocket. I'm currently in

that place where I'm excited when my phone goes off. It could be Jack. I didn't give him my number, but I'm almost certain that wouldn't keep him from getting it. Usually, I groan at the buzz since it's more often than not a fire to put out at work, or a brother asking for more budget.

UNKNOWN NUMBER

> I can't stop thinking that maybe you should be the one with the player reputation. Good girls don't kiss like that, Miss Riggs. It was too good.

Jack. Looks like he found my number. I can't help but smile like an idiot at my phone.

"You didn't hear anything I just said, did you?" She caught me and rolls her eyes.

We're in line at Brews & Books, and the smell of coffee and caramel is making my mouth water. Ignoring her comment, I look around and say, "I've never seen a line this long. This place is a brilliant idea. On a random day, it's such a great spot, but the idea to host romance authors for meet and greets during the film festival is just good business."

"Fucking smart, right? Wish I thought of it."

That gives me an idea. "You should talk to the owner and see if they would want to do a little partner pop-up for the vendor fair. Make it a date night with coffee, romance, and tattoos."

"Oooooo! I love that, Ev. Maybe we can project some classic romance movies on the building outside to draw people in. I'm going to run with this and find the owner, Kathryn, when this crowd dies down a little bit."

G's phone buzzes, and before she clicks it open, I spot Henry's name. "Why is my brother texting you?"

We move farther up in line, and while I'm reading the

menu, I'm also trying to work out why two of the people I love the most, and that hate each other, could be texting one another. At one point, I thought G was interested in Henry. In fact, she helped him get out of an unhealthy situation with his ex, but they're at each other's throats every time they're in the same room.

She instantly goes on the defense. "How the fuck should I know? I just got the text. One of his douchebag athletes probably decided they want a tattoo after a day of bro-ing out."

I text Jack back.

EVERLY

Jack, what ever made you assume I was a good girl?

I smile at my phone. What I wouldn't give to see his face with that response. I have this need to flirt and push him right back. If I'm being honest, I really want to just push him into a dark corner and have my way with him. It's almost a crime not to think about the hard bulge that pressed into me.

A deep, gravelly voice that I've gotten used to enjoying the sound of grabs my attention, and I whip my head up to look around the few people in front of me. Behind the counter, sporting a red apron, is the man I'm currently texting and have been fantasizing about for the past few nights. While I hoped he would have come into the house and sought me out after our kiss, he didn't. I wasn't going to read into it. I'm so tired of overanalyzing and planning. With Jack, I want to just go for it and not overthink anything.

"Everly, why is your famous photographer working

behind the counter at a coffee shop?" Giselle asks as she checks him out.

Without being able to look away, I mumble, "I have no idea."

Taking an order from three flirtatious college girls, I use that minute to appreciate this beautiful man. His short black hair peeks from underneath a loosely fitted black ski hat, and a black long-sleeved Henley thermal frames the muscles of his broad shoulders and sculpted biceps. The sleeves are pushed up, showing off his corded forearms, one decorated with tattoos while the other is art-free and adorned with a leather cuff. He looks like the hipster artist he likely was when he was in his early twenties. I haven't been able to close my mouth, and realize I'm parched. I swallow hard.

"There's my hot barista! Or is it a barist*o*?" G shouts and pulls both Jack's and Benny's attention to us.

That fucking smile of his is dangerous. One kiss with that man and the crush I already had has now turned into a slight infatuation. I never feel like this, interested, enamored, and hot. Too damn hot. I'm constantly flushed. Falling over myself as soon as his dimples are directed my way. But I also don't remember ever being kissed like that. And a kiss like that is one you remember. It was as if he wanted to learn what I liked while teaching me what made him feel good, creating something perfect and original and delicious with each other. God, I want more.

As the person in front of us moves off to the side to collect her drink, G and I step up to the counter. Jack reaches forward and grabs my hand, kissing my palm. I wasn't expecting the comfort of a public display of affection. But now that it's happened, I'm not mad about it. That small move just traveled its way through my entire body. I feel his lips everywhere I want them. I want to be drunk on them.

"What are you doing here?" I manage to squeak out.

"What, did you move into town and have to get a part-time job, Jack? I thought they paid you pretty well with this whole celeb-level photography thing," Giselle comments sarcastically.

"My sister owns this place. She needed some help because of the author meet and greet tonight. I was in town, so here I am," Jack says.

"Uncle Jack, we're out of almond milk. You need to push the oat milk instead." Benny comes up next to Jack and flashes a smile at both G and me.

"Uncle Jack?" I ask.

Jack grabs Benny around the neck with one arm. "Kathryn, Benny's mom, is my sister. And this handsome guy is my nephew."

"We've met. Hi, Miss Riggs." Benny smiles at me and then looks at G. "Giselle, you're looking as beautiful as ever." He sends her an even wider smile, pink reaching his cheeks as he hands her a drink. "It's after five, so here's your spiked London Fog, extra foam."

I just look at Benny and back at G.

"Benny, you are the perfect man. Why are you not older?" she says to him, shaking her head with a light laugh.

"Giselle, I'm old enough to be trained." He winks at her and then walks away.

We all just hiccup a laugh.

"Don't worry, Jacky baby. He's a great kid. I'm just here all the time since my shop is next door. Is Kathryn here? I wanted to talk to her about something after, maybe some promotional things we can do together."

Jack looks at me and then away quickly. "She's somewhere around here. I'll send her your way before things wrap up. Now, what would you like, Everly, since it looks like G has a standing order."

I order a to-go pint of a Strutt's Peak Brewery Gose and tell him I'll catch up with him later. Giselle and I take our time walking around the shop, meeting with a few new indie romance authors, finding a couple of new books to buy, and some cute bookish accessories. I look at my cup and notice in the same thick black marker, the side of the cup reads: *Beautiful.* I glance back at the bar and catch Jack's eye. He winks at me and flashes a dimpled smile my way. After we've made our way through the shop, we find a little nook up front to sit and finish our drinks. G waves over to Kathryn, and before she makes it to us, G leans in and says, "Well, it looks like your potential fling with a certain sexy photographer could be more complicated."

I look at her, a bit confused. "What are you talking about?"

"It's just that he's not here for a few weeks, Ev. If he has family in town, a family who owns a business rooted to the community now, he's going to be around. Even if it's just for visits."

"Maybe, but I don't know what it is yet. I'm not going to freak out either way. I'm not going to over-plan anything. I'm just going to go with the flow."

"That's my girl. I hope that flow decides to collide with that gorgeous human. I'm going to need to know some measurements. Like, is each ass cheek a good handful or more, or like, does his dipstick have any special features? A little curve or exaggerated head..." She cackles at my widened eyes.

Before I can respond to her lack of a filter, a beautiful raven-haired woman stops at our table, and I have to assume it's Kathryn. She couldn't look any more like her brother. Light eyes, poised confidence, a person that demands to be looked at.

"Kathryn, darling, you're looking fabulous," G says. "We have so much to talk about. Did you know that your brother is working for my best friend? This is Everly."

"It's nice to officially meet you. My brother had some things to say about working with the famous Everly Riggs," she tells me. Not exactly sure what she means, but I'm not about to wander down the path of asking for any elaboration. Instead, I smile at her and the conversation moves on.

We chat with Kathryn for a while. She and G discuss the idea for the romance movies, books, and tattoos date night theme for the vendor fair. I sit there glancing back at Jack behind the counter and find myself liking that I've met his nephew and sister. It makes him seem more real and less like a fling. But at the same time, that thought worries me. He's moving away from a quick, sexy time to something more that's going to end up shaking away my plans for just a fun, physical exploration.

My phone buzzes in my back pocket.

JACK

Stop eye-fucking the guy behind the counter.

I smile and look up. A stormy blue gaze stares back at me. The corners of his eyes wrinkle from a wide smile, and his dimples make an appearance. Right then and there, I realize that those dips on his cheeks are my sexual kryptonite. I would have never guessed that dimples could instantly make me wet. It's ridiculous, really.

EVERLY

Can't help it. He's too hot.

JACK

Stop talking about my nephew like that. He's a teenager!

That pulls a laugh out of me.

JACK

I'll find you later, beautiful.

I put my phone away and hope he does. I've made my mind up about him and I'm not interested in playing any more games. I want him. Even if it's just for a little while.

22

Jack

MY FEET ARE KILLING ME. I HAVEN'T WORKED BEHIND A counter like this since I was in my twenties and I hated it then, but now I'll chalk it up to being older and crankier. I helped my sister and nephew out today and I wasn't about to be a dick and complain.

I sent a text to Everly a few minutes ago to see if she was still downtown to meet for a bite to eat or a drink. I'm not about to admit it to anyone, but one kiss from that woman, and I'm way too eager to be alone with her again. She's the kind of person that pulls you into her world and the warmth of it makes you never want to leave. *But I am leaving, so don't get too addicted.*

"Uncle Jack, you want to catch one of the movies playing at the film festival? Tonight is horror night and I could go for a slasher and popcorn for dinner. What do ya say?"

How do I say anything other than hell yes to this kid?

"Definitely. Where'd your mother disappear to? Think she'll want to come too?"

"I...I'm not sure. She's not in the back?" Benny looks thrown off by my question.

After he locks the front door behind the last of the customers, I turn up the music. A little Bishop Briggs to close the place down.

"I haven't seen her since she was talking with Giselle and Everly earlier. I figured she would have told you if she was going to take off."

"Yeah, you're right. Sorry, I was trying to multitask. She said she had to take care of a few things and must have just headed up to the apartment when she was done."

As he's telling me this, I notice how uncomfortable he looks. Never meeting my eye as if he's lying to me. I'm not going to press it, but my sister better not have ditched us, so we'd have to handle clean-up and closing. *Asshole move.*

Kathryn did a great job marketing this place, especially around the tourists that are here for the festival. I wanted to tell her that. I'm proud of her. It's not such a simple thing to start over again, and she's had to do it many times for various reasons. But this time, it was her choice. Maybe that'll make it stick and keep her smiling.

"So why is this movie a big deal? I thought you would have never heard of these movies; aren't they just being featured here for the first time?" My movie festival knowledge is limited.

"Yes, but there're these subgenres of horror that are instantly hyped and usually gain a cult following really quickly. It hasn't happened to many mainstream films and a good chunk of the time they're foreign filmmakers. It's kind of crappy to say, but if you combine subtitles and slashers, you've knocked out like three-quarters of mainstream interest."

"But not you?"

"Not me. It's your fault too."

I laugh at that. "Why would it be my fault?"

"Gremlins. Plain and simple. I should have never watched it when I was eleven. Mom used to curse you out every night for that whole year. I wouldn't drink water or eat chicken of any kind, and I think I had to sleep in her room."

"You're going to need to find some seats up front. This is the last viewing, and I believe you've gotten the last tickets," the very quiet, stoic theater owner says as he rips our passes.

"You weren't kidding, kid. Look at this place."

It's an incredible vibe. The crowd is fairly young, with a few older patrons peppered here and there who look just as eager to be here as the rest. I've been to a select few film festivals, but the mood in the room feels more passionate and excited instead of it being about who's in the audience or just being present to be seen.

Looking around, I recognize some staff from Riggs toward the back. I'm not going to pretend I didn't look for my brunette after recognizing a few faces. I don't know why I thought she'd be at something like this. I can't remember a time when I'd hoped a particular woman was in a place that I was. It's not something I'm willing to unpack right now, but it makes me eager to see her again.

We fit our way into the aisle and talk about the movie. When Benny is passionate about something, you know it, and he has this gift of piquing my interest when he talks about it too.

"There isn't going to be a better way to see this. I think the director is here somewhere and they always do some kind of thank you or even a Q and A after the show during these types of festivals. It's a big deal to see this before it hits anywhere else. I'm glad you wanted to come."

I nudge his arm and smile at him. "This better be as good as you're hyping it, by the way."

I smile at the two guys to the right who just took their seats.

"Oh! Can we swap spots? I know those guys from the shop," Benny whispers loudly around a mouthful of popcorn.

I nod and we switch places just as the lights go down and the credits begin. It's not more than ten minutes into the movie, and I look around at the handful of rows in front of me. The shadowed outline of long hair is pulled back into a knot and the most beautiful profile sits just two rows across the aisle, watching the opening scenes. Everly's head tilts back to look at the large screen as she blindly grabs small handfuls of popcorn out of the tub and eats away.

I take in all of her. The angle of her head emphasizes her mouth, and her neck is highlighted by the lights in front of her as it dips down to her exposed shoulder. She must be wearing something similar to what she had on during our photoshoot. Just the idea of it pulls all attention to my lap. I shift and adjust, as my cock seems to remember the encounter extremely well. Watching this woman, observing her when she doesn't know I'm looking, has become my own brand of foreplay. I feel my phone buzz in my pocket and pull it out, keeping it low, trying not to distract anyone around me with a bright screen.

> Everly

> Looks like you found me. Stalker.

JACK

> Honest coincidence.

I watch her smile at that response on her phone.

EVERLY

> I like you looking at me.

JACK

> Stop flirting with me and watch the movie.

The movie lasts about two more hours and just as I'm about to tell Benny I thought it was total shit, he leans over with a huge smile and says, "That was so good! Man, I want to see it again already. Can you believe it ended up being a parasite the whole time?"

I look at Everly and see the same huge smile on her face too. Well, there's her fault: shit taste in movies. She chats with a few people next to her, some of whom I recognize from the office. As much as I want to wait for her, Benny needs to get home. It's getting pretty late, and I know Kathryn might not want him out later than this, even if it's a weekend night. I'm not able to catch Everly's eye as we leave, so perhaps I'll make sure to drop into the house before I call it a night when I get back. I'm eager to taste those lips again.

"I can't believe those guys are into the same kinds of things I am. Aside from the movie, they're all going climbing on Sunday, and I think I'm going to go with them."

"I'm glad you're making friends here. It's hard to make a move and start over somewhere new. Proud of you, Ben."

He looks at me. We're almost eye to eye these days. I only have a few inches on him, and it just further reminds me how much older he's gotten.

"I didn't have a ton of friends back home, so I'm not missing much. I like it here. Everyone I've met seems cool. They just talk about what they're into and most of it is stuff you can only do here, like snowboarding or hiking to the peak. It's pretty dope."

"The fact that you just said dope is making me think you're way cooler than I give you credit for."

"Shut it, old man. I'm insanely cool," he laughs out sarcastically.

After I walk Benny back to the apartment and we make plans for a hike, I realize it's well past one o'clock in the morning.

After seeing Everly today, all I've wanted to do is pick up where we left off in my studio at the office. She's taken up space in my thoughts, and I'm a smart enough man not to question it and just feel my way through it. I usually don't operate this way. I'm so rarely affected by the women I meet, so being left stunned by someone, hell, practically under the influence of her, the only thing I should do is cut my losses and go the other way, but there's not a single part of me that wants that. Right now, I want to just lean into it and brace for the impact.

I've been trying to understand what it is about her that's gotten me here. Wanting. Waiting. Practically changing into someone I don't recognize. I'm mesmerized by her. I could watch her charm a room, rule an empire, and then kneel before her in bed and be a happy man. That concept isn't lost on me. It's just not something I'm equipped to do. I wasn't prepared for it. I know my usual boundaries. The things I'm feeling toward her are well past them.

The women I tend to get involved with, it's physical, surface level. It's not that I'm against a relationship; I've had some that were great until they weren't anymore. I make no apologies for it and most of the time, neither do they. Things run their course and then it's time to move on. Scratching an itch for a warm bed or bringing someone sexy to show off at an event has been the majority of my encounters with women over the past few years. Less messy for them and more or less all that I can handle. I don't do vulnerable very well. There's too much opportunity for hurting someone, or worse, letting someone down. Surface-level, bird's-eye-view, and glossy are just easier to maintain.

But here I am, staring at the text exchange between Everly and me, and I'm smiling like a damn fool. Nobody has ever caught me right in the gut before, not like this.

After a gondola ride out of downtown and a quick cab ride from the station, I'm punching in the code for the fence to the Riggs' house. I texted Everly on the way here just to see if she is still awake, but I haven't heard back, so instead of detouring to the main house, I'll head to the pool house and grab some much-needed sleep. I don't mind helping my nephew and sister, but that was a full day with them, and it took time away from the photo editing I need to get done before the weekend is over.

As I walk up to the door of the pool house, I see a light on and a shadow near Everly's drafting table. I'm instantly awake, excited to see her. I expect her to respond to the noise of the sliding door, but as I look closer, her arms are crossed in front of her on the table, her head face down. I can see her steady breathing as if it's keeping a tempo to a song I want to hum. Taking another step, I just look at her wavy hair draped beside her arms, colored pencils and charcoals dropped in various places on the oversized drafting table. It makes me smile. The sight of her.

There's no way she's comfortable. I move behind her to wake her gently, but before I can, a few items in front of her and tucked under her arms grab my attention. Clothing designs sketched on faceless figures are haphazardly displayed on the desk. Multiple sticky notes about materials and accessories hang across folders and the desk lamp as I look around further. I haven't looked this closely until now. I took her warning about staying clear of her work seriously, and I've kept all of my things on the far side of the studio space. I pull a few papers out, and I realize quickly that these are the designs of the loungewear we've been photographing all week. This is what they've all been so hushed about. I didn't put much thought into it when she told me she was reviewing or approving materials out here, but it's obvious now that she lied. Their designer is not only in-house, but the second in line to run the entire company. *Miss Riggs, you've been keeping this a secret.*

She's been designing one of the most sought-after sports and loungewear lines in secret for the past five years. How does she have time to do this and all of her visible roles in the business? No wonder she seems so organized and, if I'm honest, a bit uptight all the time.

"Jack?" Everly groggily whispers my name. Shit. This doesn't look good. "What, what are you doing?" Her voice is rising now.

"You were asleep when I came in. I was going to wake you up and then all of this caught my attention." I wave my hands at the artwork displayed around her desk. "Are you? Everly, are these all your designs?" I'm in a bit of disbelief. I didn't suspect this at all. It would be such a huge asset for them to use. I don't understand why it's been so hush-hush. From one creative person to another, why would someone ever want to keep something like this so close to the vest? But before I can even begin to ask, Everly stands up so fast her chair knocks back to the floor.

She looks down at my hand and yanks the paper out of it. "Jack, this isn't okay. I asked you to stay clear of my space here, and you didn't just ignore it, you're looking at my stuff now? Are you kidding me?!"

Okay, she's pissed. Moving the sketches and swatches of materials in a temper tantrum-like state, she stuffs them into an oversized leather portfolio and hauls it onto her shoulder. She won't look at me.

How can I make this right? "I wasn't. I wasn't purposely..."

"You weren't what, looking at my sketches? Snooping through my stuff. This isn't okay. You're not supposed to... you have no right looking at any of this. I need you to leave."

I just laugh. "You're kicking me out? Are you serious?"

She stops what she's doing and gives me a bone-chilling stare. The kind that makes grown men think twice about every choice they've ever made. "I've never been more serious. Now, get. The. Fuck. Out." She looks down, gathering the rest of her bravado, I imagine. "And, Jack, if I hear even one whisper of what you found here, I'll have no problem suing you for everything you have. Do you hear me?"

Is she for fucking real right now? I know when I'm

wrong about something or someone, but I never expected her to freak out on me like this without even hearing me out. For seeing something she's made? I'm not going to fight with her, but I'm also not leaving. I know when someone has passed the point of listening to reason. She needs me to be a bad guy for whatever reason. So I walk away from her toward the bed to sit down for a minute. I need to take a moment before my patience snaps. Less than a minute ago, I was in awe of this woman, but right now I'm on the verge of spanking her for being such a brat.

"I said...Did. You. Hear. Me?"

"Loud and clear, Everly."

Standing at the door, she turns her head to the side, pausing like she has something more to say. She's breathing heavily, holding back from something. *So* angry. I understand anger and how it can completely take over your body. Right now, I'm equally annoyed that she's dismissing me and curious as to why she's so quick to do it.

I'm sitting on the edge of the bed, leaning forward, my elbows on my knees, waiting for her next move. I don't want to fight with her about this, but I also don't want her to think finding this out means anything other than me being impressed. I couldn't give a shit about what she chooses to do with her business and what she decides to market or not.

"You're pissed off and you don't need to be. Will you at least hear me out?" I'm looking up as she grabs the sliding door handle and pauses. I take that as my cue to continue. "I was going to wake you up, and then I noticed your designs. You were lying on top of them. That's all. I wasn't snooping or expecting to find that. Hell, I thought you were dealing with spreadsheets and budgets here, not secretly designing an entire apparel line. And that's not a hobby, either. That's a big deal. It must make up for at least forty percent of your company's profit. You're talented, really, really fucking talented..."

She doesn't say anything, but she also doesn't leave. She's just standing at the door. I can tell she's weighing her next move. I sit patiently, observing her, and let my eyes wander along her body. Her perfect ass filling out the black yoga pants she's wearing and the red sweater that's draped off one shoulder. Her wavy brown hair, a bit wilder than usual, draped over her other shoulder. How do I rewind to earlier today when this woman was flirting with me instead of spitting fire?

When she still doesn't say anything, I start to think this beautiful woman has one hell of a temper on her. I want that heat focused on setting each other's bodies ablaze instead. It's a good time for some honesty. "Everly. I'm not interested in anything other than *you*. I could give a shit about any of that, or why you would want to keep any of it a secret. It's incredible, but that's none of my business."

She turns around, leans against the door, and flicks her eyes up to meet mine. And just like that, the energy of the room shifts. I feel it as it billows like smoke around my body, seeping into my skin. Those big, beautiful eyes aren't angry any longer, instead they're wild, maybe even hungry, but far less hostile than moments ago. She bites on her lower lip, drags it through her teeth, and then wets both lips. And with one word, I realize she's not interested in excuses or reasoning. She wanted truth. No games.

"Beg."

Okay, maybe some games. I wait for a beat, making sure I heard that right. *I know I did.* Holy shit. I don't think about how badly that command just turned me on, instead I stand up and move toward her slowly, as if I'll scare this moment away.

"What did you just say?" I ask. If I did hear that correctly, then I'm about to understand why I've been pulled to this woman. She's not a good girl at all. She wants to get dirty. And I'm happy to bathe in it with her.

She finds her voice again. With a breathy attitude, or maybe it's pride, she replies, "You want me to believe you. I believe you. Now I need you to apologize and beg."

She wants to be in charge, change the dynamic, take back whatever power she feels like she just lost by letting go of a secret she never intended to give. Fine. I'm game.

"What exactly am I begging for, Miss Riggs?"

"Stop right there, Jack." I stop right where I am, less than ten feet away from her at this point.

I tilt my head and I'm obvious with the way I rake my eyes down and up her body. "Tell me what you want me to beg for, Everly. Forgiveness? Your mouth? Your pussy?"

"Get on your knees first." She looks at me, tilting her head, waiting for my protest. I'll let her take this moment for herself. I'll happily comply.

"I want to hear you ask nicely for my forgiveness." She pauses, playing with the feeling of asking for what she wants. "And then I want you to beg to touch me. Beg to taste me."

Well, damn. That was hot. I get on my knees as she walks slowly toward me. The air in the room is still. Like the calm quiet that happens right before it snows. As if nature is kneeling before the beauty that's about to flutter around it. That makes her the storm, and I'm ready.

Just when I think I have this woman figured out, when I put her into an assumptive box to understand better, she continues to surprise me. And now I'm on my knees, my dick straining to escape my jeans like an animal waiting for its master's next command. And oh, does it want to come out and play.

"Take off your shirt," she orders.

I pull the Henley up from behind my neck and over my head. She stands in front of me, just out of reach, but the intimacy of the moment has a hold over both of us.

"Now the belt."

I start to unbuckle my belt, and I watch her eyes roam over my chest, across my shoulders, to my arms, down to my hands that are working their way to removing what she's asked. The clank of the buckle hitting the floor breaks her concentration. It's taking all of my reserve to do this for her, give her the lead here, submit to her demands, when I want to grab her, bite her ass, lick every curve and drive into her body. I'm panting for her next direction. She knows that I'm just barely holding back. It's obvious how turned on I am, my cock trying to break through and sink into what it wants most. To what I want more than anything right now. Her.

She saunters closer and sits down in the chair that's in front of me, relaxing against the back, her eyes never leaving me. She licks her lips and then rakes her eyes down my body, assessing what she wants from me next. There is a roster of things I'm going to do to this woman, but she still has the lead. She tilts her hips up and drags her tight black pants down her ass and legs, the seductive and slow movements she's making, causing me to swallow roughly. She tosses them somewhere behind her and then spreads her legs wide in the chair. Confidently displaying exactly what she's teasing me with. My eyes are pulled to where her legs end and hand rests. I watch as she practically pets her pussy through a pair of black lace panties.

"Lose the underwear, Jack. Let me see that cock I've been fantasizing about riding."

Well, alright. A perfectly filthy mouth to match my own. Oh, the things I want to do with that mouth. My eyes flash up to hers and it's impossible not to smile. I'm salivating at every word leaving this woman's lips.

"I'll need to get off my knees, then."

She nods, as if she's giving me permission. I stand, unbutton my jeans, pull them off, and kick them out of sight, smirking down at her. She's looking me in the eyes, but I can tell that it's taking all of her willpower not to look at my cock. I pull my boxer briefs down my legs next and nudge them away with my foot. My cock juts out and practically genuflects in appreciation of the goddess in front of me. Her eyes widen slightly, and she bites her lip, staring at my hard-on, then drags a finger inside the seam of her panties.

A low growl comes out of me. "That's mine."

She moves her eyes slowly up from my cock to my eyes. "We'll see." She takes her hand away and sits up in the chair. "Touch yourself, Jack. Let me see what makes you feel good." She pauses. I can tell she wants to say more, but she's testing out how it might sound first. "Do you think of me when you do?" *Keep going, beautiful.* I tip my chin up to nod.

"The night you walked in on me, did you fuck your fist later that night?" I can't even respond, because as she's asking me, she starts to pull her red sweater over her head. She tosses it aside and moves to stand in front of me with nothing more than a skimpy black tank top and those lace panties.

My patience snaps at her closeness. I've lost any sense of sanity, because the only thing I want to do is hear this woman come. Chase every orgasm and reward it with another. Unleash every dirty thought I've had of her. I want to bury myself so deep that the pleasure she feels reaches every part of her body and my reward is her moaning and screaming my name.

23

Everly

SOMETHING IN ME JUST CAME ALIVE AND I DON'T THINK I'LL ever be able to cage it. I've never been timid in bed, but I've also never been confident like this. I like this dance of dominance we're keeping time with. The anger I felt when I saw Jack holding my sketches flipped a switch in me. I've never felt more exposed, vulnerable. Designing is a part of who I am, but I don't allow people access to it unless I grant it. And as quickly as I went from sleeping to seething, his words caught me up. What he said meant something to me. For Jack to see me, want me even after I demanded he leave. For him not to want anything I can offer him, besides to feel wanted, is what slapped me back into the moment. He made me feel desired, unbelievably sexy. And for the first time, I wasn't afraid to try something new, to not hold back, and to follow an instinct. Live in the excitement of how he'd react to a new kind of demand. And he didn't disappoint.

Every sensation in my body is primed. The anticipation

is intoxicating, and I'm drunk on it. The lustful need that's coursing through my blood invigorates me. I'm ready to give this man every inch of me. I want him to own my body as much as I want to dominate his.

I watch as he follows my order, stroking his cock for me. It's perfect, already glistening with excitement that started weeping the moment I dragged a finger under my panties. He stands before me, his tall frame and broad shoulders commanding as I look up at him. Something about his size makes me feel protected, the sculpted muscles that I want to touch and lick, and the size of his cock that's front and center, pointing at what it wants. Me.

As I stand before him, I reach out and drag my hand down his chest. The dark hair where you would expect it to be runs downward and lightens as the pads of my fingers drag to the top of his abs. His body is so well maintained, so much strength displayed through protruding muscle that ripples from his shoulders down to his forearms. His chest rises and falls quickly, keeping up with the pulse that I can see ticking along his neck. I lean in and lick the drumbeat movement, and a soft groan rumbles through him. His skin is warm, hot even, and the taste makes me crave more.

My body is thrumming with anticipation to feel him inside of me, how well he'll fill me. He continues to slowly move his hand up and down, his eyes following my every movement. Dragging my gaze back down his body, I swipe my thumb across the head of his cock, taking some of what's already dripped to his fingers, and I bring it to my lips. His hand stops moving as I suck his arousal off my thumb. The warm, slick saltiness hits my tongue, and it makes me moan, wanting to do all the filthy things I can imagine, and his reaction only fuels me more.

He opens his mouth, but no words come out. He's stopped moving altogether. His obedient nature from moments ago cracks; I can see the switch in his eyes, and in the next instant, his mouth is on mine, stealing the breath from my lungs in a hungry, almost desperate kiss. He drags his lips down to my neck and my entire body remembers how it felt to have him pressed against me from lips to hips and I'm writhing for more. I gasp as he lifts me off my feet, hoisting me up and over his shoulder.

"My turn." He takes a few long strides, then tosses me onto the bed, and I land with a bounce and a laugh. Grabbing my ankle, he pulls me to the edge of the bed, hooking his fingers into the hips of my undies and pulling them down slowly. I can tell he's trying his best not to rip these to shreds right now. He was holding back, allowing me to run the show, but not anymore. Jack is the kind of man who does whatever the fuck he wants. It's obvious in the way he carries himself. The way he runs his business. I guess that he's never met a woman that lives her life the same way. *Nice to meet you, Jack.*

He throws my underwear behind him and kneels at the edge of the bed. "Tell me what you want, beautiful." Looking me over again, he grazes his fingertips over my thighs. "Tell me you want me to drag my tongue from slit to clit, because if you don't, then I think this little game of telling me what to do might be over, Miss Riggs."

I prop myself up on my elbows so I can look at this delicious man ready to taste me and enjoy every moment of it like a Michelin-star chef's tasting menu. "This isn't over until I say it is, Jack. And right now, I want to feel your tongue everywhere. Then I want you to fuck me the way I deserve. And Jack?" I pause and wait for his eyes to meet mine again. "Say please."

He lets out a groan and a small laugh as he moves his mouth down my body. Then, as his lips drag along my skin, he says, "Please."

I spread my legs, and the moment I do, he moves from kneeling to lying his body on the mattress. Pulling my hips closer to him, he drapes my legs over his shoulders. His mouth hovers and the warmth of his breath, the anticipation of his tongue have me pulsing. "You look good down there, Jack."

He bites my inner thigh in response. I'm completely caught off guard, and I burst out a scream. Then he licks where he bit, a small smirk playing on his lips. With his tongue, he draws a path to where my thigh creases and meets my pussy. I'm so turned on that I barely recognize myself right now. I want to chase this feeling of excitement of being rewarded for saying what I want, praised for feeling confident and sexy. There's no overthinking or worrying about how I look, or if it's going to take too long. I can only be present at this moment with a man that ignites something uncontrollable inside of me. His breath trails a frantic pattern on my skin, before he drives his face, his entire face, nose, mouth, chin right into my center and murmurs, "You're so wet for me." Lick. "Fuck, you taste good."

There are no words to respond to that, so instead, I moan in agreement. Because I am. I'm so sensitive right now, I can feel my arousal dripping. The man has barely begun, and I'm already dizzy. He does as he promised. He flattens his tongue and drags it slowly from my slit to my clit. And I'm done for. I can't say a thing, never mind register a response for later, because my body is already working toward an orgasm. With one pass of his tongue.

"I was wrong, Everly," he says, catching my attention. I tilt my head to look at him. His head between my legs, chin glistening, and a wicked smile. "I thought your mouth was the sweetest thing I'd ever tasted."

It takes me a second to understand. "Oh hell," I groan.

I'm lost in his words, his hands. His mouth.

He drags his lips and tongue along the edges of where I want him to sink into me. It's too good. I'm practically screaming for the teasing to stop and never end all at the same time. "Jack, please. Please. Feels too good."

In my next breath, without warning, his fingers thrust into me and work their way in and out, coaxing me to give in and dive over the edge. With his fingers still working, stretching me with a fluid come-hither motion, he moves up my body. Dragging his lips along the curve of my hips to my waist and up to the swell of my breast, he pauses there to lick and nip in a lustful appreciation.

"Come for me, beautiful. Let me feel what I'm doing to you." It only takes three more thrusts of his fingers and my body listens to his request.

My world slows down. I'm thrown into a full-bodied orgasm that starts at the back of my knees and rolls its way like a storm raging over the ocean, higher and higher, stopping at my core to grip Jack's fingers in appreciation. It continues its path up the rest of my body, leaving a chill in its wake and a burst of white fuzz behind my eyes.

"That's it. So beautiful."

I've barely recovered and Jack is rolling my body over the top of his. He kisses me gently, palming my breast and tugging my nipple. His attentive touch sends a rush through me again. I find my way out of the haze that my orgasm left behind, and rest my head on his chest. I drag my fingers up and down his warm skin. Skating over his nipple is the last lazy movement I'm allowed.

"I need to be inside of you. Right now." I nod, and seconds later, he's lifting us both off the bed. My arms circle around his neck and my legs naturally wrap around his waist. "Don't let go." In three strides, he moves around the couch to reach his camera bag that's propped open on the coffee table, pulling out a small box of condoms.

"Very prepared," I say with a smile.

"I am," he replies, pressing a soft kiss to my lips as he walks us back to the bed. He could have easily jumped up and grabbed these, but he didn't want to let me go. And I'm wet all over again. "I was hoping things would go this way for us. I was thinking optimistically." He tears one out of the pack, giving me his full smile, dimples and all.

I was waiting for him to give me a look or something to let me know he was being cheeky about that comment, but his smile and the way he's ready to bury himself inside of me has me thinking that Jack might be telling me the truth. Maybe it's not just a line. I grab the condom from him, rolling it down onto his very hard, very ready cock. *Hell yeah, that's going to be a full fit.*

Grabbing his face, I kiss him hard, biting his lower lip, and run my hands through the back of his hair. "Get that inside of me, right now." He pushes my chest back so my back hits the mattress and yanks my hips to his, thrusting into me in one hard, fast motion that makes me gasp. It takes a moment to even moan, but then I hear him groan above me. Why is that so sexy? Hearing a grown man groan in pleasure.

"Fucking hell," he exhales. Taking a second to steady himself, he pulls out slightly and grips my hips as he pushes into me, more slowly this time. He stares at where our bodies meet. It's so erotic to watch him roll into me, to feel him drag his cock in and out, that I feel another wave ready to hit me. Our eyes meet at the same time and his thumb starts to rub in circles exactly where I want it. He drives into me, changing up the pace from a slow drag to a fast, deep thrust. My orgasm crests and hits me hard. It knocks me breathless. No build-up this time, just instant, full-bodied heaven. "That's it, beautiful. Come all over my cock...so fucking sexy."

As my legs tremble and moans turn to whimpers, Jack grabs my hips harder, possessively. I realize he's barely holding it together, ready to come undone as he drives into me one more time. I see his orgasm working its way through him, and he growls out my name as his body ripples. The gravelly rumble of his voice is like smooth caramel meeting uneven dips and cliffs of the mountains outside. It's one of the most sexually stimulating sounds I've ever heard, and like a beacon, it calls out for what's left of my orgasm.

I don't care how much of a sweaty mess we both are right now. I've never been more satisfied, felt more seductive or so complete. He leans down and kisses my chest, and I just smile at him. That small movement, the sweetness of it, has me wanting to wrap my body around him and purr.

After lying like that for who knows how long, I feel slightly dazed, punch-drunk, possibly euphoric. All I know is that's *not* something you never do again. I already want more.

He lifts his head and stares at me as I lie motionless in his arms. The only movement I can spare is my mind starting to think about how we can do that again. My words come out before I can filter any of them. "All of that was so good."

He smiles at me. "How have we not done this until now?"

"We're both stubborn, but this thing between us..." It's almost too naive to say out loud, but I shake the vulnerable thoughts away. "Now that I know what it feels like to be with you like this"—I smile, thinking about it again—"I'm not ready to stop." I'm not going to play coy. That was phenomenal, life-altering, and we both know it.

He leans up, and the weight of him draped on my chest falls away. I already miss it.

We look at each other and it confirms that whatever it is we're feeling, it can't be ignored. He rubs his thumb over my lips and continues a path down my chin to the curve of my neck and over my collarbone before he stands up, fully naked. The sex appeal of this man's body is incredible, and I can't help but stare and appreciate every contour.

"You're looking at me like you're ready for another round, Miss Riggs. And I'm ready to serve you, beautiful. So, I'm going to grab us some water. You're going to rest for a few minutes and then we're doing that again. Only this time, we don't stop until you're screaming. That last orgasm was far too quiet."

Oh, thank God!

24

Jack

THE SPACE IS SMALL, DARK, AND CRAMPED. I'VE BEEN SITTING AND waiting for what feels like a thousand years. I feel tired and thirsty, but I remember what it feels like to sit in pee for too long. My pants finally dried so I'm not going to do that again. I can hear that the grunts and screaming from the other side of the room are starting to get quieter now. That usually means it's getting late, and we can come out soon. My baby sister will need to eat when she wakes up. I found packets of oatmeal in the recycling bin a few doors down.

I feel warm thinking about eating. I'm not feeling scared. Just ready to stretch my legs and get out of this dark hell. Something brushes my arm, and I smell oranges and cinnamon. It calms me. Like a scented warm breeze, it comes from nowhere and then surrounds me. I'm not in the dark anymore. I'm not sure where, but not there. I feel something new.

I wake up slowly instead of in the typical way, which is with a jerk or jolt. It's quiet, the room the faintest color of gray and blue. It's morning, but the dawn hasn't broken yet. I smile as delicate fingers trail a path over my shoulder and down my arm, tracing the tattoos that illustrate a life I'm proud of living. *Everly.*

"You were dreaming," she whispers.

I pull her into me so that all parts of her body can touch mine now. She's so warm, soft.

"Did I wake you?" I'm always worried about falling asleep with someone in my bed, which is why I never do. Hook-ups make that easy to avoid. No explanations are necessary. My nightmares are unpredictable. The only constant is that I have one every night.

"No. You didn't. I was too busy checking you out like a creeper." She laughs. "Was it a good one at least?"

"My dream?" I hesitate for a minute. I'm not sure if I'm willing to share the truth. She senses my hesitation and pulls away from me so she can look at me.

"You don't need to tell me." She pauses and then leans closer, propping her head on her hand. "But I'll tell you something. It's a secret that I haven't ever told a single person. Ever." She smiles so big that it reaches her beautiful brown eyes. "You're in the absolute most perfect place to see the sunrise right now." She sits up and leans over me. Her hair falls in my face and her breast is inches from my mouth.

"What are you doing?"

"Here." She's moved all the pillows behind me. "Oh! One more." She leans over the side of the bed, and I get a perfect view of her delicious ass. "Now, if we shift just a little so we're facing the back window, this will be the most memorable thing you'll see in Strutt's."

We adjust as she says this, and I lean back, practically

lying down again and bringing her with me. "I can tell you with absolute certainty that it won't be the *most* memorable." I shift my eyes to meet her.

"Are you getting sweet on me, Jack?" She laughs.

"I was talking about the views from your dad's place." I never find women sexy *and* sweet. It's always either-or. Not this one, though. This one is both; mixed with charming and confident.

"Can we not talk about my father when I'm naked in bed with you? Thanks." She pinches my side, and I pull her hand and kiss it instead.

"The ranch next to his is even more incredible. You can see those peaks from their roof deck." She looks at me, raising a brow. "Never tell my father. I would never hear the end of it, but where the Muldowney Ranch sits, you can see that ridge right there, but from the other side, which means you can catch it at sunset. It's breathtaking. Probably the best view of the mountains in town."

The sky is getting brighter now. It coats the room in a brighter blue-gray than from just a few minutes ago. The sun is preparing to make its appearance. From where we lie in bed, I can appreciate the massive glass panels that make up the side of the pool house that hosts Everly's studio. I can start to see the outlines of the mountains that frame Strutt's Peak and its surrounding towns. The room is quiet with only the sound of sheets and blankets moving, and our steady breathing. In this moment, I realize how relaxed I am, even with the thoughts of my past currently at the forefront of my mind. That's never the case, and I know it's because she's in my arms. She's the difference.

"It wasn't a dream." *What am I doing?* "It was more like a memory mixed with a dream. Not a good one. I have it, or some version of it, every night. It's never the same, but just bad enough to remind me where I came from. Today's wasn't so bad."

I'm never eager to give anyone more. This admission is probably more than I've given anyone other than my therapist.

She shifts to look at me. Curious about what else I'll say, but careful not to be pushy. I tilt her chin up to me and move to give her a gentle, chaste kiss. The softness of her lips with the small moan she makes is the kind of currency I wouldn't mind being rich from.

"Kathryn and I grew up in foster care. We're not some tragic case of a bad foster system. Quite the opposite. We were adopted together. Our adoptive mom is incredible. Smart, loving, and exactly what you hope a parent could be like. I was almost ten and Kathryn had just turned five when we went to live with her and her husband at the time." I pause for a minute, looking down at my hands intertwined with Everly's. She rubs her thumb back and forth over mine. Such a soothing gesture. Seeing it and feeling her helps me breathe easier as I rummage through the guarded compartments of my memory.

"They divorced about a year or so after we were adopted. We never knew our real father, so not having an adoptive dad didn't make much of a difference to us. I'm pretty certain Kathryn and I didn't have the same biological father, but who knows. Our mother was a drug addict. I didn't know for a long time that it was why she was the way she was, but I knew she depended on something more, loved something more than she loved us. Needles, powder, pills, and drinking. Any form of a high. All of it was more important than everything else."

I look over to Everly to gauge how she's reacting to my words. It's not something I ever planned on telling, especially never to her, but she just looks back at me, without judgment or questions. Instead, she looks ahead at the sunrise, ready to listen.

"She wasn't a good person that got wrapped up in drugs. There's a part of me that believes she was always a bad person, and drugs were her savior. The universe stepped in to remove her from a world she didn't deserve. Removing her from the lives that she only ever ruined."

Everly just comforts me with her touch, not saying anything, but her eyes are glassy. All of this isn't easy to say, so I can't imagine what it's like to hear.

"I did my best to keep my sister from the world my mother brought us into, but I saw everything. Heard and felt all of it. There was so much damage, sometimes I think of it as something I may have just seen and not lived through."

I think that's where I'm comfortable stopping. "So that's what I dream about. That's what she left me with after she died, nightmares that haunt me, and the memory of a woman who was too selfish to care for us. A life that I try most of the time to forget."

I know her next question, so I answer it before it's even asked. "I've been in therapy for my entire adult life and it helps. It doesn't erase anything like I wish it would, but I find things that help clear my mind when I start to think too much, or remember too much."

She's still quiet, and I'm starting to think I'm an idiot for oversharing with this woman. We just met, had some of the hottest foreplay and sex of my life, but now I'm unpacking my heavy baggage as pillow talk? Dumb. But then she looks back at me and runs her hand along my cheek. A touch of comfort, or maybe empathy. That hand caresses down my face and the length of my arm to my hand, and she raises it toward her mouth, brushing her lips across my knuckles. I'm too stunned by the sweetness of it to say anything as she looks back out toward the insanely beautiful view in front of us. The mountain peaks would normally be the star of this show, but right now they are merely the opening act for the color that's slowly building behind them as the sunrise takes over. It's rather poetic that I see streaks of orange emerge. *A gift perhaps.*

Within seconds, every shade from burnt butterscotch to the light flesh of an apricot surrounds the mountain sky in front of us. A live canvas on display for our own private show.

My breath catches. It's almost too much.

"Beautiful," I whisper.

A reward for confiding in someone about the parts of a life that I could never control.

She turns toward me again and climbs onto my lap. The blankets and sheets wrapped tightly around our waists and her full breasts leaning against my chest. She has tears sliding down her cheeks and I feel a clench of guilt for making her feel anything but good right now. I wipe them away with the pads of my thumbs. "Don't cry, beautiful. Not about that."

She shakes her head, pushing away my words. "Thank you for trusting me with that." She leans in and kisses my lower lip softly. I meet her mouth, her tongue, and the pace. The languid movements feel more intimate than I usually allow. Pulling back, she locks her eyes with mine, not saying anything more. She leaves what I've told her and doesn't press. She doesn't try to fix anything or tell me it wasn't my fault. She just sits with the weight of what I shared.

I knew the moment I saw this woman, she was something different. After last night and this morning, I'm not sure what any of it means, but all I know is Everly Riggs feels good. She feels right where I'm supposed to be.

25

Everly

"Chocolate will always beat out Twizzlers *and* Red Vines." Jack laughs at the seriousness of my tone. "There are far too many ways to enjoy chocolate for it to be eclipsed by any form of red licorice. Now, if you're going to tell me you like black licorice too, then I might just throw you out of this place." He just looks at me in the reflection of the mirror and smiles without responding. "What?" I start brushing my teeth as he finishes with his, spitting into the sink and cupping a handful of water to swish. I keep staring at him, wondering if he's going to tell me what he's thinking right now.

"You're beautiful, you know that, right?" I start laughing, considering I have foaming white toothpaste escaping the corners of my mouth. When I look at his reflection again, Jack's smiling at me, and then leans in to briefly kiss my neck. People commenting on my looks isn't something I focus on, but with him, and the way he says it, has me feeling them rather than just hearing them. I feel beautiful with his attention on me. A few words, that from anyone else I'd probably brush past, but Jack saying them, makes my stomach flutter. I spit into the sink and then take a sip of water from the tap, giving him a big, toothy smile in the mirror.

"And no, black licorice has no place on my candy roster." We walk back into the studio, and he pulls me back into the bed piled with blankets and pillows that have been haphazardly arranged. Changing the conversation, he says, "You're different from what I thought you'd be like." I shift my head and stare up at the ceiling, our limbs draped over each other. My nerves start to run haywire as I think about how easy it is to be with him. Too easy. And then, to add to that, I remember one glaring detail. I'm not supposed to be catching feelings for this man. I'm supposed to be chasing fire, figuring out what's been missing in my bed. *The answer was never supposed to be him, but it feels like him. His big, warm, beautiful body has been missing.*

I push the thoughts away and ask, "What did you think I was like?"

"I knew the moment I saw you that we'd be good in bed together."

I adjust to prop up on my elbows, facing him, eager to hear more. "This has been fucking spectacular, so you were right about that."

"You're just more than that, though. I'm pulled to you. I crave being around you. And now that I've had you like this..." Drifting away from that sentence, he says, "Does that sound insane?" He looks at me, still confident with such a vulnerable question hanging. It makes me uncomfortable. I do feel it. This energy we have when we're around each other. It's almost visible. A mix of desire and need. And now perhaps even more. Outside of the overbearing electricity between us, there's this feeling of support and comfort.

I whisper back, "I feel it too." After a beat, he shifts forward and kisses me. I feel instantly anxious. Jack must sense it because he pulls back and looks at me, waiting for an explanation.

I steady my breathing. "How do I say this without being an asshole?" We've been talking and snuggling for the past two hours. It's probably the most fun I've had getting to know someone. I can't sleep with him again this morning. If his admission about his life did anything, it reminded me that we can't get to know one another so personally and be intimate. It'll completely fuck up the no-strings policy I was very eager to employ.

"Any sentence that starts that way will likely make you sound like an asshole regardless, so how about I do it for you, beautiful?" He raises his brow at me and untangles himself from my arms. Leaning back on his elbows, he tilts his head and says, "This has been incredible, but it isn't what either of us signed up for?"

"I don't want to be that cliche, Jack. I want to spend time with you. I like being around you." He just smiles at me again. *Gosh, those dimples are heartbreak warfare.* "I'm also incredibly attracted to you, but I don't want to get involved in something that has an already predetermined shelf life. I want more, but I know you're here for a short while and I'm not naive to think that's not our reality."

This can only end badly. He isn't here permanently and while G's "carpe diem" sex assignment has been vividly executed, I'm starting to care for this man. I like him. Like, *really* like him. I smelled him when I woke up and then proceeded to watch him sleep. Who does that? Not crazy people. Nope. People who fall too fast for the guy who's too good to be true, that's who. He's exactly the kind of man that will give me everything I physically want, but he's exactly what I don't need. Temporary. And this is the flaw with my big master plan of falling into bed with men that spark a bit of fire in me. This is the part I hadn't planned for. What would happen when I couldn't see the forest for the trees and instead had the best sex and most intimate experience of my life to then just say, *"Great time, see ya later."*

He doesn't get annoyed or pissed off at what I just said. He just looks at me, trying to read my body language, and see if I'm full of shit. Instead of getting up and leaving or working to put me in the booty call column, he surprises me and says, "You know you're damn near perfect?" I can only smile at that.

Thank goodness he can't hear all the other chaos in my mind.

"Oh, I already know that."

"Everly, if you need to cool off after last night and freak out about it this morning, then I'll give you the space to do that." He sits up and gives my lips a quick kiss before standing. I stare at his perfectly tight ass and the broadness of his back. Tattoos in patterns that travel down one side of his chest and flow onto one of his strong arms. *Those arms feel good wrapped around me.*

He walks around to my side of the bed stark naked with all of the confidence in the world, and for good reason. His cock is hard and pointing right at me, and my body perks up, thrumming with excitement all over again, yelling, *"Pick me, pick me,"* like the traitorous hoe she is. I'm trying to distance myself and his damn cock is practically summoning me to open wide.

"Eyes up here, beautiful." I drag my eyes upward to meet his. He pulls on sweatpants and starts layering on a t-shirt and sweatshirt. "I'll be whatever you think you need. Friend. Colleague with Benefits. Live vibrator. But I'm starting to understand who you are, Everly Riggs. And you and I both know you're not going to fuck anybody other than me while I'm here." I stare blankly, trying to register what he just said. "Got that, beautiful?"

While my insides are screaming, *"Yes, sir,"* I can only glare at him. My inner feminist is shouting, *"Who does he think he is?"* Just because we've slept together once doesn't give him any right to tell me who I can and cannot be with. But before I can articulate a response, he's out the door, and I'm left naked in bed, aroused all over again.

What the hell did I just get myself into?

26

Everly

As soon as the bacon starts to sizzle in the cast iron pan, that's when the smell hits you full force, and like a church bell ringing in the time on a Sunday morning, my youngest brother quite literally sprints from the stairs to the kitchen island.

"You're cooking. Why? Why are you cooking, Ev-er-ly?" Law sing-songs in a teasing tone.

I drop a death-stare over my shoulder. "Grab the tomato and slice it for me."

"You never cook breakfast. You only ever cook when you're stupid-happy or very pissed about something." He sits at the counter and props his chin on his hands. He looks like a first grader waiting to hear that sugar is a food group. "You don't look annoyed. You look extra happy, not the normal you, happy. Are you going to gross me out if you tell me why?"

"Cut the tomato, please." I give him nothing, but my

brother is like my partner in crime. We have a sixth sense about each other. And while we're the furthest in age, his twenty-nine to my thirty-four, we've always been the ones to find the best trouble and the most in common. If you got to choose cheerleaders for your life, you choose Law. He's wholehearted in everything he does, especially when it comes to being my brother. I love him for it. This is also why I'm not surprised he didn't even have to look me in the eye to notice the catalyst for my behavior this morning.

"Everly 'Pickle-Tickler' Riggs, you tell me right now, if I was going to pop over to the pool house last night, would I have found a certain photographer and a certain sister of mine tangled in a web of naughty nastiness?" His voice kicks up at the end, and I'm doing my best to not burst out laughing.

"Yolky or fully cooked?"

"Yolky, obviously. Don't try to change the subject. You're cooking and smiling. I deserve to know who I should thank for breakfast this morning."

I flick the burner off and place a fried egg on top of the tomato. The egg BLT happens to be my favorite of the breakfasts our dad would make as a kid. He always messed up pancakes and waffles. I'm still not sure how, but he did. The egg BLT is also the quickest and this morning I was starving after a full night of sexual satisfaction and an early morning of gut-wrenching honesty with my sexy photographer. *I shouldn't say mine, but he feels like mine.*

"Grab the hot sauce, please?" I swing around the counter next to Law and drag our plates in front of where the coffee cups and a French press are waiting. "Yes," I admit as I take a bite and close my eyes at how delicious this tastes right now.

When I open my eyes and glance at my brother, he's pouring us each a cup.

He stops mid-pour, gives me a side-eye, and says, "I knew it! I knew after I walked in on that make-out session at the office—totally inappropriate, I might add—that it was just a matter of time before you jumped the man." He takes a sip and looks at me. I can see him trying to size up my reactions from my peripheral vision. "You like him. Like, really like him. Did you bag a man for his meat," he whisper-shouts like an idiot, "and instead catch feelings!? Tsk tsk, Ev, that's going to get messy."

I shrug my right shoulder, trying to make it all seem like less of a big deal than it is for me. I'm trying to compartmentalize all of it. The sex was the hottest of my entire life, the talking was the most honest, and the end of it all makes me want to appreciate it and slap myself all at once. I'm not about to gush with Law about all of the toe-curling details, that's what G is for, but I'm grateful that my brother can spot happiness. It's obviously pouring out of me from a source other than work.

"You know, he's not like the other guys you've been dating or whatever you call it."

"I don't date anyone. I scratch an itch every now and then, but dating isn't what I'd call any of the last handful of men I've been with."

Biting his sandwich, he chews for a moment, then replies, "Gross. I didn't need to hear that. All I'm saying is, he's a good guy. He's not a pretentious prick, and he's not boring. Not a single one of the women that hit on him the few times we've gone out did he entertain in anything more than polite chit-chat. His business reputation is immaculate. I mean, there's some dicey stuff with a threesome, I think, from a year or two ago that followed him for a while, but I mean, look at the guy. He's bound to get around a bit."

"You don't need to make a believer out of me. I know he's a good one."

"Fine. All I'm saying is, I'm a good judge of character and I think he would be good for you. Push your buttons a little, maybe get you to loosen up some," he says, as if he's suddenly chock full of wisdom.

"You say shit like that, and I have to assume you think I'm uptight." He shrugs his shoulders. *Prick.*

"I like him, but we decided friends is a good place to be while he finishes his contract with us." He stops eating and looks at me. "He lives in New York full-time, and I don't. Long-distance never works and I'm past the age of thinking it might, so while you may be right about my glow, Jack is not a permanent fixture here. He was fun." I quickly continue, cutting off his rebuttal. "But, I'm okay with that. Last night was...well, last night happened and this morning we decided that friends will have to do, going forward."

"You are such a bossy dick, Ev. You didn't even wash the sheets before you were kicking him to the 'friends' curb? Jeez, way to hit it and run." I pinch the skin right above his armpit and he squeals like a pig. "All I'm saying is this: it's not always black and white. So what if he lives in New York? His sister and her kid live here. That's his only family, not to mention the man is a damn business mogul. And, hello, you're doing pretty well for yourself too. I don't see why you'd chuck something into a box before you had time to really play with it."

Fucking boxes. I hear him, but I won't give him the satisfaction of responding to any of it.

"Okay, you've already made up your mind here, but

since I can't just leave it, I'll say this too...when was the last time a man made you feel"—he raises his hands and points from my head to my feet—"like that?" *He's right, of course.*

I ignore him and instead shift the discussion. "I need to wrap up the last few summer designs before I submit them to the manufacturer tomorrow. Do you want to have a look beforehand?"

"Nope!" Law says, popping the *P.* "The designing and choices for the apparel are all you, Ev. You never need my feedback. I'm just the one to push you, that's all. Don't forget to include some kind of unisex bag for climbing. Michael's been complaining about how much he hates the fanny pack trend from last season. He's annoying me."

We both clean up after eating and I pour us another cup of coffee each. Law passes me the creamer and says, "I get in early and every day, like clockwork, Jack is coming out of your office. He goes in with two cups from that new place you like, and he comes out with just one." I already had a feeling it was him, but hearing it and having Law witness it makes me feel excited and cared for, even if it's for something small, like a coffee. "All I'm saying is, he secretly brings you coffee, he makes you smile...I mean, he's making the rest of us assholes look kind of bad, but that's besides the point. What do I know? I'm about to research sex club destinations, not ways to find a life partner."

I snort my coffee and start choking. "You're ridiculous. I hate you a little bit. I didn't want a visual of that and you."

"You're welcome." He kisses my forehead and strides out of the kitchen, yelling, "Love you, Ev," in his wake.

The rest of the day ticks by as I draft some new styles, feeling motivated and inspired for the rest of the line that I need to submit tomorrow. My mind drifts to Jack and I think about what life would have been like had I stayed in New York City after graduation. If I really tried to find a place in the fashion world instead of packing up and heading home. Would I have still ended up here in the long run? In Strutt's Peak? In bed with Jack Deacon?

The vibration of my phone knocks me out of my haze.

JIN

> Everly, we have an issue with Q1 motivation. We need to address it before tomorrow's meeting with the rest of the board. Can you meet for dinner?

EVERLY

> Of course, but wouldn't it make sense to discuss it with my father?

JIN

> He's sitting across from me and suggested you join us after we wrap up our trail ride today.

This is why you don't sleep with your dad's friends or colleagues. My father is a lot of fun, but it's hard to decipher if this warrants my time, or if it's a ploy just for Jin to see me. Jin's a good person, and while we left things on the platonic side before I escaped from our last overnight, I can't help but wonder if he has some kind of ulterior motive with this request. On a weekend, nonetheless.

EVERLY

> Let's get some dinner at The Mogul. I'll see you guys there around 7 p.m.?

JIN

> Let's make it 8. See you then :)

27

Everly

THERE ARE TONS OF PERKS OF LIVING IN STRUTT'S PEAK, BUT some of my favorites are the unique places where you can enjoy delicious food and an incredible drink. The views and vibes alone are more worthy of daily appreciation than when you fold in the talented chefs, mixologists, and sommeliers, who relocate to tourist locations like ours, and it's better than New York City's and Chicago's food scenes combined.

"David, I swear you're more like a mind reader than a sommelier." I lean into my dear friend as he delivers me to our table. A Grey Goose shook so cold that ice chips skim the edges of the glass with a twist of an orange slice floating on top welcomes me. I'm the first to arrive, which is how I like it. When I feel like I'm walking into an unknown business conversation, I'd rather have the upper hand and make the location my home-field advantage.

"My darling, when you tell me you're making a late

dinner reservation on a weekend, I can only assume it's business and you'd rather not be doing it today. That, or you're dumping some unlucky man and he doesn't know it's coming. Either of those calls for a clean, stiff drink to start." David leans in, kisses the air beside each cheek, and holds out my arms, assessing what I'm wearing. "Based on your choice of clothing, I'm guessing it's business?" I'm wearing tailored black suit pants with a camel-colored cashmere sweater. Since this is a mountainside restaurant, and I had to ride the gondola to get here, I'm also wearing my furry snow boots. I may be all business, but I'm a Colorado girl, and you don't fuck around with dumb shoe choices when you're on a mountain.

"It's a bit of both, maybe." He smiles. "Please do a tasting menu and bring along a chilled white when my guests arrive. Oh, and my father should be here as well, so please bring him-"

"I know what he'll want. Not a problem, Miss Everly."

I nod and smile as my old friend walks away. I've known David for my entire life. He's been a fixture, much like a lot of folks in this town. You tend to get to know everyone; the gossip may not have to travel too far, but it travels fast. David was born and bred here, and most of the town knows he's the best sommelier this side of the Mississippi River, but what only a select few of us know is that he is part owner of this place and a half dozen more just like it spread throughout the west. The man is smart, loaded, and wants to work every day the universe will let him. His words, not mine. While some like to mistake his service role as a lesser-than job to some of the billionaires that roll into town, what they don't know is that his net worth nuzzles right near theirs.

His property butts up against our family ranch, and he and my father are business partners in what they like to call "side-hustles." Most would call their side-hustles life changing investments. Like my father, David had the opportunities to leave Strutt's and live around the world, but he chose to stay. There's pride in knowing where you came from, loving it, and staying put to build your happiest life.

A beat later, David comes back with a bottle of sparkling water. "How's Callen handling the bustle of the upcoming season? A decent amount of idiots getting arrested yet?" I ask. David's son Callen is now known around here as Sheriff Callen Muldowney. To me, he will always just be Callen. We grew up together. One of the most crush-worthy of men, and then he went ahead and became a cop, and now has the whole uniform thing going for him. He's delicious.

I crushed hard on Callen for a lot of years, but the feelings were always platonic on his side. It wasn't until he was elected sheriff that he told me if he was attracted to women, which the light should have gone off right there for me— spoiler, it didn't—that it would have been the two of us all the way.

I fell in love with him even more that day, but I wasn't doing myself any favors by hanging on to dead hope. And then had thought maybe he was bisexual. Yeah, I was in deep there for a while. It was a low point for me, thinking that my friend who trusted me in sharing a part of him that wasn't, and still isn't, public knowledge, would just change his mind. I know that's not how any of it works, but Callen, well, Callen, a lot like David, is the kind of man that you root for and hope is, in some way, a part of your life. I was being stubborn about how he was going to be a part of mine.

David just smiles as he takes the menus back. "Callen is Callen." He sighs. "You know him, he'll complain that people are only getting dumber and that tourists are the bane of his existence, but he loves it when it picks up around here." I just smile. Callen has always been a person riled by chaos. He thrives in it like Henry. So I know exactly what David means.

David looks over my shoulder, and I turn quickly. I've been misinformed.

Jin walks toward the table. Full swagger. His confidence was always the thing that attracted me to him the most. After that, it ended up being anticipation and then nothing. Flat soda. Total disappointment followed by self-loathing for using him to scratch an itch. But now, he approaches, and I can only find a bit of anger stirring in my belly. I thought my father was coming, and that this was pure business, but now I'm worried he's looking for a weekend pick-me-up. My mind immediately runs to Jack.

"David, great to see you again." He extends his hand out as he approaches.

"Mr. Cormick, excellent to see you again, sir." David turns my way as he leaves, and an unspoken nod has me thanking him again for the stiff drink.

"Jin, is my father joining us? I was under the impression this was a business meeting and he was going to be here." I sit and cross my arms.

"No, I just left the ranch. He won't be coming, and I already spoke with him about my concerns and the reasons I wanted to speak with you. Actually, I wanted to speak with him first before I went ahead and spoke with you. I have some things I want to address, and I needed his"—Jin shifts uncomfortably, and all of a sudden, I'm sweating—"...his approval to approach you with what I'm thinking."

My mind is reeling right now, and I'm anxious that I'm going to need to have a repeat conversation with him about how much I respect him, but we're far better as colleagues. "I'm going to be honest here, Jin. I was expecting to deal with a work-related crisis, and now I'm-"

"Everly, don't," he cuts me off, and I uncross my arms. Taking the last sip of my drink, I look up and see David coming our way with a refill and a bottle of chilled white wine. *Good man.* "This is work-related. In a way, it's more about you and not about Riggs Outdoors. I want to fund you." I look at him, confused, waiting for more. "I want to be your investor. For the apparel and accessories that I know you're behind. I want to offer you the opportunity to do it. Do it big and make it exclusively your brand."

"My brand is the Riggs brand. They're the same."

"Yes, but they shouldn't be. I'm seeing what's going on from a numbers perspective, the industry, and how your brand could disrupt the current space if it's nurtured properly." I let him continue, but I'm already starting to get defensive in how I'm responding to him in my head. "I wasn't going to approach you about this until I spoke with your father first. I didn't want anything I said to you about this to make it feel like I was going behind his or your brother's backs about what my intentions are with how we could separate and build this as your own."

Right there is where he loses me. "What are you talking about, Jin?" I take a long sip of my refreshed drink. "First, you aren't even supposed to know about my role in the apparel and accessories part of our business, but that's a moot point now, apparently, so let's move on. This isn't something I'm willing to discuss. I mean, I'm being groomed to run Riggs as soon as my father is ready to retire." He moves to interrupt me, and instead I hold up my hand to stop him. You never interrupt a woman on a roll, ready to tell you exactly where to shove your current bullshit. "Hell, who do you think has been running it so efficiently for the past handful of years?"

He sits back coolly to my clearly fired-up tone. "You, obviously. You're a damn rockstar, Ev. We all know that. That's exactly why I wanted to talk to your father first. I wasn't about to poach you or plant an idea in your mind without getting clearance from Asher beforehand."

"You told my father that I should leave and pursue something on my own?" I laugh. "I'm sure that went over well. He's been so damn happy to have me at the helm with him."

"Of course he has. Please tell me you've thought about this before? You had to have wondered what it would be like to go out on your own. *Not* just be a part of the family business?"

"Nope." I pop the *P* to exaggerate, but of course I've thought about it. I thought about it when I left New York City, but I made my choices and I've accepted making decisions that impact other people and staying committed to them. Especially now when we're at a huge turning point for our company.

"Well, out of all the things you've ever said to me..." He raises an eyebrow, clearly remembering the time I said to him the dimple in his ass could also operate as a soup bowl. In my defense, it was after a lot of drinks and my filter got thrown off and exchanged for the mouth of a very thirsty and aggressive woman. "The fact that you're telling me it's never crossed your mind, I feel like is your way of telling me you're not ready to talk about this."

"Damn right I'm not," I say defensively. "Jin, I'm also very wealthy and so is the rest of my family, so if this is something I wanted to pursue and have funded, I would have done it. With *my* family. Not you."

He leans forward on the table and rests his fisted hand on his temple. "You and I both know that if you thought about this for real, then you would agree that an investor is more than just money, but the connections, doors, and details."

He's got me there.

"All I'm saying is, think about it. If you've never thought about it, then now's your time." Jin shifts back and takes a sip of the Scotch neat sitting in front of him. It was meant for my father, and immediately I feel like a traitor for even entertaining this conversation for as long as I have. Smiling at me, Jin continues. "You're an incredible woman, Everly. There's so much more that you can be doing, and I think you'd be crazy not to even consider it."

My eyes dart up to him. He knows what he just said may have pissed me off beyond repair. You never call a woman crazy, regardless of context, *dumbass*. Jin leans forward and grabs my hand.

"Don't."

"I shouldn't have phrased it like that, but I know you, and I know you're fiercely loyal to your family. But, I recognize the difference between family and business. And what I'm talking about is business. Life-altering business, Everly." He looks up and over my shoulder, then instantly drops my hand. "Shit!"

Pushing back out of his chair and standing, he moves

toward the back corridor of the restaurant. Jin yells out to a woman who's running away, "That's not. Kat, wait!"

He turns back to me while he's still moving in the other direction. "Everly, I'm sorry I need to go. Please don't be angry here and shut this down. Just think about it." And before I can even respond, Jin is jogging out the back exit.

I have no idea what just happened. In so many ways. I'm pissed off, annoyed, and quite frankly, ready to rip someone a new asshole. How could my father, out of all people, be on board with this? I whip out my phone and send a text to him. I expect him to walk me through everything he discussed with Jin. Does he want me out of the company? Is he just ready to pass the torch along to one of my brothers instead? Dread hits my stomach, and I'm practically sprinting to the gondola to get back down to town. Damn mountainside restaurant.

28

Jack

"I'M NOT ONE TO GOSSIP, BUT IT'S MY RESPONSIBILITY TO LOOK out for the folks in this town. Men like you waltz in here, fluff a lot of feathers, and then prance on out with a fuller dance card, leaving heartbreak in your wake. I won't even get started on how you're taking local business away as well. That's a whole other conversation we'll have." Lenny McKenna holds on to my forearm, waiting for me to respond to her dutiful accusations.

As soon as I stepped into the gondola, I knew I was in for a brutal assault by the sixty-something self-appointed town squire. There were a few snowboarders who jumped off a few stops earlier, and it didn't stop her from loudly declaring me "the big city manwhore" as soon as I sat down. I was almost positive, after being here for a few weeks now, that Strutt's Peak may have been without the nosy know-it-all who typically comes with a small town like this. As it turns out, I just haven't been approached by any of the vultures yet. They've just been watching, circling, and waiting to spar when I was alone.

I just smile at her. I'm usually pretty good with charming older women, but I can tell this one is going to give me a run for my money. "I came here to do some work for the Riggs family. My sister and nephew just moved into town as well."

"Oh, I know your sister. She's a tough nut to crack, that one." She rolls her eyes. "Your nephew, however, is just a doll. He helps me find some of the best books in that store. Real talent, that one. I hear he likes to climb. Makin' a name for himself on the mountains with the help of Michael Riggs. Good boy, that one too. A little awkward, but those Riggs kids have been through a lot, and they all turned out alright, if you ask me." I didn't, but she keeps going anyway.

"Except for Lawrence. He's a pain in my ass." She tuts and then nudges my shoulder. "I hear you're getting cozy with Everly, though. We all thought she might have been asexual, not that there's anything wrong with that. I'm not one to judge, but she's so damn gorgeous I was hoping she'd bat for the girls-only team, if you know what I mean." She nudges me again and then looks ahead as the gondola dings for its next stop. It makes me laugh. I know exactly what she means. My girl is damn gorgeous. Hm, my girl. I haven't thought about a woman in that way before. As mine. Without being able to overthink it, Lennie knocks me out of my head as she gossips on. "I figured out I was a lesbian after twenty-seven years of marriage to my darling Paul. We stayed married after I came out, and made it work for both of our needs. Saint of a man. He's been gone now for damn near a decade. The fucker was my best friend and decided to have a heart attack while he was having sex with his girl-friend. Such a cliche, right?"

This woman just keeps talking, and it's nice to listen to people who like to share the chaos of their own lives. It's incredible the things you can find out by simply saying nothing. However, Lenny McKenna might be the worst kind of talker. The one who talks to fill the silence. The one who will think we're friends after she word vomits all over me.

I've always been a good listener, an observer. It helped me survive as a kid countless times and not just the horror that was the first nine years of my life. It's what made the foster care system and adoption bearable. Manageable. I could learn how to stay on people's good sides without testing limits that could end with me or my sister learning more lessons that ended in tears. It's helped to build my business and most of the companies I currently own. I'm a silent partner. It's been working in my favor for most of my life.

Years of therapy meant I had to be on the other side of it, talking about all the shit that happened and about how things made me feel. It was never easy. Still isn't. Anybody who has gone through and survived abuse or trauma knows that saying anything about it out loud, acknowledging it, is like experiencing it all over again. It was for me, at least. Listening to others. Hearing what my therapist would suggest about how to move on from it all and working to live with it. It keeps my anger at a manageable level.

"Is it true, then?" She looks back at me, waiting for some kind of response to a question I'm sure I've missed.

"Is what true, Mrs. McKenna?"

"You call me Lenny, kid. And don't insult my intelligence. You look like, well...you." She motions up and down, pointing from my head to my feet. "And she looks like the gods favored her most when she was made, so I know that if you two were in the same room, sparks would turn to fire-works *real* fast." She's right, but I'm not willing to feed the town gossip monster. Instead, I smile at her as she stands to get off the stop.

"She is a beautiful woman. You've got that part right. The rest, well…" I smile at her again. "We're just friends." And just as she stands and turns to get off the gondola, with a smirk and a huff from not getting her dirt, the door opens, and the topic of our conversation is standing right there. Everly Riggs, angry and out of breath, might be my new favorite. She looks up from studying something on the ground intently, lost in thought. The moment her eyes meet mine, I feel the electricity. There's some kind of magic swirling around that woman, because I felt her before I saw her standing there. Warmth and knowing. If I believed in magic, then I'd say my soul has found its equal, and it signals my body, letting me know that she's near. But I feel more comfortable with the idea that it's simply an intense attraction. A physical need to be with her again.

Before Lenny leaves the gondola car, she looks between the two of us, smiles to herself, and shakes her head. "Friends, my ass," she mumbles as she leaves. If the town gossip had an inkling before, now she has a first-hand glimpse of the way this woman looks at me. I'm looking at her in the same way; like I want to save her, comfort her, kneel before her, restrain her, burrow deep into every part of her body. She can call it whatever she wants, but it's not any version of friendship that I've had. It's more.

Everly steps into the gondola car, and instinct tells me that she needs to be in my arms. She closes the gap between us immediately and wraps her arms around my neck, burying her face in my chest. Throwing her legs on each side of mine, she straddles my lap. I lean into her and grip tighter.

"Hey, beautiful," I whisper, as I breathe in the smell of her, *oranges and cinnamon fusing right to my senses.* She takes a deep breath the same way I did when she wrapped herself around me. When she leans back slightly to look at me, there's a fire in her eyes, and the plumes of smoke are billowing out, surrounding me. I want nothing more than to taste her skin again. I kiss the inside of her wrist that's turned toward me, resting on my shoulder.

The gondola tilts me forward, and her back, as it starts to glide out over the mountain. Each stop is marked with the time in between each station. From here to our next is just over eight minutes. We have eight minutes alone right now, and I can do a lot in that amount of time. And damn, do I want to. I look at her mouth, lips slightly parted, and then raise my eyes to hers, making sure I'm not reading her wrong. She doesn't say anything. She licks her lips and rocks forward, grinding down on my already hard cock. Her smirk answers my unspoken question. *It looks like she wants to go for a ride, and I'm all about giving this woman anything she wants.*

29

Everly

"THERE IS A CAMERA OVER YOUR SHOULDER, WHICH MEANS I'M not going to fuck you here, but I am going to make you come so hard that you'll forget about whatever just ruined your day." Jack's low, gravelly voice sends anticipation rushing through my entire body. I rock into his lap again, and I can feel how much this man wants me. The gondola is quiet, empty, with only the two of us on this stretch of the ride. Only the darkness from outside of the gondola's windows surrounds us. We're high enough up that nobody can see anything other than the shadow of the occupants in the car.

Jack drags his knuckles over my chin and grips it between his thumb and pointer, pulling my mouth closer to his. I watch and wait for him. I feel the warmth of his breath as he moves closer. He licks his lips, readying his assault. It's been a while since I've been angry like I was, and now it's morphed into a need to be consumed by this man in any way that he'll allow. How can being wrapped in his arms be exactly what I needed without even knowing? He should be upset at me for being so hot and cold with him, but he's not. I want him to control these next few minutes alone together. Make me feel something good, because I don't want to think right now. Not about my career, not about new choices, not about the disappointment I feel toward my father, and not the frustration I just left behind with Jin.

"Hey, friend," his deep voice whispers. Followed by the flash of his smile.

"Hi," I quietly answer back, knowing he's teasing me after our last conversation.

"I'm going to ignore what we talked about, and instead I'm going to kiss your perfect mouth. Is that what you're asking me for, beautiful?"

I nod and draw my body closer. He drapes one arm around my back, resting his hand low on my hips. Jack kisses me softly and slowly, coaxing my lips to part, hypnotizing my tongue to move with his in a seductive roll. The way he kisses me is a contradiction; it draws shivers over my skin and warms my core all at once. Soothing and exciting with the same touch. He trails his fingers from my chin down the front of my jacket, unzipping it fully to find the hem of my sweater.

Moving his mouth to my neck, he trails open-mouthed kisses to right below my ear and growls, "I know you're wet for me right now. I want to make you so needy for my cock, baby, that you're going to come just hearing what filthy things I'm going to do to you when we get home. How does that sound?"

If any other man called me "baby," I'd shut it down, but from Jack's lips, it fuels me. I'm so turned on that I can only hum in agreement and tilt my head so his mouth has easier access to devour me. He bites my neck. "Answer me."

Anticipation and a twinge of pain rumble through me. "That sounds exactly like what I need right now." There's no clear thinking. No lines drawn or feelings shielded. I'm dripping at his words and movements. This man has me any way he'd like me, and I'm so ready for it that I'll beg if I need to.

And just as I'm thinking it, he says, "I'm going to make you work hard for my cock tonight. And Everly"—he pulls back and looks me in my eyes and down at my lips—"if you're good and you do exactly as I say, then I'll reward your beautiful mouth."

I've never wanted to be more obedient in all my life. His words ignite a swoosh of heat throughout my body, and I can feel my cheeks burning. This is the fire I've been waiting for. His roaming hand moves up underneath my sweater slowly, and as he grazes the underside of my breast, he changes pace and yanks the cup of my bra down, allowing it to spill out into his hand. The soft cashmere fabric grazes against my nipple and sends another shiver through me. The pad of his thumb rubs the hardened flesh back and forth lightly, teasingly.

His mouth captures mine again. Now with purpose, his tongue searches for mine, and then moves with a slow intention that coaxes my inhibitions to leave as I give my body over to him completely. I jerk my hips toward him, hoping to grind myself against what he's promising. He may have been hard when I sat on his lap, but that was just a glimpse of what has now swelled into the most satisfying promise of what I get to play with later. I'm instantly reminded of how well this man fills me, fits me, and delivers pleasure so graciously.

"That's right, beautiful, take what you need. Grind yourself against me," he growls out.

The only response I'm capable of is a soft moan. He pinches my nipple hard, and it catches my breath. A flutter of excitement hits me and whatever state my panties were in before is irrelevant. They're soaked now as I find deep blue eyes focused on my mouth. I can only smile. I feel so powerful being able to turn this man on simply by following his lead.

The hum of the electric gondola is the only other sound to fill the small moments of quiet between my breathy moans and Jack's delicious promises. He smells like caramel, and it makes me crave tasting more of him. He moves his hand from my hip and pulls me closer, never stopping his torturous rubbing and plucking of my nipple with his other hand. As he leans back in his seat, he brings his thumb to my lower lip, and I nip at it playfully.

Jack pushes his thumb farther into my mouth, and I lick the pad, barely tasting anything other than the need to return some kind of pleasure. He hums so deeply that it almost sounds like a rumble. *He likes that.* Sucking his thumb deeper, I swirl my tongue around it, grazing my teeth slightly on his warm, wet skin. "Are you giving me a preview, baby?" He pinches my nipple again, and it rolls a new wave of pleasure through me. "You want me to fuck this pretty mouth?" I open my eyes, not even realizing I had closed them. Meeting his again, the soft icy blue has turned darker now, more like the stormy ocean. "Will you open for me? Take all of me down that tight throat?" He moves his thumb out and pushes his pointer and middle fingers into my mouth. I suck and lap at them without an ounce of shame. He takes another shaky breath in. "Fuck, I want you so bad right now."

Before I can even think of a response, Jack sits up and pulls the top of my sweater down, stretching the neckline below my breast, and wraps his mouth around as much of it as will fit in his mouth. He shifts up just enough, so his bulge grazes my core, dragging his teeth over my nipple. Pulling back, he unbuttons my pants, drags the zipper down, and takes the fingers that were just in my mouth and drives them under my panties and right into my pussy. It takes my breath away, and he groans. He pulls me into him closer, his palm grinding into my clit and fingers working a punishing rhythm, and at that moment, I lose it completely. I unravel. I strangle out a moan as stars explode behind my eyes, the intensity of my release starting from the backs of my knees and making its way up throughout my body, pulsing violently exactly where my body craves his.

I rest my forehead on his shoulder as the world comes back into focus. The thought of what we just did makes me smile, and I tilt back to look at the sexy man who just turned me to putty in his hands. His satisfied smirk shows off one of his dimples, and my body swoons in response. He's so damn pretty, it's almost worth complaining about. He removes his hand from my pants, bringing his fingers into his mouth, sucking them clean. "You're my favorite taste," he says, and then he buttons my pants back for me, shifts my sweater back into place, and the gondola dings as the interior lights brighten. Just in time for the bell. I stand up slowly, feeling punch-drunk, and smile as I start to zip my jacket.

"Did that help?" he asks as he stands, and the gondola comes to a slowing stop.

For a few minutes, as we moved quietly across the sky, I completely forgot why I was angry. The only thing that mattered was to submit to this man, this stranger turned lover, then friend, and now...who knows.

It was freeing.

"It did. You know it did." I didn't want to think about what it meant, or what happened earlier today with Jin, or how I needed to confront my father. *And myself about what I want.* "Thank you, Jack."

We step out of the gondola and walk along the station's pathway toward the waiting taxi line. Jack hooks his pinky to mine to hold my hand, and without thinking, my fingers intertwine with his. The feelings I have when I'm around him scare me and excite me, but I know myself, perhaps too well. I can only handle so much life-altering thinking for one day.

When I pull my hand from his, his confused look hits me in the gut, and part of me regrets popping the bubble of lust we just built. I can't forget the upheaval that is starting to take shape in my life, though. If I push it aside and jump into bed with him again, as much as I want to, I'll hate both of us for it. I have too many unanswered questions.

Knocking myself back into the moment, I walk faster to catch the taxi a few feet from where we've stopped. "I'm sorry, but I can't go home with you right now. I have some questions that my dad needs to answer, and I need to do it now before I lose whatever edge I have left."

He doesn't say anything, but then again, I don't know that I want him to. The playfulness and excitement we held just moments ago are replaced with a cold seriousness of my doing. His tough exterior shifts back in place. Jack simply gives me a nod, turns, and walks away. As I pull away from the curb, steadying my resolve, I send a text to my father, letting him know I'll be there in a few minutes. I look up and notice that it started to snow. Staring back toward the station, my eyes search for Jack, but he's nowhere in sight. I've just messed up whatever we might have started. Friendship or otherwise.

30

Everly

I LOOK AT MY PHONE AS THE TAXI PULLS UP TO THE RANCH. IT'S only eleven-thirty and I know for a fact my father is still awake even though he hasn't answered my text about stopping over. I'll likely find him outside around the firepit or working in his study.

"Thanks, Gina." I give the taxi driver a wave as I finish sending her payment.

"You betcha, Everly. Have a nice evenin'. Gimme a call if ya need a lift back home."

"I'll probably just stay here tonight, but thanks. If I do, then you'll be the first number I dial. You workin' all night?"

"The bunnies started arriving last week, which means the rich old coots are comin' in on the red eyes and late flights. Those cream puffs tip the best, so I don't mind working late this time a year." Gina's one of a handful of locals who drive around town for a living. She also is the elementary school crossing guard and one of Michael's fishing guides in the warmer months from June through August. She got me home safe a few times in high school when a call home to my father to pick me up after sneaking out was the last thing I'd ever want to do.

"Looks like you're not the only one making a late-night call at your dad's." Gina tips her head toward the police cruiser parked in the roundabout of the ranch driveway.

"Have a good night, Gina." I push the door closed behind me and she pulls away. What on earth could Callen be doing here right now? My dad better not be getting into more trouble, or worse, plotting something that's going to require a hefty clean-up. With our annual Riggs Family Tree Lighting event coming up, I can only imagine the interference he might be running with the local police to look the other way about something he's got cooking.

Before I reach the front steps, the door swings open, and a smiling Sheriff Callen Muldowney walks through. Laughing about something, he turns back, and my father moves to the doorway, leaning against the frame, smiling. Something tells me not to yell out to them, so instead I stand and watch. Something about the exchange seems personal, private, and I feel like I should have called and not just texted before showing up.

My dad reaches out and fixes something on Callen's uniform and then grips his shoulder. They must have sensed me only a short distance away, because Callen looks over toward me and smiles. "Well, if it isn't the biggest troublemaker in the Riggs clan."

I make my way over to them and lean in to hug my long-time friend. "Shouldn't I be saying that about my old man since you're here? What did he do now?" I quirk my eyebrow and take in the beauty that is Callen Muldowney.

"Give me a break, Everly," my dad tuts. "Callen was just returning some of the equipment I lent to the department for their recent training." I lean over and kiss him on the cheek.

"Hey, Daddy."

"Ash, thank you again." Callen hitches a crooked, charming smile at my father. "Everly, it's always a pleasure seeing you." He tips his hat and walks backward toward his cruiser. "Oh, by the way, Quinn, down at dispatch, mentioned something interesting to me. Something about security footage earlier from the gondola. You wouldn't know anything about that tonight, would you?" He smiles at me.

"I have no idea what you're referring to, Sheriff." We exchange a silent game of *let's not ask and we don't have to tell*, then he shakes his head with a smirk, heading to his cruiser.

We both watch as Callen turns down the driveway and I use those few minutes to pull my head back to the reason why I'm here. "What's going on, pumpkin? Why you here so late?" I just look at him and my dad knows the face that I'm giving him means he's about to get an earful. "Okay, let's get a drink first. I feel like we might need one for this."

After pouring us both two fingers of bourbon, we sit around an already blazing fire on the outdoor patio. The Colorado sky is pitch black. Being so far away from a city means no light pollution, making the stars come to life at all angles. It's one of the things that I knew I'd always miss if I had never returned from New York City.

"I had dinner with Jin." I look up over my glass at my father's unreadable gaze. "But you already knew that. I thought you were going to be with him to discuss issues that the board might have had, but instead, I was knocked sideways. Without any support or warning."

Still, no response, no emotions, as if he's conducting business right now. I suppose, in a way, he is.

"Jin knows more than he should, and to top it off, the son of a bitch suggests I leave the company, swipe the apparel line away, and start my own business!" My voice is raised now, and I remember again why I'm so angry at all of this. "Did you tell him about the apparel? About my designing?"

He just stares at me to continue my tirade.

Fine. Hold on to your hat.

"You're my father, but let's just put that aside for a minute. You're the CEO of this company and I'm your VP. Why on earth would you disclose one of our key business assets to him without discussing it with me first? And on top of that, he made it sound like you gave your blessing about me just up and leaving the company! I mean, Daddy, what the hell is that?!"

Still no response, but I'm not done either.

"You had no right to blindside me like that! You've betrayed my trust, not to mention a very thick non-disclosure agreement about the exclusive apparel line. Are you trying to push me out? Do you not want me to take things over anymore?"

He tilts back the rest of his drink and sets it down on the table just to his right. "Are you done?"

"No! I don't know. Yeah, okay, I'm done. For now," I answer, taking a deep breath.

"When I started Riggs, I never imagined it would turn into what you kids have made it over the past few years. You're all so brilliant. It makes me proud. And sad at the same time. You all pour so much of yourselves into building it that I'm starting to see that maybe I've been doing my job as CEO far better than as your father." He shifts forward and leans his elbows on his knees. Looking down at his clasped hands, he continues, "I fell in love with your mother when I came to Strutt's Peak. I never planned to stay, but I was running from my responsibilities back at home. Your grandfather wanted me to stay in Montana and take over his ranch, but I wasn't ready to give up my dreams, even if I didn't know what they were yet, just to grow old on a boring ranch." He laughs. "Look at where I ended up in the long run."

I smile at him. "You may be on a ranch, Daddy, but you did it your own way."

"That's exactly my point, pumpkin." He looks back at me, and for a beat I see his eyes water slightly. "You work so hard. Always harder than your bone-headed brothers when they were younger, trying to prove that you were as good as they were. And, sweetheart, you never had to prove anything. Those boys know, along with everyone in this town, that you've always been the best of us."

"So why are you trying to get rid of me, old man?" I tease.

"I'm not. I want you to see what you have at your disposal. You've helped me build the business into something I couldn't have dreamed up on my own. You've built up incredible knowledge and managed to make some good coin along the way. You could do anything you want and if that means you stay and run this business, then I'll be thrilled. To have all my kids run this when I'm ready to retire is incredible, but, pumpkin..." He taps my knee with his foot to pull my eyes up to his. "You running Riggs was never my dream, kiddo. My dream for you and your brothers has always been to find what makes your heart beat faster and to go for it. If you tell me that running it, that it's your dream, then I'll support it, but you and I both know that designing those clothes and accessories is where your heart lies. And if you put your head into it, then you might just discover what I did all those years ago."

I smile at my dad, waiting for what I already know he's going to say. "What's that, Daddy?"

"Building something on your own from nothing is humbling. You've got it in you, Everly. Out of all of us, you're the strongest. Smarter than all of us and a hell of a lot more creative."

I sit with what he's said for a few minutes without saying anything in response. My dad could always hurdle wisdom in a way that leaves me questioning my entire life. "Why tell Jin about the apparel line?"

"I didn't. He figured it out on his own. I'm not quite sure how, but he's smart and has great gut instincts. He came to me out of respect for our friendship and business relationship before he approached you. You know you don't need an investor. If you didn't want to sink your savings or trust into it, then I'd back you silently if you wanted."

My head is spinning a little here; my dad is good at that. Turning my anger into logical thoughts. I wouldn't even know where to begin unraveling myself from Riggs Outdoor, telling my brothers I'm leaving, and then starting up on my own. And that's when it happens. A twinge of excitement hits me.

"I see you working this out in your head."

I just look up at the star-filled sky. "Daddy, how would I even do this?"

"One step at a time."

"I don't want to leave Strutt's."

"I don't want you to either. But, kiddo, the world is easier now. You could be here when you wanted, then wherever you needed to be, with a quick flight. Hell, most of the world works from home now, so life is malleable. Bend it to make it work for you."

We sit together in silence for a while. Listening to the breeze and the firepit crackle. And I know that I can't just abandon this idea. It's already started to take shape. In a matter of two conversations throughout just a handful of hours. And just like that, my world is about to change.

"Now, tell me more about Jack Deacon."

"No way are you moving into that topic so easily." I laugh.

Grabbing the bottle of aged bourbon, he teases, "I know you like that man. He's a good one too, I can tell."

"There's not much to tell, Daddy." He quirks a brow my way, knowing I'm totally full of shit.

"You sure about that?" he asks.

"Jack is..." I pause and try to choose my words because I could say so much, but why give my father a false hope for a happily ever after. "Jack is complicated. Smart. Obviously very good-looking, but he's also really sweet. And a good handful of other things, but the most important one is that he's leaving. He's only here until after the New Year. He goes back to his life in Manhattan, and that's it."

My father resumes his stoic glare as he sips his drink. He makes a harrumph sound, which usually means he's going to give his opinion, even though I really, really don't want it.

"What, Daddy? Out with it."

"Pumpkin, the fact that the biggest issue you have is that

he's not going to be around here for too long is reason enough to see where it goes. I've never liked any of the idiots you've dated. Even Jin. Smart businessman, but kind of an asshole otherwise."

I laugh, spitting some of my drink out with it. Of course, he knows about Jin. *Damn small towns.*

"And the fact that your life might be looking a little different and less permanent here soon too seems like a good reason to mingle with other not-so-permanent things. Take it from your old man. I've let the love of my life believe that there were more important things. The secret is, there isn't much that's more important than figuring it out together. Sometimes it works out and sometimes you discover it wasn't right, but, pumpkin, you have to let yourself try."

31

Jack

"All I'm saying is there's no reason why a New Yorker, if you could even call yourself that, would choose to root for the Mets *unless* they hated the Yankees." I turn and laugh at Law's exaggerated movements as he tries to understand the logistics of my baseball loyalties.

"It's simple. I've always liked the Mets, but I am also a New Yorker, so if the Yanks are playing the Sox, especially in a postseason game, I'm going to root for my home team." I turn the waffle iron as I plate another. "And any New York team is my home team." Law pulls out the syrup from the cabinet, along with cinnamon. "How are you a Red Sox fan? You live in Colorado."

Plopping the condiments on the counter and moving toward the whistling teakettle, the youngest Riggs brother is riled up, and it's hilarious to watch. Michael chimes in from the far counter where he's cutting strawberries. "Law's buddy Hernandez plays for Boston. Don't let my brother give you shit about what team you back." Michael yells louder in Law's direction, "Two years ago, he was a Dodgers fan!"

"Michael, I don't remember asking you to participate in this conversation."

A loud thud draws our attention to the other side of the room, where Henry stomps toward the kitchen. The guy is massive. We can all hold our own in a room, but Henry is the guy you hope is on your side in a brawl. "How are you guys talking about baseball? It's the off-season. Can we move this conversation to the Lakers, maybe? That's a conversation I can get behind." Dropping in the seat next to Michael, he asks, "There enough for me? I'm starving."

"Tons of bacon under that towel, and I got you. This waffle is almost done. It's all yours."

When I started making breakfast this morning, I hadn't intended to feed the whole house, but I like being in the thick of this crew. I knew Everly never came back last night. I waited up for her, but after around 3 a.m., I assumed she decided to stay at her father's ranch. As much as I'm trying to be distracted by her brothers right now, the only thing I'm doing is waiting for her to come home.

Waffles always make me feel better, so as soon as dawn broke, I went out to the market downtown to get what I needed for a big breakfast. While I was out, I ran into Lenny McKenna again, who proceeded to call me out on my "lies" after she saw the way Everly "eye-fucked me like an omega in heat." I have no idea what reference that was, but I got her message loud and clear. That I'm not fooling anyone.

If her nosy ass only knew.

"This bacon tastes like that spot in Hell's Kitchen. Law,

what was it called? Something about your mom?" Henry barks out after inhaling two more pieces.

"I love that place! They had the fries with those cheese curds. What the hell was the place called? And the boozy milkshakes!"

I pull off the fourth crispy Belgian waffle from the iron. I'm finally ready to dive into the breakfast I've been making for the past hour. "When were you guys in New York?"

Michael looks up from his plate and takes a sip of coffee. "We'd go out to see Ev all the time when she was in school."

"Law was probably there the most." Henry pretends to shield his mouth, and then whisper-shouts, "If you haven't noticed, Law practically lives up our sister's ass."

Law chucks a piece of melon at Henry, who intimidatingly catches it. "I love our sister and New York City was incredible. I lost my virginity the summer of her sophomore year out there. After that, I thought women in New York were on an entirely new level."

"Dipshit didn't realize that it was his fake ID that got him into places where women assumed he was older than sixteen," Henry goads at his youngest brother.

"It was my good looks, you asshole. And I was a horny motherfucker back then." Law laughs.

"Back then?"

Law ignores Henry's chide and keeps talking. "But we went out there a lot. Not just me. Henry, you stayed out there for a whole month at one point, looking for that girl from the bar, so don't bust my balls. Everly thought about staying there. After college, I mean, to make a go of the whole fashion thing, but in the long run, she decided she wanted to help build the family business. We all came to that conclusion too, in our own time, but she started the train. After that, it was easy to come aboard." He shoves a piece of waffle into his mouth. "If you haven't noticed, she's kind of a force."

I look up as I bite into the crispy warm waffle and answer, "Oh, I've noticed."

"She's spent the majority of her life taking care of us, in one way or another, and it feels wrong not to ask the guy she's been smiling about lately what he's doing with her." Law pours us each another round of coffee. "So? It wasn't rhetorical. What's your plan here? You look at her like she's a plate of waffles." He takes a bite off his fork and gestures to his almost empty plate. If he only knew how precise he is with that comparison.

I can feel three pairs of scrutinizing and overly protective eyes on me. I didn't think I was going to have to do this right now, but I suppose now's as good a time as any.

"You messed up already, huh?" Michael throws down his blatant honesty. Henry and Law just bark out a laugh, and I can only shake my head because he's not wrong.

"I haven't messed it up. I'm not sure she wants anything serious in her life right now." Pushing the plate in front of me, I lean back in my chair to give this conversation the attention it deserves. I look at each of the Riggs brothers and lay it out for them in the most honest way. "Getting involved with her was the last thing I expected when I took this job. Then I met her. In this room, actually, and my world tipped on its axis a bit. I mean, she's fucking gorgeous, that was obvious right away, but the more I get to know her..." I just shake my head, because I'm not sure I should be telling this to her brothers. It should be her to hear this.

Michael clears his throat and looks at me in a way that tells me to listen carefully. "We are the tides and she is the moon." *Not what I was expecting.* He pauses, realizing maybe that was too profound. "It may sound like too much, but to us, in our family, she is the force that keeps all of us moving. Always has been."

I glance around the counter to see if Henry or Law will chime in with more than just this poetically deep statement, but instead, I'm left with silence. How do I respond to that? No wonder she's never put her desires ahead of the family. They depend on her in a way I can truly understand from what I've been through, but that's a lot of weight to bear. I only had my sister. Everly has three, four, if you count her father, that looks to her.

"That seems like a lot of pressure to put on someone."

"Michael just means that she's important to us. She's our sister, but she's also our best friend. Geez, practically a surrogate mother, without us realizing it for the better part of our teenage years. We want her to be happy. And quite frankly, there hasn't been a person to come into her life that has ever really made her happy, so we're skeptical." Law lifts his shoulder. "I like you, Jack. I think you're one of the few people that might be able to keep up with Ev, but you're never going to find an ally in us if she's not happy. Just laying out some truths before you decide your next move."

Henry just grunts next to me and gets up to clear his spot. "Take it however you want, Deacon, but it comes down to this. If you're just fucking around while you're here and you're not interested in more, then you're a bigger idiot than I thought. And I'd take this conversation as a warning. If you make my sister regret spending time with you, then you're going to regret ever meeting the lot of us. Clear enough?"

There's no need to get in his face, even if I normally would never let someone talk to me like that. Instead, I just look him in the eye and say, "Clear." I watch Henry leave the room and head back to his space while Michael keeps his eyes pinned on me.

"I...hmm, how do I say this without sounding like the weird one? Sometimes how I say things, no matter how honest, they sound wrong. I'm not great at reading the room." He rubs the back of his neck, searching for how to say whatever else is on his mind. I give him the space to do it. "My father told me a long time ago that Everly is the person you watch, mimic, and protect. Most don't get me, not in the way that she does. I like things done a certain way and I have trouble keeping my thoughts calm. So yeah, my sister is my moon. It may sound dumb or over the top to a guy like you, but it's my truth. If you're not interested in someone as big as the moon, then, like Henry said, take this as a suggestion to move on."

Law just smiles at his brother and holds up a fist. "Dude, you said it just right."

I lean over to Michael. "She's lucky to have you guys. I feel the same way about my sister." I pause. "Different reasons, but I understand, and I would be saying the same thing if someone swooped into her life. In fact, I have sent similar warnings to someone before, and I can assure you it wasn't wasted breath."

I should have known some kind of talk like this was coming. The problem is, she's made it clear that this thing we have, no matter how much I try to avoid the realization of it, is not going to be more than what she wants. And after last night on the gondola, it needs to remain light and fun.

"You assholes coming or not?" Henry barks from the garage.

Law grabs the plates from the counter and piles them in

the sink. "We're going to try and get in some time at our buddy's MMA gym. You want to come?"

"Thanks, but I'm going to hang back. I'll go next time."

"Alright, man." Law pauses and looks at the mess of the kitchen. "Thanks for breakfast. Those were damn good waffles."

I'm sitting back, feet kicked up on the counter, finally able to dig into my waffle and strawberries. I feel relaxed even after the Riggs brothers' interrogation and warnings. I respect them and their relationships even more now, to be honest. My body is still buzzing when I think about Everly. The woman makes me dizzy. She looks at me like she wants to devour me and then cools off as soon as she starts to think outside of the moment. It's how I usually operate, but apparently not with her.

She's gotten under my skin, pushed her way deeper than I ever would normally allow, and I'm not even sure when it happened. I'm sitting here, in her house, no less, and my brain shifts to the shape of her mouth and how right it feels to kiss her, how I don't want any other lips meeting mine or anyone else's tasting hers. All the parts of her that make me feel good, feel something other than defensive. I like how she listens, and how she doesn't try to fill silence because she's uncomfortable with it. She lets me breathe around her and it's not something I ever thought about wanting until now that I've had it. It's a crazy realization for me to come to, but if she felt the same way, I'd stay. Make it impossible for her to choose anyone else. I'd do whatever was necessary to be with her, to make this feeling grow and change only for the good.

"Make yourself at home."

I flick my eyes up to find her leaning against the doorframe of the kitchen, a wicked grin on her face. I keep my feet propped on the counter as I eat another bite of my waffles. Smiling at her, I'm trying to cover any trace of the thoughts I was just having. I should be pissed off at her for the way she left me at the station, but I'm not. I've been waiting to see her. And that's obvious from me being here. In her house.

"Did you make breakfast? It looks like you fed my brothers based on the disaster here." She walks over to the refrigerator and plucks the creamer out. Hair piled in a messy knot on the top of her head, she shifts to take off her sweatshirt, and I'm rewarded with seeing a strip of her beautiful skin as she raises her arms above her head.

This woman sets me on fire with a simple tease of her lower back. And her brothers think *I'm* the one that's the threat. She shifts her weight to take off her boots. Seeing her sweatpants slung low on her hips and a black tank top hugging the rest of her curves, I shift in my seat, making room for the growing tension in my pants.

"I did. It was a morning for waffles. Too bad you weren't here. They're good." I take another bite.

Everly pours herself a cup of the coffee left in the French press and adds a splash of cream and then a squeeze of maple syrup. Then she walks next to me and hops up on the counter, scooting her bottom closer so that I'm forced to drop my legs off and sit up. She holds out her hand, asking for the fork. I shake my head and instead spear a piece with a strawberry slice and move it toward her mouth. She opens and takes the offered bite.

"Thank you." She shimmies closer, and I open my legs to make more space for her feet to rest. As she finishes her bite, her gaze meets mine.

"What happened?" I cut another piece, stab it with the fork, and move it to her. She opens her pillowy lips and takes another bite. Feeding someone shouldn't be a turn-on, but right now my dick strongly disagrees.

She finishes chewing and takes a sip of her coffee. "A lot."

I sit up straighter and push the plate to her side, scooting forward in the chair and lifting her feet into my lap. Without overthinking, I take her right foot in my hand, start rubbing my thumbs into the arch, and begin working the tension from her body. She looks at me as if I've just thrown her off by my actions, but I can't help it. I want her to talk to me and I need her to feel like she can.

"Is that all you're going to give me?" I ask.

She takes a deep breath. "The more time I spend with you, the more I want to give you."

Liking the sound of that, I keep kneading her foot and work my way around her ankle, coaxing her to relax.

"There's someone that wants to invest in my designs. Well, one of our current investors wants to go into business with me, exclusively. Taking the designs that you now know about and turning it into my own thing." She pauses, looking for my reaction, but instead I study her foot and keep moving. I want her to keep talking. "It would mean I wouldn't be a part of my family's business any longer and that I'd be starting from the ground floor again. And..." She pauses, and I can tell she's working through this out loud for the first time, perhaps. "I mean, it would be a lot of hard work and scary to go all-in on it, but it might be incredible. The most amazing part is that I know I can do it, and I don't need an investor, but it would be a smart move not to take on the initial costs myself, but well..." She pauses again.

I look up and meet her stare.

"I would be blowing up my life to do this. I'd have to split my time in Strutt's and New York, probably, as I set everything up, for at least the first year. And that's assuming I'd make it past the first year."

"Blowing up your life doesn't have to be a bad thing. It just makes it more exciting." I offer my perspective a bit. "The scary stuff is always the most worth doing, but you already know that."

"I'm sorry." She leans forward and drags her hand down her leg to meet my fingers that have been busy moving up to her calf. "Last night I was an emotional wreck when I boarded the gondola, and after you..." She stumbles on her words. "After we..."

"After I worked that orgasm out of you..."

"Yes, after that." Her face flushes at the acknowledgment of our ride together. "I wasn't expecting to see you, and then when I did, all of my angry energy just turned into needing your hands on me. And then after that, I pushed you away, and I'm sorry. I like being around you and I want to be around you while you're here. You make me feel things. Delicious things, but things that I wasn't prepared to feel. I was all-in on a great night of sex and what it's snowballing into scares me."

Something that feels a lot like happiness mixed with nerves washes over me as I absorb her words. I stare at our hands as we lightly tease each other's fingers, then I lean forward, resting my chin on her legs. "Can I tell you something, beautiful?"

She looks back into my eyes, and I grab her hips tight and pull her down from the counter in front of me and into my lap so I can be closer to her. "I want to be near you, and that might seem like something light or small to say, but I don't ever feel that way. With anyone. Not many people know me. Really know me. I don't let them. It's easier to be a good time, or a fling, or just a friend who listens, but with you..." I stop to breathe her in and even after a night spent away, she still smells like oranges, but now mixed with the sweetness of maple syrup. Even the way she smells brings me a sense of ease. "With you, it's easy to just go with it. Not overthink any of it. It doesn't make me want to run from you, it makes me want to run right at you."

It's as if my words were flint because within seconds the fire between us is lit, and her lips meet mine with urgency. And the only thing I know, the only thing that is certain, is that in this moment, she is mine.

32

Everly

THE WAY THIS MAN KISSES ME IS AN ART FORM. IT'S NEVER THE same. The rhythm of his movements is ever-changing and complimentary. Soft, deep, chaste, wanton. Hands cupping my face, tugging my hair, dragging down my thigh. There's nothing presumptive. I get lost in the softness of his lips and the confidence in how they meet and tease mine. The way his tongue sensually dances with mine, seeking with intention. Jack's mouth is the only thing I can focus on. The determination of his lips, the way the scruff on his face rakes along my chin and upper lip as he shifts, his hand fisting my shirt at the back and the other as it grips my waist. I wrap my arms around his neck and drag my fingers through his hair, as the man kisses me as if I'm his air.

"I want you so badly right now, Everly." He drags his mouth to my neck and nips, then stands and picks me up with him, bringing me back to the counter behind me. I push him back slightly and look at his sexy mouth for a moment. Then, my gaze lifts to his. His eyes search mine for the reason why I'm pushing him away.

I drag my hand down his chest slowly. He watches, waiting to see what I'm going to do. Jack pulls some kind of newfound confidence out of me. A sexual bravado that must have always been there, but one that's been tamped too far down over years of mediocre chemistry and hurried experiences. The way he looks at me makes me feel like the bottom just dropped out from beneath my feet.

My hand moves from his body to my own, and I wedge it into the rolled band of my sweatpants, gliding it lower, and dipping into the waist of my already soaked panties. I swipe my two fingers along the edges of my core. The space that I'm craving for his mouth to venture and play. A come-hither motion that sets me off and has his eyes fixed on the movements beneath the garments. I pull my hand out, and before I can even move toward him, he doesn't miss a beat, taking my hand in his and bringing my fingers into his mouth with a groan.

Then, as if unleashed, he's yanking the top of my tank top down and rolling my nipple between his finger and thumb before diving forward to suck. "Jack. I need you, please." I don't even know what I'm asking for other than him. More of him. I want to flood my senses with him.

He answers my plea and pulls me off the counter, spinning me around with my back to his front as he grinds into me. The groan and gravel in his voice turn me on even more as he tells me, "I'm still hungry, beautiful." And with that, he pushes me forward so my belly and chest rest on the cool countertop. From behind, he rips my sweatpants and undies down my legs, leaving them bunched around my ankles before I can even register the movements. Grabbing my ass cheeks in each hand aggressively, he spreads them up and apart, making room for his face to be buried deeply. He licks my pussy from clit to slit with a flattened tongue and back again.

"Oh my God, fuuuuuuckkkk." I can only push out swear words and then his name in between moans after that. He works his mouth and tongue over me with such ambition that if eating a woman out was a career path, Jack would be the mogul. My legs shake. From behind, the way his mouth feels, and the way he couldn't care less about just diving into me, feels forbidden and exquisitely indulgent. He grabs my ass tighter. I think he even slaps it, but at this moment, I'm so far gone in a state of chasing the euphoria and the anticipation of an orgasm, that he could do anything to me, and I'd let him.

"That's right, baby." He grips one ass cheek while working two fingers into me, and somehow reaches around, rubbing light circles directly on my clit. This man needs no guidance. Whatever homework he's done, or instincts he has, are irrelevant; he works my body like he knows the coding and algorithms for my orgasm to spill over at the exact moment he wants it to happen. The thrusts of his fingers move with greater intent, and I'm so wired, I move to meet them. "That's it, beautiful. Fuck yourself on my hand. My cock is so hard right now, just watching your ass move and the taste you left on my tongue. So fucking good."

"Jack..."

I want all of him to be touching me. His mouth and hands. He curves his fingers and they hit exactly that place that brings an instant flash of heat. I can feel my orgasm starting to wind through my body.

"That's it. Give it to me. Come for me, beautiful."

And I do. A cataclysmic wave of rolling darkness takes control of my body, moving up the backs of my thighs, low in my belly, through my core, and taking over every remaining part of me. The chaos of it feels like the ocean pulling me under, and I can't do anything other than surrender. Let it toss and turn me until it's had its way, and only then can I resurface and breathe. How incredible those few breathless, frenetic moments feel.

I lie still until the things around me and the person who sent me into the most exquisite experience come back into focus. Jack turns my face to look at him and kisses me lightly. I smile, and then I realize I'm lying ass up across the counter in my kitchen, where I also live with my three brothers. *Did I just black out?*

This realization must register on my face because Jack quickly says, "They're not here. They left just before you came home. Don't worry."

I stand up slowly and smile, my eyes half-lidded, still recovering from the bliss. Without saying anything else, Jack pulls my tank top and bra off. "What are you...?" Then he pulls my sweatpants and underwear that are still draped around my ankles off my legs completely, taking my hand and leading me to the stairs across the living room.

"I'm not fucking done with you yet."

"Let me grab my clothes. I can't just leave those..."

Jack stops and smiles, jogs back to the pile I just left behind, grabs them with one hand, and then stalks toward me. He's quick, and as soon as he approaches, he picks me up and hoists me over his shoulder. I squeal and laugh as he carries me, swatting my ass cheek as he trots up the stairs. We make it to my room, where he drops me in the center of my bed.

"Everly, I need to be inside you right now. I'm so fucking turned on, and my dick feels very left out of all the fun." Jack drags his shirt over his head and quickly unbuckles the belt of his jeans. In just a few short movements, he's naked and his heavy cock points directly at what it wants. Me. I've never been the woman to gawk at a man the way I do him, but I can't help but stare. I can't just let him sink into me without tasting him. It's only fair and I've never wanted to taste and lick a man more in my life.

"You're looking at me like you want to devour me."

As Jack crawls up my body, I take in his handsome face and the perfection of his toned and muscled body. Before he can settle between my thighs, I push him over and move on top of him. Kissing his plush mouth, nipping at his bottom lip. "I don't want to devour you. I want to savor you. That orgasm was..." I blow air from my lips, trying to articulate just how amazing he made me feel. "My body is still buzzing from it." I start to move down his torso. "It's my turn to play for a bit."

He grabs my shoulders to stop me. "I'm already so close to coming, Everly."

"Good. I want to taste all of you."

He groans, whispering, "Fuck," before he sits up higher on his elbows to watch me.

I sink back on my knees, popping my ass up in the air and tease him with my mouth. Drawing a line with my tongue, I move from the base of his cock to the edge of its crown and across the slit. When I slow down enough to dip slightly and taste the bead of excitement that escapes, Jack bucks his hips and groans. I love how much I can turn him on and prolong the orgasm I know is so close to escaping him. Flattening my tongue down to the base again and back up, I wrap my lips around him and swirl the tip into my mouth, pulling him to the back of my throat.

"Fuck, baby. You're going to kill me here."

Wrapping my hand around the base of him, I work his cock with both my hands and mouth to the point where I know he can't take it any longer. With a final pull, I pop him out of my mouth and crawl up his body. I need him inside of me and now. He grasps my hips to help as I move and position him right where I want him. As I rub him against my pussy and drag him up and down so he hits my clit, I already know it won't take long to lose control all over again.

"You're so sexy. Goddamn. That's it, baby, take what you want from me."

I sit down slowly, taking my time to get used to the fit of him. The stretch hurts so good it drives a shiver down my back. Buried to the hilt, I start to circle my hips and grind. We haven't taken our time connected like this yet, being able to ride him and draw out each thrust and pull of my hips so that I can feel the push and drag of his cock. I'm so concentrated on how it feels that I haven't looked up. Jack's hand on my chin jerks me out of my lustful daze and it pulls my eyes back to his. Those ocean blue eyes.

"You look like you were made to sit there. Savoring the way my cock fits you." He hooks his thumb into my mouth so I'll suck on it, and I do. "You take everything I give you, beautiful." He lets out a moan. "So ready to please."

Without warning, he tugs my arm forward and my chest meets his. He wraps his arms around my back, fusing us together, holding on for what comes next. Then he begins to fuck me from below, hard and slow, bottoming out each time, hitting me so deep that words leave me, and my fingers dig into his shoulders.

"You're so fucking perfect for me. Fuck, beautiful, I can't hold back here."

He grips me tighter and pulls his mouth to mine as his hips kick up faster, changing the pace and connection completely. The hypnotic motion just moments ago was a slow dance, a promise of what's to come. A seduction. But now, as he drives into me urgently, that seduction was nothing more than an appetizer to this. He fucks me with abandon, holding my body tight to his, as the only part that is able to move is his cock, as it surges in and out. I have no choice but to hand over all control. We move together so beautifully, even the sounds of sweaty skin, and each other's moans are poetic. Turning me on even more, readying me to drop completely over the edge.

"Everly, fuck, I'm going to come, baby." Jack shifts slightly. If I hadn't known before, I know now he's not satisfied unless I'm coming undone with him. He pushes deeper into me, still at a piston's pace, and I can feel the rush of my orgasm starting to take over my body once again. He tightens his grip around my body, pulling me flush with him, and the pressure is just enough that we explode around each other. I feel warmth flood me, as he swears and moans deep into my ear.

The way this man moans during his release is now one of my favorite sounds. It gives me such a high hearing him unravel and knowing that I'm responsible for it. As we pant into each other's skin, he loosens his grip. I have tears in my eyes because the gravity of that orgasm and the way he pushed my body were nothing short of incredible.

"Woman, you might have just ruined me," Jack rasps out and laughs.

I can only smile. I wipe away the tears that start to spill

over the corners of my eyes. The rest of my body can barely move. We lie quietly with one another for a few minutes, maybe longer, as time also doesn't seem to register for me right now. So that's what I've been missing. That's what people write songs and books about. That level of lust and undeniable connection that can't be articulated, only experienced.

I start to drift off, even though I can feel our orgasms dripping out of me. The responsible part of my brain is yelling loudly to get up and pee while figuring out a way to have a conversation with him about STD testing. We didn't use a condom, and while I'm on birth control, that doesn't keep me safe from whatever decisions about sex Jack's made before me. And even with that in mind, I still feel like heaven. I'm not cavalier about things like this, but I don't want to hit the accountability wagon just yet.

I'm moved gently as Jack gets up, and I can only groan at the loss of his warm body that was surrounding me.

"Beautiful, turn over for me," he whispers.

I roll over and groan, opening my eyes as a warm cloth startles me between my legs. I just laugh and sit up. "I can do that."

"My mess. I will clean it up." He smiles, thoroughly cleaning me with light movements. When he's finished, he grabs the fluffy duvet from the floor and drags it up the bed as he lies next to me. I move toward him and drape myself over his chest, resting my head in the crook of his neck.

"We didn't use a condom. I haven't done that before. I'm usually much more aware of what I'm doing, but I lost all track of common sense for a few minutes there," he says.

"Yeah, we kinda did, didn't we? I don't have any lurking STDs, and I'm also on the pill."

"A bit careless of us." He rubs his hand behind his neck and looks back at me. "I never have this conversation, because I never don't use condoms. Shit, that sounded…I don't know how that sounded, but you don't need to worry about me either. In case you were. Worrying, that is."

I tilt my head to look at him. "I'm glad you said something. It was careless, but it felt so good not to care."

It's the most nervous he's ever seemed. I respect his assertiveness, but it's also a turn-on that he can be aggressive and in control and then tell me how he feels, even if it makes him vulnerable. Jack is not what I assumed or ever expected. And contently lying here in his arms, a place I rarely find myself comfortably with men, I don't want to move. I could easily drift off, but I need to tell him how I'm feeling. I want to give him more of me than mixed signals and sex. *I'm starting to fall for this man.*

"Jack?" I whisper. His breathing has started to even out. While I was overthinking for the past few minutes, he managed to fall asleep. I kiss his chest and nuzzle back into him. What I have to say can wait, for now.

"No!"

I'm jerked awake by a yell, and I move away as Jack shifts and twitches. "Please." He grunts and moans.

"Jack." I touch his shoulder and shake him slightly. He opens his eyes. "It's only a dream, baby. You're okay."

He rolls to his back and rubs his eyes with the heels of his palms. Embarrassed or angry, I'm not sure what he's feeling, but I need him to know it's okay. "You can talk to me about it. It's okay."

"Did I hurt you?" He sits up, worried, searching my face.

"No, not at all. You just woke me up from yelling and moving. I'm fine." He drops back to the bed and lets out a deep breath. I don't want to push it if it's something he'd rather not talk about. Since this is the second time this has happened, and after what he's already told me, I know these are more than just nightmares. I rub his arm up and down to let him know it's okay.

"I don't sleep with people because of this. I'm never sure how aggressive I become, but I never want to put anyone in danger because I can't control what's going on in my mind." He looks over at me. I can see that he's deciding how much he wants to say. "I'm so fucking damaged, Everly." He searches my eyes for a response, but I'm not about to agree with him. We all have things that make us feel that way, some worse than others, and in Jack's case, his traumas don't ever go away. "My therapist told me once that we hold on to the bad memories because those are the ones that affect us the most deeply, but the reality is, all of it was bad. There weren't any good memories. Other than my sister. And even then, every moment with her, I was anxious that I wouldn't be able to keep her safe. The first decade of my life, I wouldn't wish on my worst enemy." He takes a minute, and then shifts to face me. Sitting up, he drags a hand through his hair, rubbing his neck. "Are you sure you want to hear any of this?"

"I'll listen to anything you want to tell me, Jack. And you don't even have to do that if you don't want to. I'll just sit with you and let you work through it silently, if that's what you'd prefer." I hook my pointer finger with his and shift to hold his hand. "I don't look at you or hear what you tell me and think you're damaged. I just see someone who's strong, a person who has worked hard to create a life he can respect, someone who protects who's important to him. There's nothing about that kind of person like that I would call damaged."

He just smiles softly, and then I'm met with silence. I meant what I said; I don't want him to share anything with me that he's not willing, but I won't let him tear himself down for things he can't control. "There's a lot to tell and I want to tell you, which isn't something I ever feel like doing. With anyone. Even Kathryn and I rarely bring up life before we were adopted. I suppose for her, whatever she remembers is what I tell her. She was too young. I'm jealous of that, to be honest. I've done just about everything to forget it all, and most of the time, I do. Until I sleep. Memories find their way back to me when my guard is down."

The room is bright. If I had to guess, it's probably mid-afternoon by the way the warm colors of the sun hit my white bedroom walls. It's the first time that I really search and study Jack's face up close like this. The way his stubble surrounds his chin and cheeks. And then slopes above the bow of his upper lip. The lines that form between his eyebrows when he's speaking about heavier things. The way his dark eyelashes blink away the emotion that threatens to spill from his ocean eyes. As I listen, I find myself getting lost in the details of how his mouth moves with certain words and the way his throat buoys when he chooses to stay silent.

"I don't remember too much before I was about five or six years old, but it wasn't like one day things went to shit. I just didn't start remembering most of it until then." He shifts to sit up higher against the headboard and looks down at our entwined hands. "We lived in an apartment that I never left until I was nine years old, surrounded by my mom's addiction and the actions that came along with it. Only when she died did we get to experience a normal life."

I don't want him to stop talking, but my eyes are already beginning to water, and I feel like after I hear more, the weight of it will be just as heavy as to why he feels comfortable enough to tell it to me.

"There were men that always came and went. We lived in a studio, so that meant when they came, I had to hide. It was either an oversized wardrobe or under the bed. The wardrobe was where I'd prefer because sometimes they'd be there for days. I was never allowed to come out. I had made that mistake a couple of times. I saw things I never had any business of seeing at that age. And I could never unsee those images and erase the feelings that came with them." A tear spills down one of his cheeks, and he wipes it quickly, with noticeable resentment. "It all damaged me enough that I can't fucking forget any of it."

He looks at me again, wiping the tears that are quietly pouring down my face. I don't have any words for him. There's no comfort in words, so I hold his hand tighter.

"I was seven or eight when I wished my mother would die. Every day. Who does that? Who wishes for their parents to die?"

I know it's rhetorical, but he looks at me as if he's searching for an answer, so I give him one. "Survivors do. Someone who fights to survive the hell that a parent puts them through."

"Well, I got my wish. I was nine when it happened. She couldn't pay off her debts, which wasn't anything new, but this day, it was enough of a reason. The men who had always come decided she wasn't worth the trouble any longer and killed her. That time, we were under the bed. I cradled my sister under that bed for almost three days straight before the police found us. The best thing to ever happen to us was her death, and not a single day goes by that I don't thank the universe for it."

Jack wipes the tears from my face and kisses my lips softly. "The memories follow me. It's my penance for wishing my mother dead, but I'll take it. My sister is safe. I have an incredible nephew. And I have a life that I'm proud of. But, I never fall asleep with anyone. I never know which memory will wake me. And until you, I've never felt the need to tell anyone about it."

I move toward him, sitting on his lap, and facing him, I cradle his face with my hands, brushing my thumbs over his lips, a move he's done to me repeatedly. I kiss him with all the feelings I have swirling through me, compassion, sympathy, *love*. "Thank you for telling me." I wrap my arms around his shoulders and neck, hugging him tightly. "You are so much more than what I expected you'd be, Jack. But none of those things are damaged or broken."

He doesn't say anything else after that, but he lets out a long breath that has me wondering if he's been holding it in along with his secrets. A heavy burden now lifted, or perhaps enough of a past dredged up that he's letting it settle itself back into the dark. We hold on to each other, brushing our fingers along each other's skin, lulling one another until we both drift off again.

33

Jack

I DON'T REMEMBER FALLING ASLEEP, BUT I HELD THIS beautiful woman in my arms so tightly, afraid if I let any space between us, she'd snap out of it and want to leave. Run as far away from the broken man as possible. But she didn't. She hasn't pulled away at all, and that doesn't terrify me. It thrills me and makes me believe I could be worthy of this woman. I didn't come to Strutt's Peak thinking I would stay for long, but as I hear her breathing so close, feel her nuzzle into me to keep warm, I don't know that I have it in me to walk away. Why would I walk away from something I've always wanted?

Yesterday we spent most of the day in bed together. Always touching each other in some way. Sometimes it was nothing more than drawing small circles on her arms or Everly dragging her fingers through the short hair at the nape of my neck. I don't know that I'll ever be tired of touching her. The only break was while we ate Chinese takeout for dinner. As soon as we were done, we came back to her bed and watched a double feature.

Over salty buttered popcorn we argued which movie could be considered the best sequel of all time. I said Godfather: Part 2, and she scoffed adamantly, saying that it has to be Terminator 2. So, we watched both. I held some part of her the entire time with a few intermissions for sex and a shower, and then sex in the shower, but we always came back to holding the other. Part of me was afraid if I didn't hold her in some way while we lied in bed, that I'd wake up and realize I had dreamt it all.

"I can hear you thinking, you know?" she whispers, her head laying on my chest.

"Oh yeah, and what am I thinking?"

"Hmm, let's see..." She sits up, moving to rest her chin on my chest to look at me. "You're thinking that falling into bed with me is the most pleasure you've ever experienced, and to show your gratitude you're going to bring me a hot coffee and maybe something with carbs in bed."

"You're good. I could go for a coffee." I drop a kiss on her lips and move out of bed. When I turn back to look at her, she's burrowed under the covers and is already back to sleep.

I make my way into the kitchen without seeing any of her brothers, which, to be honest, I'm glad. I'm on a mission, and I want to get back into that bed as soon as possible. The clock above the door reads six-forty-five, and I pull out everything I need to make us breakfast. It seems like the perfect time to make another batch of waffles.

All the ingredients and waffle iron are where I left them last. I work quickly, brew coffees, and find a tray so I can carry it all upstairs. It's not lost on me that I'm making my comfort food for her, and it feels different, to feel like I'm taking care of her in a very small way. Something a part of me craves to do with the people I care for. And I do. I care for her. No, more than care. Fallen. I've fallen hard for her, and it knocks me back. I don't know exactly when it happened, but just that it has. And I'm happy. I'm freaking out at the weight of it. About falling in love with her, but I'm so fucking happy, I think I smiled the entire time I made breakfast.

34

Everly

WE SPEND THE REST OF THE DAY IN BED TOGETHER AGAIN, only breaking away to shower and deposit our dishes in the sink downstairs. It's the laziest and most fulfilled I've ever been. After, he brought me breakfast in bed, which, by the way, I highly recommend. A small little Level Up coin should have popped up because seeing a shirtless man, with the kind of body that Jack has, with his boxer briefs slung low as he carries in a tray of waffles to me in bed, has elevated my partner goals. His choices were elite. I hoped for coffee, and he went full-breakfast.

The man also managed to make me a version of a Hungry Eye, mimicking my drink obsession from Books & Brew. I've been won over by breakfast foods. I'll never tell him, but I'm sure I've given it away by the sounds I made while eating. Not to mention the big fat smile that sat on my face from the first bite to the last sip.

"There is no way a place that serves only rice pudding

could be your favorite place in New York City." I can only laugh at his admission. "I was expecting something artsy like the MET or The Public Library!"

"Don't be so judgy! Tell me yours." He pulls me back into him. Hugging me from behind, he drapes his arms around me and plays with my hands.

"There's a hidden bar inside of Grand Central. I can never remember its actual name, but my friends and I named it Secret Bar. It's not obvious to find, but once you do, it has a Great Gatsby vibe to it. High ceilings and a lot of dark greens and golds. My favorite bartender would make me a drink that he named The Everly. It was an Old Fashioned with a splash of Aperol. That's the secret ingredient that Law is always trying to figure out, by the way. He still hasn't gotten it, and it's killing him." I laugh because I haven't thought about the place in a long time, and it was one of those places that just never leaves you.

"I'd like to try it. The way your bartender makes it. In New York." He smiles at me, and my body warms at the sight. "I know the place, by the way. Great vibe. I could see you being there."

Those dimples of his come out like secret weapons. This man knows how to wield his assets, there's no doubt about that. I brush my hand along his jaw, feeling the scruff that's started and touch the elusive dimple in his right cheek. "These are panty-melters."

He smiles wide. "Oh, I know." *Cocky bastard.*

"I think I might be heading to New York soon. All of a sudden, there are a couple of reasons to be there for a bit." He raises his brow, waiting for me to elaborate more. We spend the next hour talking about business, specifically what I'm planning to do with the apparel. My apparel. I've been non-stop running different ideas and scenarios in my mind ever since Jin suggested it because, as mad as it made me, it opened my eyes. "It's a gamble and it makes me nervous. Like, who do I think I am to just change directions completely in my mid-thirties?"

"A badass, that's who."

"Well, yes. That might be true. I'm excited, though. It's been a long time since I've felt excited about something." I smile at him. "And someone..."

"If there was anyone to do this, beautiful, it's you. Your talent is only part of it. You are a force." He kisses me again and smiles. "You took your father's company and turned it into a brand that's dominating the sports and outdoor industry. I've done my homework, Everly, and that was you. As soon as you stepped into that role was when Riggs started on its current trajectory." As he's talking, all I can think about is how much I want all of this. The new career. The life I've always been too afraid to go after. *Him.*

We talk more about New York. How we can make seeing each other work when I'm planning to kick-start things. "I have some shoots that are taking place out of the country in late January, but I'll be back in New York by mid-February. What do you think? Want to take a chance and see where this goes?"

I lift my shoulder nonchalantly. "I guess." I can't hold in the laughter as he pinches my side. "Of course, I want to see where this goes. Jack, I'm in this if you are."

He pulls us back so we're lying flat on the bed again and turns his head toward me. "I'm in, beautiful."

35

Jack

TIME MANAGES TO MOVE SMOOTHLY ALONG, EFFORTLESSLY even. The ease at which I meld into the life that Strutt's Peak offers is natural. My days are filled with editing photos and working through visuals on a few remote projects, I pepper in work from other ventures when needed, while my nights are choreographed between climbing with Benny, watching football with Law, and being wrapped up in conversations and moments with Everly.

Thanksgiving comes and goes in a blink. Dinner with Kathryn and Benny meant a burned turkey, but we managed to make the most out of all the sides and some good rolls. Benny escaped after a few hands of cards to catch a movie with friends. It was relaxed, and it felt comfortable, a new normal. The holiday ended at the Riggs' ranch where Everly's entire family, including her best friend, their neighbor David and his son, Callen, who is also sheriff, waited for me to join them for dessert. As usual, her father's spread of pies and after-dinner cocktails was over the top. Endless football games were playing on a wall of oversized screens. There were individual platters for every guest that included eight different variations of apple, pumpkin, buttermilk, and pecan pies. It came and went, but it felt so much like something I could get used to.

The light from outside is highlighting the edges of the covered windows in Everly's bedroom. There's just enough of a yellow tint to tell me it's well past sunrise and morning has officially broken through. I pull her warm body into me closer and burrow my face in her hair and neck. *Oranges.* No nightmares last night. That's more than two weeks without one. Somewhat of a record for me.

I notice my phone lighting up on Everly's bedside table and sit up to grab it. *4 Missed Calls Benny, 6 Unread Text Messages Benny.* I pull myself out of bed and kiss my girl on her head, trying my best not to wake her. It's only just after five in the morning.

"Are you sneaking out on me?" She catches my hand and pulls my arm back toward her.

"I was trying not to wake you. Benny is trying to get ahold of me, so I'm going to head over there to see what's going on." I sit and brush a few pieces of hair out of her face. *She's so beautiful. In so many ways, I'm learning.*

"Tell Benny I said hello." She smiles and kisses the inside of my wrist. I lean down and brush a quick kiss across her lips.

"I'll see you at the Tree Lighting tonight."

"Jack?"

I turn back and smile at her. "Yeah, beautiful?"

She just smiles and shakes her head. When I shut the door behind me, I can hear her laugh softly and I can't help but smile at the sound. I call Benny back as soon as my foot hits the stairs.

He picks up on the first ring. "Uncle Jack. Um, I'm sorry...I didn't know what else I should do. I just figured you would."

"You call me for anything, anytime. What's going on?"

"Mom. She hasn't been home. Sometimes she stays out late, but she didn't come home this morning like I thought she would, and now I think...shit, I don't know what to think." He takes a minute to finish and my stomach drops, like falling off a cliff, only to be jerked awake a moment later. The problem is, I'm not dreaming right now, and it's the first time I wish that I were. "I'm nervous that something happened to her. She usually calls or texts me that she's fine, but she's not answering her phone, it's just going straight to voicemail."

"I'm on my way to you, kiddo. Hang tight." Kathryn is not the kind of person to just stay out all night, at least as far as I'm aware. I'm not an idiot; maybe she has a one-night stand or something, but I know she isn't seeing anyone, so not answering her phone just makes it feel like something's off. I'm even pissed she left him home all night alone, if I'm being honest. I know he's seventeen, but he's still a kid in my book.

By the time we head down to the sheriff's station, Kathryn still isn't answering and we both have tried calling and texting repeatedly. We're past the point of waiting for her to surface. Every hour that ticks by makes me more anxious. I've run my hands through my hair so many times at this point that I look disheveled. I don't want to make Benny any more nervous, so I'm swallowing down all of the what-if assumptions. It's obvious that she didn't just lose track of time doing something.

"I've called the hospitals and clinics in Strutt's and into the next two counties. They don't have anyone with her description as a patient," Benny says quickly. "She drinks sometimes, so I called all the bars in the area too. Half of them didn't even answer, but the ones that did weren't much help." My chest tightens at his admission. The sheriff looks up at me to confirm what my nephew is saying. I feel blindsided. An outsider looking in at my sister's life. Out of the loop.

"She drinks *sometimes*...?" I just stare at him, clenching my jaw. He gives me an awkward one-shoulder shrug. "How bad, Benny?"

He doesn't say anything. My head is pounding. I pinch the bridge of my nose, trying to put pressure at the pain. How could I not know she was drinking heavily again? She squashed that issue years ago, right after Benny was born.

"How bad is it, Benny?" I raise my voice louder to speak above the ringing in my ears. I'm so upset, I'm on the verge of punching a wall. But I know that's not going to solve anything and my nephew doesn't deserve to be on the receiving end of it.

"You don't know the whole story with my dad, okay." He rubs his hands on his thighs, wiping off sweat and frustration. "It's bad," he chokes out, fearing that their secret can't be kept any longer. "I thought she was doing better since the last time she got in trouble for it, but she drinks. A lot. More than I think she should. More than Dad thought she should too." He looks up at me, finally meeting my eyes, and his are glassy. It makes mine water too. I pinch my eyes closed, letting a few tears escape, and quickly wipe them away. "She's never not come home for this long, though. I've had to help her to bed or the bathroom before, but she's never been away like this." I center myself, take a breath, and feel a new wave of responsibility hit me. My time to be angry and upset about this will have to come later. Now it's about finding Kathryn and making sure Benny has someone in his corner.

Sheriff Muldowney wrestles through some papers and asks us both questions about her behavior lately and a description of what she was wearing the last time Benny saw her. He brought a few pictures they can use.

"She hasn't been out of contact for more than twenty-four hours yet, which means I can't assign her as a missing person." The sheriff nods and continues to make sure we're on the same page. "I'm going to have my guys make some additional calls and take a trip down to County General Hospital just in case they're too slammed to do a good enough check. I want both of you to keep your phones on and alert me if she responds to any text or call."

The sheriff moves his attention to my nephew and says, "Benny, we're going to do our best to find her. If she's still out of contact by this evening, then we can escalate her to a missing person and that will allow me to reach beyond our county."

He shakes Benny's hand and then asks that I stay back for a minute. I wave Benny on to meet me in the car. "Listen, Jack, call the ex-husband and feel it out. If you catch a strange vibe, let me know. I can't do much right now since he's out of state, but I don't want to drag my heels on anything until she's back at home."

"I left him a voicemail already. I have a couple of other people I can call in the meantime." After shaking his hand, I rush out of the station to find my nephew looking like he's ready to start crying or hit something.

I drive his truck back to their apartment, and instead of filling the silence, I think about all the signs I might have missed. There's a gnawing feeling in my gut that this is going to come back to bite my sister in the ass. I'm almost sick at the thought of it being anything more than her passing out somewhere.

"I need to open the shop for a little while. We need to make some money and we're not going to do that if the shop stays closed today," Benny says, looking exhausted.

"Money isn't anything you need to worry about right now, Ben. If you guys get into a jam, I'm always here to help. Your mom knows that too. I have more than enough, so you guys don't have to add it as something else to worry about. If you want to open and take your mind off of things for a bit, then I'll help you."

He thinks about it for a minute. "I kind of want to go hiking. Mind if I call Michael and see if he's free?"

"Michael? You mean, Michael Riggs?"

"Yeah, he's been working with me on the indoor wall, and during the last climb, he mentioned he'd be up for going out on trails sometime. The weather might not be ideal right now, but-"

I cut him off. "I wouldn't mind, but Michael and most of the town are going to be at the tree lighting thing tonight. I know it's not really what you had in mind, but I have to take some photos to finish up the job for them, and I promised Everly I would go. Want to help me out? Come with me?"

He nods. "Yeah. That's good. I'd be down for that."

"Listen, your mom is going to be okay. And whatever is going on with her, I'm here to help. You're not alone in this. Got it?" I feel like I'm a hypocrite for even saying it, because I haven't been there for her or him. They have been alone.

He just nods and tears start to fall down his face. He whispers out, "Got it," as I wrap my arms around him. I don't remember when it happened, when my favorite little person turned into a grown man, but I want nothing more than to shield him from all of this. The harsh realities that life can throw at us. I feel like a piece of shit for not seeing what was going on with Kathryn sooner. That I was too distracted with my bullshit not to see my nephew shouldering a burden he has no business taking on. It feels too familiar. A responsibility that he shouldn't have had to take on. I feel like I've failed by allowing my history to repeat for my nephew.

My phone vibrates in my pocket. Text from an unknown number. As soon as I read it, I know exactly who it's from. I don't have time to deal with him today.

UNKNOWN NUMBER

Where's Kat? She hasn't answered me.

JACK

None of your fucking business.

UNKNOWN NUMBER

I'm serious. Where is she? She's not answering her phone.

JACK

Fuck. Off.

Well, it sounds like my dick-douche of a brother doesn't know where she is either.

UNKNOWN NUMBER

Real fucking mature. I'm worried about her.

JACK

Too late. Go fuck your hand, Jin.

36

Everly

"ANSWER YOUR PHONE. I'M TRYING TO HEAR THIS!" I LEAN over and pinch G's arm. "Did you hear me? Answer your damn phone, or turn it off."

My whisper-shouting gains a glare from Henry across the large table that my entire family is all sitting around. With fifty tables spaced throughout the outdoor tent and ten people at each table, this year's event is one of our biggest. My father started the annual tree-lighting event years ago when we were just kids, as a way to bring the community together and decorate our new offices for the winter season. It's not just about the holidays, but about the most lucrative time of year for our town.

Each year it grew in both attendance and details. Now, instead of lighting just one large Evergreen Tree that stands tallest on our office property, we light everything green that touches Riggs Headquarters. It's a lot. But that's how we roll.

Our building overlooks our cute and quaint downtown

of Strutt's Peak. And though it's a gondola stop from here to there, my father and the mayor decided to extend the lighting down the mountain to bring more attention to our town's businesses. So now we light up half the town and it's quite the sight.

"It's not my phone, Ev," she says.

"Then what's buzzing?" G just stares ahead at the stage, purposely not looking at me, and sips her dirty martini. It prompts me to take a sip of mine. And the buzzing starts again. Louder this time.

"Nudge Law and see if it's his," I tell her. She just looks ahead, ignoring me. "Never mind. Law. Law!"

Shushing echoes from the table behind us. Lenny McKenna doles out her best death glare and shifts to whisper something to her girlfriend that turns their attention back to me. Lord only knows what rumors that woman is wielding.

G just starts laughing quietly and leans back in her chair. "Tell me that noise is not coming from you, please?" I beg and then begin to realize exactly what that noise might be.

Leaning over, she smiles and whispers, "I didn't want to be bored. I found a pair of underwear in a gift bag in the office of my shop, so I figured I might as well make this night a little more exciting. What? Don't look at me like that. It's not even that loud." She shifts, uncrossing and recrossing her legs. "Oh, oh, oh!" She blows out a long breath. I watch as pink creeps up her neck and onto her cheeks. "I don't even know where they came from, but I put them on, and they started vibrating. It was like a sign from the sex gods. Stop looking at me like this is surprising behavior! I need another drink. And to move around. Want something?"

"You shouldn't be allowed out in public sometimes," I grumble. "I'll just come with you."

We both get up quietly from our table and make our way to the back of the tent toward the massive bar. It's the perfect time to survey the space as everyone's attention gathers forward. The opulence of the tent rivals the most lavish of ballrooms. Law and his team have outdone themselves. Four oversized chandeliers float above the center of the space, and what must be yards of draped white fabric weave throughout it, framing the warm light which gives the entire space a romantic feeling. Collections of multiple-sized pine trees are arranged around the space, each bathed in twinkling white lights and flocked with fake snow. Actual snow started to fall outside earlier this evening, making the night feel as if a little touch of magic might be surrounding us.

I pull my phone out of my purse to check if I've missed a call or text from Jack. I was expecting him to arrive earlier this evening. A cocktail hour kicked the festivities off, but he didn't show. I was looking forward to having him at my side before the event started. It's time to let the gossips collect their rumors correctly and see us work the room together.

I see a cocktail waitress out of the corner of my eye. "Would you mind bringing another round to everyone at my table, please?" I know my brothers are equal parts anxious and excited about the next part of the event to begin.

"Sure thing, Miss Riggs. Are you all set?" she asks. I nod and smile. "I have a quick question if you don't mind. Are *all* your brothers up for auction tonight?"

"They sure are. You plan on bidding?"

"Nah, too expensive for me right now. Henry is looking rather good these days, though. Much better than when we were in high school, that's for sure."

G interrupts, "Those drinks aren't bringing themselves over there, darlin'." She pulls her eyes from the waitress and starts to survey the room.

I smile at the waitress, hoping to gloss over the snarkiness of my best friend. Then I turn back to Giselle, who is flirting with the bartender. "G, that was rude."

G lifts her shoulder in a shrug and plucks a green olive out of her drink.

"There's a tall and handsome photographer staring at you so hard right now." G shimmies closer to me and nods her head toward the far side of the room. The sight of him elicits a full-body reaction. He looks incredible in an all-black Tom Ford suit, black shirt, no tie, with the top couple of buttons open. Black-tie be damned because that man right there does whatever the fuck he wants. And everybody pays attention. God, I feel like genuflecting, because I am so far gone for that man, ready to worship all of him. I can guarantee if I was able to pull my eyes away, there would be at least a dozen other people staring in appreciation. There are very few men built like him. Tall and fit is common, but not with his swagger and confidence. His dark hair is cut tight, and it accentuates the ocean blue eyes that I've been lost in for some time now. The smile that he wields as a reward for any daft human that might be brave enough to keep staring. He makes it impossible not to smile back. With one hand draped in his pocket and the other holding the lens of his camera, he is arrogantly very aware of what he does to me, and mouths, "Hi." The artistic, casual photographer vibe he's portrayed for weeks is completely gone. Now, he looks like a billion bucks.

A surge of excitement rolls through my body. If Jack was steel, then I was the flint. From the moment I saw this man, it was an attraction I couldn't escape. And I barely tried. Now when I'm near him, I feel excited and nervous and ready to lay it all out for him. *Let's just call it forever.* The moment we're in the same space, these sparks kick up and it's impossible to ignore. This fire that we've been playing with hasn't died down, it's only gotten stronger.

I wasn't sure if *this* existed. The idea of connecting with someone in this way feels like I'm a little crazy. It isn't something I was prepared to handle. Looking at a person and craving their touch as well as their time, wanting to spend hours together just to hear what else they have to say. It's not organized or planned. It's simple and chaotic, but even those contradicting words don't do it any justice. When I think about it now, there was no way to avoid him. The moment Jack set foot in Strutt's Peak, my life was irrevocably changed. Call it profound. Call it fate. Maybe even inevitable, but the most accurate, most right thing to label me is his. I am his.

I'm so in love with him, it's dangerous. It's a feeling that I haven't had the privilege of knowing before him, but I know that's what it is. Love. I have never thought about love this way. Logically, it wasn't probable, but the hopeful romantic in me did just that, it hoped. I hoped I'd catch a piece of it at some point in my life. And right now, I feel almost certain that this man was designed for me, and I for him.

37

Everly

THE SMELL OF SNOW AND BURNING WOOD SURROUND US AS glasses clink and break the spell that I've just floated under. My attention pulls back to the room, and I smile as I watch my father take the stage and welcome everyone who came to celebrate with our town. From locals to tourists and important families from across the county, all eyes are on the man that makes this town feel like something extra special.

The mayor flips the switch, and everyone erupts in a cheer as the town of Strutt's Peak lights up like an actual Christmas tree. Running the entire perimeter of our office property and down the mountain to all the businesses that line Main Street, white lights surge, and some even twinkle. The band starts to play one of my favorite Christmas songs and it douses everyone into the holidays. Just like that. With the flip of a switch. It's incredible. The kind of winter wonderland that sparkles and breathes life into a season that otherwise would feel cold and dark.

Within seconds, the magic I'm feeling comes to a nasty little screech and crash. The universe grabs me by the ankles, flips me over, and pile-drives it all into the ground. Three things happen at once and in what feels like slow motion. Less than five feet in front of me, Jack's smiling face and carefree demeanor wash away. Jin Cormick cuts off Jack's trajectory toward me with a smirk. I'm trying to understand why these two men are so affected by one another. The only thing that registers is they know I've slept with both of them. That much is clear.

Then, my father announces the upcoming auction. Giselle erupts with some kind of gasping hyena-like orgasm that half the room must have heard. Somewhere in all of that, Henry is holding up a remote control across the bar, which has now sent Giselle into an all-out rage that has her walking up to him and punching him right in the gut. He wasn't expecting it because he folds over, and she storms off.

"Jin?...The fuck?" Jack growls as he steps around from Jin's physical cock-block.

"Everly, please tell me you're not sleeping with him," Jin snarkily pleads in front of me, and my head rears back slightly at his bluntness. His tone is arrogant and not like the usual Jin I'm used to dealing with. I say nothing in response because aside from it being none of his business, I'm still working out why it would matter and how they know one another.

"Are you in town about Kat?" Jack asks, coming up beside me.

Jin shakes his head and smiles deviously. "I'm surprised she didn't tell you. I've been living here for a few years now.

That's how she found the coffee shop. I helped her get it off the ground."

Connecting the dots, or at least trying to, I say, "I didn't realize you knew Kathryn." I piece together who he must have chased after from our meeting the other day. He yelled out *Kat*, and then, I hadn't thought anything of it, but now maybe it makes more sense.

"My sister," Jack answers.

Jin corrects, "*Our*. She's our sister." He looks at me. "Adoptive sister. And this..." Holding back whatever he was planning to say, he continues. "And it looks like you're already acquainted with my brother." Nodding down at our clasped hands, he lifts a brow. Somewhere in the uproar, I must have grabbed it. "Looks like you've moved on, Everly. But not up, unfortunately."

Fuck my life.

Jack looks back and forth between Jin and me. He lets go of my hand when it registers what Jin just meant.

The tap of the microphone sounds around the tent, drawing everyone's attention to the stage. "Ladies and gentlemen, please get your checkbooks ready for tonight's annual auction." My father's voice bellows through the room, and Law comes up next to me. He must read the situation and instead of questioning, he pulls me from whatever fray is happening between the man I've been falling for and his apparent brother.

How has my boring life gone to this level of disorder in mere moments?

"Excuse me, gentlemen, I need to steal my sister away." Law wraps his arm around my shoulders and redirects us toward the stage. He leans down once we're out of earshot. "Whatever that was all about...it didn't look good, Ev."

I have no words to even respond to him.

"There're the rest of them. Everly and Lawrence, get on up here," my father beckons to us in a showman's tone.

I have to shed whatever I was just feeling and put on my best, most confident, town-badass boss face as we walk up the stage stairs to kick off tonight's auction.

"Ladies and gentlemen, as most of you are aware, we like to turn this night into more than just lighting things up and ringing in the holidays. Last year, between the silent auction and this, we were able to do quite a lot." He pulls up a card. "Last year, we fully funded the outdoor sports after-school and weekend program for any Strutt's Peak resident between the ages of five and eighteen. There was enough left over to provide transportation to and from for anyone who needed it. And we outfitted Strutt's Central High with new skiing and snowboarding gear for their outdoor activities programs."

My father searches my face, realizing I'm not totally present with what's happening up here, but he continues. "We also introduced a new equine therapy program led by my son, Michael, for children and adults at Strutt's Learning Center. And while I'm more than happy to auction off my children"—he gets a nice laugh out of that one—"no, really, who's going to finally take them off the market already?!"

Super funny, Dad.

"I'm a proud member of this community. Our pledge is always to do what is necessary so that the people in this town are thriving, happy, and feel cared for. With that being said, get your checkbooks out, and let's get this auction started."

The room erupts in a round of applause, but my attention is pulled to the two men I just left. I watch as Jack and

Jin bring their attention away from my father and back to one another as they continue their heated discussion. *Please don't let anyone throw a punch right now.* There's more going on there than it being about me.

"You all know my beautiful children, Everly, Henry, Michael, and Lawrence. They've done incredible things with our business and continue to surprise me with their talents, in the most wonderful ways." My eyes water as my father pauses and looks right at me. "I'd like to remind you that the winners will have twenty-four hours with whomever they've bid on. Additionally, I like to encourage you to know the areas of business my children are responsible for, their connections within the industries they are a part of, and to utilize your time, should you win it, wisely. This isn't just about a date or the exclusive resort reservations that come along with it."

The crowd laughs and a few shouts chime in, saying, "Whatever you say, Ash!"

Another person from the far side of the room hoots, "Law, you ready for me!?"

Law leans over with a wide, fake smile and through his teeth, he whispers, "Remind me why we say yes to this every year? I don't have a good feeling this time."

"First up is my beautiful daughter, Everly. As Vice President of Operations, she's done incredible work at transforming Riggs Outdoor into what it is today. Working her way from the mailroom to the boardroom, my darling girl holds our family together, and can go toe-to-toe with the best of you all on the slopes." A bit of a laughing murmur breaks out around the crowd. Almost every daredevil in this room has been on a run with me for a time or two.

"You name the outdoor sport and she'll beat your time.

And she'll do it more gracefully," While my father wants to keep the "advertising" of each of us about our business expertise and the outdoor sports we play, most of the bidders want a date and dibs on the all-inclusive resort stay that comes with our twenty-four hours together. "As always, Riggs Outdoor will match each of the final bids."

I look back around the room. I'm not seeing Jack and Jin in the space I left them, and now I'm anxious that they took whatever was brewing between them outside.

"Let's start the bidding at one-hundred dollars. I've got one in the back. Can I see two, two-hundred up front." My father carries on the bidding while the crowd builds the dollar amount. Within a few minutes, and a four-way volley, the bidding hits five thousand.

"Ten-thousand," a deep, familiar voice yells out. The crowd makes an exaggerated gasp, and everyone draws their attention to Jack in the far corner of the bar.

"Fifteen," Jin responds with a raise of his left hand.

What is he fucking doing?

My father shifts uncomfortably and looks at me quickly, almost asking silently what the hell is going on.

Dad, if I knew, I'd tell you.

"That's fifteen thousand from Mr. Jin Cormick. Do I hear fifteen-five?" my father croons through the room.

Standing no more than a few strides apart, both men are squared off to one another, and I'm feeling a wave of disgust work its way through me. They both know what they're doing. A public pissing match at my expense, and I don't like it. The room sees it as friendly banter by two men with deep pockets for one of Strutt's most eligible, but the way I see it, it's something else entirely. This is about them, and now I'm just along for the ride.

Jack yells out, "Twenty-five."

"Fifty," Jin responds.

Jack kicks back the rest of the vodka in his glass and yells back, "Seventy-five."

My father looks at me, asking if he should call it right here or let them keep going. Instead of responding with a nod or shrug, I raise my arm and shout, loud enough to pull everyone's attention away from the battling douchebag behavior in the back.

"One-Hundred thousand."

"Accepted. Miss Everly Riggs wins her own bid at one-hundred thousand dollars."

The room is quiet. My brothers peer over to me, not understanding what's going on. And before I can think twice about any of it, I watch as Jack and Jin rush out of the tent with the sheriff.

I just gave Lenny McKenna enough gossip for the next three months.

38

Jack

"Mr. Deacon. Jack? Jack, please come with me." Sheriff Muldowney taps my shoulder just as Everly shouts one-hundred thousand dollars to knock our bids out. I can't even process what I just did, but I know it wasn't good. More than that, it also has very little to do with her, and we just dragged her into our decades-long list of bullshit.

"Sheriff, what's going on? Is it Kathryn?" Jin yells out behind me as we exit The Riggs Event. "I have a right to know what's going on here. She's important to me."

"You have a funny way of showing it, you piece of shit," I growl out.

"Gentlemen, I don't know what your history is, but right now, I'm here to speak with Jack regarding his sister, yes. If you'd like Mr. Cormick to come along down to the station, that's up to you. Otherwise, Mr. Cormick, I'd ask that you back up and let me conduct my business."

"Is she okay?" I rush out.

"I'm about to pick her up and thought it would be smart to have you with me. She's okay, but I got a call from one of my deputies about twenty minutes ago. He was called out for a drunken disorderly at Grizzly's Tavern. It's a dive just outside of Strutt's."

Muldowney looks at me, and I can see a flash of empathy coming with the next phrase. I've seen that before. "She's in rough shape, Jack. And I know you don't want to hear this, but you need to." He pauses, looking at Jin and then back to me. "This isn't the first time we've gotten a call about her. I didn't want to say anything earlier with your nephew present, but she's been on several "do not serve" lists in town. This is the first time we picked her up from Grizzley's, but I'd say it's about the third or fourth time overall that my guys have been called out to bring her home."

I look over at Jin. Just by the horrified look on his face, I can tell he had no idea. "I didn't..." He chokes back tears. "I didn't know. I mean, I knew she struggled when Benny was younger, not long after she had been married, but I thought it was managed. I didn't know."

I feel nauseous and out of breath. Like I've been kicked in the gut, knocking the wind out of me. How didn't I know about my sister having a drinking problem, especially at a level like this? I feel helpless. In the dark. That's not a feeling that sits well with me. I had one job, and that was to keep her safe. I've been failing at it for years, apparently. But, right now, it's not about me or how I've failed her. It's about getting her home.

"Let's go get her, Sheriff." I nudge my chin at Jin. "He can come."

39

Everly

WHAT AM I MISSING? THIS EVENING WENT FROM HAPPINESS with a twinge of excitement to a raging pile of hot garbage. What total shitbag thing earned me the karma of Jack and Jin being brothers? How would I know any of that? It's the kind of bullshit hand I'm dealt, just as I find the exact person I've been holding back for.

"Adopted brothers? Ev, I'm going to go silver lining for just a second...there's probably a limited number of women in this world that could check off 'fucked brothers' from their bucket list." The death stare that I throw at my best friend leaves her unaffected.

"G, *that* was never on my bucket list." I tilt my head back and stare up at the cold night sky. Plumes of white puff out from my mouth as I try to replay tonight's insanity.

She grumbles. "It was on mine. Ticked that off in college, but they knew it was like a tandem, tag-in kind of thing, so whatever."

I take another swig of the limoncello and pass it back to her. "I haven't heard that one. You'll need to tell me the details when I'm not wallowing in my own bullshit someday."

"Ladies, are we staying out here for a while?" my dad yells out from the kitchen door. We've been out on his patio around the firepit for the last hour. I'm sure we're keeping him up, but I don't want to see my brothers right now and delve into their bullshit tonight. There's something comforting about being at the home you grew up in when your life takes on shitstorm status.

"Ash, are we cramping your style? You have a hot date coming over or something?"

My dad just shakes his head and smiles at her. "Giselle, please. Hot dates are the last thing on my mind. I was only going to bring you girls heated blankets if you're going to be out here longer."

"Yes, please!" G yells back at my dad. "Oh! And is there any chance you can make us some of your popcorn? I need something to balance out what I'm drinking."

"You got it. Anything else, princess?"

"Nope. Love you, Ash!" G is one of few people who can order my father around and have him answer easily with only yeses.

Sitting with silence between us and a crackling fire, my mind drifts to places that make me feel so uneasy. *Can Jack really be angry with me?* It's not something he has a right to be mad about. Visually, they look nothing alike other than the fact that they're both tall with dark hair. There is no way I could have known, which honestly is what makes it all the more frustrating. Whatever bad blood is between them, it doesn't need to involve me. It shouldn't. Jin and I were over before I even met Jack. It may have happened the same day, but regardless. One door closed and another opened.

"You're having a big conversation with yourself right now, huh?" G chimes in, breaking my thoughts away.

"Whatever was happening with him tonight wasn't all about me. I know Callen came in and brought him to the police station, but I have no idea why. I'm angry that he's not answering his phone. How do you go from feeling like the most important person to someone to just being cast aside?"

"I think you're jumping to conclusions too quickly. Before you think the worst, just wait for him to call you back or text you. Give him the benefit of the doubt, and go from there, but stressing out over it tonight isn't going to make anything better."

"Thanks." I smile and look up at her.

"You never have to thank me, Ev. You know that, but you're welcome." She shifts and sniffs the air. "Oh my deliciousness, I can smell the popcorn from out here."

A beat later, my dad is delivering two big bowls of popcorn and heated blankets. After depositing a kiss on each of our heads, he turns in for the night. After the success of the evening from his perspective, along with each of his kids having their level of chaos happen during the auction, I'm sure the old man is ready to turn in.

"Honestly, I never looked at the big house and land as something I ever wanted, but this..." G shakes her head and smiles at me. "Heated blankets you can plug into a chair around a firepit in the heart of winter is next level boujee shit right here. I need this whole setup in my life for forever." We both start laughing. The little luxuries we have sprinkled into our lives are pretty incredible.

"So are we going to talk about it?" I ask as I peek over my

bowl of popcorn toward my friend. While my evening was a bit jilting, hers was somewhat unexpected.

"Nope." She pops the *P* and carries on drinking limoncello and eating the seasoned popcorn.

"You punched Henry. Is he the one that gave you those ridiculous panties?"

"I said no, Ev. I'm not ready to talk about anything regarding your brother. I'd rather not have to lie to you, so let's just leave it. Can we?"

"We can leave it. Tell me when you're ready." I lean over and squeeze her hand.

She wipes a tear from the corner of her eye quickly. "But we can talk about how Michael is going to prom with Lenny McKenna's kid."

"Oh my gosh, can you believe that? I don't think I've ever seen Michael get more flustered in his entire life. He was practically begging one of us to bid on him. It's too good!"

"I paid her. Gracie McKenna. I paid her fifty bucks last month to clean out my office, bathroom, and waiting area. She did such a great job, I'm having her do it every couple of weeks. At least I know how she's spending her money now." We both start laughing uncontrollably. The look on my brother's face when nobody else would bid against Gracie McKenna was a mix between sheer panic and chaotic embarrassment. For someone who hates to be in front of a crowd or given extra attention, this was probably the epitome of people gawking at the sight of an eighteen-year-old kid bidding for a grown man to take them to prom.

Michael will make sure she has a fantastic time and will be nothing but respectful, but I think he was hoping for someone his own age or older to be his bidder. Not an eighteen-year-old with a very obvious, long-time crush.

"Law is going to end up cleaning horse stalls. Mr. Burwell is still pissed off at him for shaving dicks on his herd of sheep when he was in high school. Every year Mr. Burwell bids, but this year he must have convinced others to cap it off."

"Law is lucky that it's an old man that wants revenge and not one of the many girls he's fucked and screwed over in this town." I just nod, because G is right.

"You're right. He's a bit of a slut".

"Hey! No slut-shaming here. Law likes to play the field. I respect that. It's not his fault he has a big appetite. I don't think he promises them anything other than fun. If he does, then yes, he deserves the wrath, but I think that's why it's just the old man that wants to torture him. I think most of the women bidding were hoping for a piece of the good time."

We sit for a little longer. Both of us stop taking sips. Our popcorn ran out when we stopped listing all of the out-of-towners we didn't recognize.

"Nope." G just looks up at the sky again.

"I didn't say anything."

"You were going to, and I'll say this once and only here. Your night ended up being a bit of a mess, and I'm taking pity on you, but if you ask me again, I won't get into it. Deal?"

I nod.

But then she continues. "I saw the wildebeest in the bathroom earlier. The redheaded dickbag was talking to her minions about how she was going to get Henry back after she won the bid tonight. I remember what he was like after her, Ev. It wasn't good. As much as I hate him. And I do. I fucking hate that smug meathead. I won't allow her to come back into his life and destroy him again. No one deserves that woman. Even my worst enemy, apparently."

I just stare at my friend. She's trying hard to mask it, but I see it. She cares about him. More than I bet she even realizes. The thing I learned about her a long time ago was to let her talk to you about it, never approach her. She'll spook and never speak of it again. So instead of letting on, I just smile at her and appreciate that she saved Henry from some destruction at the hand of the worst human on the planet.

"Not to mention, if anyone is going to make him miserable for a full twenty-four hours, it's going to be me. That fucker has no idea what he's in for!"

We shuffle inside and both decide to head home, even though the sun is starting to peek through the horizon line. I want to curl up in my bed, sleep the last day away, and figure out my next move from there.

When I finally make it home and wrap myself in my cozy bed, I toss and turn for hours. It feels empty and things feel so uneasy. I'm craving Jack's arms. I send him one more text before I fall asleep and hope I hear back once I wake up.

40

Jack

"What do you mean, you don't know?! How could you not know you have a problem, Kathryn? When you're making up lies and leaving your son home alone for days, *that* should have been the first clue." I'm seething as my sister tries to talk me out of why picking her up at a local bar so drunk she couldn't stand isn't her fault.

"Jack, I'm saying I don't know what to do. I know I have a problem. I've tried fixing it for years. Years! I never thought I'd end up like this. With my brother staring at me like I'm a fucking disappointment. And my son..." She gestures to my nephew across the room, crying as he watches us lash into one another. "My son is crying because of me. Do you know the level of failure I feel right now? No, you don't, because you're not a father. You have no idea what my life is like, so don't stand there judging me right now."

I drag my hands down my face. I've pulled my hair so hard, I'm surprised I don't have bald spots. I'm so angry, but

I know that it's not helping right now. I'm not even sure if I'm madder at her or myself for not seeing this.

A text comes in from Everly.

> Is everything okay? I saw you leaving with the sheriff.

"What are you, texting your girlfriend right in the middle of this?" she yells. "What *is* it about that woman? She has you and Jin by the balls, and you're both too stupid to see it."

I can't deal with any of that right now either. My mind is so focused on my sister, I can't even unpack the idea that she was with Jin at some point and where that leaves us. Jin, that fucking piece of shit, is a constant thorn in my side. Even now, I bet he has something to do with Kathryn flying off the handle.

"Everly doesn't have anything to do with this, Kathryn. We're talking about you."

"No, we're talking about my life and that woman is fucking herself into the middle of it, with two of the most important...You don't even see it! I fucking saw them together; he was fawning all over her." I'm not interested in who she wants to blame or change the subject on, but I know that's what she's trying to do. Part of me also is clawing at the idea that the woman I've fallen for has or had a relationship with my fucking stepbrother.

"Enough! Kathryn, enough!"

"I need help, Jack. I thought coming here was going to fix all this for me, but it's just made everything worse. I can't control my emotions. One thing triggers me, then I'm drinking. I'm so tired of being in this spot. Hating myself. Feeling guilty and then just pretending like it didn't happen. I'm exhausted."

My sister, when sober, is smart and articulate, but her drunk last night was an entirely different person. One I didn't recognize. Aside from slurring and barely standing, she was belligerent. We've been talking in circles for hours now, the sun having made its appearance hours ago. Nobody slept, just cried and yelled.

"Mom, we can check you into a program. Maybe start you on a better course," Benny's voice chimes in.

Kathryn starts crying harder. "What kind of failure of a parent am I that my son has to say those words to me? Jesus, I'm such a piece of shit. I'm so sorry, baby. You don't deserve any of this." She looks up at me through tears, and I feel like a kid all over again. "Just like Mom, huh, Jack?"

I move to wrap my arms around her, but Benny moves faster. I hang back to give them a moment. And instead, I say, "You're nothing like her. Don't ever put yourself in that category, Kathryn." How could she think that? She's not her. "Let me call around and see what programs there might be. What do you think about taking some real time off, just you, working with people that can give you tools that'll support you in making better choices." It's not a fix, but a start.

Her bloodshot eyes find mine above Benny's shoulders. Before she can say anything, I decide that there is nothing more important right now than making sure these two are cared for. A job that I've grossly let fall so far away that my sister is about to check into rehab, leaving my nephew virtually parent-less in the meantime.

"I'm going to stay here for a while with Benny. I'll make sure he gets through until the end of school and stays active with climbing." All of my businesses and responsibilities that need to be tended to in New York can be done remotely from here, and anything that can't be, Luce can fill in during my absence.

Kathryn nods yes over Benny's shoulder as tears continue to spill down her cheeks. "God, what about the shop?"

"The shop will be fine. We'll keep it running, but I'm going to put up some help signs." I'm not sure if I should mention this or not, but while everything is on the table right now, what other harm could it do?

I shift my weight and take a breath for what I'm going to say next. I need to pay attention or at least find some inkling as to how Jin could have set all of this chaos in motion.

"Jin came with me when the sheriff told me where you were. He left before you saw him. I didn't want him upsetting you any more. I know it had something to do with him. Always does. Why is he here, Kat?" She looks up at me.

Instead of answering, she directs her attention to Benny. "Benny, sweetheart, can you get me some aspirin and my fuzzy socks out of my top drawer?"

Once he leaves to grab her requests, she shifts uncomfortably. I already know just by her body language that what I assumed is right. It was him that caused her to tailspin into last night's bender. For the life of me, I don't understand why. They've always been more of a support for each other than anything. She knows better than to bring him up with me, but I didn't think he'd cause her any harm. Not like this.

"What did he do?" I ask and shift forward in my chair, leaning closer to her. I'm not sure I want to know, but if he hurt her, then I'm going to make it right.

"It's not something he did to me. It was me. A reaction. I saw him with Everly Riggs two days ago, and it just looked like more than friends or colleagues to me." I continue to stare at her. My anger is surfacing because the idea of Everly spending time with Jin after she and I have been together is already making my thoughts drift. "Why? I know it's not on my behalf that you'd be upset about that. Everly and I just started seeing each other. It's still new. So what is it about Jin, Kathryn?"

"You're seeing her? What does that mean?" She huffs and mumbles to herself. "No, you know what. I'm not surprised. You two fight over everything. Why not another woman. Fucking typical."

I don't miss what she says: *another.* He and I have been fighting over my sister's attention for years. "Don't change the subject. Why would seeing Jin with Everly fuck with you so much that you flew off the handle? And don't even think about lying to me right now."

She sits still and doesn't respond. We remain like that, in silence, for at least five minutes. I know Benny is taking far longer to get her aspirin and socks, but the kid is smart, and he knows we need to hash things out without him being witness to it. She's so stubborn, or maybe she's just choosing not to lie to me.

When she refuses to even look up from her hands that are picking away at her nail polish, I decide to fill the quiet. "We have a lot to talk about, so I don't know why you're choosing to say nothing. Like, why is Jin backing the coffee shop? I could have done that for you. You only needed to ask. Financially, you don't need to worry about anything. You know that. But why ask him? Why haven't you mentioned to me that he was even living here, in Strutt's Peak?" I know she's not going to answer me, and I'm getting madder by the minute. "What is it about our brother, Kat, that's gotten us to this moment?" At that, Benny comes back into the room, obviously overhearing some of it, and shoots me a glare to stop.

Over the next few hours, and with the help of Luce, I manage to get Kathryn set up with a program just over the state border in Wyoming. It'll be her home for the next three months. If she can focus on herself for a chunk of time before she folds the stresses of her life back into it, then maybe she'll feel better equipped to battle this.

I also make a few additional calls, one to her ex-husband again to let him know what's going on, specifically for Benny's sake, and then another call to Jin. My brother offered to pay for her treatment. I don't want his money involved in this and I demand that he sign the coffee shop and property that it's on over to her. To my surprise, he does, without me offering to buy it from him or a fight. Kathryn is going to need a job and to keep busy when she's back. Losing the shop is not an option and well, he got her into the mindset of owning the place, but I don't want him holding any claim over her.

Around six, I realize we've gone all day without eating, but my stomach sinks when I think about how I'm finally going to respond to Everly. There's so much baggage I'm bringing to the table right now. So much that I need to focus on and adjust my life for.

How could a single day change so much? We just talked about keeping this thing going between us, but I don't know that I have the capacity to keep this part of my life moving and start a relationship with her. I don't do relationships anyway, and this is a good reason not to start now. I could never equally split my time so that someone wouldn't be neglected. I can't allow that to be Benny. I type out a text that

I already know is a mistake, but I can't think or do anything else right now. I'm drained.

> **JACK**
>
> Kathryn was in trouble and is going through some heavy stuff. I need to focus on her and Benny for the foreseeable future. I'm sorry.

It all feels like too much. When things get complicated, that's when it's time for me to step away. I don't like leaving things so unsettled, but I need to focus my attention on the people who need me. Right now, that's Benny and Kathryn. I've already let them down. I wasn't there or aware, and it was almost too late. I'm not going to feel that way again and be the reason my nephew is left to figure this out. I never want him to be left to pick up the pieces like I was as a kid.

> **EVERLY**
>
> You're telling me this in a text?
>
> Fucking coward. After all that we've said to each other? I'm not going to chase you. If you want to talk to me, you know where I'll be.

She's right. I am. I'm too afraid to pull any energy away from the family that needs me. Too afraid to show her exactly how I've failed my sister, and too proud to admit that I'm hurt by any kind of relationship she's had with my brother. But most of all, I'm terrified of what I'd be asking of her if I were to pull her even further into my life. It's less collateral damage to leave us as a happy memory. I can't handle failing her too.

41

Everly

IT'S BEEN A WEEK SINCE I CALLED JACK A COWARD. AND HE responded with silence. Not a fight or an explanation. No words of any kind that let me know that what he was asking for was space or support. Just a text that shoved me aside. I don't think I'm a needy person, but let's be honest, every person that's in it with someone, in a real relationship, needs reassurance when there's chaos. Maybe that's the answer that I keep trying to avoid. It wasn't anything other than some great sex and a pinch of intimacy. That and the connection that I've been craving. I got what I asked for, something that punched me in the gut, set my world on fire, and it all ended up being nothing more than temporary. Exactly what I originally planned for, and what I didn't end up wanting. He turned into so much more.

The days have flown by, but at night I'm stuck, practically paralyzed with thoughts of him. How can two people go from being naked and memorizing things that can make a dimple pop to being nothing to one another? That's the motion that always makes me feel helpless, the everything, and then the nothing. Add in lack of clarity and barely any closure, and it's a recipe for feeling like total and utter shit. I'm not a fragile woman or one who stares at the past for too long, but I was falling in love with that man. How do you walk away from a fall? I can only assume, from my minimal experience, that you don't. You keep falling until you hit the ground. I wasn't done falling, and here I am, already hurt, and I'm not even sure I've hit the ground yet.

In a handful of days, I've moved along the entire spectrum of feelings from hurt to sadness, right into anger and self-improvement. I function much better when I'm pissed off, and I wish I could stay in that headspace. Anyone from the outside looking in would think that life is running as efficiently as ever. I beast-mode at the gym with Michael two times a day. I chopped my hair shorter, so now it sits right above my shoulders. I even made the final decision that I'm going to relocate to Manhattan for the next few months to get my apparel brand off the ground. I think I decided it right after my father gave his blessing for it, but I put all the pieces in motion this week to make it happen. Find something to focus on and annihilate it. That's what surviving a fractured heart looks like, right?

I'm wrapping up work at Riggs Outdoor as the vice president, but I'm officially the proud lead designer and owner of my apparel line, Apre´s Eve. I have partners lined up, a marketing plan ready to be executed, and an exclusive deal set already with two big department stores. My first task as soon as I get my real estate underway will be to build a small team that's motivated and hungry enough to grind away some long hours.

"I have more than enough room for you to stay at my apartment in SoHo, Ev. I'm not going to be there unless you want me to be, so you could consider it yours for now."

"Jin, I want my own place, but thank you for the offer. There's a building I'm looking at when I arrive tomorrow morning that I think will be perfect. It's enough room so I can make it my studio as well. At least until we can find a storefront. And it's in SoHo."

"You said we. Does that mean you're accepting the offer?" He leans back into the counter, watching me work my way around the room.

I stop for a minute and look up at Jin. The man that stirred the pot, tried to mark territory he had no business in claiming, and who set my current course of a career in motion. I'm pissed off at him, and if this was a few days ago, I probably would have called him a lot of names before letting him through the door.

"Everly, if looks could kill, the one you're giving me should have me drop dead any minute. And before you say anything else, I know I owe you an apology. I knew what I was doing at the event, making it sound like we were an item and then bidding on you. It was shitty to put you in the middle of the mountains of shit I have with Jack."

I've been waiting for that apology since the moment he called and told me he was coming over to discuss his offer. "I'm very good at compartmentalizing when it's necessary, and with you, it's necessary because I think what you did was a real asshole move, Jin. That wasn't being a friend to me. That was being a prick. I'm not ready to forgive you for it, but I am ready to move on. I want your investment, and I want your attention on building my brand, but that's all. We're colleagues and there are no more lines to cross, so please remember that. I do not consider you a friend right now. I'll take you on at the full investment you outlined, but you're only getting a twenty-five percent share."

"Everly." He smiles to cut me off.

"I'm not done. You can take it or leave it. I don't need the start-up capital and I don't need your real estate in SoHo, but I do need your eye for building this brand properly. And I need your operations and fulfillment connections to be able to execute the contracts I've already signed. If you still want it at half the percentage that you were originally asking, then I'll move forward. If not, then you can leave, Jin."

He lounges back in his chair and watches me as I fold the last few garment samples into my bag. "You can ask me about him, you know." I don't look up. My chest feels heavy even at the mention of him. I don't know how I feel today, but the thought of hearing his name is already making my eyes blurry. "There's a lot he's dealing with right now. Kathryn is away in rehab, so he's stepping in to be there for Benny. You heard from him?"

"I'm not talking about him with you. But I know what's going on with Kathryn, and no, I haven't heard from him."

He mumbles, "Stupid asshole." And while I agree, I'm not looking for his support when it comes to anything involving Jack. "He'll be sticking around here for a while. In Strutt's."

I already knew that Jack had planned to stay in Strutt's Peak for longer than his contract with Rigg's Outdoor, at least through Christmas, but since his sister's issues with alcohol came to the surface, I had been so consumed with our relationship that I didn't think that it meant he'd be in my town long after I left.

"My brother is complicated. You already know at least that much, but for what it's worth, I'm sorry I made a mess of things for you that night, even before the sheriff showed up about Kat. I knew you two were seeing each other, and I'll be honest, Jack and I don't mix. We never have, but it was wrong of me to insinuate that we were anything more than friends at that point."

I zip up the final garment and look around the pool house. With all of my design materials gone, the space looks bare and kind of sad.

"It's a deal, Everly. At your demands." He moves to shake my hand and finishes it with a hug. "We're going to make a lot of money together."

"Oh, I know." I smile at him, still not happy with him, but mature enough to move past everything.

The sound of the sliding door opening has me turning. Something had me knowing it was Jack before I saw him. The jaded part of my heart wants me to think that it's a helpful warning, being able to know whenever he might be near, but the still hopeful part of my heart knows that it's something more than a warning, maybe a reminder that if we can figure out our way through this, he's made for me.

Jack raises his voice. "The fuck are you doing here, Jin?"

Jin doesn't respond, just laughs to himself, shakes his head, and grabs his jacket off the chair as he stands.

I turn to Jin, ignoring Jack's intrusion. "I'll call you once I'm settled. We can discuss what comes next from there."

Jack stands in the doorway in his running gear of gray sweatpants, a black hoodie, and sneakers, taking in the scene. Jin leans into my ear and whispers, "Give him hell, okay?" I smile and watch as he leaves, knocking Jack's shoulder as he passes him out the door. They say something to each other, but I can't hear it. I don't want to. It's not about Jin anymore.

Jack settles his glare at me. "The fuck was he doing here, Everly?"

"*That's* how we're doing this, you asshole?" My body is buzzing with adrenaline. If he wants to start angry, then I've got plenty to dish out. *Here we go.*

"I've left you numerous text messages. A voicemail. I even emailed you to make sure you were able to at least deliver the work that you've already been paid for, I might add, but you know what I've gotten in return? Nothing. No response. Not even a damn emoji, Jack."

He drags his hands over his face and through his hair, then slamming the door behind him, he stalks toward me. I'm so mad, and a barrage of other emotions that I can't process. My body is shaking, shivering like a snap of cold just passed through the room. I know he's going to try to touch me, and I don't want it. I can't. I don't trust that my anger won't hold steady with him. I'll make bad choices that I'll end up hating myself for, so instead of moving away, I hold my ground and put out my hand to stop him.

"Don't."

He looks at me and then around the space, noticing that it's practically cleared out but a few boxes stacked near the kitchenette, along with my garment bags. "Where's all your stuff?"

I shake my head. "Nope. You don't get to ask questions. What are you doing here, Jack?"

He steps closer, so that my outstretched hand, meant to stop him from coming closer, is flattened on his chest. I push him off, but instead of staying back, he holds it there. I can feel his heart racing, his chest moving wildly up and down beneath it. My anger starts to crack.

"I don't know what I'm doing. I know I'm fucking this up." He lowers his voice. "I just keep fucking things up by what I do or don't do." He rubs the back of his neck and pulls at his hair, so visibly frustrated with himself. "I'm trying to be there for the people that need me. But I can't stay away from you any longer. Look at me."

I keep my eyes on his hands instead. I don't want to look at him, because he's either going to kiss me or tell me good-bye, and both of those things I'm not prepared for. I don't have the bad bitch energy I need for a confrontation like this. I want to be mad at him. I want to be understanding. I want to run away. I want to run into his arms. I'm all over the map and I have no idea what's right.

"Look at me, beautiful."

42

Jack

I STARTED MY RUN OVER AN HOUR AGO WITH NO PLAN IN MIND other than to run and sweat. When I'm not working or spending time with Benny, then I'm punishing my body by running, lifting, or climbing. Anything to numb out the anger and shame I feel for not seeing what was happening to my sister, what I'm doing by pushing Everly away, the carelessness in which I didn't pay enough attention so that my nephew was left with too much adulting when he should have been enjoying being a kid. It's a repeated spiral of guilt that I can't seem to stop.

Today was no different, but I got lost in my thoughts and without even realizing where I was going, I ran right to her. *What have I been doing?* I'm so fucked up by what's been happening with my family that I've completely fucked over the best woman to come into my life. I'm punishing myself. I don't deserve to be with someone like her, and she shouldn't want to be with someone like me.

Broken, useless, and chuck-full of baggage that just won't go away.

But I'm here now and as soon as her beautiful hazel eyes meet mine, I move so quickly it doesn't give her any time to overthink. My mouth collides with hers and though I know she's upset with me, she doesn't push me away. How could kissing her feel so good?

It's familiar and comfortable, mixed with a levity that pulls a measure of stress right from my shoulders. I move my lips across her jaw and back, and she pulls my bottom lip into her mouth. What was urgent and riddled with purpose turns into a vehement battle of our tongues. Messy, angry, and I don't think anymore, I just need to feel her.

My hands wrap around her waist, and I hold her flush against my body. If I move too far away, I'm afraid she'll never want me back. I glide my hands down and scoop her up from under her thighs. A small yelp escapes her, clearly not expecting me to hoist her up in my arms. She wraps her legs around my hips, arms around my neck, never stopping her lips from working soothingly over mine, and everything I've been beating myself up over, the worry and anger, they fall away, and I feel like everything is as it should be. Me here, with her.

I've craved this incredible woman every moment of every day that I've stayed away. Right now, my reasons seem irrelevant. I'm not about to unpack any of it, because nothing else matters but feeling her. The way she's moving, I'm not sure if she wants me or hates that she wants me, but neither of us is stopping.

She moves her hands down my body with intention, into my sweatpants, and pushes them down enough to pull my cock from out of my briefs. We have the same plan, fuck each other, and forget about everything other than how our bodies feel when we're together, the release we've been longing for, the warmth.

Her skirt makes it easy on me, and I push it up her hips, tugging her wet panties aside, and the feel of that alone makes me ache. She drags my cock through her wetness, up and down, mixing our arousal. With abandon, she lifts her legs, using them to pull me closer, and claws at my shoulders to move faster. She thrusts her hips forward, and I impale her in one fast movement, pinning her into the wall we've moved toward. I'm buried to the hilt, immediately dizzy with my desire for her, never wanting to stop. But I pull back to stare at her, making sure this is what she wants.

"Don't look at me like you have things to say. I'm not interested in talking right now, Jack. I only want to feel you. Nothing else."

So, instead of words, I move my hips slowly and press into her even deeper, punishing her for being as cold to me as I have been to her. Once she starts moaning, I know I'm hitting her exactly where she wants. I reach my hand around and grab her jaw, pulling her mouth to mine.

"Fuck." I pull back to look at her. There's only passion there, no forgiveness. She bit my lip, and I can taste copper.

"Don't fucking tease me right now. I want you to fuck me, Jack."

I kiss her again and do as she says, pulling back almost completely out of her and thrusting back into her again, hard. It shoves her body against the wall, closing any space that's left open between us. It's the most in control I've felt in days. She's giving that to me. Over and over, I push into her, drawing out screams and moans from both of us. Nothing is loving or sensual about this, but it's exactly what we both need from the other. A punishment, not to her, but only to myself. I don't get to make love to her right now. I've lost that privilege. With a sheen of sweat on her face and neck, I lick down, while keeping pace.

"Don't stop. Don't you fucking stop, Jack," she says between breaths.

Within moments, she clenches around me as her orgasm takes over. She moans so loudly in my ear that a warmed chill cuts through my body, and I follow her over the edge. I come so hard, I lose any inhibitions and yell, "No! Fuck, you feel so good." I have no control over what I'm saying, so I stifle the animal that she draws out of me and quiet the love that is simmering just beneath the surface. Afraid of letting it bubble over, I sink my teeth into her shoulder. It's not hard enough to hurt her or draw blood, but just enough to feel as much of her as I can. Claim her.

We lean against one another, breathing heavily, fighting ourselves to savor this and hold back from returning to this moment, the room, whatever awaits us next. I can't bring myself to move out of her. I'm afraid of what that all just meant. I'm unraveling. I'm not okay, and I'm not about to drag her down with me.

When we let go of one another, that'll be it. We both know it. I don't know how to tell her to wait for me. Maybe after all of this with my family, when it smooths over, I'll be ready for her. How do you tell someone you *might* be ready for them later? And how do you do it without a timetable? She deserves more than that. More than me, and my fucked up perspective. The shit cards I've been shuffling around for my whole life.

I steady myself for what I'm about to say. "I came here to give you closure. To give me closure, because I don't have enough right now to focus on you and what we could be together." She leans back to look me in the eye. She's trying to understand, but if I can't understand it, how on earth can I expect her to get me? "My nephew and my sister are the ones who need me, and I need to pay attention now. I've pushed them to the sidelines for long enough and now after everything that has happened...Kathryn's is a recovery program a state away while Benny has to be in therapy, and I need to make sure that kid finishes school and doesn't fall down the same holes I've fallen down. I am supposed to be responsible for her, and I fucked up. I didn't see what was going on right in front of me."

We finish untangling from each other. I tuck myself back into my pants while she moves her skirt down and over her thighs. She grabs a towel to clean herself up, and after a minute, with so much silence in the air, she looks up at me and smiles. "I love you, you know." My heart feels like it stops before picking up its speed.

What? After that, she's going to tell me she loves me?

She tilts her head, studying my movements, and there aren't any. She's left me in a paralyzed state by her words. "You're not to blame for anything that's happened, Jack. What matters is how you deal with it. You can't prevent people from making choices and choosing the wrong thing, even if you did know what was happening with her. There's nothing you could have done to change her decisions. That's not how life works. It happened, and now, just like her, you deal with it. You're a good man, so don't start believing that you're not." She looks down, and I'm so overwhelmed, desperate to say something but not sure what, when she looks back up at me. "Be there for them."

I have no idea how to navigate this. I was preparing for goodbye, not a confession of love and support.

She continues. "By the scowl on your face, I'm going to guess that you weren't prepared for me to say that." She pauses and moves over to the sink, washing her hands and drying them.

As she leans on the counter, she looks at me, and I watch her completely gain control of the situation. *There she is, my boss, my fighter. Shit, how I've fallen for this woman. Hard.*

"Be there for them, Jack. I just wish you could have realized that it never had to be a choice. Me or them. Shame on you for thinking it had to be and not respecting the honesty we had."

So that's what it feels like to be put in my place. Shown how I should have handled a situation I've been failing to figure out. It sounds so simple now that she's said it. Fuck. I bite my cheek to keep my chin from shaking. I bite harder to keep the blur and threat of tears behind my quickly crumbling stoic veil.

Less than a beat later, she says, "I'm leaving." That knocks me back into reality and out of my head. "I'm going to be spending some time in New York, getting my business off the ground."

"Wait, what? The apparel?" I ask, sounding accusatory and panicked for not knowing.

She nods and smiles. "You missed a lot when you decided to ice me out."

"I didn't mean-" She cuts me off, holding up her hand.

"I've lived most of my life hoping something like us would happen, but I never thought it would break me the way that it has. And the worst part is that you barely did anything. You treated me as if I was nothing more than a good fuck. Even after we said things to each other. Things that, to me, meant it was so much more than sex. I started to think that…" She stops herself from saying more. "I don't know what I am to you, at this moment…I don't have it in me to care."

I'm not processing any of this right now. It's too much. Too many emotions I don't know how to navigate like a damn adult. I can't understand why she isn't angry and pushing me out the door. I'm better with anger. I understand it. This, I don't understand. "What was that just now, then?"

"That!? Jack, you and I both know that if you have to ask." She smirks at herself and shakes her head. Then she looks up, as if something in the universe is going to help to not let this all just disintegrate around us. And it makes me feel sick. "That was the end. You said it yourself, it was closure. So let it be closure. That was us saying goodbye. Just like you wanted."

43

Everly

"He just left. I told him it was goodbye, and then he just left."

"I don't get it?" G takes a bite of her grilled cheese sandwich and a swig of some kind of purple drink.

"What's not to get? I was about to punch him. Then we fucked each other. Really fucking hard too, like I still feel it, for fuck's sake. And then he asked what that was. I told him it was goodbye. And then he left. He didn't even argue with me. It was the easiest out, and, G, that pisses me off more than anything. He didn't even put up a fight." I swallow the emotion that keeps trying to surface. I can't cry anymore over this. It won't make it hurt less or change it.

"Oh. Well..." She chews a massive piece she just bit off. With her mouth full of crunchy, buttery bread and what must be a quarter pound of cheese, she continues. "You left the part out where you jumped the gun and told him that it was goodbye. Why'd you say that if you didn't mean it?"

"No, I meant it. I told him I loved him, and he looked at me like I was about to burst into flames. The man LOOKED AT ME LIKE I WAS INSANE! Like, how could I possibly tell him that? I know he's dealing with shit, and I know his life has been, well, you know what, I don't even know what his life has been like because I barely know him. I barely know him, yet I'm in fucking love with him. What is wrong with me?!"

"Okay, okay. Don't yell at me. I'm trying to understand everything that happened so I can get a handle on what you need right now. Do we hate him? Are we mad? Just tell me so I can be that!" she says, my ever-loyal friend.

"I'm angry at him. I'm angrier at myself for going for it. I never go for it. He would have never been something I would have gone after if I had just kept to my list. I feel stupid, and I'm not a stupid person, G. I was worried about him and his sister, thinking he was mad about Jin and that he needs space. But he's blaming himself for his sister's spiraling, and now I think he's just broken and drowning. And while I want to be there for him, I can't if he doesn't want me to be. I'll drown right along with him. I know it."

"That's way heavier than the fling I thought you were supposed to be having." She stares at me. Provoking me.

I can only glare. "He practically busted his way into the pool house like some crazed, sexy lunatic on a mission and, of course, Jin was there, which was like the worst possible person."

She chokes on a piece of her sandwich, interrupting me. "Jin was there! Why was he there? Please tell me you didn't fuck him. Everly, this is like a telenovela."

"Stop it. I didn't fuck Jin. What is wrong with you?" I scoff. "Jack took one look at Jin, yelled something, like, *why the fuck is he here.* Jin leaves and then Jack basically growled at me. That growl was like permission to rip at each other. As soon as it was over, I knew we weren't going to survive the rest of the day. It felt wrong in every way possible. He told me in not so many words that he couldn't do us right now, and then I told him I loved him. I knocked him over with it, but I hoped, oh, God, G, I hoped that he would just tell me he felt it too."

She gives me a sympathetic smile. "But he didn't."

I shake my head, trying to hold back the tears that are blurring my vision. "He froze. He said nothing. So I told him I was leaving, this was goodbye and then he left."

I throw my hands in the air and slap them down on my thighs. "He just left."

"And now you're leaving, and it doesn't feel..." She looks at me to answer, but I have no idea what to say. "...Right? Or over?"

"Oh no, it feels over. But I don't know if it feels right. And now I'm supposed to go and start a whole company on my own, with his brother, no less."

"Stepbrother. Foster brother? Adopted brother?" She scrunches her nose.

"I have no clue, but I feel like Jack could have been it. I felt it. I felt it with him. It never was like that with anyone else. I want to shake him and yell at him. Why isn't he seeing what I'm seeing?" I look over to my friend with watery eyes and wet cheeks, hoping for some knock-my-socks-off wisdom to help make this hurt go away.

She wipes her mouth and leans on her hands, taking in the chaos I've just unleashed. "Because maybe he doesn't feel the way you feel. I see what you see, but that's not how it works. I know you feel it and want him to, but the reality is...

that's not how it works." She smiles at me, empathy in her eyes, because I know her tough exterior and aloofness with men are there with purpose. I hate that she's right. "So, what do you want to do now?"

I don't want to feel so defeated. It's evident in how I'm sitting, breathing, living. "I don't know, G. Curl up in a ball, burn down the patriarchy, wear no bra for a year, make my business so incredible that Jack becomes just a story I'll smile at fondly someday. I have no clue."

"Well, I'm pretty sure you don't want it to be over, but I think you need to move forward. You're going to be in New York for the next few months, and you're going to be elbows deep in being a badass starting her business. So do *that*. Aside from FaceTiming me, dive into life there until you're ready to come back here. You already know he's going to be in town for a while, so you know where to find him if you feel like you want to chase him. I'm not saying that you should do that at all, but for now, stop trying to make it feel right and just move forward for a while."

I smile at her. She knew I needed to hear that.

"But, Ev, don't chase. I want you to be happy. Hell, even I thought he might have been the guy, and I don't even believe in this whole one person for everyone bullshit." She shrugs. "But no matter how much you want someone to be that thing you've been hoping for, it's okay to wake up and see it for exactly what it is or who they are. The forest for the trees and all that."

I nod, working to hold back the burst of emotion that's creeping up again. "It was fire between us, G. You can't just make that happen. It's either there or it isn't. I've never had that before. It was so consuming to be near him. I didn't think I believed in that kind of connection with a person. I mean, I hoped, but I kind of thought it was all just hype, that people just said it because it was romantic. It was more than physical, and it was *very* physical." I smile at the memory. "Even that first time I kissed him, I felt like I was with someone who could keep up with me. I didn't have to lower my expectations or feel bad about being successful. It was respect, mixed with dirty, delicious sex...and he was sweet. Oh my gosh, he was sweet. Below the facade of being this big deal and a prickly asshole, the fucker was actually sweet!"

"Stop. Life is too damn short to be wasting it on a man who can't handle a woman at your level. And, babe, you're a level up for most. Jack is a fucking disappointment. And believe me, he'll realize it even if he hasn't already. That's when you decide what you want to do. He might have been all of those things when you were together for a minute, but when it came time to show up, he didn't. So maybe he'll realize he messed up the best thing to probably ever walk into his sad life, but then it's up to you to decide if he's enough."

I love her optimism, but right now I'm not interested in holding on to a maybe. For me, it was all or nothing. I chose all. He chose nothing. And now it's time to move on.

44

Jack

THREE WEEKS. IT TOOK ME THREE WEEKS. ROUGHLY TWENTY-
one days. Five hundred and something hours before I realized I had made the biggest mistake of my life. That's how
long it took to fully register that I choked, shut her out, and
probably lost the woman I'd fallen in love with. It hit me
with a jolt, like the universe had enough of watching me
drown in my choices. The moment I left her at the tree lighting, the moment I stepped out of that pool house. The
moments I left her, repeatedly, I knew it was a mistake. It's
all I feel like I've been doing lately.

But, that was yesterday.

Today, I'm sitting across the street, completely
enchanted all over again by the woman that I walked away
from and let believe she hadn't been something worth
fighting for. I always thought I was a brave man, but I'm too
terrified that being here isn't enough. That jumping on a

plane to get to her and tell her I'm sorry was a rookie call. I knew I had to see her, and that was as far as I thought this through. What kind of man does she really think I am if I won't fight for her, and now I'm just going to stroll in that front door and say what? "I messed up. Can we have a mulligan?" All I did was react and never thought about what I was doing with her.

It was so easy to fall into bed with her, fall at her feet, fall for her. I never pretended with her, it was always honest, but now I feel like I'm nine years old again. I chose to dive under a bed and hide instead of staying in the light with her.

I watch her move around the room, talking to staff, organizing styles, doing fittings for models and athletes. Some of them are even my friends. Marcus, currently the youngest starting quarterback in football history to bring home a Super Bowl, is front and center, taking selfies while Everly laughs and types on her phone.

I'm almost paralyzed watching her. She's beautiful, probably even more than I realized, if I'm being honest, the whole package. That was obvious from the first week I spent in Strutt's. Sexy, funny, kinder than most people I've ever met, not to mention her ambition and talent. She's one of those people you can't help but want to be around. I get it now, probably feeling it more than it was ever intended, but she is the moon. Her brothers were right.

Maybe we would have met no matter what. No matter the circumstance or the place that life chewed and spit us out into. There are too many coincidences and connections between us to think we would have never been in each other's orbit. Of course, one of those mutual acquaintances had to be my brother. *Asshole.*

I watch Jin lean over and kiss her on each cheek. The dimple on her left cheek peeks through and it pisses me off. The kiss is not intimate, more like a hello between colleagues or a goodbye between friends. They've been in meetings all morning. I've seen numerous brand ambassadors come and go in the past few hours, ranging from athletes to a few models. She's been busy building her new life.

Jin walks out the door and pulls his phone out of his pocket. I don't know what compels me to do it, but I dial his number. He's only listed on my phone as Unknown. I stopped knowing who he was a long time ago. A brother, a friend turned disappointment, then to an enemy. I watch him look at his phone, deciding whether or not to answer. To my surprise, he picks up. "Jack. Is Kat okay?" I see the nervous look on his face. He cares about her, but his actions in the past have told another story, and I'll never forgive him for it.

"She's fine."

"Benny?" he asks.

"Also fine."

"Then what?" he huffs out.

I can't let it slide. "Why are you in New York right now?"

He looks up and around. Then he meets my gaze from across the street where I sit on the same bench I have been for the past few hours. As he starts walking my way, he says, "Immaturity. It's not a good look for you. What, are you stalking her now?"

I hang up as he hops up to the sidewalk and over the bike path in front of me.

"I wanted to see her. This was as far as I got."

He nods slowly and sits on the open space of the bench I'm sitting on. "The fuck you doing, Jack?"

I keep silent. I don't know why I called him.

He stares at the side of my face. "Sitting out here makes you seem desperate." Taking a pause, it finally registers. "Holy shit, you love her, don't you?"

I don't answer. It's practically a rhetorical question at this point. *Of course, I love her. Dumbass.*

"If you got out of your head, then you would have done your research and would know that she's my business partner now."

"Oh, I'm aware. It's a smart move. That doesn't mean I like it."

The uptight asshole, whom I've known for the vast majority of my life, leans forward. Elbows to knees, dropping his head to level with me. "You and I are never going to agree on much, but I can tell you one thing: you don't deserve her."

I give him a side-eye glance. *This is something we can agree on.*

He continues. "Not like this, at least. Let her get her business started; she's got the world practically falling at her feet right now. Give her a minute to gain her footing before you blow it up again. I know she cares about you, but let me tell you, brother, if you aren't serious about her, then stay away. She doesn't need you. That right there is the kind of woman that if she wants you, then you're the lucky one. Not the other way around. Don't mistake that for a minute."

I'll never admit this to him, but he's right.

Pulling out my phone again, I send a text. I'm going to need all the help I can get here.

JACK

I need your help.

LUCIFER

What did you fuck up now?

45

Everly

"*LADIES AND GENTLEMEN, WE'RE STARTING OUR DESCENT INTO Manhattan. Please bring your seats and tray tables back into the upright position. The flight crew will be around to collect any trash and help you stow anything necessary as we approach. We'll be landing in about twenty-five minutes. The local time is six-ten in the morning and if you're on the right side of the plane, you can take a look out to the horizon and see a beautiful sunrise coming up over the city. Welcome to New York.*"

I push back the tears that are threatening to fall over my watery eyes as I take in the beauty of the city. It's been more than a month now that I've been surrounded by the liveliness of this city, and I'm going to blame my sudden emotions on just coming off of a seven-plus hour red-eye flight from Los Angeles. It had nothing to do with thinking about how the sunrise this morning was too close to the mornings Jack and I watched it in each other's arms. Nope, definitely not that. It was absolutely the red-eye.

About an hour later, my Uber finally makes its way into my SoHo neighborhood, and while it doesn't feel like home, I am happy to be back after a week filled with schmoozing buyers and rubbing elbows with pseudo-celebrities. I've given away more of my apparel at this point than sold, but I know how the game is played. If it's going to be worn, then it has to be seen.

I wave to my doorman as I hustle to the elevator, and I just think about how I want to do nothing today other than put on something cozy and sleep. Maybe I'll figure out food at some point, but I need to sleep. My brain is in a weird haze between a headache and the need to think about everything that still needs to be accomplished this week. I get off the elevator and I'm greeted by the most delicious smell of salty bacon. There's no way my trust-fund neighbors are cooking at seven-something in the morning on a Sunday.

I walk up to my door and find a brown shopping bag on my welcome mat with a tag that reads: *Everly*. Nothing else, just my name. I roll my suitcase into my loft and drop my bag on the counter, alongside the bag that's doused in the magical smell of greasy, crunchy heaven. I might be out of it, but I know I didn't order breakfast. I abandon everything and drop my jet-lagged body on my bed and send out a text to my brothers.

EVERLY

> Whoever ordered me breakfast this morning gets to come to the model shoot next month. Thank you. Love you, miss you.

MICHAEL

It wasn't me. But I want in. What are they modeling?

EVERLY

The usual. Comfortable lingerie. Why are you up? It's 4:30 a.m. there?

MICHAEL

I'll book tix. Board meeting prep today and need to get in a workout before. Love you, Ev.

LAW

STOP BLOWING UP MY PHONE!

2 EARLY!

46

Jack

"Before you step one more foot through that door, I'm going to warn you that I have a very bad temper when it comes to assholes who hurt the most important woman in my life." Giselle leans forward on the front desk of her shop. I knew I wasn't going to be greeted with open arms, but I probably underestimated the fact that she's a wild card.

"I deserve that, but I need to talk to you." I push the rest of the way into the shop.

"You need to talk to Everly, not me, Mister Disappointment. Figure your shit out without me getting involved. I'm serious. My loyalty is always with her, so if you think you'll get anything other than an aching set of balls after they meet my steel-toed boots, then you're dumber than I thought."

"I need to know if she's moved on. If she's happier without me."

Giselle stares at me as if two heads just sprang from my stomach. "Like I said, not happening."

"I know what I want to happen. I know I've made a huge mistake, but I need to know from you, and only you, if she's happy where she is right now. If she's moving on and not looking back."

She crosses her arms over her chest, the intricate designs of her flowery tattoos that run the length of her arms glaring at me somehow too. I knew coming in here was a long-shot, but I mean what I say, if Everly is better off with us in the past, then I'll leave it. Leave her. Let her move on. Giselle is not a person to sugarcoat anything, and she'll know if her best friend wants to leave what we had in the past.

"I had such high hopes for you, ya know? I didn't think you were such a pansy penis to come and look for a way out of fighting for the woman that we all know you're being stupid about."

I give her a nod. But an out for myself isn't why I'm here. If I was selfish, I would have rushed her storefront when I was in New York and told her how much of a mistake I've made, but this isn't something I'm dumb enough to take so lightly. Everly needs to see what I want from her and not just hear it. *I know her.* Words only mean so much; they only get you so far before you have to make the big moves. Do the big scary things that could leave you more broken. But she's worth it.

"Giselle! For fuck's sake, please? You don't owe me anything. You're right. I can't imagine having a person like you in my corner. Everly is so lucky to have you, but I need you to tell me if she's going to be better off without me. And before you say anything else, *I* won't be. I won't be better off without her. I already know that. I want to be everything to her, but I don't want to hurt her any more than I have."

She looks at me, studying if I'm bullshitting her right now. I'm not.

"I'm not..." I shake my head and choke back the emotion in my throat. "I hurt her, and I have to live with the fact that I hurt the woman who means more to me than I thought possible."

She raises her eyebrow and then turns to walk to the back of her shop near her tools and inks. She nods at the seat for me to sit.

"I'm going to add to your tattoo. That ending line needs to be better finished off, and it's been bugging me ever since I met you." She starts to pull black latex gloves on and sits down on her roller stool to my right.

I roll my sleeve up my forearm and she starts prepping. She wipes the area with an alcohol cloth and then shaves around my arm, since the lines she's referring to run around its entire circumference.

After a few minutes, she gets to work. Silently, she pulls the skin taut and dips her micro-thin needle into the black ink. I sit calmly and know that this is a good sign. I hope. There's a fifty-fifty shot that I come out of here with an angry dick drawn on my arm, but it's a chance I'm willing to take.

"I came to this town a decade ago, after a lot of shit went down, and it was hard not to fall for it. It's a small town, which, I'll be honest, I thought I'd be highly allergic to after a while. But turns out it was where I was meant to be. It's home. The longer I'm here, I kind of think it was always meant to be."

"How did you find it?" I ask.

She looks up from her work and shifts to grab another small cloth to rub away the excess ink. "I have a pretty good memory, so when I was researching places that I'd like to try out and that would also be a good place for me to open a shop, I stumbled across Strutt's Peak on a map, it seemed like a sign."

I let her continue. "Strutt's Peak is named after a scientist, mathematician, actually, but not because he found the place or anything like that. It's a bit more poetic, to be honest." She looks up at me. "I'm about to blow your mind, so keep up, okay, Deacon."

"I'm listening," I say with a smile.

She looks back down and continues the tattoo while talking. "John William Strutt was a British mathematician, like mucho brilliant, but the most interesting thing he did, in my opinion, wasn't what he was most known for. You keeping up with me here?" She looks up for a second to make sure I'm paying attention. I nod. "Strutt was also referred to as Lord Baron Rayleigh. I don't understand how people get these titles, being rich or born into a family that thinks very highly of themselves and the land they oversee... I don't fully comprehend it, but that's not the point. My point is, Rayleigh's Scattering is the theory or explanation of why the sky is blue. How we see the way the light scatters and why we see it as blue, or at certain times of day dark blue or pink or orange."

She dips the needle again and continues. "I picked this place because of what it promised. If there was a place that existed that was named after the person who could finally explain why the sky was blue or why we could see certain colors at certain times of day, then fuck yeah, I was taking that as a sign. My world was very dark for a while, and I needed something more than light. I needed to find a way to add color to it again."

She looks up and smiles. I believe in making things happen, not the idea that everything is destined to happen without being able to do anything about it. But I also believe there can be parts of life that are unexplained, coincidences, even a bit of magic. Call it whatever you'd like, but Giselle telling me this is hitting me in the gut. "Then everything kept falling into place. I found a tattoo shop owner that was ready to retire, and one night I met Everly. That night it was it. I knew I was home."

I raise my brow. The loudmouth best friend is quickly becoming one of my favorite people with this and I think I see where she's going here, but instead of interjecting I let her keep talking and tattooing.

"And you're telling me this so I'll stay here?"

"I'm telling you this, because from one artist to another, you don't leave a place that paints your life with color. You listen to the signs that are thrown in your face. You stay. You figure it out."

She wipes the last of the lines, and I give it a turn to look at her work. She is good. "Came out nice. Thank you," I tell her.

"She's sad. She's put on her badass heels and is doing great out there, but I know she's not eating much, which for her is very out of character. The girl loves food." She looks over to me, leveling what she's going to say next. "She's not over you. Yet. But I wouldn't waste too much more time. She's a fucking catch."

I smile. "I know." I got what I came for, or rather, hoped for. A sign that I'm doing the right thing here, not just for me or what I want, but for her.

"How did you know that, by the way? About Strutt's Peak?" I ask.

"Like I said, really good memory." She taps the side of her head. "It was a question I fucked up for my physics final my senior year. It's the grade that held me back as the salutatorian and not valedictorian. Pissed me off, so it was hard to forget."

Before I turn to leave, I have to ask her to do one more thing for me. She's not going to like it. "Please keep this between us. I know that's asking a lot, but I'm promising you that I'm going to make this right for her. I just need a little more time."

"I can't promise that. If she asks, then I'll tell her you came to talk to me. So, don't make me regret this, Jack. Do you hear me? I have no problem drugging you and tattooing a dick on your face. Just putting that out there."

And with those words of encouragement, I pick up my phone and make a call. Time to go big, because I'm not going home.

47

Jack

"DID YOU MAKE YOUR MOVE ON THAT GIRL YET?" I ASK MY nephew as he laces up his shoes and claps chalk on his hands.

"No way. She wasn't interested in me. She heard I was your nephew and thought she would be able to get a selfie with you if we hung out. I heard her talking to one of her friends."

"I'm sorry, man." If I could keep a bubble around this kid to hide hurt from his world, I'd do it in an instant, but I know that's not how it works.

"Nah, it's all good. I ended up meeting this cute little thing during one of my shifts last week. She's a little older, just started at the University last fall. We've been texting, so I'll see where it goes." He smiles at me proudly.

"Nice. You're being smart?" That comment gets me a look. The kind that is followed up with either embarrassment or a bark to shut up. I throw up my hands in surrender. "Just asking. Don't get defensive. I hope I get to meet her."

We start working our way up the massive wall, and I notice as I'm making my way about twenty feet off the mats that my belayer on the ground has changed. Normally, that doesn't happen; the belayer is the person giving me the proper slack and rope so I can move up the wall easily and safely.

"Ah, fuck," I say to myself as soon as I see who's taken over.

Benny looks at me and then down to the ground and yells out, "Hey, Michael!"

When Benny asked to burn off some energy tonight after school, I told him sure before realizing where we were headed. He pulled into the Riggs Rock Wall facility and assumed I wouldn't run into any of the Riggs men. They run the big business, not work in the rock wall or mixed martial arts facility. I'm positive I'm their least favorite person right now, even after delivering their rebranding package and photography. I knew they were happy with it, but after reviewing it with their marketing teams and the board of directors, I didn't stick around to shoot the shit or grab a bite. I'm not an idiot. They liked my work. What they very clearly don't like is me right now. And I get it, I messed up with their sister. Big time.

"Hey, you know Michael asked if I'd like to work the kids camp here this summer," Benny says as we both make our way upward.

"Is that right? And what do you think? Want to stick around this summer and make some extra money before school in the fall?"

"I've been thinking, Uncle Jack..."

I look over at him, already knowing what he's going to say, but I let him get it out before saying anything to shoot it down.

Benny grabs the next grip and he's moving toward the horizontal edge, which needs some solid strength to handle. He's coasting through it and talking to me like this is easy stuff. It's definitely not. "I've been thinking I want to defer school for a semester. Start up in the spring instead so I can do some climbing around here until it gets too cold, and then maybe head south for a bit. Do some exploring on my own for a while. Maybe see if Dad wants to come for a bit, too. I don't know. I'm just not ready to start being an adult yet."

That wasn't what I thought he was going to say. Benny has been through a lot. Way more than I initially thought. Between his parents' divorce, which had been edging toward a demise for the last five years, playing referee between the two of them, his mother heading into rehab, not to mention all the pieces that led her there, the kid could use some time on his own. Figure out who he might be. He's had to step into a roster of grown-up roles he never should have been in to begin with. I don't blame him for wanting some time to breathe on his own.

"I think it's a good idea. You're going to have to clear it with your mom when she's back, but I'm sure she'd support whatever you feel you need, kiddo," I say as I smile at my very grown-up, sweetheart of a nephew.

"You're getting really good at..."

The rest of what Benny says falls away, as does my body as I plunge off the wall. My ropes don't stop me with too much slack I've been pulling. My harness jerks my body quickly, and with a grunt, I abruptly stop. Dangling only about five or so feet from the ground, I see Michael to my left, smiling at me.

"What the fu–" With another grunt, my ass hits the matted floor.

"Try to be more careful in my facility, Jack." Michael passes the ropes off to his colleague, then he stalks away.

"Uncle Jack, you alright?" Benny yells from his spot just below the top of the wall.

I stand up, ass sore and pride a bit wounded as people stare. This is going to hit the rumor mill nice and fast. "All good!"

I walk over to the locker room and shake off what just happened. I wasn't planning to see any of the Riggs brothers. I hadn't thought about what I'd tell them when I did. *Rookie move.* I feel like I owe them an explanation, but I'm not about to walk into their lair without a plan or explanation.

"Are you fucking kidding me right now?" I say it, but I'm not expecting any sort of response from the brick house of a man that stands in front of me on the other side of the men's room. Henry Riggs, not one of the most welcoming men to begin with, but we bonded over some beer and mutual athlete friends. Right now, though, he looks like he's 'roided out and ready to rumble. I'm not a man to back away from a fight, so I know what's coming. This asshole is going to knock me in the face and I'm going to let him.

"You're not even going to fight back, are you, you piece of shit?" he barks out at me.

"What do you want me to say, huh? I fucked up? Yeah, I fucked up royally, but I'm trying to make it right. For everyone." He doesn't let me say much else. In three behemoth-sized strides, his full fist connects first to my stomach, and as soon as I wretch over in response, he drives an elbow into my lower back, right into a kidney. I'll likely piss blood for the next few days. *Great.*

I'm lucky his ham-hands didn't pop me in the nose, a far more visible assault that wouldn't go unnoticed in this town. Serving up coffee and books with a broken nose wouldn't be too ideal. I should thank him for keeping it to the body, only the wind's been knocked out of me, and I can't take a full breath yet.

"That's enough now." The soothing voice hovering from the doorway is from none other than Asher Riggs. It bellows through the empty locker room. What did they send out a group text that I was here?

I watch as his shined-up loafers come into view and he crouches down, grabbing my elbow to help me stand. "Thank you, sir."

"Don't thank me, son. Who do you think called my boys? I saw you pull in a little bit ago. My staff has been told to let me know whenever you show up on any of our properties. You're just lucky you were at the wall and not in the MMA gym. Would have been bloodier, I gather. We couldn't let you just stay in town without acknowledging what kind of state you decided to leave my daughter in."

He claps his hands together and continues. "But, now, since that's all out of the way, grab that nephew of yours and come to the ranch for some burgers. We have some things to discuss." And with that, he walks out of the locker room, like the damn Godfather of Strutt's Peak.

The only one missing was Law, and if I know him, he won't be missing the next show.

"Mr. Riggs, this might be the best burger I've ever had, and that's saying somethin' 'cause I've had a lot of burgers in my life," Benny confesses with a mouthful of what might be his third or fourth burger. To be fair, they are really good.

"Benny, you need to stop calling me Mr. Riggs. It's just Asher to you." He turns around from the grill and sits back on the bench to take another bite of his meal. "You just have to use good meat. You can taste if the cows have been mistreated," he says.

Law just laughs, interrupting. "Oh please, old man."

"It's true. Good quality beef and a good amount of salt, pepper, and a little crushed red pepper for good measure will make the best burger of your life."

"Jack, you want another?" Michael gets up and holds up his empty lager.

"Yeah, that'd be great."

A few hours later, we're sitting around the firepit enjoying the brisk evening. Law brought out the bourbon, and Ash cut some cigars for each of us. Michael and Benny made their way inside to talk about the summer program after graduation, leaving me out here with Henry, Law, and Ash.

"We heard about what's going on with Kathryn. I hope she's doing better," Asher says in a concerned voice.

"She's doing her best right now. She's in a program down in Wyoming for the next couple of months. There's a lot of work ahead of her, but my sister is a fighter." I swirl the bourbon in my glass and meet their looks with a tight-lipped smile.

"You are too, from what I've gathered." Asher looks at me, and I glance around the firepit. It's clear that Law and

Henry aren't privy to the same information that Asher somehow is aware of, and I'm thankful for that.

I nod at him and take another sip.

Henry sits quietly, as usual, with his irritable presence hovering like a solemn bodyguard, making you aware it's there, just in case it's needed. Law relaxes in his chair, staring up at the sky, tapping his fingers on the edge of his glass as he puffs on the cigar.

Asher pulls my attention back with a clearing of his throat. And I imagine this is when he tells me to get out of dodge and stay away from his daughter. This is why his next few words throw me off a little.

"I like you, Jack." He puffs his cigar.

I chime into the silence, "But?"

"But nothing. I like you. I like the kind of man I think you are. And more importantly, I like the way my daughter is when she's around you."

"How's that?"

"Happy. And not in a way that she is when she's with us or at work, but that kind of happy when you've found your partner, your other half. She's a romantic deep down. She's been waiting for someone like you. I'd hate for her to be disappointed."

I'm not sure what to say to that, but I feel it too. I know it. She makes me feel that way too. I've just been too distracted to appreciate the importance of it.

"Jack, loving someone isn't the hard part." Asher takes a sip of his drink, and I know he's about to unleash some wisdom on me that's going to stick. What I wouldn't give to have a father like this in my corner. "It's not the love that's hard. It's staying." He leans forward, resting his elbows on his knees, and takes a puff of his cigar. "Life gets hard, messy, but you stay because it's better when you're doing it with someone who can set your soul on fire, cool you off when you need it, and make you laugh at the end of it all."

"I hear you, sir."

"Then make it right. She's outpacing you, and if you don't get your head out of your ass, she's going to move on with someone who can."

While I never expected this night to turn out like this, I'm happy that it did. After another hour and bringing the conversation back to business and the great response they've seen with the new brand roll-out, Benny and I shake hands with each of them and head out.

Law gives my hand a tighter shake and says, "I'd love nothing more than to be friends with you, man, but you continue to hurt my sister..." He drifts off, and then says, "Just make it right."

I give him a curt nod. "Thanks for not hitting me, by the way. I would have taken it, but I appreciate it."

"Oh, Jack, don't misunderstand my lack of aggression. I want you to work it out with Ev, but she's our moon, man. You're going to have a long night ahead of you. Sorry, not sorry in advance." And with that, he claps his hand on my shoulder, and my stomach rumbles.

Three hours later, I realize exactly what he was sorry, not sorry about. The fucker must have put something in my drink. I barely made it to the bathroom and haven't left it since I got home. Good play. I can't even be mad at them. I fucked their sister, fell in love with her, and then fucked it up. I'll take the punishment and move forward with my plans to make it right. In the morning.

48

Everly

"How is it possible that Giselle still hasn't been out here? I don't get it," Law says.

I just shrug. I have no idea why she hasn't come to New York, but it doesn't matter to me. I see her on FaceTime calls at least every other day, sometimes more. Last week, she called me from the shower, asking if I could tell her if her waxing lady gave her a true Brazilian because she couldn't see a certain angle on her ass crack. She's an over-sharer, with no boundaries, but I'd rather have that than to miss her.

"I don't know. She's been really busy and can't just cancel clients. Or so she says."

Henry makes an annoyed grunting noise, and we all stop what we're doing to look at him.

"You're not fooling anyone, bro. Stop acting like you hate her." My eyes meet Law's. We both know Henry will never say otherwise, but there's no way he would spend so much time and effort grumbling after her if there wasn't some-thing else there. She's never done anything to him other than push some buttons, but we all know that it's a matter of minutes before he either storms out or chucks an object at Law's face.

"I just have to grab my phone, one sec. I'll meet you downstairs," I yell from my bedroom in the back. My brothers arrived in town last night to observe and to give their two cents on the models that are coming through today for our social media sessions. They took credit for something I know for a fact now they had nothing to do with. After the second Sunday in a row of a mystery bag arriving on my doorstep, chuck-filled with crunchy bacon, crispy Belgian waffles laced with bourbon butter with vanilla bean maple syrup, and sliced strawberries, I realized it was from Jack. I don't know how, but every Sunday morn-ing, I wake up to his—and now *my*—favorite breakfast sitting outside of my door. It's been going on now for about six weeks, and while I'm not sure what *exactly* it means. It means *something*.

"Ev, there's a bag at your front door. It smells like bacon," Law yells from the other side of the loft. "Did you order breakfast? I thought there was breakfast catered at the shoot."

"Just leave it on the counter, please."

I walk into the kitchen from the hallway and drop my phone into my bag. I pull my winter hat on and throw a scarf around my neck. March in New York is colder than December, most days. It's not Strutt's Peak cold, but if the wind zips through the avenues just right, you'll think frost-bite could creep into anything that isn't covered.

"Where's your coat?" I keep my momentum and move to

the door. "What?" Law's arms are crossed, and he's stopped at the kitchen counter in front of the takeout bag.

He stares at me, waiting for me to flinch, and asks, "How long has he been delivering you breakfast?"

Of course, he'd realize it was from Jack. It's not worth lying about it, so I tell him, "Six weeks. Every Sunday at eight-thirty in the morning, I can expect it to show up on my front step."

Law just looks at me, expecting me to say something else, but there's nothing else to say. I haven't processed it. I just eat it and then go on with my day. It's one of the only things I'm eating regularly. Between my busy schedule and the bit of depression that's snuck in, I'm mostly living off of coffee and protein bars. Sometimes Thai or sushi from the places around the corner, but I can only do takeout for so long.

"You haven't seen him? Texted him?" he asks.

I brace myself for this, because thinking about him is one thing, but talking about him is another. I don't want to feel the sadness that's just sitting on the sidelines, waiting to take over my steeled reserve. I shake my head. "What? Don't look at me like that. I don't know. I'm afraid that if I talk to him in any way, then I'm going to have to figure out what we are to each other. And I don't know. I don't have all the answers. It's not in my court. He could call or text me if he wanted to, but he hasn't."

"The guy is somehow arranging for you to have breakfast every week. Wouldn't you think it's nice to say thank you, or at least *something*?" I just look at him, because I've purposely tried not to acknowledge that there's no reason for me not to at least text him. I just decided to live in my bubble right now, knowing he's thinking of me, but I'm not ready for anything more than that. Plus, it's not in my court. I'm not going to chase him. I can't. Call it stubborn dignity.

I shift my weight on my feet and lean against the counter. He asks, "Are you dating someone else?"

"No," I bark out at him and scoff at the idea that I'd just move on like that. Even though I should be doing that. Moving on. I open the bag and dig out a piece of bacon to distract my emotions from surfacing.

I look up fast, as worry creeps into my gut. "Wait, is he? Is he seeing someone else? Law, tell me what you know. Are you still hanging out with him?" Law just looks at me out of the corner of his eye and smiles.

"That's what I thought." He smirks.

My stomach flips, like I've just gone over the highest point on a rollercoaster, and I throw the bacon piece back into the bag. "What's that supposed to mean?"

"It just means I needed to know if you were over him or not. Clearly not. Now, I just don't understand why you're both being dumb and aren't together."

"That's not a question for me, Law. He knows how I feel. It's on him to do something about it." I steady myself from the discussion and walk out the door, with Law trailing behind me. We walk into the cold air of the morning, meeting Michael and Henry on the sidewalk out front. The cold knocks me back into a more stable frame of mind. I don't want to start down the path of "what ifs" and hopeful thoughts. I haven't even fully pulled myself back together since my last interaction with Jack. I can't trust that I won't unravel completely if I start talking to him again, and then I figure out it's just Jack feeling lonely.

There's a part of me that knows that's not the case, but after you've been hurt, self-preservation hardens any thoughts of hope. I'm not prepared for anything more than realities. We walk to the storefront and studio that are now headquarters for my brand. Several people are crowding the small lobby as my assistant works to move people around and keep the day organized. The photographer is set up, and we take seats along the edge of the space to watch him work.

It takes about twenty minutes. Between my brothers causing a bit of a commotion to get breakfast from catering and to find a place to sit. It's Michael that notices first. He goes wide-eyed and chokes on his coffee. He looks at me and starts laughing.

"You alright, man?" Law chimes in. He takes a bite of his bagel and sips his coffee, surveying the models lined up and sprawled out.

Henry looks at me and smirks. Got him. Now I just wait for Law to catch up.

"Um, Ev?" Law says between bites.

"Yes?" I exaggerate, batting my eyelashes at him.

Law is looking at the set again and finally taking in the models he was so eager to come into town to observe and he begins to register that I got him. I got him good. "Why are there only men in sweatpants, shirtless, on your set?"

"What do you mean?"

"Ev, come on!?" Michael and Henry just start laughing now. "Why are there a dozen TikTok thirst traps laying all over the place half-naked? This isn't what you promised!"

"It absolutely is. I said I had a big shoot with models wearing comfy lingerie. Everybody knows the sexiest lingerie on a shirtless, well-cut man is low-slung sweatpants."

He plucks his jacket from the chair behind him and

stands up. "Fine. You got me. I am going back to your apartment, and I'm going to make Bloody Marys because I'm not sitting here watching dudes, who are making me rethink my gym routine, by the way, without drinking something stronger than Starbucks."

The four of us erupt in laughter. God, I miss spending time with them. I think that's why we all were on board for so long with living together. We had too much fun together to let life and being busy be the reason we didn't share little moments. It's the first time I realize that part of our lives is over. Even though my time in New York isn't permanent, when it's time to be back in Strutt's Peak, I'll need my own space.

The photoshoot ended up being exactly what I was hoping for, chaotic success. Aside from being a photoshoot to show off next season's styles, it was a jackpot marketing opportunity. Most of the "models" we hired were brought in for two reasons; they could wear the hell out of my men's line-up, and they each had no less than a quarter of a million followers on their social media platforms. With a limited run of the apparel they were wearing, it is exclusively available through Riggs Outdoors' new website. As an exclusive, today only push, we managed to bump traffic to the Rigg's website, and I took a full percentage of profit from the sell-out. It was a win-win for everyone and a perfect case study as we roll into buyer meetings over the next few months.

"You're moving out?" Michael practically slurs at me. After our fair share of drinks during dinner and now on our third or fourth round of Old Fashioneds at our secret bar, we're all half in the bag.

"I'm just ready to have my own place. And I love you guys, but I don't want to run into any more women in the hallway after one-night stands, okay? I can't even believe I put up with it as long as I have." They look at each other as if I'm missing something. "What?!"

Henry looks up from his drink. I can tell he wants to say something, but instead, he just shakes his head and says, "It's a smart move, Ev. I'll miss having you around like that, but I get it."

Law squints his eyes at the bartender from where we sit. "Are you fucking kidding me!"

We all turn our attention to where he's looking.

"Aperol?! It's fucking Aperol that he uses in the Old Fashioneds!" His eyebrows are up so high on his head, they practically meet his hairline. His face is a mix of excitement and total anger. "You knew!" He pointed at me.

I've known for a long time what the secret ingredient was, but I couldn't tell him. It was too easy. And if I'm being honest, all these years of him trying to figure it out have been hilarious and appreciated. Some of his concoctions have been even better, in my opinion, but I will also never tell him that. I'd never hear the end of it.

"Everly, you knew this whole damn time, and you didn't tell me. It's been a decade of trying to figure this out, and you knew! I feel bamboozled. Who are you even?"

Henry, Michael, and I just laugh uncontrollably. Law joins in, and it might be the most I've laughed with them in years. It's the most fun I've had since I've been here. I haven't thought of Jack once. *Damn it!*

49

Jack

"Do you think she's going to be okay? After all of this?" Benny asks quietly. It's been over an hour of driving now, and he hasn't said much. I knew he would be anxious and worried today. I am too. It's been almost three months since Kathryn checked into this rehab program. We all know that the hardest part for her is what's next. Remaining sober when she's dealing with her everyday life. Our mother never even got this far, so already, she's ahead of where the worst could exist.

"Your mom is one of the strongest people I know. And she's not a coward, she's not about to back down from this fight. I know she's going to work really hard." When I look over at my nephew, I don't see the adult he's becoming, but a nervous kid who wants nothing more than his mother to be the grown-up for a while. I didn't realize how long he'd been covering for her, and not just socially for her being out drinking or upstairs in their apartment sleeping it off.

He's been the one making sure the bills were paid when they arrived in Strutt's and the refrigerator stocked with food. I'm pissed at her for that. For making him rush into adulthood.

"I know. Do you think she's going to understand about me taking time off after graduation?"

"I don't know what she's going to say, but you've got me in your corner. And I'll be around to check in on her while you're living your life for a bit, kiddo."

"Thanks, Uncle Jack. For staying. For everything, really."

I reach over and squeeze his shoulder. Getting to spend time with him was a privilege, not a burden. This kid stole a part of my heart when he was born, but the man he's becoming has made me so proud, and I appreciate him even more. I thank the universe for letting me know him, learn from him.

Five hours later, with my sister in the passenger seat, we're on our way back home. *Home.* There's never been a place that's ever felt more like what that word is supposed to mean than when I've been in Strutt's Peak. I never thought a physical place would give me all the things I didn't realize I had been searching for. *Family. Real relationships. Love.*

With tears in her eyes, she gets a complete recap from Benny about everything he's been doing. Most of it, she already knew from phone calls. But talking in person just sits differently, and I know she wants to absorb his energy with all of the excitement behind some of what she's missed. "It sounds like you've done even more than I thought since I've been gone, kiddo. I'm proud of you. How did your chem lab project turn out?"

I look at Benny in the rearview mirror as he squirms. I know he didn't do the best on that one, but his GPA is high enough that even if he pulls out of that class just passing, he'll still maintain a B+ average.

Kathryn looks over at me. "I guess not so great, then?" She turns around to look at him in the back seat.

"I'll still be able to pass the class, but there's no way I'm going to bring home anything higher than a C at this point."

Kathryn lifts her left shoulder and surprises him by saying, "Can't be great at everything, my love. Now tell me about prom. Have you decided if you're going to go yet?"

The rest of the car ride is light on conversation. I can tell more than anything she just wants to catch up on the little things she may have missed. I know there's more she and I need to say to each other, but right now, this is about her and her son.

After a few minutes of silence, there's a song that comes on from the playlist that Benny made a while ago. John Mayer croons about the things that parents pass on to their children. Will it wash out in the water, or is it always in the blood? I can tell they're both listening to the lyrics, and out of the corner of my eye, I see my sister shield her eyes.

She looks over toward me, and without words, we squeeze each other's hands. Her watery eyes meet mine, and we smile at each other. She unbuckles her seatbelt and climbs into the back with Benny, and I turn the music up a bit. I can hear her apologizing to him and vowing not just to make promises but to show him she's worthy of being called his mother.

I wipe away the tears as they spill over to my cheeks before they can reach my chin. The tension that had been pulling throughout the day has finally loosened, and I'm relieved to see two of the most important people in my life begin to heal.

50

Everly

IT'S BEEN SIX WEEKS SINCE I'VE SEEN MY BROTHERS IN NEW
York. About three months since I've spent time with my
best friend in person. And it's been six months since I've
seen Jack Deacon. I hate myself a little for measuring time
so precisely. Time since I've kissed that man, fucked him
so unapologetically, and then he disappeared from my life.
I guess that's what I'm left with, friggin' yearning. That
must be what it is, because it sure isn't my dignity. How
did I get here? To this place where I'm even annoyed at
myself for not moving on. I've moved every other part of
my life forward, except for the one that probably counts
the most.

It's Sunday and I'm back in Strutt's Peak, which means
Sunday dinner at the ranch. And because the weather is
beautiful, there'll be lots of grilled meats. When warm
weather hits Strutt's Peak, we never dare to do things inside
for too long, especially cook or eat. When June hits, it's offi-

cially the summer season, and all the laid-back, outdoor fun that comes with it.

I'm happy to get out of New York for a while. That city has parts of my heart; anyone who's spent time there always leaves a piece of their heart with it, but I'm a Colorado girl to the bone. I need to see the mountains. I need people to smile at me as I walk downtown, and I need, more than anything, to spend time with my family.

"Are you kidding me!" I yell as we drive down the long stretch of road to the ranch.

"What? Holy shit, what? Did I almost hit something?" G grips both hands on her steering wheel and frantically looks in her rearview mirror.

"No, no, you didn't hit anything. David Muldowney has a sold sign on his property. I didn't even know he was thinking of selling. I kind of wish I knew."

"Fucking hell, Everly. Don't do that shit while I'm driving. I thought I either hit an animal or there was a naked man with his dick swinging on the side of the road or something." She looks back out her rearview.

"I've been waiting for you to say something wildly *you* since you picked me up. It took"—I look at my wrist as if to exaggerate the time—"way too long."

She looks over at me, still smiling from our fit of laughter, and in true Giselle form, she calls me out on what I've been trying desperately to avoid. "Have you talked to him?"

"No."

"Why not?"

"He knows I'm back in town by now. It's on him to come and find me. Nothing has changed since I left. I told him how I felt, and he didn't. Which was kind of like him telling me in a way. I'm not moving on, but I'm still pissed off. And hurt. And honestly, the man isn't poor or unable to travel, so if he wanted to make a grand gesture or if he wanted me in his life, then he would have come to New York to see me."

"He did."

I look at her, my head spinning. We're pulling into the driveway to the ranch, and I can see my dad and Law on the front porch, watching us approach. "What do you mean, he did?"

"He went to see you right after you left. I don't know, maybe a few weeks after you were settled. We had a very"— she clears her throat—"heated conversation about what a piece of shit I thought he was for what he did to you, and he told me he went out there to see you, but he didn't want to ruin the life you were restarting." She waves her hand in the air as if swatting a fly. "Such a penis move. I can't even call him a pussy, because our flowers are elaborate and beautiful. Penises are a one-trick pony, so yeah, he was acting like a below-average-sized penis. Then I told him he didn't deserve a woman like you and some other things. I haven't seen him much since then."

"I talk to you every day. Wouldn't that have been something that you should have told me? I don't know at *any* fucking point?" I'm so upset right now as soon as the car stops, I rush out and slam the door.

Giselle follows behind me, slamming her door shut, too. "Don't be pissed at me. I don't know what you idiots are doing. I have my own bullshit going on. How am I supposed to know that you weren't going to speak to him, or that he was going to send you breakfast every Sunday? Like, what is that? Why not take the easy way out, and text each other at least! You both know how to text like most immature people when they want to say things they don't have the balls to say in person."

I stomp up the porch stairs to the house. My dad and Law sit there watching and know better than to interrupt.

"You're my best friend, G. You tell me shit about the guy that I'm crumbling over."

She stops and yells, "HA! Exactly, you were crumbling. Fucking falling to pieces. Over a guy! I'm supposed to tell you that he went to see you, but then backed off? What is that going to do?"

"You. Tell. Me." I push into the house and stomp over to the bar for a drink. "I'll take anything at this point. Even water, to throw in my face, because I'm floored that my best friend would just leave out a very important piece of information like that fact that he came after me!"

"Fine. Well, I'm telling you now." She continues to shout at me and moves into the bar beside me. I notice Michael coming in from the back patio and Henry creeping out from the kitchen with a towel slung over his shoulder.

"What's going on? Why are you fighting-" Law just shakes his head at Henry to shut him up. They all know better than to say anything right now.

Giselle yells at him, "Stay out of it, Hank!"

Michael walks toward us just as I'm pulling out two shot glasses. G unscrews the cap to the vodka and starts to pour. I watch my brother, silently warning him not to speak. G pushes the overflowed shot glass toward me and picks hers up. We don't say anything else and just shoot it back. The burn going down shakes a bit of the rage out.

"Ackk! Fuck. Dad, where are lemons?" He just points to the bar top, and I suck on a wedge while I pass G another.

"So you told her about the Muldowney Ranch, then?" Michael asks cautiously.

I look at my dad accusingly. "No, he did *not* tell me. I had to see the sold sign on my drive in here. Why wouldn't you tell me that David was thinking of selling?"

"Shut the fuck up, Michael," Law says through gritted teeth.

I look at Law and then back at Michael. I take in the awkward, nervous glances that Henry is giving my father now. "Why? Why shut the fuck up?"

"Pumpkin, why don't you take a minute and breathe. You two showed up like a tornado and a hurricane, ready to do some serious damage, so forgive me if I'm not eager to be throwing anything else at you right now."

"Dad, give me a break. I found out my best friend held out some really important information from me, and I'm reacting to it. We're fine." I feel like I'm out of breath again.

"Are you two operating on the same menstrual cycle?" Michael asks. *He's so dead.*

G holds her hand up, stopping my response. "Michael, I'm going to chalk that remark up to not knowing any better. And then I'm going to hold you to a higher standard for next time. If you *ever* bring up my menstrual cycle again in reference to my mood, I will make good on that promise of tattooing your face when you sleep. Got it?"

"Yes?" Michael shifts very awkwardly and backs away toward the patio door from which he initially came.

"I'm not one to joke about tattoos, Michael. Or my period," G grits out.

"Got it. I'm going to just make sure the grill is all cleaned up and ready for the steaks."

Giselle looks over at me, and we both just smile. We

walk toward each other and wrap our arms around one another. Without saying anything else for a moment, we just hold on. Something tells me that she needs it, maybe as much as I do.

She mumbles on my shoulder, "You forgive me?"

"Always."

She leans back, holds my shoulders, and looks at me. She's searching for the truth and finds it. I know her and she'd never intentionally hurt me.

"I just thought..." She pauses like she wants to say more, but she's not sure exactly what to say.

My father breaks up the thought by shaking the shit out of his cocktail shaker. I wipe the tears that fell. I'm far too emotional when it comes to arguing and apologizing with G.

"Pumpkin, I've got a vanilla bean and lime-infused vodka with just a splash of coconut milk. I think you'll like this one. It reminds me of that trip we all took to Hawaii right after Henry came back from Japan."

I walk toward the bar. "That was a great trip. He was extra grumpy, if I remember correctly, always so snarly. Oh! Law had the boob-shaped tan line on his face."

Henry starts cracking up, a full-body chuckle, remembering the prank. My dad too.

Sipping on the drink, I take a look around the room. There's something about coming home that makes me breathe easier. Safe. Happy.

Taking another sip, I hear the rumble of a motorcycle. It pulls my attention to the front of the house, and my heart rate picks up, maybe even skipping beats that should be there. I watch Jack, with his confident swagger and stupid, sexy face get off his Harley and walk up the porch steps.

What is he doing here? My palms are instantly sweaty, and I'm frozen in place. I wasn't prepared to see him here. He moves closer, with a bottle of wine in each hand. *Is he coming for dinner?* Through the front door, and down the foyer steps, without even looking up, he says, "Ash, I brought the pinot instead. I'm pretty sure she likes this one better." Then he looks up, sees me, and stops dead in his tracks. All the worry drains from my body. Instead, as soon as we see each other, it's as if I can breathe again. My heart beats at its normal pace, a familiar heat passing through my shoulders and settling into my cheeks.

A big smile takes over his face, both dimples coming out as he says, "You're here."

I blink for a minute, trying to register his words. "I'm here. Why are you here?"

My dad breaks my attention by clearing his throat, then says, "You didn't get my text."

Wait. I look between my father and Jack now, trying to work out any logical reason why these two would be speaking without my knowledge.

"What's happening? Why are you texting Jack?" I ask my dad.

I look around the room quickly to see if I'm the only one surprised by Jack being here right now. Except for G, all of the men in the room are clearly waiting to see the type of response I'm about to dish out. They all *knew* he'd be here. I look over at Giselle.

"Nope, don't glare at me. I didn't know he would be here, honey. I promise. Especially after that car ride, I would have said something," G says, clearly as surprised by our current guest as I am right now.

I turn to look at my dad again, trying to understand this

surprising dynamic. "Daddy, you invited *him* for dinner? W-why would you do that?"

Jack cuts in and answers instead. "I asked him if I could be here. I have some things I need to say to you. Things I need to show you, and I knew if I didn't do it right, I wouldn't get another chance." He moves closer, more slowly now. And I feel the dam of emotions I've been holding back break.

My eyes are already betraying me by watering up so quickly that tears begin to spill over. The man just started speaking, and I'm already a crying mess. The truth of the matter is, I need to hear everything he has to say, but now that I see him, in the same room as him after all this time, I just want to wrap my arms around him and hope he never lets go.

51

Jack

"I'm listening," she says as her chin quivers. It's killing me that I've made such a mess of this and that it's taken me this long to clean it up and set it right. I place the bottle of wine I brought onto the bar, then move closer. Close enough to see tears rolling down her cheek and to be reminded that she smells like my favorite color. The way she affects me is like a punch to the gut, mixed with a welcoming home and fire-burning need to touch her skin, absorb her warmth, strength. Being close to her again makes me feel lighter, happier than I have been. *God, I missed her.*

I'm so nervous. Afraid that she's going to tell me to fuck off and that she doesn't love me anymore, not the way that I'm ready to love her now. I don't want to be too late. I steel my reserve so that my voice doesn't shake the same way that my hands already are.

I look around quickly and so does she. We watch Asher and Law make their way out to the patio doors, both giving me tight smiles and nods of encouragement. The guys knew I was planning to talk to her today, but it wasn't supposed to be until later tonight. I feel a twinge of guilt for cutting their time with her short, but I've waited long enough. *Too long.*

I've come to more than appreciate this family. After the day at the rock wall and dinner with them later that night, I've seen them often. Henry's been helping me with some renovations at my new place, and Law always pops over with dinner on Friday nights. He tells me he's taking a break from dating, but I think he's been dumped royally and needs to lick his wounds without the rumor mill catching wind of it.

The fact that I don't even need to ask for some time alone with Everly, they already know that I don't want to do this with an audience says enough. I can't say the same for Giselle, who is sitting and watching us as if we're the penultimate episode of her favorite TV drama.

"Giselle?" I ask and look up at Henry as he walks back toward her.

"I'm not about to leave her alone with you. Oh, no. I'm staying right here until I know she's going to be okay," she says with obnoxious gumption.

In an exaggerated exhale, Henry says, "No, you're not. Let's go." He doesn't wait for her to get up, he just hauls her up under her armpits and walks with her outside. I don't catch many actual words coming out.

"Such a killjoy, you big oaf! My girl needs me right now. Put me down before I jam my boot right into..."

As the commotion settles, Everly looks back to meet my gaze.

She says, "I've missed you." And with that, I release the breath I didn't even realize I was holding. In two short strides, I make my way to her. Without missing a beat, she wraps her arms around me and buries her face in my neck. I've never held on to anyone so tightly in all my life, and I have no interest in ever letting her go. I made a lot of bad calls when it comes to this woman, but the one that ruined everything was saying nothing at all. *Never again.*

"Will you let me explain some things? Things that have been going on that you probably don't know about since you've been in New York. Well, even before that." I wipe a tear away from her cheek and she mimics the same motion on the other.

"I don't want your excuses, Jack. I just need to know what you want from me. I can't move forward unless you spell it out for me. I'm a smart woman, and I refuse to be stupid about this. About you."

I brush my thumbs under her chin and pull my hands from her face down her neck, tilting her up to look at me. "I want everything you're willing to give me. I want you. All of you. I've never wanted something so much in my entire life."

She closes her eyes, hopefully absorbing my words and not readying to shatter my existence.

I'm filling silence, because she needs to hear everything. She deserves all my truths. "The biggest mistake of my life was not running after you. Staying that day after you told me how you felt, and not figuring out how to talk with you about what was going on with me. I handled all of it wrong."

I pull her hand over my chest so she can feel how nervous I am. My heart racing, chest rising. I take my breath and exhale my love for her. "I fell for you hard. Probably started that first time I kissed you in the studio, beautiful. You knocked me sideways with that mouth of yours, and then everything afterward was better than I thought I ever deserved. After you told me you had fallen in love with me, I wasn't ready to hear it, but it never meant I didn't feel it too. And I should have said that." I take a breath. The next part she doesn't know about yet.

"I went to New York when I realized how badly I fucked up in shutting you out."

I pull my eyes from our entwined hands to her sparkling hazels. "Giselle just told me you came to New York. Why the big secret? If you came to fix it, then why not stay and come talk to me?"

"I saw you in your store, running the place." I kick up a laugh. "Like the boss you are, and I was proud of you. I am so proud of you. I watched you for almost an entire day from across the street like a damn stalker and realized that if I was going to come into your life and blow it up again that I needed to do more than just tell you how I felt. I needed to show you that this wasn't just a fling for me. I don't want to *just* date you. I'm not looking for temporary."

I pull her closer to me and drag my fingers through her shortened hair. "I'm such a goner for you, Everly. I should have told you. I'm so sorry I pushed you away."

She looks at me for a long minute, searching for something. Perhaps her way of making me sweat for being such a dick, for taking so long to get out of my own way and in front of her at this moment. She steels herself, grips the fingers that are twined with hers and stands taller.

"Beg."

I bark a laugh out because it wasn't what I was expecting her to say. If she needs me to beg, then I will. I'll do anything she damn expects from here on out.

"Alright, beautiful. You're the only person I'll get on my knees for." I drop in front of her and look up at her wild hazel eyes, and I already know she's forgiven me. That she's mine. Smiling, I obey her request. She deserves nothing less. "Please. Forgive me. I'm so sorry it's taken me so long to show up for you. For this. Us. I'll work my ass off to make it up to you every damn day."

Mirroring me, she smiles, big and bright. The dimple in her left cheek, which I've learned only comes out when she's truly happy, truly smiling, is there. "That was good, but I feel like I'm going to need to think of some kind of penance now."

I can see her wheels spinning. Hopefully, she comes up with something deliciously dirty. I'll take it. Right now, at this moment, she's smiling at me, and that is worth more than any kind of currency or exchange. I pull her down to me and brush my mouth over hers. Our lips are slow, but my body is quick to remember what she does to me when we touch. Warmth. Sparks. *Fire.*

I break our kiss, only to lean my forehead to hers and finally tell her what I've been working up to say. "I'm so in love with you."

"I know." She pauses and then says, "You sent me waffles."

"Yeah, I made you waffles. They were the only thing I could think of to try to make you feel better. They always do the trick for me. Did they help?"

"A bit. Every Sunday, always warm, like clockwork. Wait, you made me waffles?"

"Well, Luce made them for you. When I was there, I showed her how I made them and paid her...a lot...to make them for you every Sunday, with farmers' market strawberries and extra crispy bacon, and then she had to deliver it."

"Tiny little Asian woman, big hair? Looks kind of mean?"

"That's Luce. The evilest and most selfless friend I've got."

"I saw her creep away from my door through the peephole one morning, and I just assumed she was an UberEats driver. I'll have to tell her thank you when I meet her."

"Good, you can come and meet her now. She's getting my new place in order, and I want you to see it."

Everly looks at me quizzically. "You're not staying at Kathryn's anymore?"

I shake my head.

"Strutt's Peak is home for me now." I pull her close again and wrap my arms around her body. She pulls me closer, wrapping her arms around my shoulders, her fingers running up the back of my neck, through my hair. She kisses me, and it feels so good. Relief and worthiness flood through my veins. Hearing that she can forgive me, after everything, stupid mistakes, bad choices, time, distance. I've never had anyone choose me. And that's what she's doing, and I'm not sure how I'm worthy of it, but I'll work at trying to prove it to her every day. If she'll let me.

Everly

Jack pulls me along a stone-cut path stretching from my dad's ranch and into the wooded landscape along the width of the property. Now that it's dusk, any light left from the day is fleeting. I hold tightly onto Jack's hand and listen as he fills me in on what's been happening with his sister and nephew. I knew from the Strutt's gossip train that Kathryn had been frequently fall-down drunk at the local bars, that the last time it happened was the night before the Tree Lighting and that's what had pulled Jack from the event. She chose to go to rehab and re-enlist in therapy to work through it. What I didn't realize was that it meant Jack stayed in town, taking care of his nephew and keeping Books & Brew running smoothly. He joined her in therapy.

"I know I didn't handle any of it right, Ev. I should have told you what was going on instead of assuming you couldn't exist with me while I was dealing with it. He looks toward me again, closing his eyes and pausing with a squeeze to my hand. "And as far as Jin is concerned, I'm sorry I behaved the way I did. He and I never got along, ever since we were kids. It's always a competition between us about something. Most of the time, it was about my sister's attention, but that's my shit. Anything else I say will just be an excuse." He smiles and then says, "Kathryn always says how much we're alike. Maybe that's why he pisses me off so easily."

"I wasn't happy with him either. We ended things and left it as friends before you and I met, so I was thrown as to why he acted like we were anything more at that point. He was just as much a prick as you were." I stop walking for a minute, wanting him to hear me when I tell him this. "You both make it difficult for other people to see it sometimes, but you're good men. You have that in common."

He doesn't respond right away, instead he brings my hand that he's holding to his lips and kisses it. We continue walking, and I can tell he has more he wants to say, so I stay quiet and let him work through it.

"Maybe. I never liked the way he assumed responsibility for Kathryn. They weren't the same, not the way she and I were. And then after a while, everything was a competition and not a friendly one. So then you came into my life, and I find out that you've had or have a relationship with my brother, of any kind, and it instantly pissed me off. That wasn't fair to you, but I wasn't thinking, just reacting."

He's right, that wasn't fair. I squeeze his hand and tell him, "You could have asked me what was going on, how I knew him. I would have told you anything you wanted to know."

Jack rubs the back of his neck with his free hand. I can tell there's more to unpack. It's a lot of family drama, but if he wants to move forward, I need to hear it. Understand it at least.

"Jin disappeared for a handful of years, and Kathryn took it pretty hard, losing another person in her life, our life. She was young, pregnant by some kid from our neighborhood that she was wrapped up with, and then one of the people she grew to depend on just left."

Without thinking, I say, "Another thing in common." He looks over at me, questioning what I mean. "Disappearing."

His face changes quickly, caught off guard by the admission. He stops walking and pulls me into his arms, holding on tightly and burying his face in my neck. "You're right," he whispers. "I'll do better, Ev. I promise you I'll do better." He pulls back, kisses my forehead, and then leans his head against mine. The tenderness of it makes me feel his words, not just hear them. He grips my chin and kisses me gently.

I smile at him, and though it would be easy to get lost in his ocean blue eyes or fall daintily into the sweetness of his touch, he needs to know I hear his words, and he should hear mine too. "I'm going to hold you to that. I won't stick around for another apology," I say, leaning in to press another soft kiss to his lips. "I love you, but I love me more, and I won't allow myself or the life I've built to come crashing down, because I've chosen to trust you. That's what this is, for me, trusting you to put us first, respect me enough to include me in your life, and to trust me in return, even if it's messy."

He threads his fingers through mine and squeezes my hand. "I understand". The corner of his mouth kicks up, and before a full smile takes over his face, he says, "Damn, I'm in love with you."

We walk around a curve in the pathway, and it's then

that I can see the Muldowney Ranch house in the distance. I've walked this property dozens of times, but I was so wrapped up in what we were saying to one another that it hadn't registered where we were headed. The ranch looks different from the last time I ventured over here. The outdoor space is lit up with big, round bulb patio lights strung around the space. It's surrounded by beautiful orange, pink, and blue wildflowers and pristine green landscaping. The barn house and guest house in the distance are lit as well.

David Muldowney, while a refined sommelier, is also a cowboy at heart, and his tastes reflected it. His home was adorned with all shades of wood and plaids. The main house was a deep russet log cabin framed by heavy greenery around the outside. It looked very different from what's standing out in front of me right now. And then, as I look up at my dream home in awe, my thoughts come back to me. This walk was leading us to Jack's new house...

"You bought *this*? The ranch, I mean, *this* ranch?" My voice kicks up at the end, in complete shock.

This fucker just smiles at me, hitting me with those dimples. "C'mon," he says, knocking me down a peg. I am so overwhelmed, I can't even get my feet to move. He tugs my arm, leading me toward the house. The bright white siding and oversized black framed windows make it completely new. Refreshed and modern, but it still maintains some of its rustic charm with distressed wood patio furniture surrounding an oversized outdoor fireplace with a massive hearth.

I'm still rendered speechless as we rush forward. Jack pulls open the sliding glass door, which really should be considered a wall, since the pristine glass runs the length of almost the entire house. There is nothing remaining of the dark aesthetic that stood here before. Instead, it looks like Chip and Joanna Gaines crossed paths with Frank Lloyd Wright, and the result is an architectural work of modern farmhouse art. It's incredible.

As we enter, a loud, New York-infused accent comes from the open refrigerator. "You only have some local bourbon shit stocked in your bar. Jack, that's not acceptable and you know it. Next time I come here to help your stupid ass, I need more variety. Oh, shit!"

"Forgive me, Luce. I'll have it stocked next time." Jack laughs while shaking his head. "I thought you might like to meet Everly, finally."

A gorgeously confident Asian woman saunters my way with a level of confident swagger that makes me instantly like her. Her lips stained in a bright purple gloss and nails almost as long as her fingers in the same shade greet me with a closed smile and a firm shake.

"Lucy," she says. "And thank the universe, you're stunning and you look like you can hold your own in a room. I was afraid he went and fell for a debutante, or worse, some crunchy granola who makes her own soap or some shit."

"Luce," Jack growls.

"It's nice to meet you, Lucy. I was told you're the one to thank for my Sunday breakfasts these past few months. They were delicious."

"Don't mention it." She kicks her thumb at Jack. "His sorry ass paid me well for it." She moves toward the oversized couch in the living space and picks up a black furry coat and matching hat. "My work here is done." She looks at Jack with a scowl. "For now, at least."

"Luce, you don't have to go."

"Give me a fucking break, Romeo. I've had enough bonding time with you to last me the rest of this year. Call me next week, and we can talk about your contracts and that gallery in Chicago."

She turns around before leaving through the front door. "Everly, treat him right. He may be stupid a lot of the time, but, you know, MEN! This one, though, deserves only the best."

Without responding, I give her a quick nod and lean into Jack's arms. We watch as she pulls out her phone and starts barking directions at someone on the other end.

I can hear the smile in Jack's voice as he says, "Now you've met the devil herself."

"All five feet of her. She seems exactly like the kind of friend I'd imagine you'd have. She doesn't seem awful enough to call her that, though. I really thought her name was Lucifer. Does she know you have her saved as that in your phone?"

"She doesn't seem that bad, because she's probably tired. You got the tame version. She's probably on her way to consume the soul of an unsuspecting man she met on her flight out here."

Jack turns me and places a soft kiss on my lips. I wrap my arms around his neck and nuzzle into him. "I want to show you a few things. Some upgrades since you may have last been here."

Jack leads me through the renovated home, and in every room we walk through, there's something unique to love. Starting with the kitchen, it's not the typical bright whites and monochromatic tones. Instead, the marble counters rest on top of deep blue cabinets adorned with brushed gold fixtures. The dining space and living room flow into each other, making the space feel big and bright. But it's the back wall of windows that runs the length of the space that makes it feel massively special. It frames the beautiful outdoor living space, the sprawling field just beyond it, and I'd bet in the daylight, you can see the mountains of Strutt's standing tall behind it all. The artist in him did the place justice. It's breathtaking.

"I didn't realize this place was even for sale or that David had any plans to relocate. How did you know? I haven't been gone all that long for all of this to happen."

"It wasn't for sale. But everything has a price. It took David a bit of convincing to sell it to me, but I knew if I wanted you in my life that I was going to have to pull out all the stops. You said how much you loved the view here, so..."

"Jack," I whisper. I'm not about to play dumb and think I didn't play a role in him buying this place, but to hear that he did this out loud, I'm overwhelmed with happiness.

I don't need a ranch and an insanely expensive home to know that he's it for me. I won't find this again. This feeling that lights up between us, the electricity, the understanding, and the all-consuming need to be near him. And now that I know how he feels, I know this isn't something you explore and meander through. Even after the tears spilled, I want to go all-in now, dive with no hesitation, because I know I won't be lucky enough to find this again. Not in this lifetime.

There's not much furniture or personal things in any of the spaces yet; it's still being painted and finishes missing. He was waiting to complete it with me. We walk down the hallway, then up another flight of stairs and, as we hit the top, my breath hitches. The entire top floor is floor-to-ceiling windows. And because it's the highest point of the house, you can see above the property line of trees and out to the most breathtaking view of pitch-black darkness speckled with stars.

"Out there, just above tree line, in the morning, you'll see that view you love so much," he tells me. I can hear the excitement in his voice.

I'm not sure what to say, so I stay quiet, trying to understand the emotions swirling around me. It's too much, and it's going to end up coming out as a mess of tears.

Jack looks at me, trying to read what I'm not saying. "You told me it was beautiful and you were right. It was the best view I had ever seen." I finally blink.

"I tend to be right about a lot of things," I joke.

"Almost." He pauses and comes up behind me, wraps his arms around my waist, and kisses my neck. "This view only gets better when you're in it. And it's the only view I want. This isn't my place, Ev, this is ours. If you want it to be."

I become very aware of my breathing. Slowing down this moment to absorb all of it. Relish in it. I'm always so busy rushing into what's next and waiting for the other shoe to inevitably drop that I never just breathe in the good moments, the great moments. This is one of them.

He peppers kisses along my neck and whispers, "Move in here with me. Make this a home with me."

I smile wide and turn around in his arms to face him. "I was planning on it."

"I'm serious, beautiful." His dimples pop in to frame the very amused look on his face.

Meeting his smile, I whisper back, "So am I."

As soon as I say it out loud, I know it's right. I can hear my best friend objecting to the speed of it. Today was a whirlwind. It started with barely being able to imagine how I'd feel if I saw him. That was this morning, and now we're living together and loving each other by nightfall. G would say something in the way of, "Maybe date for a while before you live together?" or "Maybe make him work for it a bit more before you saddle yourself to just one." But I'm not interested in practicing cautious decision-making anymore. Not with Jack.

While there's a part of me that thinks about life very logically, I know that there's a catch: logic can only make you so happy. After a while, it takes out the interesting things, and you're left with a lot of smart decisions on paper, but not much else. It's where I've been residing for most of my life, always smart on paper and never too indulgent. It's been productive, but damn lonely. And it didn't keep me from getting hurt.

I'm a successful woman in my mid-thirties who can afford a home on my own and all the little luxuries that I want. In a nutshell, I don't *need* a man in my life to survive and thrive, but I *want* one. This one in particular. So if this doesn't work out, if Jack ends up being a control freak with an urge to adopt twenty-five feral cats or if he develops a distorted view on domestic gender roles, then I can revisit the idea of having my own place. But, for now, I'm going to live with the man I'm in love with, in the house that he's built for us, in the town that I adore and call home.

"I've figured out what you're going to do to make it up to me." I kiss his plump bottom lip and give it a nip. "You're going to love me."

He brings his hands to my face, rubbing his thumbs along my chin. It's the simplest of gestures, but the size of his hands on me in this way makes me feel so cared for. Cherished.

"That's already done, beautiful. I plan on never stopping."

"Good. Then I want you to worship my body. I want your mouth everywhere my blood pulses. I want your hands on every curve. I want your tongue to tease me, and your cock buried so deep that I'll feel every breath it takes to fuck me good."

He groans at my words. "Everly, usually a punishment or penance is a task that you *don't* want to do."

Jack drops to his knees and rests his forehead on my stomach. I run my fingers through his short dark hair, and he wraps his arms around my middle.

"I'll worship you every fucking day, beautiful. You don't even need to ask."

Nuzzling his face into me, he takes a deep breath, as if he's trying to breathe me in and borrow the same air that's already coursing through me. He takes his time undressing me. He lifts my shirt just enough to kiss the skin above the seam of my pants and then sits back on his heels to start his promised task.

The quietness of the house amplifies every movement, hitch of breath, and the significance of this moment. Choosing to love each other. None of it is lost on me.

Our chests rise and fall with loud breaths, sucking in more air in anticipation of our promises and movements. His masculine smell is layered with something dark and sweet, like caramel or coffee. It makes me want to lick the air around him, taste his smell. He moves his fingers and hands along my body, exploring and remembering exactly what sends shivers across its surface.

We languidly fall into a rhythm of a love that soothes the hurt and misunderstanding. With every touch of his fingertips and dip of his tongue across my body, the feelings I've been trying to keep away and smother for months awaken with intent.

I want to do more than take right now. I want to give. I pull his chin up to stop the trail of kisses and praise he's been forging along my thighs. Instead, I need Jack to look at me and see that if this is going to be the type of love that I know we're capable of, then he needs to allow me to worship him too. I need him to know that I am moving forward, no penance is necessary.

"What do you need from me, beautiful? I'm literally on my knees in front of you, ready to do anything you ask." He kisses and licks the thumb I've been brushing across his lower lip.

"I want to feel how hard I make you just by the promise of what I'm about to offer. I want to taste you. And then I want you to tell me how well I please you when I pull your cock to the back of my throat and suck."

He growls, "Fucking hell, Everly." Then, he stands, and without hurry, he unbuckles his belt. I can see the desire in his eyes, and I can tell it won't take long to have him unraveling. I already see the outline of his cock trying to break free of his pants. *So eager.* There's something so satisfying knowing that I can make him that excited with only a kiss and a few dirty words.

"I haven't been with anyone else. I wanted to get over the hurting, but I couldn't even think about being with anyone else, let alone meet someone for a date or casual sex." I wait to hear what he has to say. I'll try not to be upset if he'd been with another person while we've been apart, but I still hope he hasn't.

"Look at me." I tilt my face up to look at him. "There was

nobody else. There is nobody else. You're it for me, beautiful. I'm sorry that I couldn't let you hear that sooner, but I'm telling you now. I've never wanted another woman the way I want you. I *crave* you. Your laugh, your kindness, your fire. All of it. I don't want anyone else. How could I go back to ordinary when I've found what I was made for? And beautiful," he pauses and kisses my lips softly, "I was made to love you."

As he kisses me again, we both smile. Hearing words like that, feeling them, and not just hearing them. Not just love, but more. And with these emotions swirling, I can't help but want to show him, make love to him, get sweaty with him until we're drained of all the rest of the bullshit that hasn't been flushed out yet.

Our kiss closes the seriousness of our conversation, and we both know that right now, it's back to feeding what our bodies crave. Each other.

"Are we good?" I ask.

"We're good. Now take out those beautiful tits. I need to see them."

I pull my shirt over my head and throw it to the floor. Jack pushes his pants down and off his legs so that he's only standing in front of me now with his black boxer briefs, his erection ready to spring to life and meet my promises.

Instead of taking my pink-laced bra off, I pull my breasts up and over the top, letting them spill out. On a groan, Jack fists his cock in his hand and gives it two hard tugs. I can already see the tip glistening with his excitement.

"Open that pretty mouth for me." I lick my lips and part them as he brushes the tip of his cock around my lips. "Stick out your tongue." I do as he says and get my praiseful reward. "That's my girl. Look at how pretty you look, so eager to please me."

He pushes a few strands of hair away from my face and tucks them behind my ear and then pushes his cock into my mouth slowly. "That's right, beautiful. Take all of it." He pushes forward, and with a slow roll of his hips, he slides in and drags out of my mouth. I close my lips and keep my tongue flat so it can glide along from tip to shaft and back again each time he enters and exits.

The dominance in his movements and the care in his voice have my panties drenched, and I'm craving some kind of friction. I shift to relieve some of the pressure that's already building. Jack reaches down and plucks at one of my nipples and rolls it between his fingers. Just that concentrated movement alone increases the hunger, but instead of moving my mouth away from the task I've been given, I squeeze his firm, rounded ass, and pull him forward. His cock hits the back of my throat, and instead of gagging or pulling away, I pull him toward me again.

He understands what I need and doesn't ease back. I relax my throat and breathe as he grips my hair and starts to fuck my throat.

"Fuck. Your mouth feels so good," he growls out. "Look at you taking my fat cock like such a good girl."

Just as I get used to the movement, he pulls away and kneels in front of me, mimicking how I'm sitting. "I am a very lucky man. Another minute, and I would be spilling into that beautiful mouth of yours. But I want a taste of what that was doing to you, how much sucking my cock turned you on."

Without being able to respond, Jack shifts and grips me under my thighs, pulling my weight up. I wrap my arms around his neck, laughing at the quickness of his movements as he guides us down to lie on the plush carpet.

"The last time we were together, it wasn't nearly enough. I don't ever want to leave each other like that again. I need to make up for it. I hope you don't have any plans tomorrow, because I don't plan on sleeping much tonight, beautiful."

"No plans, just you. Now stop talking and put that mouth to work, Jack."

He growls, bites my nipple, and then flattens his tongue and runs it back and forth to soothe the twinge of pain. He mimics the movement on the other side, and before I can catch my breath, his mouth covers me at the core. With an open mouth and heated breath, he teases my clit. He does it so softly that it feels more like he's blowing air above me than gliding the tip of his tongue up and down. Repeatedly, punishingly. He works me up into an aroused mess and then leans back, looking at my eager body to survey what he's done. I buck my hips toward his mouth in protest for more. He gives me a smirk, flashing those dimples again.

Time doesn't register for me in any traditional sense, only in the build and anticipation for Jack's mouth to satiate me. He repeats all of it, over and over, edging me toward my orgasm and then retreating, only to do it all over again.

My moans are loud and needy. "Jack, please. I need more. Please."

They echo throughout the massive room. But instead of complying, he stops and blows a cooling breath over the wetness that's engulfed me and then thrusts fingers into me, filling the void that's been aching. It's exactly what tips me over, spilling my orgasm throughout every muscle. The darkness behind my closed eyes fades into a snowy-white fuzz, and my body keeps its pace, writhing and riding it out.

When I open my eyes, I'm met with Jack's heated gaze. I look down at our bodies as he pulls my hips up, the backs of my thighs hitting the front of his, and then I watch as he slides into me. The sight of it turns me on. Watching him move inside me.

In one fast push to the hilt, he fills me, and I'm knocked back again into an orgasm that has me screaming out his name. The delicious, devious feeling of my body taking what it needs from him, and its result is complete and utter pleasure.

"That's it, beautiful. You feel so incredible. This pussy was made just for me," he groans out.

I've never been so easily manhandled, and it's so satisfying. He maneuvers my legs up so he can flip us over, so I'm lying on top of him now. Our sweat-slicked skin is the only thing that keeps time, and shows how long we've been lost in each other. He wasn't joking about taking his time and I'm not sure how he's held himself together this long. I've already come apart countless times, each more intense than the last.

I sit up and grind down on him slowly, rolling my hips so he has no choice but to hit the deepest parts of me. He watches my body, his face intent and hungry, as he gives me the lead to control the pace. His need to come apart soon is starting to seep through. The resolve he's built to keep this going is fading fast, and I can tell that he's more than ready to come. The tightness of his jaw, the tilt of his chin upwards. "Everly, fuck. You're so damn sexy."

Tilting back, I give into one last sensation. I ride him so well that he hits even deeper, and I start to unravel all over again, only this time he's right there with me, and we ride out our orgasms together. The feeling of it is so consuming and overwhelming that tears sting my eyes and start to roll down my cheeks. We lie there together. I'm on top of him, unable to move, only able to feel the wake of emotions quivering through me. Feelings that I won't be able to articulate.

Jack quickly realizes and says, "Beautiful, no, no, no." He shifts out from under me, with worry in his voice. "What's wrong? Did I hurt you?"

I just shake my head, trying to find the words that can convey the magnitude of emotion that's running through me. "I've never felt that. The lust and the love part together before. I didn't know that it could be like that. The intensity of it, and I'm not even sure why I'm crying. But, oh God, Jack, please tell me we can make that happen again." I smile through the tears.

He barks out a laugh and kisses my sweat-soaked neck. "I love you so much, beautiful. And yeah, we can make that happen again. I may need a minute or two, but I plan on doing that with you countless times."

And we do. Countless times. We didn't sleep that night, instead we showed each other how much we missed each other, respected each other's bodies, and craved one another's touch. We talked until the night fled and the morning crept in.

When the sun started to peek from behind the mountains, it painted the sky with broad, exaggerated strokes in every shade of orange I could imagine. It was the first morning in our home, in the warmth of each other's arms, where we truly began loving each other. It was when color seeped into every part of my life that had been so rigidly black and white for so long. It's when our love story really began.

EPILOGUE

Everly

"THERE ARE ONLY TWO QUESTIONS YOU NEED TO ANSWER tonight. Are you ready? It's not what you're thinking either. Okay, here it goes. One, because my hair is currently tipped pink and my dress is this shade of red, will I be mistaken for a real-life cupid? Like, should I just go all in and find some exaggerated heart jewelry or something?"

"That's not a serious question, G. What's number two?" I finished putting on the lip liner that matches the dark ruby-colored lipstick I'm trying out tonight.

"Fine. It was a valid concern for a minute. Your head went there. I saw it, I know it did. I don't want to overplay a part, ya know?"

"G, you look friggin' amazing. You're always a ten, but tonight you look like a damn prize, and you know it. What's question number two?"

Ignoring me, she says, "You look incredible, Ev. See, you need to add a little color to your wardrobe now and then.

Gold sequins are your jam right now, and with that lip color, damn girl."

It's not my normal black or white, but when I saw the dress, I had to have it. A gorgeous deep V-neck, floor-length cocktail dress that happens to sparkle gold.

She smiles and passes a glass of champagne to me as I finish applying the lip stain that makes my makeup pop tonight. "You look like this glass of champagne. Jack is going to try to make you leave early. DON'T DO IT! Do not Irish goodbye on me tonight." She clears her throat, and I know what question is coming before she asks it. "Is everyone going to be there? I haven't heard you mention all of your brothers, and I want to know what level of alert I need to be on before I walk into that tent."

Before I can even answer, she downs her drink and tops it off with a small hiccup.

"Everyone will be there, yes. Henry included. He just got back last night. I saw him at dinner. And before you ask, he looks fine, but beyond that, I have no idea where he was. He wouldn't tell me, but I know better than to ask. He only said that he had to take care of a few things for a while."

"Okay, that was a segue. My second question is, do you have anything, anything you'd like to tell me?" She glares at me.

"Like what?" I smile a big cheesy smile and refuse to make eye contact. "I have no idea what you're asking about."

"Fine, whatever.. I won't push, but I know you, Everly Riggs. You're a shit liar." She points at me. And she's right. I'm a crap liar. I always have a tell, and Giselle is a hawk for bullshit.

"Why are you acting so weird?"

"You're being weird. I'm just nervous. I'm fucking

nervous, that's all. I knew I should have never let Ash talk me into being auctioned tonight. Too many pissed-off people in this town. Now Henry is back, damn it. God, let's just get in there so I can drink something that's going to get me drunk enough to be auctioned off like the fucking prize that I am."

There it is. She said yes to my father, which honestly is the only possible answer when he wants someone to do something for him. He asked her to step in for me this year since I didn't want to be auctioned off.

We're no sooner at headquarters, never mind in the tent, and Giselle is practically sprinting to the bar on the other side of the room for a drink.

My dad looks at me and laughs. "Is she okay?"

"Daddy, I have no idea. She's freaking out." I lean in and kiss my dad on the cheek. Always looking so debonair, his salt and pepper hair is slicked back, and instead of wearing a bowtie this year, he opted for an ascot and a black velvet jacket. "You look great, Daddy. It's very Bond meets Hefner."

He barks a laugh. "Oh, please, your brother had some favor he had to pay and that meant all of us wearing fucking ascots."

"Dad, this is a statement. Stop trying to make it like you aren't feeling good about yourself right now. I had very explicit instructions on attire," Law barks back, quirking his eyebrow at me.

I stifle a laugh. "Where's my guy? I haven't seen him yet."

"Jack's over at the bar, talking to Henry and Lenny. She had some big news to tell him about the boats for next season, and Henry had some new guys coming in to build out the fishing lodge. I think they wanted Jack's help on visuals."

I smile at my brother. Law leans in and kisses my cheek. "You look stunning, Ev. Gold was the right choice." He winks and looks at my hands.

Then Dad clears his throat, gathering my brothers' attention. "Alright, kids, let's get this party moving. I'm going to grab my drink and then do the welcome speech."

I catch Jack's eye from the other side of the room. His gorgeous dimples make an immediate appearance as he looks me up and down. My body buzzes when he looks at me like that.

The man can wear a tuxedo, I'll give him that. While I prefer to see him in jeans and a Henley most days, I'll take the billionaire in a tux look, too.

And that's what I learned when I was discovering all the details about the love of my life. That he's not just a world-renowned photographer. Nope. The man is worth billions. With a *B*. He sits on the board of a variety of technology companies and sporting brands, as well as Riggs Outdoor as of a month ago. He's also an investor in each of those companies and a variety of small art galleries up and down each coast. The man has a larger investment portfolio than my father, and you would never know it. He's not on any fortune lists and would never flaunt it. He'll tell anyone who asks that he's a photographer, but he really is a businessman and an exceptionally great one at that. Self-made, smart, and so fucking sexy.

As he walks closer, my stomach does a somersault, taking in every deliciously masculine angle of his face and body. A body that had mine quivering for a good hour after an onslaught of orgasms earlier today. Life is pretty damn good.

"Beautiful. That dress is giving me all kinds of feelings

right now. We might need to leave a bit early." He leans in and kisses my lips and then drops his mouth right beneath my ear, leaving another that has me shivering.

"This is our party, baby. We're not leaving early."

The tapping of the microphone pulls our attention to the front of the room. "Good evening, everyone. I'd like to welcome you all to this year's Annual Tree Lighting in Strutt's Peak." The audience claps, and my brothers each give their supporting hoots and hollers.

"Quite a lot has occurred over this past year with my family. While my daughter Everly moved on from the family business to start her own, very successful apparel line, our latest Strutt's Peak transplant Jack Deacon decided to take a seat on our board of directors and work alongside my sons to help bring our brand even more success." Jack gives him an appreciative smile and nods, but instead of stopping at that, Jack grabs my hand, and we walk toward the stage.

"Oh, okay, it looks like they're going to join me up here. Jack, did you want to help me kick the night off?" My father laughs, slightly caught off guard as we approach.

I speak first. "Actually, Daddy, we both do." My father hands the microphone over and steps off to the side, looking at me curiously. Initially, I wanted Jack to do most of the talking, but now that I'm up here, and I look out at the people who make up this town that's as much of me as I am of it, I feel like I should be the one to share the news.

"Good evening, everyone. You all look incredible this evening." I look out over the crowd of familiar faces. "On nights like tonight, it's easy to see why Strutt's Peak is so important to my family. My brothers and I have grown up here with each one of you as neighbors, colleagues, friends, and, in extension, family." I look over to Jack. "And now, it's our home." I smile over to my brothers and Giselle, who are now standing in the back of the room, all attention on us. I think they assumed Jack might be proposing tonight, but we have an even better surprise for them.

"Which is why Jack and I thought that tonight would be the perfect night to share our news and celebrate." Curious eyes watch as I stare at Jack through watery eyes. I nod and pass the microphone to him, because I know I may not be able to finish without ugly crying.

"Last night, I asked the love of my life if she'd spend the rest of it with me." Cheers and hollers begin, but Jack cuts them off. "And she said yes." The entire room erupts into even louder cheers, and my father wraps me in a strong hug, tears escaping and flowing down his face.

"Congratulations, pumpkin. He's a good man. When he told me he was planning to ask, I gave him my blessing. Until him, I wasn't sure anyone would have gotten that from me," He laughs. "I'm so happy right now."

"Me too, Daddy. Me too."

My brothers, like the goons they tend to be, storm the stage and yank each of us into bear hugs. They each kiss me and mumble congratulations. All of them, including Michael, give Jack a back-slapping hug. I think they each have a little bromance with him. He seems to have that kind of effect on people.

"No wonder you were okay with me looking like a cupid. I'm like your engagement mascot, for fuck's sake!" Giselle laughs out and wraps her arms tightly around my middle. She pulls back and wipes a tear from the corner of her eye. "My best friend in the world is getting married, and I knew it, by the way, I fucking knew you were hiding something!"

Jack

The excitement of the room isn't lost on me. A room full of strangers just a year ago, are now congratulating and toasting to mine and Everly's happiness. It didn't take long to make changes so that the life we wanted together worked. Everly hired Luce to take over for her in the New York office, getting things off the ground there so that Everly could focus on the designing side of things. My dear Luce, whom I'm still quite certain is the devil, did not disappoint. Now Everly is there only once a month or so and spends most of her time in her office on our ranch or working from Brews & Books.

"There is not a single person here who I have any interest in taking home tonight, and that is such a disappointment. With this much money and champagne in one room, there should be at least one dumb schmuck here who wants to be tied up," Luce continues on her tirade. She looks past me and quirks an eyebrow up. I look over my shoulder and watch as Michael sheepishly sips on his seltzer, trying hard to not make eye contact. "Luce, don't. That's my brother-in-law."

She pats my chest before moving toward Michael. He's so fucked. "Congratulations, by the way. She's too good for you. You know that, right?" I look over at my wife and catch her eye. She shoots me a smile, both of us still holding on to a little secret.

What everyone doesn't know, and I'm not sure we'll ever tell them either, but this morning, just after sunrise, we exchanged vows. We didn't want to wait to say those words to one another. To tell each other we would love one another forever and make that promise to honor the other every single day. We were already doing it, since the moment we got out of our own way. So, when I asked if being married was something she would want, she said, "Let's not wait any longer." We could do the important piece together, just us, and then tonight celebrate with everyone who mattered. We could throw a big wedding and a party later, but we wanted something just for us. Why wait?

The Colorado sky put on a bit of a show for us too. Orange is still and might always be my favorite color. It was the brightest, painted across the sky with pinks and yellows burning around it as I told the love of my life that I would spend every breath from there on out honoring her as my wife. It was nothing I ever anticipated, being able to love someone like this and feel it back so equally. I'm a better man because of it, or maybe I just keep trying to be so I can be worthy of it.

I rarely have dreams anymore. Sometimes when I'm stressed, but even then, they're nowhere near what they used to be. I don't know what that means, but I'm happier for it. I spend most of my time doing things that I'm good at with the people I love. Now I spend less time worrying about remembering what happened in my past or trying to protect people from things I don't have control over. Instead, I grow my businesses. I take pictures; it will always ground me, seeing things through a lens and then perfecting it.

I spend time with my sister, getting to know her again and helping when she asks for it. I still think Jin is a prick, but he spends a lot of time with Kathryn, and I've come to realize that I'll need to accept it if I want her in my life. And Benny, well, he's off in Costa Rica right now. He met a girl, and they started "exploring." And I remember being nineteen; I know exactly what that means, even if Kathryn thinks he's just hiking. I don't know when he'll be back, and I miss him like hell, but he's finding his way.

"You ready to sneak me out of here, Mr. Deacon?" Everly says, as she walks toward me with two tumblers of scotch in her hands. I take a sip and smile at my beautiful wife. I know that tone, and it's laced with promises that have my dick on high alert.

"What are you going to do for me if I say yes?"

She smiles at me and takes the last sip of her drink. She looks down at the diamond adorning her left ring finger and then looks up across the room. Everyone she loves is dancing, enjoying what's left of the evening.

"Oh, my love, it's not what I'm going to do for you, it's what I expect you to do for me."

I shake my head and smile. "And what's that, beautiful?"

With the sexiest smirk that starts at her eyes and moves to her mouth, she says, "Beg."

THE END

I HOPE YOU ENJOYED PEAKS OF COLOR!
Get ready for more of the Riggs family with Henry and Giselle's story, Hide and Peak.

Alluring. Sexy. Liar.
The newest stranger in Strutt's Peak has a mouth as loud and captivating as the bright tattoos drawn all over her body. But she's no stranger to me. Because I've met her.

I've kissed her lips.

And I'm the only one who knows her secret.
She's supposed to be dead.

Now, I hide the truth and keep her safe. Pretend we never
met. Try to forget I ever touched her. Ignore that she's
always around. She's my sister's best friend now, but before
that, I wanted her to be mine.

My family runs one of the country's most successful winter
sports brands, making me high-profile, a target for small-
town gossip, and national recognition. All of it, dangerous
for her.

The stakes are too high. I know the rules. So why can't I
follow them? How am I supposed to stay away from her
when all I wanted to do was find her? How can I hide her
and keep her safe when what I really want is to make her
mine?

THE RIGGS ROMANCE SERIES CONTINUES WITH...

Henry & Giselle's Story

Michael & Grace's Story

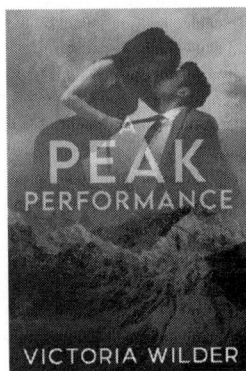

Law & Tessa's Story

MORE BY VICTORIA WILDER

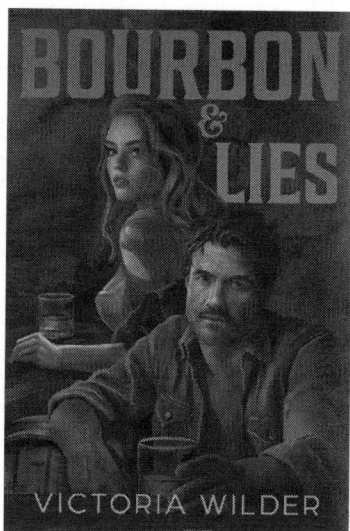

The Bourbon Boys Series (Book 1)

ACKNOWLEDGEMENTS

Thank you is the least I could say to the people whom have helped me along the way. A few words don't seem like enough, but since that's what I have to work with, here we go...

There is this incredible community of people on Instagram, the Bookstagram community, that is filled with readers whom consume romance passionately and fantastically support each other. To all of you, you may not even realize it, but you're such incredible motivators. Between saucy images, gorgeous edits, and original photos, they spark imagination and made this writing escapade even more fun. You happily feed and nurture my reading obsession. I am constantly inspired by you. Thank you.

A special thanks to a few indie authors whom maybe without even realizing it, made an impact. Elsie Silver and Nikki Castle, thank you for always answering my questions and going out of your way to connect me with the right people. That kindness and those details are what made this book come to life. Abby Millsaps, thank you for having some *real talk* with me. Your words were the push I needed. All of you are fantastic writers, but most importantly, fabulous humans.

Thank you to my beta readers, Pam, Erin, Cathy, Sarah, Christina, and Myrna. Your feedback has been so valuable. Thank you for your time, encouragement, and friendship throughout this process.

To my editor, Mackenzie, thank you for being exactly the kind of support I needed. Your guidance made this story come together better than I thought it ever would. I feel like I lucked out with an editor that gets this genre and me so well. Thank you for your cheerleading in the margins, and your genuine excitement for this couple. Cheers to this one, and all of the stories to follow. I'm psyched for what's next!

If you had told me, when I was a kid, as I watched my Mom read voraciously at the kitchen counter grasping onto romance paperback classics, that I would be just like her when I grew up, then I'd have called you crazy. Not a single person is as sharply smart or incredibly cool. But most days when I'm not writing, I'm reading at the kitchen counter grasping my Kindle which is filled to the brim with romance. Mom, turning out even half as amazing as you is a life goal. Aside from being an elite hype woman, you are one of the best alpha readers. Thanks for cheering on this chaos.

To my hubs, thank you for being *my* male main character. You're exactly the kind of man my hopeful romantic heart craves and adores. To my kiddos, hopefully, you don't read this until you're grown-up...and, even then, I wince a little. I love you every day.

Last and most, I'd like to thank my sister, Blair. You're the ultimate alpha reader, sounding board, and support system. Cocktails and read-aloud's with a side of cackling are my favorite. Without you, these characters and their messes would still be locked somewhere inside my head. Thank you really isn't quite enough, so instead, with a way too enthusiastic fist in the air, "*we stole a car!*"

See you at Sunday dinner.

A SIP FROM BREWS & BOOKS

THE HUNGRY EYE

Ingredients

- 8 oz cup medium or dark roast coffee
- 1 to 2 shots of espresso
- ⅓ cup oat milk *any milk can be substituted*
- ¼ teaspoon cinnamon
- Zest from 1 orange
- 2-3 teaspoons of brown sugar
- 1 cup of ice *optional*

You can drink this hot or cold. *Everly prefers it over ice.*

1. Position a small strainer over your coffee cup while brewing. Place the orange zest inside the strainer. Allow the espresso and coffee when brewing to run over the zest and into your cup.
2. Stir the brown sugar, if you prefer less sweet then opt for 1-2 teaspoons.

3. Add your milk of choice, Everly's version is made with oat milk (unsweetened). You may want to add a splash more considering the espresso will make this drink darker than a basic coffee.

If you choose to drink it over ice, try shaking it up in a cocktail shaker to get it insanely cold and frothy.

While Jack may not be able to deliver this to you secretly, you can always re-read Chapters 22 and 23 while you drink it.

ABOUT THE AUTHOR

Forever a hopeful romantic, author Victoria Wilder writes contemporary romance with deliciously witty and wild characters. Her stories range from small-town swoonworthy men to fiercely powerful families and lead characters whom aren't afraid to ask for what they want.

She's an east coast girl, always chasing the next season and living it up with her husband, two kiddos, and dog, Linus. When she's not reading or writing, you'll find her training at a kickboxing class or finding an excuse to sink her feet in the sand at the beach.

She believes in the power of a great story. That words have the ability to change the trajectory of your life. And that a new pair of sneakers can be just as powerful as heels to put you in the right mood.

instagram.com/authorvictoriawilder
tiktok.com/authorvictoriawilder
bookbub.com/authors/victoria-wilder

Made in the USA
Columbia, SC
27 June 2025

60015581R00215